Praise for *Maclean*:

A finalist for the 2005 Rogers Writers' Trust Fiction Prize and one of Globe and Mail fiction reviewer Jim Bartley's "Bartley's Top Five" books of 2005.

"Note to book-chat pooh-bahs: This book merits a media flurry.... Donaldson's simple device of inserting John's ghastly war memories directly, without preamble, into the body of the main narrative pays huge dividends. Without writerly display, he communicates not only the ambushing of John's psyche by old traumas (his past is always present) but the unfathomable fact of life's random doling out of horror and beauty."

— The Globe and Mail

"With sharp, incisive prose, Donaldson illuminates one ex-soldier's search for peace that left this reader humming along to the barely remembered 'Pack up your troubles in your old kit bag...'"

— Ottawa Citizen

"*Maclean* may be modest in scope, but readers should be lavish in their praise of this fine novel."

— Fredericton Daily Gleaner

"Allan Donaldson's first novel, *Maclean*, is a finely detailed study of a man buffeted by fate whose story stays with you long after you put the book down....A small, hard but brilliant gem of a book."

— Halifax Chronicle Herald

the CASE AGAINST OWEN WILLIAMS

ALLAN DONALDSON

Vagrant PRESS

Copyright © Allan Donaldson 2010

All rights reserved. No part of this book may be reproduced, stored in a retrieval system or transmitted in any form or by any means without the prior written permission from the publisher, or, in the case of photocopying or other reprographic copying, permission from Access Copyright, 1 Yonge Street, Suite 1900, Toronto, Ontario M5E 1E5.

Nimbus Publishing Limited
3731 Mackintosh St, Halifax, NS B3K 5A5
(902) 455-4286 nimbus.ca

Printed and bound in Canada

Author photo: Marjory Donaldson
Interior design: Jenn Embree

This novel is a work of fiction. Names, characters, places, and incidents are either the product of the author's imagination or are used fictitiously. Any resemblance to actual persons, living or dead, events or locales is entirely coincidental.

Library and Archives Canada Cataloguing in Publication

    Donaldson, Allan
    The case against Owen Williams / Allan Donaldson.
    ISBN 978-1-55109-776-3
I. Title.
PS8557.O51C37 2010   C813'.54   C2010-903052-4

We acknowledge the financial support of the Government of Canada through the Book Publishing Industry Development Program (BPIDP) and the Canada Council, and of the Province of Nova Scotia through the Department of Tourism, Culture and Heritage for our publishing activities.

 *for Marjory*

CHAPTER ONE

Dominion Day, 1944, fell on a Saturday. Elsewhere across Canada, the shipyards and factories worked on without ceasing, turning out the materiel of victory. But in Wakefield, New Brunswick, population 5,783, nothing that was postponed until Monday was going to lengthen the war by one second, so the town took its holiday as usual and staged the parade that in some form or other it had staged every July 1 since 1867.

In front of the cenotaph a small reviewing stand had been set up, decorated with red, white, and blue bunting, and as noon approached a thin crowd of people—the patriotic, the bereaved, the lonely, the poor, the idle—began to gather near the courthouse. They waited on the sidewalks in such shade as they could find, and as the town clock began to strike twelve, they heard from out of sight up the street the drums and bugles of the local company of the Royal Canadian Army Cadet Corps. It was the signal for the reviewing party to descend the steps of the courthouse and take their places on the stand—the mayor of Wakefield with his chain of office, Captain Ernest Fraser of the Seaforth Highlanders of Nova Scotia, and Colonel (retired) J. MacGregor Blaikie, late of the 85th Infantry Battalion, now honourary commander of the local branch of the Royal Canadian Legion.

There was a minute of expectancy, and then around the curve of the street, under an arch of elm trees heavy with summer, the parade appeared, led by Corporal Drost of the RCMP in his dress scarlet and a colour party of the Legion bearing the Union Jack, the Red Ensign, and the Legion banner. Behind them marched the brass band of the local militia, and as the colour party approached the reviewing stand, it took over from the bugle band and struck up "The Maple Leaf Forever." Colonel Blaikie and Captain Fraser saluted. The mayor stood stiffly at attention. The band passed and was followed by a company of the Legion, then the bugle band and two platoons of cadets, and finally, not so much the climax of the parade as an ignominious afterthought, a platoon of Captain Fraser's Seaforth Highlanders.

As they passed, Colonel Blaikie pointedly dropped his salute, and there was a scattering of derisive whistles from the crowd. Captain Fraser had known that marching them would be a mistake, but Area Headquarters had ordered them to be marched, so marched they had to be.

The difficulty about Captain Fraser's Seaforths was that they were what had become known popularly as "Zombies"—men who had been conscripted but who had refused to volunteer to go overseas and could not under existing law be forced. Now with the casualty lists rolling in once again from France, they had become an object of furious debate in Parliament and of growing unpleasantness on the street.

Most of the Zombies were hidden away in camps in the West, where they were supposed to be waiting to repel a Japanese invasion, but some of them were scattered around the country, guarding things the army had decided ought to be guarded. In Wakefield, they guarded a makeshift basic training camp that had been set up in the summer of 1940 on a big island in the middle of the river, used to train one battalion through one bitter winter, and then abandoned.

The buildings that had been run up still stood there, unused and useless—jerry-built huts already rotting away under their leaky roofs—but four times a day a guard detail of half a dozen Seaforths marched down Main Street and across the bridge to the island, and the detail they had relieved marched back. It was an operation that had about it, like many things that went on in those days, an atmosphere of dreamlike absurdity, and it was possible to imagine the army forgetting about the Seaforths altogether and leaving them to march back and forth there forever.

It had befallen Captain Fraser to command the Wakefield Armoury, the Wakefield Basic Training Camp, and this platoon of military outcasts, not because he himself was a Zombie, but because he was thirty-nine years old with eyesight too bad to allow him to be assigned to a combat unit. Nevertheless, as he watched the platoon slouch past, not so smart even as the high school cadets, and as he saw out of the corner of his eye Colonel Blaikie drop his salute, he felt that something of their disgrace inevitably rubbed off on him, and he resolved once again to set about pulling strings to get some kind of overseas posting. Or, failing that, any posting anywhere away from this dismal hole and these dismal misfits.

When they had passed, Fraser ended his salute with the snap he had been taught long ago before the war. He shook hands with the mayor, saluted the colonel, and descended the reviewing stand, revolving in his mind some act of vengeance for the day's humiliation. A route march would be the thing. On Monday, a punitive route march for sloppiness on parade. March the little bastards in full kit until their legs fell off. He would have Sergeant MacCrae see to it.

At seven o'clock it was still hot, and the sky was filled with gathering thunderheads—tall galleons of cloud that sailed in from the west in fleets. In the late afternoon, there had been distant rumblings to the north, but in Wakefield there had been no rain, only sudden, odd little gusts of wind that raised tornadoes of dust along the roads and then subsided as abruptly as they had come.

With the approach of evening, there had also come clouds of blackflies and mosquitoes, nowhere more of them than around Daniel Coile's house on the Hannigan Road a mile west of town. It stood at the top of a high bank above a creek, which here spread itself out during the spring floods over acres of interval land, then retreated in the summer, leaving behind it stagnant ponds where blackflies and mosquitoes bred by the billions.

Unlike most of his neighbours, Daniel Coile had never built himself a summer kitchen, so the temperature in the house after supper had been cooked was in the nineties. With all the doors and windows open, the flies and mosquitoes found their way through the rotting screens and into the house, where they buzzed from room to room until they eventually blundered into one of the ribbons of sticky paper that festooned the ceilings or were squashed with a swatter by Matilda Coile.

For himself, Daniel Coile didn't give a shit about blackflies or mosquitoes, nor for any god-damned man who ever walked neither. What he did give a shit about was his good name and the obedience due him as a father.

"She ain't gonna talk to me like that," he said, sitting up very straight in his chair by the kitchen table. "She ain't gonna talk to me like that and go on livin' under my roof. I'll give her one she won't forget in a hurry. I'll give her one that will make them soldiers think twice before they run around with her. By Jesus, them bastards better not cross me."

Upstairs in the bedroom she shared with her younger sister Unis, Sarah Coile half-listened to the rhetorical rise and fall of her father's voice, not making out the words especially and not particularly trying to or needing to. She had brought a pailful of hot water upstairs from the tank on the side of the kitchen stove and poured it into a large wash basin, and she was standing, naked except for her pants, in front of the mirror on the dresser, washing herself. She was a well-built girl with the kind of opulent Edwardian figure that still turned up occasionally on dirty postcards or flipcard peepshows at carnivals.

Her sister was sitting on the bed.

"I don't have to stay around here," Sarah said. "There's all kinds of jobs in places like Saint John. There are girls makin' a dollar an hour buildin' ships."

"Where are ya gonna git the money to go down there with?" Unis asked.

"Never mind," Sarah said. "I can git it if I really want to."

She washed her armpits and under her breasts, lifting one after the other, then stopping to look at herself, admiringly, in the mirror.

"Papa said he wasn't gonna let ya go to the dance," Unis said.

"Papa can go to hell," Sarah said.

She towelled herself dry and got dressed in clean underwear and a white dress that she had bought earlier in the week and sneaked into the house when she got back from work. From the back of one of the dresser drawers, she took out a tube of lipstick and a compact of rouge and put them in her purse. Then she went downstairs, and Unis trailed after her.

Her father was still sitting at the kitchen table, drinking a cup of tea. He eyed her wrathfully from under his heavy brows.

"So where are you goin' all dressed up like the Queen of England?" he asked.

"I'm goin' to see Vinny," Sarah said. "Maybe we'll go to the movies."

"Or to that dance hall," he said.

"Maybe," Sarah said.

"You ain't goin' to no dance. No daughter of mine is gonna hang around in no dance hall."

He started to get up.

Sarah stopped by the door and turned on him.

"You better watch out. You lay a hand on me, you're gonna be sorry."

"If you go to that dance hall, you needn't bother comin' back," he bawled at her. "If you ain't gonna do what I say, you ain't gonna live under my roof."

"That suits me."

She pushed out through the screen door and slammed it behind her.

The band that night at The Silver Dollar had three fiddles, a guitar, a banjo, and a mouth organ. The man who played the mouth organ could also play bones, and he liked to step dance, playing the bones off his elbow. They were playing a waltz now, not putting much into it, and there were only a dozen couples on the floor, dancing in the slow, bored way people dance at the start of an evening.

Sarah sat on a chair on the right side of the dance hall where the female stag line always sat, just as the male line always sat across from it on the left. Sarah knew or half-knew all the other girls in the line, but she didn't join them. Instead, she sat a few chairs away and watched Vinny and her boyfriend, Brick, as they shuffled around among the other dancers.

Brick was a big boy, over six feet, over two hundred pounds, and he was nicknamed Brick because of his mat of red hair. Vinny was only the latest in his succession of girls, and it had surprised Sarah when Vinny had told her that Brick had begun taking her out. Vinny was pretty, but she was barely five feet, barely a hundred pounds, and there didn't seem to be enough of her to be a girl for someone like Brick. Sarah knew it wouldn't last, and she felt sure that she could take Vinny's place when it ended, but that wouldn't last either. With Brick, nobody was going to last.

She turned her attention to the male stag line on the other side of the hall. It was a good deal shorter than the female stag line. It always was. Once, four years before, when the battalion had been training on the island, it had been the other way around, and she still heard stories from the older girls about how in those days any girl no matter how homely had half a dozen soldiers chasing her to go to dances, to go to movies, even towards the end to marry them. But she had been only twelve then, too young for it to do her any good. And the thousand men of the battalion had left, and so had several hundred men from the county, and the twenty or thirty Seaforths who had arrived a couple of years later didn't begin to make up.

There were half a dozen of them in the stag line now, sticking together as they always did, not dancing yet until things had sorted themselves out a little, waiting for the strays whom no one was going to fight over. Sarah knew them all, more or less. Some she had danced with. Some she knew about from other girls. The rest of the stag line was made up mostly of sixteen- and seventeen-year-old kids who in spite of all the stag girls would end up with nobody because they didn't know how to dance or what to say to a girl when they did. Sarah hardly looked at them.

The set ended. Vinny and Brick came back, and Brick went off to the canteen and got a bottle of ginger ale and three paper cups. Sarah and Vinny got up, and the three stood tight together while Brick poured rye into the bottom of the paper cups and then topped them up with ginger ale. It was against the law to drink in a dance hall, or anywhere else in public, but at The Silver Dollar this was interpreted to mean that you didn't openly show the bottle, so that if the Mounties arrived, the owner could claim with something like the truth that he hadn't seen anybody drinking.

Brick hadn't stinted on the rye, and Sarah still had a finger in her cup when the band started up again and a local singer in a white cowboy suit slid into "It Makes No Difference Now." Vinny dropped the rest of her drink into Sarah's and went out again with Brick.

Sarah sipped the drink and watched the soldiers on the other side of the floor. Some of them now and then watched back, but none of them made a move, and she was still there holding her empty cup when the number finished.

"Take your partners," the man who played the bones shouted, "for the first reel of the night. And here's Daddy MacDade to call."

An enormous fat man came down the hall at a heavy trot, like a milk cow someone had thrown a stick at, and heaved himself up onto the stage.

The reel brought out most of the soldiers from the stag line, and even some of the kids who couldn't dance one to one but could be hauled and pushed through a reel. There were enough for two lines almost the whole length of the hall. Daddy MacDade did a little step dance and gave a whoop. The band threw itself at "Soldier's Joy," and the evening began to take off.

Sarah didn't get one of the soldiers. She got a soft, pimple-faced boy named Herbie Booth. But with a reel it didn't matter. What mattered was that he got her out there, so that while he clomped around, getting lost in the clockwork down the middle of the lines, she was breaking the ice with some of the others.

"What are you doing with that jerk?" one of the soldiers asked her as they spun.

"Tryin' to git rid of him," Sarah said. "What are you doin' with that scarecrow?"

After five minutes, "Soldier's Joy" abruptly stopped and Daddy MacDade shouted, "Now waltz them partners," and the band struck up "The Tennessee Waltz."

Herbie was somewhere in the confusion as the reel broke up, and Sarah slipped away. A lot of the dancers were getting rid of one partner in hopes of a better one, and Sarah saw close to her a soldier she had danced with the week before. His name was Owen Williams. He would do, for now anyway. She took his elbow and swung herself into his arms.

She saw him blush. He wasn't much taller than she was, slightly built, with rather pale skin and very thick black hair. On his chin and along his jaw line, even though he was close shaven, there was a dark shadowiness. He smelled faintly of some kind of shaving stuff and of something else, something like leather, some sort of army smell, different from the smell of farm workers or garagemen.

"I'm Sarah Coile," she announced. "Remember me?"

"Yes," he said, "I remember. I'm Owen Williams."

"Are you now?" she laughed. "I thought you were Hopalong Cassidy."

The floor was still crowded with the dancers the reel had brought out, and Sarah let herself be pushed closer to Williams than he would have brought her on his own. He wasn't a bad dancer, but stiff and nervous, inclined to hold her at arm's length. She put her head on his shoulder and hummed along.

"'I was dancin' with my darlin' to the Tennessee Waltz.' I like that song," she murmured, "don't you?"

"Sure," he said.

She looked at his dark eyes, recognizing in their depths a look he would not have wanted her to recognize.

"I had a couple of drinks," she said. "I'm feelin' a little tipsy."

"All change," shouted Daddy. "All change."

The fiddlers sawed their strings tunelessly, and someone took Sarah's arm from behind and turned her around away from Williams. It was Huddy Foster, one of Brick's friends, a drinker, a fighter, small, wiry, quick as a weasel. Sarah was afraid of him, but she couldn't get away.

The band started another waltz, and Huddy danced away with her. There was nothing shy about Huddy. He danced her close, one leg almost between hers, his hand low down on her back. When the dance finished, he followed her back to join Brick and Vinny, and the four of them went outside. They stopped in the shadows back of the dance hall, and Brick took his bottle out and passed it around. There was no ginger ale to put into it this time, and Sarah was conscious of the heat of it going down.

When the band started up again, they went back to the dance hall together. Huddy walked beside Sarah, and she worried that he might be trying to take her over and wondered how she could get rid of him. But inside, he and Brick went off together, and after five minutes, an old boyfriend of Vinny's came along and asked her to dance, and she went off with him. When Brick came back, he was alone. She had thought he might be angry about Vinny, but he didn't seem to care.

"Let's you and me do it," he said.

Like Huddy, he held her close, his belly rock-hard against her.

"Why don't we go out for a drive some night," he said. "We could go over the lines some night maybe and go to a movie."

"Vinny wouldn't think much of that."

"Vinny don't own me."

"I know. But she's my friend. She's been a real good friend to me, and I don't want to make her mad."

The hard strength of him excited her, but in spite of the rye she still held to the knowledge that no matter what they did together she wouldn't last either.

"Well," he was saying, "we wouldn't have to tell her, would we?"

After the dance, they went back to the place by the wall that had become their spot for the evening. Vinny was alone, and Sarah thought she saw a flicker of jealousy in her look when she saw her with Brick. But nobody said anything about anything. They simply watched the crowd.

Further along the wall, Sarah saw Williams looking at her. She met his eyes, not signalling anything exactly, but not breaking the thread either. In the end, it was he who looked away, but after a few seconds his eyes drifted back to her. She put both her hands up to her head and with the palms slowly pushed her hair back from above her temples, lifting her breasts inside her dress and letting them slowly descend, watching Williams all the while as she did.

But when the music started, it was Herbie Booth who got to her first. She told him no, and he smiled his foolish smile and just stood there. Out of the corner of her eye, she saw Williams hesitate and then come on.

"I had this dance promised," she told Herbie.

"Did you want to dance with him?" Williams asked when they were out on the floor.

"I wouldn't dance with him if he was the last man in the place."

"You were dancing with him before."

"That was just a reel. That don't matter."

As they danced, she moved closer to him and again put her head on his shoulder.

"What did you do before you went into the army?" she asked.

"I had a job with a lumber company," he said.

"You mean sawin' up logs?"

"No. I worked in the office. I did accounts and stuff like that."

"You been through high school?"

"Yes. In Fredericton."

She looked at him.

"I never got through grade eight," she said. "My father said no one needed no more school than that, not a girl anyways. Not boys neither unless they were gonna work in town jobs. So I had to quit and go to work. I work at the dairy now."

"What do you do?"

"I wash milk cans mostly. There's a big machine. But I'm gonna git a job on the ice cream counter maybe the end of the summer."

They danced in silence while she thought about all that. She hadn't known that he had been through high school. Not many people who came to The Silver Dollar had been through high school. Mostly they worked on farms or in garages or drove trucks. And mostly they lived in places like her place.

"What does your father do?" she asked.

"He's dead. He had a farm. My mother went on running it, but she died a couple of years ago too."

"So you ain't got nobody?"

"Uncles and aunts. Cousins. Things like that."

"No steady girl back in Fredericton?" she asked teasingly.

"No," he said.

The dance ended, and they stood together, awkwardly, in the middle of the floor.

"It's gittin' awful hot in here," Sarah told him. "Why don't we go outside and git some fresh air?"

"Sure," he answered with a touch of…what? she wondered. Surprise? Shyness?

"I'd like some ginger ale to take out," she said. "Would you git me some? I'll give you the money. I ain't tryin' to make you treat me or nothin'. It's just hard for a girl by herself up there."

"I'll treat you," he said. "We just got paid."

She went with him to the canteen and stuck close to him, so that Huddy or somebody like that wouldn't think she was free and try to pick her up.

When he had got the ginger ale, they went out. All the light had gone from the sky now, and it was filled with stars. Sarah took Williams's arm. They picked their way along the darkness by the side of the hall and found themselves a spot at the back a few yards away from another couple, who were standing close together talking in low voices. Williams also had a small bottle of rye, and they spiked the ginger ale.

They drank, awkwardly, without speaking, and when they had finished and thrown the cups away, she lifted her face towards him, and he kissed her briefly, his lips closed, his body tense.

She put her arms around his neck, so that her breasts pressed against him. When they had started to grow towards their present heaviness, they had embarrassed her, but she understood their power now and would not for anything have traded them for Vinny's little-girl figure.

She could feel Williams's heart pounding heavily even through his thick tunic.

"Do you like me?" she whispered.

"Yes," he said.

"I like you too," she continued to whisper.

He kissed her again, this time putting his arms around her, and she saw his eyes close. Then suddenly he stiffened and drew away from her. Three figures had crept around the corner of the hall and were watching them.

"Hoop and drive her there, soldier," one of them shouted.

"Don't pay no attention to them," Sarah told him, low so they couldn't hear. She was afraid that Williams might get lured into a fight.

Inside, the music started. The peeping Toms waited for some response from Williams, then drifted away into the darkness.

"Don't git yourself smothered in them big tits," one of them shouted back.

"Let's go back and dance," Sarah said. "I came here with Vinny, and I better let her know where I am. If you'll walk me home, I won't need to go with them. It isn't very far. Would you do that?"

"Yes," Williams said. "Sure."

They didn't see Brick and Vinny at first, so they danced. She sang along with the music, her face down against the rough wool of Williams's tunic. "You are my sunshine, my only sunshine."

Later she saw Vinny and Brick and waved at Vinny.

When the set finished, the band played a few bars of "The Bear Went Over the Mountain." This was the signal for intermission. The band climbed off the stage, and among the dancers there was a general move towards the canteen.

"Would you like something to eat?" Williams asked.

"No," Sarah said. "Let's go outside again."

"What about your friend?"

"She knows I'm with you."

There were more couples outside this time, their cigarettes glowing along the side of the dance hall and around the parked cars.

"Let's go somewhere there ain't so many people around," Sarah whispered.

She took Williams's arm and led him towards the darkness at the edge of the woods. As they faded into it, someone whistled shrilly and gave a wolf-howl.

CHAPTER TWO

Tuesday, July 4. Twelve miles away across the border, the Americans were celebrating their independence. Corporal Drost, his hour of glory at the head of the Dominion Day parade mercifully behind him, sat at his desk in the RCMP office reading the Saint John paper.

There was a double headline. NAZIS BLASTED FROM LAST MAJOR SOVIET CITY. SHARP OFFENSIVE IS LAUNCHED ON CHERBOURG. Inside, there were the day's casualty lists for the province with the photographs of six of the dead in a neat block. Elsewhere, Drost read that the Cardinals were continuing to run away from the Pirates and that the Browns were still ahead in the American League. In Saint John, one of the movie houses was playing *Jane Eyre* with Orson Welles and Joan Fontaine.

He finished scanning the paper, and got up and looked out the window. The RCMP establishment in Wakefield was across from the rear of the courthouse on a little side street. Across the street and just behind the courthouse stood the county jail, a square, red brick building with a little crenellated tower and a yard enclosed by a high wire fence.

As Drost stood studying it, wondering vaguely once again what purpose the tower was supposed to serve, the telephone rang.

"I'm phonin' about my daughter," the woman's voice said—a country voice, nasal and raw-edged.

In the background, there were other voices and a sound of dishes being rattled.

"She's been gone since Saturday," the voice went on, "and I just been to town and she ain't been to work for the last two days."

They always began in the middle and worked both ways from there.

"Could I have your name?" Drost asked. "Then tell me what happened."

"My name's Matilda Coile," the voice said. "My husband's Daniel Coile. We live on the Hannigan Road. You know?"

"Yes, I know it. So what about your daughter?"

"I said. She ain't been home since Saturday. She went out on Saturday night, with a friend of hers named Vinny Page, to that dance hall on the Bangor Road. And she ain't been back. I went to the Page girl's house because I thought she might be stayin' there, but they ain't seen her neither, not since Saturday. Then I went to the dairy where she works, and they ain't seen her neither. I think somebody better start lookin' for her."

"Does she have any friends, any relatives she might have gone to stay with?"

"She don't have a lot of friends. We got a lot of relatives, but she ain't at none of the ones I asked. And why ain't she at her job?"

"Does she have a boyfriend?" Drost asked.

"Not that I know of. But she might have and didn't tell us."

"You didn't have a fight with her on Saturday night, did you?"

On the other end of the line there was a silence.

"Maybe she's run away," Drost suggested.

It was a great time for running away because there were so many new places to run away to—the forces, the merchant navy, the factories, and all the new stores, restaurants, boarding houses, and hotels that these gave rise to.

"She didn't take no clothes. She wouldn't leave her clothes if she was goin' away somewheres."

"What do you think happened?" Drost asked.

"I don't know. I keep goin' over it in my mind, and I don't know."

"What does your husband think?"

"He don't know neither."

"Could I speak to him?"

"He ain't here. I ain't home. We ain't got no phone. I'm at the canteen on the Bangor Road."

"Well, Mrs. Coile, I think I'd better come out and talk to you and your husband together."

"I never told him I was gonna phone," she said. "He may not like it."

"Mrs. Coile, I can't institute a search without talking to your husband."

Another, longer silence.

"All right," she said.

"Now where do you live?"

Drost took down the directions.

"Okay," he said. "I'll be out in an hour or so."

Drost had only two constables—Hooper and MacDougal—in a detachment that before the war had had four. He had sent Hooper out to deal with a car accident across the river. When Hooper came back, he would turn the office over to him and go out and get the rest of the story.

Instead of coming back after dealing with the accident, Hooper had decided on his own to make a patrol and had burned up half a tank of gas driving around the country for nothing, so it was nearly three o'clock when Drost turned off the Bangor Road onto the Hannigan Road.

For the first couple of hundred yards, the Hannigan Road was flanked by small houses on town-size lots, then abruptly the pavement ended, and the houses gave way to woods on the left side and on the right to an abandoned church and its graveyard, and then to an alternation of patches of wood and small subsistence farms. Whether it was the ground around here that was no good or the people or both, Drost didn't know, but the farms had an air of desolate, generations-old poverty: two-storey houses trailing randomly added ells and sheds; unpainted barns, some with their backs broken, some mere boardless skeletons; chicken coops, pigpens, fields full of rocks and rusting machinery, small potato fields, smaller vegetable gardens.

The Coile place was just beyond the top of the long curve that brought Hannigan Road around to parallel the Bangor Road a quarter of a mile away through the woods. The house was well back from the road, and the driveway had wheel ruts so deep that Drost drove down it at walking speed to avoid taking the bottom out of the car.

Halfway down, he was met by the inevitable dog, this one large, long-haired, muddy-red, which ran snarling and barking beside the left front wheel. When Drost stopped, it drew away a little and stood with its teeth bared, its hackles up, growling murderously. Drost studied it through the open window and decided that it was the kind that only attacked if you ran away from it. Or if someone set it on you. He hated these vicious curs that confronted him almost every time he drove into a farmyard, and he would gladly have paid five dollars for the pleasure of taking out his revolver and shooting this one.

He got out, and the dog crouched and growled harder but made no move.

From behind a screen door at the front of the house, a man stood watching him. He would have been there ever since the dog started to bark, but it was only now after Drost had braved the dog that he pushed open the door and came out.

Drost recognized him as someone he had seen on the streets in Wakefield, a man somewhere in his forties, unshaven with a pasty, unhealthy-looking face and black hair going grey, medium height, a hundred and eighty pounds maybe, twenty of it fat around the middle. He was wearing bib overalls, a grey flannel shirt, and gumboots.

"Daniel Coile?" Drost asked.

"Yes, I'm Daniel Coile," the man said.

He had small eyes set close in against his nose, and he studied Drost with deliberate hostility.

"Your wife phoned me and said you had a daughter missing," Drost said.

"So she said," Coile growled out of the side of his mouth.

"I can't start a search unless I have more information," Drost told him.

"You gonna be able to find her?"

"I don't know," Drost said. "I may not even try."

Behind Coile beyond the screen door in the dim interior of the house, Drost made out the figure of a woman. Coile stood unmoving, watching him with his mean little eyes, and Drost considered getting back into the car and driving off. What held him back was the feeling that this may have been what Coile wanted.

"Why don't we go inside," Drost said, "so that you and your wife can tell me what happened?"

Coile shrugged, grudgingly pushed open the screen door, and led Drost down a hallway towards the back of the house.

Matilda Coile was nervously waiting for them in the kitchen, a middle-aged, mid-sized woman bare-armed in a well-worn, sleeveless print dress. Drost noticed that on the left side of her mouth there was the suggestion of a harelip, but in spite of the lip, Drost could imagine that she might once have been quite pretty, and he wondered what had brought her to marry a pig like Coile.

Drost put his cap on the table and sat down. Mrs. Coile hesitated, then sat down across from him, smoothing her dress over her lap. Coile stood with his back to them by the window that looked out over the creek while Mrs. Coile told Drost again the story of Sarah's disappearance.

"When I talked to you on the phone," Drost said, "I got the impression that there might have been some sort of argument before she went out."

"I told her I didn't want her goin' to no dance hall," Coile said.

"And what did she say?"

"She lied," Coile growled. "Like she always does. She said she was goin' to the movies. But she never went to no movies. I knew she wasn't."

"Mrs. Coile," Drost said, "I can understand your being worried, but it looks to me as if your daughter has simply run away."

"But she ain't taken none of her things," Mrs. Coile said. "I know she wouldn't leave without her things."

"She could send for them. Or come back for them later."

"But where could she go?"

"To some of the relatives you didn't check maybe. Or to some friend you don't know about."

"One of them men she meets at that dance hall," Coile said. "Brick Smith and his crowd. She thinks I don't smell liquor on her when she comes back. She thinks I'm a fool."

"Okay," Drost said, "I'll see what I can do, but I'm short-handed, and I can't spend a lot of time. And I have to tell you that I can't make your daughter come back here if she doesn't want to. It might help if you could give me a photograph."

While Drost sat at the table and Coile stood looking out the window, Mrs. Coile went upstairs and came back with a snapshot. It showed two girls and a boy standing in front of a verandah.

"That's Sarah on the right," Mrs. Coile said. "And her friend Vinny. I don't know who the boy is."

Sarah looked a little like her mother but without the disfigured lip. She was also bigger than her mother, taller apparently, fuller, her heavy bosom accentuated by a blouse that was tucked tightly into her skirt.

"Okay," Drost said, "I'll take this for a few days. Now describe her."

Sweating inside his tunic in the heat of the kitchen, Drost got out his notebook and took down the details that the photograph wouldn't tell him. Five-foot-six, maybe. Brown hair. Brown eyes. No moles or scars. Left-handed. Dressed up for the dance in a white dress when she left.

He was weary of this, but dutifully he spent another half-hour getting the names and addresses of relatives and friends Sarah might have gone to.

"What do you think's happened?" Mrs. Coile asked.

"I think she's run away," Drost said. "It happens all the time. She's legally of age. She can do whatever she wants."

"She's a whore, that's what she is," Coile said.

At five o'clock the sun was still high, the afternoon heat undiminished, and Drost felt sticky and irritable. Having stopped at the Pages' on the way back to town to find out what Vinny might tell him that she had not told Matilda Coile, Drost now sat facing Private Owen Williams across a folding trestle table in a small room at the armoury.

"I understand you know a girl named Sarah Coile," he said.

"Yes," Williams said, "I've met her."

Drost studied him, waiting for more than that for an answer. Williams seemed nervous, but that, Drost knew well enough, meant nothing. He had come to the armoury with the idea that Williams might have set Sarah up somewhere as something more than a dancing partner, but he had needed only one look to make it clear to him that Williams would be incapable of anything so daring. Drost judged him to be nineteen or twenty, but with his bitten fingernails and his scared eyes, he seemed more like a grubby high school student than anything else.

"Where have you met her?" Drost asked.

"At dances."

"When was the last time you saw her?"

Williams hesitated, and Drost saw him calculating and wondered why.

"Last Saturday night," Williams said. "At The Silver Dollar. What's the trouble? Has she done something?"

"No. We just want to locate her, that's all."

"She works at the dairy in town," Williams said.

"I know that, but she hasn't been there since last week. And she hasn't been home either. I thought you might have some idea where she might be."

"No," Williams said. "I haven't seen her since Saturday night."

"When did you last see her there? What time?"

"I don't know," Williams said. "I danced with her a couple of times, and when intermission started, she said she wasn't feeling good and asked me to walk with her a ways."

"And?"

"We went outside. There's a shortcut she knew through the woods back of the dance hall, sort of a trail, and after a little ways that came out onto a road. She said she lived just a little ways up the road, and she would be all right now."

"So she went on by herself?"

"Yes."

"And you? Did you go back to the dance hall?"

"No, I went back to the armoury."

"By yourself?"

"Yes."

"Her parents say that she didn't come home, and she hasn't been home since. What do you make of that?"

"I don't know," Williams said.

"Do you think she might have been meeting someone else?"

"I don't know."

"Maybe saying she wasn't feeling well was just a way of getting rid of you, so she could meet someone else," Drost suggested.

"I don't know."

"Did you watch her walk up the road?"

"No. I just went down the road the other way to the main road. I stopped at the canteen out there for a soft drink, and then I walked the rest of the way back here."

"And you haven't seen her since? You haven't heard anything about her? No one around here has said anything?"

"No."

"Did you see her dancing with anyone else?"

"Yes. Once with a young guy. I don't know his name. And once with a guy named Huddy. He was in a fight out there a couple of weeks ago. And once with a guy named Brick who was there with her friend."

"You seem to have watched her pretty close," Drost said.

Williams flushed and shifted in his chair.

"Do you think she might have been more interested in one of them than in you?"

"I don't know."

"She didn't say anything about going somewhere else after the dance?"

"No."

"Did she say anything about what things were like at home? She didn't say anything about wanting to run away or anything like that?"

"No."

"What did you talk about?"

"Nothing much," Williams said. "Just about the dance and the people there and stuff like that."

Drost looked at his watch and then at Williams, wearily. This was a waste of time, he thought. The whole thing. He got up.

"Okay," he said. "I guess that'll do, for now anyway. If you hear anything about her from anyone, I'd like you to let me know."

He went down the hall and out onto the street past the guard, one of the rotation that stood out there uselessly twenty-four hours a day with an unloaded Lee-Enfield .303.

Tomorrow, he thought, he would give Hooper the list of names he had got from Matilda Coile, and since Hooper enjoyed driving around the country so much, he would send him off to see what he could find out.

Drost sat at his desk. Constable Hooper stood in the middle of the office, all regulation six feet of him, handsome, blond-haired, scrubbed, clipped, square-shouldered, the very image of everybody's image of the Mountie. Near the window that looked out at the jail, George Carvell, high sheriff of George County, slouched in an armchair tipped precariously against the wall, a tall, casual man in his late forties with a prominent scar across the left side of his forehead, the only outward damage that had been done to him in his year and a half in the trenches.

Drost had met him the first day he had taken over the Wakefield detachment the previous October. It had been Carvell's habit to drop in on Drost's predecessor, as the mood took him, for a talk and a coffee, and he had simply continued the habit with Drost. At first Drost had been polite but distant. He didn't want to antagonize the sheriff because he had learned as a good Mountie that you don't antagonize people if you can help it. But as a good Mountie, neither did he like the idea of a non-Mountie hanging around his office, listening to the traffic.

It had gradually dawned on Drost, as it must have dawned on his predecessor, that he needed Carvell more than Carvell needed him. There wasn't a person, a house, a farm, a road, a woods track in George County that Carvell didn't know about or couldn't find out about in an hour. Without him, Drost would still have been floundering helplessly, struggling to extract even the most innocent information from people whose minds became vacuums the minute he stepped out of the car in his uniform and addressed them in his Upper Canadian accent. Without Carvell, he would still have been blind and deaf.

So there Carvell sat that July afternoon with his legs stretched out as if he owned the place, and it never crossed Drost's mind or Hooper's not to say what they had to say in front of him.

"There's nothing," Hooper said. "Not a thing. Nobody has seen her. No one knows anything about her. I went to every name on the list except one that I couldn't find, and I went to some other people that they said might know something about her. Nothing. I went to the railroad station and the bus stop. Nothing. Nobody had seen anyone like her."

"Do you think that she might have got on a train or a bus without them noticing?" Drost asked.

"That's possible, I suppose," Hooper said.

"But Matilda Coile said she didn't take any of her clothes," Drost said.

"You said she had a fight with her old man," Hooper said. "Maybe it was bad enough that she didn't dare go back for her clothes. Maybe he threw her out."

"Maybe," Drost said. "It still seems odd though."

"Maybe she's set up with some guy and doesn't want to be found," Carvell said.

"I wondered about that too," Drost said. "I wondered if maybe she'd been set up somewhere by Williams. But he's not the type. He's a child."

"He's the last person who saw her?" Carvell asked.

"The last person we know who saw her," Drost said. "He said she told him that she wasn't feeling well, and he walked her to the Hannigan Road and left her there."

"Maybe she did go home," Hooper said.

"And then?"

"She had another fight with her father."

"And then?"

"I don't know," Hooper said. "I was just thinking."

"What do you know about Daniel Coile?" Drost asked Carvell.

"Nothing that's new," Carvell said. "That place he lives on is the family place. The old man died a long time ago. Dan had a lot of brothers and sisters. I don't know where the brothers went. Some of the sisters are married and live around here. Dan's wife came from out near the border, and the talk is that Dan married her because he had to. I guess they were a pretty rough crew out there for a while. They drank, and Dan used to knock his wife and the kids around. But he's slowed down, and a few years ago, the wife got religion, and I haven't heard much about either of them lately."

"What about the daughter?" Drost asked.

"I don't know," Carvell said. "But I wouldn't be surprised if she were a little like the mother at that age."

"I wonder what I should do," Drost said. "I don't think I'd better put out an alert this soon, but it's beginning to look funny. I wonder if I should go out to the dance hall and look around. Just so that everything's done right before I start the rumours flying."

Carvell looked at his watch.

"I'll come along," he said. "Nice day for a walk in the country."

The Silver Dollar was a long, wooden, one-storey building standing in a ragged clearing of dirt and weeds that had once been part of a farm, now failed, vanished, and mostly overgrown by bushes and small trees. From the front peak of the roof a round sign, painted silver, hung out over the front door with the name, The Silver Dollar, printed around the edge. The centre of the sign had been decorated with a couple of dozen bullet holes of assorted calibres and one charge of bird shot fired at close range. The door was closed, and there were shutters on the windows, not to keep out burglars, which they wouldn't have done, but to dissuade the local bucks from shooting out the windows.

Drost parked at the back out of sight of the road, and he and Carvell got out. There was no one around. Drost had been out to The Silver Dollar often enough at night but never during the day, and the quiet seemed unnatural. Instead of the usual uproar of music and rage, there was only the backdrop of bird calls and somewhere, everywhere and nowhere at once, the intermittent shrillness of a cicada.

They walked from the dance hall back towards the woods and entered along one of the trails that led out of the parking lot, following the route that Williams had described to Drost the day before. At what had been the edge of the original, much larger clearing, the overgrowth of bushes gave way to taller evergreens, and then the track came out into a long, narrow clearing that was growing up in bushes and small evergreens.

"This is the end of the Birch Road," Carvell said. "The land here wasn't any good, and the road was just left to grow up. It comes out over that way onto the Hannigan Road."

"This is where they went, according to Williams," Drost said.

They wound their way through the small trees. A little further on, they came out onto the Birch Road proper although it still wasn't much of a road, more dirt than gravel, with a strip of weeds down the middle. A quarter of a mile or so from the back of the dance hall, they emerged onto the Hannigan Road.

"This is where Williams says he left her," Drost said. "She went off up the road towards home, and he went down the other way."

They stood and took stock. To their right, toward the Bangor Road there were houses, and Drost could see a woman in an apron standing on a front porch watching them, her eye caught no doubt by his uniform. To their left, the Hannigan Road swung away uphill toward the Coile place. Fifty yards from where they stood it was joined by another road that ran away from them eastwards back towards town. This was Broad Street although it wasn't broad here or anywhere else. But then neither were there any birch trees on Birch Road nor had anyone named Hannigan, so far as anyone knew, ever lived on Hannigan Road. On the upper corner of the intersection of Broad Street and Hannigan Road, there was an abandoned church and its graveyard. Drost and Carvell crossed the road and wandered, more or less aimlessly now, up past the end of Broad Street and turned into the graveyard over a crude cedar-log culvert.

The doors and windows of the church had boards nailed across them, and the graves around it were untended, overgrown, as if their occupants had long passed out of memory. At the back of the churchyard beyond a weathered cedar-rail fence, the ground dropped away sharply through a tangle of alders and chokecherry bushes. A couple of hundred yards away, where the ground rose again, Drost and Carvell could see through the trees the roofs of some houses and a squat church steeple roofed with sheet metal that shone silver in the sun.

"You can't see it from here," Carvell said, "but there's an old gravel pit down there where people sometimes go to drink. Do you want to have a look?"

"Okay," Drost said. "Then we'll go back. I'll let it sit for a day or two, and if she still hasn't turned up, I'll put it on the wire."

They walked back out of the churchyard and around onto Broad Street. Down the Hannigan Road, the woman who had been watching them from her verandah had been joined by another woman and an old man. A hundred and fifty yards along Broad Street, they came to the road that led down into the gravel pit. It was more a track than a road. The grass had begun to creep into it from the edges, and there was a deep channel down the middle where the rain was eroding it away. There were recent car tracks all the same, straddling the erosion channel.

The pit didn't look big enough ever to have been a government or commercial operation. More likely it had been used by farmers as a source of gravel for their own driveways, but it didn't look as if anyone had hauled out of it for a long time. The ground in the middle was still bare, but grass and weeds and small bushes were growing around the edges under the broken banks, which like the road were eroding away, exposing the roots of the small hardwoods at the top. In some places, the banks had collapsed completely, so that instead of a cliff face, there was now just a slope on which stood in some places the dead, whitened trunks of trees that had been brought down when the bank collapsed.

It was perhaps that broken earth, those whitened skeletons of trees, stirring remote associations, which made Carvell recognize almost at once what the smell was that hung in the air.

It was nearly seven-thirty when Hooper, standing beside the patrol car, saw the two cars and a small van approaching up the Hannigan Road. Hooper's face was still pallid, the faded freckles of his childhood showing through his tan. He had been violently sick earlier, and he felt vaguely sick still and also humiliated.

Below him in the pit, Carvell was sitting in the shade on a little ledge of earth that had slid down from the top of the bank, grass and all, and formed a kind of natural bench. Drost paced slowly, obsessively, around in the middle of the pit, looking at, without really seeing anymore, the scattered testimony of the pit's social life. Bits of paper and boxes, most of them soaked and dried and bleached, though one Sweet Caporal cigarette box looked new. Bottles, some whole, most broken. Black Diamond Demerara Rum, Moosehead Ale, Sharpe's Pure Vanilla Extract. A couple of French safes. Some dried shit.

At the western end of the pit towards the abandoned churchyard, partly screened by high grass, in a little hollow among some of the older piles of earth from the collapsing bank, a green canvas tarpaulin was spread, its corners held down with stones. Above, among the trees between the churchyard and the edge of the pit, Drost could see figures moving again, three men this time, creeping forward as if stalking something.

"Get out!" Drost shouted. "Get out. Get back on the road."

The men stopped and stayed where they were, standing completely upright now, straining to look.

"Get out!" Drost shouted again, his voice trembling with rage. "Get out or I'll have you arrested."

The men hesitated and then slowly disappeared backward into the trees. On the opposite side of the pit, there were more of them, kids this time.

"Hooper!" he shouted. "Get them out of there."

This had been going on—going on and getting worse—for nearly four hours. While Carvell had walked back to the car and driven to town to get Hooper to report to Fredericton, he had stood guard over the obscenity that had lain uncovered in its little hollow until Carvell had come back with Hooper and the tarpaulin.

It had started almost at once, a man and one of the women who had been watching them from the verandah earlier edging inquisitively down the road into the pit. What they had seen, he couldn't tell, but his driving them off had only excited their curiosity more, and the word began to spread. They began creeping cautiously down the road. They began slipping up to the edges of the pit through the trees. And the more he drove them off, the more they gathered, and there began to seem something sinister, something ghoulish, in the persistence with which they bore down on him. Once, rattled, alone, at the end of his resources of self-control, he had started to unholster his revolver with the idea of firing a warning shot into the air before his reason resumed control.

Then Carvell and Hooper had come back, and Hooper had taken one look and been sick. Drost had sent him up to the top of the road to keep watch on the crowd, fifty at least by then, probably a hundred and fifty by now, that had gathered along Broad Street.

And through all this he had tried to think. Carvell had said that he was certain that the figure under the tarpaulin was Sarah Coile. And so far as it was possible to tell, it looked like the girl he had seen in the photograph. And the clothes were right. Nevertheless, it was an assumption, and someone would have to make a positive identification. But so far he had done nothing about getting in touch with the Coiles, and he wondered how long it might be before word spread up the road to them.

"They're coming," Hooper shouted from halfway down the pit road.

Relieved, Drost followed him back up, and he was waiting with him when the two cars and the van pulled up behind their own patrol car.

In the passenger seat of the first car, beside his driver, sat Detective Staff Sergeant Grant. The second car was driven by a corporal named Kroll, whom Drost had met once or twice but whom he knew mainly by reputation as part of Grant's criminal investigation team. This represented something of an elite, a good place to be if you wanted promotion badly enough. The constable driving the van he recognized as the provincial dog man from

Moncton, a hundred and fifty miles away. If he had been brought from there today, that was quick work even for Grant. Maybe he really was God.

Like the others, Grant was in uniform, and as he got out of the car, all six-foot-two of him, and put on his cap, he was an impressive figure of authority. He looked at the crowd on the other side of the street, and their chatter died as abruptly as if they had been figures in a movie whose sound had been turned off.

"Quite an audience," he said to Drost.

"Yes," said Drost. "They've been a problem."

Grant looked at them. Behind the trees at the edge of the pit above the tarpaulin, two young men in gumboots and mackinaws were poised, looking down.

"Reynolds," Grant said to his driver, "get those god-damned hillbillies the hell out of there."

Then he went out onto the road and faced the crowd.

"This is a police investigation," he said, "and you are to stay away from it. The next one who crosses this road will be arrested for obstruction of justice. There isn't going to be anything for you to see, and the best thing you can do if you want to stay out of trouble is to go home."

He waved his arm at them, a wide sweeping gesture as if he were shooing away a herd of cows. Like a herd of cows, the crowd stirred within itself, fell back, reformed a little further away, and stood watching, dumbly.

Grant turned back to Drost.

"All right," he said. "Now let's see what we've got."

At the bottom of the road, Carvell was waiting. Carvell had heard of Grant but had never met him. If Grant had ever heard of Carvell, he gave no sign of it.

"George knows the ground better than I do," Drost said. "And when we thought we might have a problem, he came out with me to have a look around. He was the one who knew about this gravel pit."

"That was helpful," Grant said.

Together the three of them walked across the pit. Drost took the stones off one side of the tarpaulin and lifted it, and they stood looking down at the figure beneath.

"You say her name was Sarah Coile?" Grant said.

"Yes," Drost said, and before he could qualify it, Grant interrupted.

"Have you got a positive identification?" he asked.

"No," Drost said. "Not exactly."

"Well," Grant said, "before we start chasing around, maybe we'd better make sure who it is we're chasing around over."

"She fits the description we had of Sarah Coile," Drost said. "I saw a photograph. The clothes are right. And George feels sure that it's her. He's seen her around town."

Grant glanced at Carvell.

"It's too big a coincidence," Drost said.

"Famous last words," Grant said. "Where did she live, assuming it's her?"

"About a mile up the road out there," Drost said. "I didn't send anyone up there because I didn't have anyone I could spare. And I didn't want to cause any more stir than there was already until you got here with some more men."

"Any idea how she got down here?" Grant asked.

"No," Drost said. "Down the road presumably."

Grant looked around the pit and up at the trees that fringed the top.

"Have those people out there been on the ground?" he asked.

"Not down here," Drost said, "but some of them were partway down the road before I chased them off, and they've been around the edge of the pit up there. I only had Hooper and George here. It was hard to control them."

"Couldn't you have got some help from the town police?" Grant asked.

"They'd have created more problems than they solved," Drost said. "You don't know the town police."

"No," Grant said, "I don't know the town police, but if those people have been all over the place, our dog is going to be useless."

Through all this, the figure from under the tarpaulin lay staring blindly up at the sky. Grant gestured, and Drost gave her back her privacy.

"Have you found anything?" Grant asked. "What about the rest of her clothing?"

"Nothing," Drost said. "Nothing down here. All this rubbish seems to be old. We haven't looked in the bushes."

Grant looked around the pit, and as he stood meditating, Kroll and the dog man from Moncton came down, Kroll with a camera and tripod. Grant introduced them perfunctorily. The name of the constable in charge of the dog was Martin, which Grant anglicized in spite of Martin's obvious Acadian accent.

"Do her first," Grant said to Kroll. "Then the area—everything."

"We might as well try the dog," he said to Martin, "since it's here, but we're not going to find out anything."

Martin went back up for the dog, and Grant turned back to Drost.

"You say that no one has seen her since Saturday night at the dance?" he asked.

"No. Not that we know of anyway," Drost said.

"Funny no one found her before this," Grant said. "That's almost four days. You think she's been here that long?"

"I don't know," Drost said.

"You say she went to the dance with some friends, but she left with a soldier named Williams?"

"Yes," Drost said. "Williams said that she told him she wasn't feeling well. According to Williams, he walked her out to the Hannigan Road just out there and left her to walk home by herself."

"What time did Williams get back to his barracks?" Grant said.

"I don't know," Drost said.

"You haven't checked his story?" Grant asked.

"There wasn't any reason to especially," Drost said. "Until we found her here, we thought we were just dealing with another missing persons case. Since we found her, we haven't had time."

"Okay," Grant said. "But there's lots of time now. Tell Hooper to go back to town and go over all the ground again. Tell him to find out when Williams got back to his barracks and to check everything about his story that he can. Do you think he can manage that?"

"Yes," Drost said.

"And while he's there, get him to send someone out here to pick her up."

As Grant had foreseen, the dog was useless. It was a German shepherd, dark-grey, thick-coated, alert to everything. It was the best in the business, and Martin was very proud of it, but the trail it might once have followed was cold, and there were scents everywhere. It went around the pit on its lead, snuffling the ground, stopping every now and then to look at Martin, eager but unsure of what it was supposed to be looking for. After a while Martin took it back to the van and came back to help the others with the ground search.

Kroll finished photographing everything worth photographing and followed them around carrying his camera to record anything new, but they found nothing but the remains of nights much longer ago than the night the girl had been brought there.

Halfway through the search, an ambulance arrived. The body was loaded onto a stretcher, covered with a clean sheet, and Reynolds and Kroll carried it up out of the pit. Then Daniel Coile arrived. Drost told him what they suspected, and Reynolds took him to town to confirm it.

Finally, when the light was beginning to fade, Hooper came back.

"It doesn't add up," he said. "There's almost an hour missing. He's been lying."

"Well," Grant said, "it looks as if we have an open and shut case."

CHAPTER
THREE

Lieutenant Bernard Dorkin, awaking from a troubled sleep, became conscious of the clatter of metal-shod boots on a metal staircase. He rolled over onto his back on the crude army cot and looked at the room. The walls were a bilious institutional green. From the ceiling an unshaded light bulb hung on a cord. On a clothes rod along the wall, his uniform, dispossessed of him, hung on a cheap wire hanger among a line of cheap wire hangers. There was a wooden chair against the wall, on which he had placed his kit. And that was all. Apart from the uniform and the kit, it might have been a more than ordinarily spacious jail cell.

Dorkin looked at his watch. It was just after seven. He willed himself to get up and went over to the window and ran up the blind. The sky was cloudless, and there was the look about it already of a hot day. Below his window, there was a small gravel parade square, bordered on the other three sides by a collection of ramshackle sheds. Beyond these, he could see larger brick buildings dropping away down the hill towards the creek that divided the town in two. On the other side of the creek, the roofs and gables of white wooden homes showed through a dense canopy of leaves. In the early morning sunlight, they seemed an image of small-town tranquility—an image more attractive certainly than the one he had formed in his imagination of a ramshackle farm town full of hillbillies and horseshit. When he had arrived the night before, it had been too dark for him to see any of this, and in any case he had been too exhausted and too angry at being there at all to give a damn what the town looked like.

This time yesterday, he had been two hundred miles away at Camp Utopia on the Bay of Fundy coast, where for two years he had served as a provost officer, dealing with the usual trail of soldiers' offenses—drunkenness, disorderly conduct, assault and battery, petty theft, damage to property, paternity—while he waited for what he had heard rumoured was going to be a favourable response at last to his request for a transfer to an infantry unit and an overseas posting. As the casualties mounted around Caen, a reinforcement crisis was brewing, and what was going to be an ill wind for the Zombies was going to be the wind of freedom for Dorkin.

It was this that he had hoped to hear about the day before when he was summoned into the presence of the Officer Commanding, Camp Utopia. Instead, he was ordered to report that afternoon to the senior Provost Officer, Colonel Meade in Fredericton, on a matter of urgent importance. As was the way, he wasn't told what the matter of urgent importance was. He was assigned a Jeep and a driver, and an hour later he was being bounced along the coast road through the early morning fog towards Saint John en route to Fredericton.

When he arrived in the early afternoon, he found that Colonel Meade was in a meeting, and he waited for over two hours in Meade's outer office while a CWAC clerk, blonde, attractive, and remote, typed and answered the phone and took down messages and departed and returned and went away with files and came back without them. There was clearly a flap on, and the longer it lasted the more uneasy Dorkin became. Finally, Meade arrived, expansively apologetic, with a briefcase and an armload of folders.

Colonel Kenneth Meade was a man in his fifties with an ample figure and a taste for formal rotundities of speech, a staunch monarchist, a staunch imperialist, a man whom it was not difficult to find ridiculous if one forbade him his premises. But in his few dealings with him, Dorkin, though a very junior officer, and half his age, had always found him open and friendly, and partly in spite of himself, he had come not only to respect, but rather to like him and to feel that he was in some measure liked in return.

The office into which Meade ushered Dorkin was furnished as it might have been in a civilian firm rather than an army H-hut. There were heavy curtains, a heavy oak desk, bookcases of real wood, opulent, upholstered armchairs.

Meade dropped into the chair behind his desk and sighed heavily.

"You're wondering," he said, "not unnaturally, what this is all about. Well, what it's all about is the Williams case. You've heard about the Williams case, of course?"

Dorkin nodded. Everyone had heard about the Williams case.

"The preliminary hearing is tomorrow, as you may also have heard," Meade continued, "and what all this has been about today is making some decision about what attitude the army should adopt to the proceedings."

It struck Dorkin that it was a little late to be getting around to deciding that, but he kept the observation to himself.

"There has been a view abroad from the beginning," Meade said, "that the army should wash its hands of the whole affair by giving Private Williams an immediate dishonourable discharge and leaving him to be tried as a civilian. The first advocates of this view were Williams's commanding officer, Captain Fraser, and the commander of the local branch of the Legion, Colonel Blaikie. Blaikie has a lot of influence with important people, and he's been bombarding people here and in Ottawa with letters and phone calls for a month. What Blaikie and his people are arguing is that Williams will bring the uniform into disrepute if he is tried as a soldier. And they point out that Williams is a conscript who was brought into the army against his will and who has refused overseas service—that he is a Zombie, in short—and that therefore he has no right to involve the army in his infamous crime and certainly no claim to any assistance from it, legal or otherwise."

Meade paused and lit a cigarette.

"The trouble with this view," he went on, "as I have spent several hours pointing out, is that it assumes Williams to be guilty before he has even been committed for trial, let alone convicted.

"What was decided yesterday and then argued all over again today was that for the time being the army should adopt the compromise of sending someone with a watching brief to the preliminary hearing tomorrow and make a further decision after that. They didn't want anyone too senior, and of the people who were available we thought you seemed the most suitable. You have no objection?"

"No, of course not," Dorkin said.

He had learned long ago that what you can't help in the army, you may as well pretend to like.

"Good," Meade said. "I was sure we could rely on you. Now, unless he has found one today, I understand that Williams does not have legal counsel. Before the hearing, you should see him and tell him not to say anything whatever during the preliminary hearing unless he has got legal counsel. We've already told the magistrate that you're coming, and he'll probably give you the right to examine witnesses, but I don't want you to do that. You're not to give the impression that the army is conducting a defence for Williams. I want you to listen and form an opinion of the evidence and come back to me and report. Then someone somewhere will have to make some clear decision about what is going to be done."

So it was that an hour later Dorkin was back in his Jeep on the way up the river to Wakefield, and here he was this morning looking out the window of his spartan quarters in the local armoury.

He got into his trousers and shirt and took his shaving kit and went off towards the officers' bathroom to shave and shower. His room opened onto a walkway above the back end of the drill floor, which doubled as a dormitory for the garrison of Zombies. Between the rows of double-decker bunks that lined the wall, they were getting themselves put together under the eye of Sergeant MacCrae, who had looked after getting Dorkin and his driver settled the evening before.

The evening before, Dorkin had also met Captain Fraser and had recognized him at once for what he was: one of those pre-war reserve officers who after supper a couple of evenings a week had played at being soldiers so that other nights of the week they could drink Scotch in the local Legion Hall away from their boring wives. When the war started, in the days before anyone really knew what was what, they were called up, given real commissions and jobs they were incompetent to fill and for a few months officered a good part of the Canadian Army. Then reality set in, and most of them found themselves shunted off into dead-end postings like Wakefield.

Thanks to previous encounters of this sort, Dorkin took all this in in a moment, and he saw that in that unguarded moment Fraser had seen him take it in and had put him down as a hostile presence. Talking from the height of his rank, Fraser had hinted unmistakably enough that he regarded Dorkin's being sent, even as an observer, as an intrusion on his authority and a questioning of his judgement. It was clear that he would have liked Williams hanged without even the bother of a trial and that he saw Dorkin as someone who might somehow sully the purity of these feelings. On his side, Dorkin had hidden behind his subordinate rank to stay clear of any argument, but he did not want to have to deal with Fraser again this morning or any other morning.

When he had shaved and showered, in more or less cold water, and got himself into his uniform, Dorkin hunted out Sergeant MacCrae to ask where he could breakfast and was directed to the town's main hotel, a great four-storey barn of a building with a balcony from which a Union Jack hung out over the street. Three-quarters of an hour later, breakfasted, feeling a little better about things, he walked slowly up Main Street through the centre of town and off along a little side street to the George County jail and his first business of the day.

Dorkin had never seen a good-looking jail, and this one was particularly ugly. It was a square, two-storey building, constructed of some kind of cheap orange brick, and it was much too wide for its height so that it seemed to be crouching by the sidewalk like a gigantic toad. There had been some half-hearted passes at ornamentation which seemed somehow only to enhance the ugliness. There were remembrances of medieval stonework, pointed windows of vaguely ecclesiastical shape, and at one corner a squat tower topped with truncated sandstone battlements.

Dorkin mounted the steps under the squat little tower, pushed open the door, and found himself in a short hallway with barred windows on one side, an open door on the other, and a much heavier, closed door in front of him. There was a stale smell and somehow an atmosphere of darkness in spite of the morning sun that was pouring in through the barred windows.

Dorkin went to the open door. Inside, a tall man in an immaculately tailored grey suit was sitting behind a desk smoking a cigarette. He was fiftyish with a clean-lined, rather English face, dark hair going grey at the temples, and cool, hazel eyes. Dorkin noticed the thin scar that angled down across one side of his forehead.

"Good morning," he said. "I'm Lieutenant Dorkin. I've been sent up from Area Headquarters. I'd like to talk with Private Williams for a few minutes before the hearing."

The man rose and held out his hand across the desk.

"I'm George Carvell," he said. "The local sheriff."

Some wry twist in the voice made it sound like a parody of a line from a western movie.

"You've come to represent Williams?" he asked.

"No," Dorkin said. "I'm just here to look on and report back to Fredericton."

"He's not going to have any counsel then?"

"No, not so far as I know. That's why I want to talk to him."

Carvell raised his eyebrows.

"Captain Fraser gave me the impression that the army was sending someone up to act as counsel."

"No. Captain Fraser must have misunderstood the situation."

"He should have counsel."

"I agree," Dorkin said. "But the army's view, at the moment anyway, is that that is not its responsibility."

"It's a nasty affair," Carvell said.

"It is," Dorkin agreed. "In more ways than one."

"Well," Carvell said, "I'll take you out back."

He led Dorkin out to the door at the end of the hallway and took out a ring full of keys and inserted one into the lock.

"The dungeon," he said.

Beyond the door there was a line of cells on either side of a corridor. They were empty except for one in which a man who looked like a tramp was lying curled up on his bunk facing the wall.

"Thirty days for drinking and fighting in public," Carvell said.

From a door at the end of the corridor, a grotesquely fat man emerged.

"Henry Cronk," Carvell said. "Our county jailer. Lieutenant Dorkin is here to see Private Williams."

"I can lock you in," he said to Dorkin, "but there's an interview room down here where you'll be more comfortable."

"I would prefer the room," Dorkin said.

"Open up, Henry," Carvell said.

Henry rattled his way along a ring of keys until he found the right one and turned it in the lock. He managed to convey a sense of ritual importance to the unlocking of the door, a sense of some imminent moment of high drama, as if the door were going to open on someone fabulous, like Bluebeard or Jack the Ripper. Instead it opened on a prisoner who looked as harmless as any Dorkin had ever seen. But then, he thought, Dr. Crippen would also have looked harmless. And Sweeney Todd. Even Adolf Hitler, whom someone very unlucky had just failed to kill with a bomb a few days before. Williams was the first murderer, putative or otherwise, whom Dorkin had ever seen.

Williams had been lying on his bunk, but he got up warily when the door was opened. He was not wearing his battle dress but a rumpled work uniform.

"This is Lieutenant Dorkin," Carvell said. "From headquarters in Fredericton. He wants to talk to you."

Williams hesitated, still wary, watchful. Then he saluted perfunctorily, the kind of salute that in the wrong place to the wrong officer could get a soldier put on a charge.

The room that Carvell showed them to was like other rooms Dorkin had sat in with other prisoners in other jails. It was furnished with a plain wooden table and four plain wooden chairs. On the table, there was a small tin ashtray that would have been quite useless as a weapon. The window, of course, was barred.

Dorkin sat down at the table and motioned Williams into a chair opposite him.

"You can smoke if you want to," Dorkin told him.

"I don't smoke, sir."

He sat hunched forward with his fingers hooked nervously over the edge of the table. Dorkin noticed that the nails were bitten back almost to the quick. He seemed to remember that Williams was twenty or thereabouts, but there was something of the pimply adolescent about him. In spite of the jet black hair, his skin was white, untanned and untannable, like that of the Irish girls Dorkin had gone to school with in Saint John.

"Why are you wearing clothes like that?" Dorkin asked. "Where is your uniform?"

"The Mounties took it the night I was arrested, sir," Williams said.

"You didn't get another uniform?"

"No, sir."

That would be Fraser's doing, Dorkin thought, with the idea of distancing Williams from the army and himself.

"You still don't have a lawyer?" Dorkin asked.

"No, sir. My uncle tried to get one in Fredericton, but he couldn't find anyone."

"Your uncle?"

"Yes, sir. My mother and father are both dead. My father got gassed in the war. He couldn't work much, and he died when I was ten years old. My mother died a couple of years ago. They had a farm in Carnarvon, but that went to my uncle for debts or something."

"I see," Dorkin said. "Well, if you can't afford a lawyer, the court will appoint one for you. You can't be tried without a lawyer."

"Maybe after today I won't need one," Williams said.

Dorkin affected not to be surprised by such naivety.

"All I did was walk that girl a little way from the dance hall and leave her," Williams said. "I didn't do anything to her."

Dorkin studied him. He sounded confident enough, but he had had over three weeks to practise speeches like that.

"That may be," Dorkin said, "but I think I'd better warn you that a prosecutor doesn't usually go to a preliminary hearing unless he is reasonably sure that he has a chance of his case being sent to trial."

Dorkin saw Williams's face whiten even further, and the fingers dropped from the table edge into his lap.

"But I didn't do anything to her."

"I'm sorry," Dorkin said, "but I have to warn you. They evidently feel that they have enough evidence to justify a trial, and that is what will probably happen."

"What will happen today?"

"They're going to present the evidence they have to a magistrate. If he thinks it's enough to make it seem possible that you are guilty, he'll set a trial date in two or three months. If you had a lawyer, he would contest their evidence. Since you don't, you shouldn't say anything yourself at all. You'll only get yourself in more trouble. When you're asked if there's anything you want to say, you should say that you've been advised not to say anything until you have a lawyer to represent you."

"But then they'll think I'm guilty," Williams said.

"No, they won't. It's the normal thing to do in the circumstances."

Williams stared across the table at the window beyond which the leaves of a maple tree stood against the sky, and birds came and went, and the ordinary world went on. Dorkin was afraid Williams was going to start to cry.

"Do you understand?" Dorkin repeated. "You shouldn't make any statements in court. Or to anyone about any of this until you get a lawyer. But listen to what is said so that you can tell your lawyer when you have one about anything which doesn't seem to be an accurate account of what happened. Do you understand?"

"Why couldn't my uncle find a lawyer?" Williams asked.

"I don't know," Dorkin lied. "There may not have been anyone who was free to take the case."

No one would take it, Dorkin knew, because it was a case where there was nothing to be gained—not money evidently and certainly not glory. If Williams were convicted, his lawyer would be seen as having chalked up a well-deserved defeat in defence of a bad cause, and he would have to endure such guilt as he might be capable of at having a client hanged—for if Williams were convicted, he would unquestionably be hanged. Everyone—the law, the army, public opinion—would certainly see to that. And in the unlikely event that Williams was acquitted, his lawyer would be seen by the public as a clever scoundrel who had contrived to subvert the course of justice.

The lawyer whom Williams would end up with, Dorkin knew, would be some court-appointed incompetent who would simply go through the motions of a defence because in his heart he wouldn't even want to win. Dorkin studied Williams and realized that he was almost certainly talking to a dead man. In the interest of his own peace of mind and his perhaps already fading belief in human justice, he could only hope that Williams was indeed guilty as charged.

The central court of George County was a majestic room some sixty feet square and two storeys high with a spectators' gallery at the back which made it seem a little like a theatre. The judge's bench was on a raised platform about four feet above the main floor. To the right and lower was the witness box. Down one side wall was the jury box, down the other a long table. Facing the judge and completing the rectangle, were two long tables, the left for the defence, the right for the prosecution. Behind these, separated by a low rail, there was seating for a couple of hundred spectators. The room was panelled in oak and filled with light from four tall windows along each side.

When he had left Williams, Dorkin had presented his letter of introduction from Meade to the presiding magistrate, Thurcott, a prim little man with rimless glasses, an old friend of Meade's with the same unmistakable air of good family. But this morning, behind his polished manners and his surface assurance, he was clearly nervous. Like Dorkin's, his normal clientele had been guilty only of petty crimes, where a little blood might have been shed, but no life had been taken and none was at stake. He was very unhappy that there was no defence counsel, and in its absence he arranged that Dorkin be seated at the table where the defence would have sat if there had been one.

There Dorkin now waited, surprised and a little intimidated by the unexpected magnificence of the setting in which he found himself. Behind him, every seat on the main floor and in the balcony was filled with a small fraction of the crowd that had assembled over the last hour. The rest were outside, filling the sidewalk and street near the jail, hoping at least for a glimpse of Williams as he was led in, creating an atmosphere suggestive to Dorkin of what it must have been like at a public hanging.

At five to ten, there was a commotion behind him, and Dorkin turned to watch the arrival of the prosecution: two attorneys followed by half a dozen assistants with briefcases and papers. Most of these people Dorkin did not know, but there was one whom almost everyone would have known if only from newspaper photographs.

H. P. Whidden was one of the wonders of the provincial bar. Nearing sixty now, massive, with a great mane of white hair combed straight back, he was an extravagant courtroom performer. Florid of phrase, grandiose of gesture, his specialty was the emotional appeal to high principle and noble sentiment in the service of whoever could afford his considerable fees. That the government had appointed him special prosecutor for this trial was a mark of the importance that someone in authority attached to securing a conviction. That Whidden had accepted it was a mark of the publicity the trial could be expected to attract—and of the fact that he felt sure of winning.

Twice when he was a student, Dorkin had attended trials where Whidden had appeared. Once he had heard him speak at the law school, and afterwards, as one of their most promising students, he had been introduced and had shaken the great man's hand and been given the famous pointed scrutiny that had made him feel a little like a witness who had just given himself away on the stand. Dorkin had never heard what the H. P. stood for, but he recalled a much-told story in which some witty judge had once said to Whidden, "Don't give me no sauce, H. P."

Leading his entourage today was his junior partner, Donald McKiel. Thirty years old, tall, lean, bespectacled, he was as great a contrast to Whidden as calculation could have devised. Dorkin had been in residence with McKiel, a freshman when McKiel had been in his final year. McKiel had been one of those frightening rarities, a student who had decided exactly what he wanted to become before he ever arrived at university and pursued his goal with unswerving singleness of purpose. No booze, no late nights, no dames. Some squash, at which he was very good, to keep fit, a movie or a game of bridge now and then to clear the head.

It was possible to imagine Whidden, even at sixty, destroying himself through some spectacular act of folly. Not so McKiel.

As they settled themselves, the clock on top of the post office down the street began to strike ten, the sound at first just registering above the buzz of conversation, then silencing it. In that silence, Thurcott emerged from the door behind the bench and took his place. Then from another door to the side, Carvell and a deputy sheriff escorted Williams to his place at the table along the side to Dorkin's left.

He was dressed as Dorkin had seen him earlier in his rumpled work uniform, which made him appear as if he were already a convict. As he sat down, obviously stunned by his surroundings, he seemed the very image of abject guilt brought before the bar of justice.

Thurcott tapped his gavel, cleared his throat, and began. They were here to conduct the preliminary hearing of Owen Thomas Williams, private in the Seaforth Highlanders of Nova Scotia, lately of the County of York, in connection with the death of Sarah Elizabeth Coile of the County of George, who met her death by foul play at some time between July 1 and July 5 this year of our lord 1944.

"The Crown is to be represented in these proceedings by special prosecutor H. P. Whidden and assistant prosecutor Donald McKiel. I regret to say that Private Williams is not represented by counsel. Is that correct?"

He turned to Williams, and Williams mumbled something inaudible.

"You understand that you yourself have the right to question witnesses if you wish," Thurcott said, "but I must warn you that anything you say will constitute evidence in this case and may be used against you. Do you understand?"

"I have been advised by Lieutenant Dorkin that I should not say anything until I have a lawyer," Williams said in a low voice, as if reciting a lesson.

Thurcott turned to Dorkin.

"I realize that you are not here to represent Williams," Thurcott told him, "but you are naturally free to seek clarification of any of the testimony that is presented, if you wish."

Dorkin nodded, disguising the nervousness he felt under the scrutiny of so many eyes.

"We may proceed then," Thurcott said. "Mr. Whidden, if you will call your first witness."

Whidden rose slowly, leaning forward with one hand on the table.

"I beg to inform you, sir," he said, the rich voice booming effortlessly, "that I have turned this part of the proceedings over to my assistant, Mr. McKiel."

A murmur of disappointment ran through the spectators, and McKiel rose and called Corporal Drost of the RCMP.

Corporal Drost, in full dress uniform, sat with a small notebook discreetly in his right hand and began the story of the discovery of Sarah Coile: the phone call from her mother, the interviews with Vinny Page and Williams, their futile enquiries, his expedition in the company of Sheriff Carvell to The Silver Dollar and their walk through the woods to the Hannigan Road, their investigation of the churchyard and their arrival at the gravel pit.

"As we descended the road," Drost said, "we became aware of a very pronounced smell, and on the west side of the pit, we came across the body of a young woman whom Sheriff Carvell thought he recognized as that of Sarah Coile. This was later confirmed. It was lying in some tall grass and weeds in a small hollow between two mounds of earth, and there had been no apparent attempt to conceal it. The body was lying on its back, fully clothed except for the lower undergarment, and it was obvious from the condition of the body that it had been the object of an act of violence and that it had been there for some time."

Drost stopped and looked at McKiel.

"Mr. Magistrate," McKiel said, "we have photographs which were taken at the scene by the RCMP photographer."

From behind, one of Whidden's assistants passed McKiel a heavy brown envelope. He extracted a pile of photographs and murmured something inaudible to the assistant, who made his way to the bench and placed one pile in front of Thurcott and another in front of Dorkin.

Nothing in Dorkin's experience had prepared him for what he saw. The first photograph had been taken near the feet of the body. The white dress was pushed up almost to the waist and except for a garter belt, stockings, and one shoe, the body below that was naked. One leg was lying straight out, the other slightly bent. The arms were spread a little to the sides. The chest seemed thrust upwards, the head thrown back. The mouth was open, forming an almost circular black hole, around which the lips seemed somehow to be rolling outwards from inside. The eyelids were partly open, but between them there was only an obscure darkness. The face was covered with patches of discolouration so that it would have been impossible for the uninitiated to know whether it was the face of a woman of eighteen or eighty or the face of a woman at all.

The next photograph was a close-up of the face, making its hideousness more hideous still. The next one was of the extended leg, and Dorkin saw that what he had taken in the first photograph to be dirt of some kind on the stocking below the knee was in fact a place where the stocking had been torn away and the flesh beneath hideously lacerated.

Dorkin went quickly through the rest of the photographs. There were three taken from further away designed to show the location of the body in the pit. There were photographs from each side showing the peculiar arch in the back, in one of which Dorkin noticed the second shoe lying beside the outstretched leg. There was one taken from the head looking down the body in which the face was thrown backward, pointing straight at the camera, as if blowing towards it its foul breath of decay.

Dorkin turned the pictures face down on the table and pushed them to one side. He became aware that Drost was concluding his testimony, explaining in his flat policeman's voice how he had summoned expert assistance from Fredericton.

Drost descended, and his place was taken by Detective Staff Sergeant Grant, who had sat on many witness stands and did not carry a little notebook. Unlike Drost, he was not in dress uniform but in everyday brown. Even McKiel shifted his tone of voice a little in the direction of deference when talking to him.

Grant crossed his legs casually, leaned one elbow on the arm of the chair, and continued the account of the investigation: the photographing of the body, the collecting of the nighttime debris around the pit, the failure to locate the missing undergarment, the futile attempt to pick up a trail with the dog, the futile attempts to find footprints or car tracks clear enough to take casts of for later identification.

"Is it your opinion," McKiel asked, "that Miss Coile met her death at the place where her body was found?"

"We found no evidence to suggest otherwise. My own opinion is that she did. If someone had been carrying the body away from some other site, I presume that he—or they—would also have taken more pains to conceal it."

"Thank you," McKiel said.

Grant recrossed his legs, surveyed the courtroom, and resumed.

"Once the investigation at the scene was well in hand and the staff was available, it seemed obvious that the first line of inquiry should be concerned with Private Williams, who was the last person known to have seen Miss Coile alive. I was naturally concerned that he might have heard of the discovery of her body and that this might have consequences which I wished to avert. Consequently, while the search was still continuing at Broad Street, I dispatched an officer to check the story which Private Williams had given to Corporal Drost the previous day.

"As a result of this inquiry, we found a number of serious discrepancies in Private Williams's account of his movements on the night of July 1. Witnesses will be called later to testify to this. As a result of what we had learned, in company with other officers, I went to interview Private Williams again about nine-thirty on the evening of July 5, when darkness had made further operations at Broad Street impossible.

"I asked Private Williams if he were willing to describe again his movements on the night of July 1. He agreed, but he seemed very nervous. He then gave substantially the same account which he had given Corporal Drost, and he agreed to sign a statement which we had drawn up summarizing his testimony. When I pointed out that his account did not agree in the matter of times with what others had said of his movements that night, he seemed to become even more confused and said that he had been drinking and that he must have been mistaken in the account he had given of these times. He also asserted for the first time that he and Miss Coile had stopped to talk for a while outside the dance hall.

I should make clear that Private Williams had been issued the customary warnings.

"We then told him about the discovery of the body of Miss Coile and informed him that he was to be charged with her murder. I secured a warrant for his arrest, and he was remanded in custody to the county jail.

"At the same time, I seized the uniform which Private Williams had been wearing the night of July 1 together with his other clothing and boots. These were sent to the forensic laboratory for testing for blood stains and so forth. I also seized Private Williams's personal possessions, and I have submitted an itemized list of these. We did not find among them anything which we know to have belonged to the deceased. On the day following the arrival of the body at the mortuary, an autopsy was performed by Dr. Pierre Bourget."

Grant departed and Dr. Bourget ascended the witness stand. He was a man in his middle fifties, lightly built with a long Gallic face and immaculately dressed in a grey suit. His expression, his manner in general, created an impression of detached, sardonic melancholy. Like Grant, he sat his chair with negligent ease. He summarized for McKiel his qualifications as an expert witness and began.

"On Thursday, July 6, I conducted an autopsy on the body of a young woman which I was told was that of Miss Sarah Coile of Hannigan Road, George County. I was told that she was sixteen years old. She was five feet six in height, and she weighed one hundred and fifty pounds at that time. She may have weighed more earlier. At the time of her death, she appeared to have been in good health. However, she was well into the second month of pregnancy."

There was a rustle of whispering in the court, and Bourget waited imperturbably for it to subside.

"At the time of my examination, I would say that the subject had been dead four or five days. I understand that she was seen alive around eleven o'clock on Saturday evening, July 1, and I would say that death must have occurred within twenty-four hours of that time. Because of the lapse of time and the hot temperatures to which the body was exposed before it was discovered, it is impossible to be more accurate than that. An examination of the contents of the stomach suggests that the subject had not eaten anything substantial within four hours of her death. Blood tests revealed the presence of alcohol in the blood in a concentration of .09, but the accuracy of that measurement might be open to question in the circumstances. If this were accurate, it would be enough to cause some impairment of physical function and no doubt of judgement, but would not result in what could be called real drunkenness.

"The subject had been the victim of a succession of acts of violence. The cause of death was unquestionably suffocation, apparently by having a cloth, perhaps an article of clothing, stuffed into the mouth and held over the nose. Small fibres were found in the subject's teeth, which under microscopic examination proved to be rayon. In addition, the face and upper body of the subject had been battered by a blunt object of some kind—a club, a piece of metal, a stone perhaps. There were fractures of the left cheekbone and the front of the skull, and there were thirteen contusions on the upper body and arms. In view of the absence of bleeding, it would seem that these injuries were inflicted after death. In addition, the right ankle of the subject had been gnawed through almost to the bone by some scavenging animal. This had also clearly happened after death.

"Examination also revealed the presence of semen in the vaginal tract, indicating that an act of sexual intercourse had taken place sometime within a few hours before death although it could conceivably have been afterwards. There were no signs of violence in the genital area, but minor abrasions there, or elsewhere, might have been obscured by the deterioration of tissues after death.

"In summary, the probable sequence of events was that the victim had sexual intercourse at some point not long before her death. She was then suffocated, at some time not later than twenty-four hours after she was last seen. After death had occurred, she was subjected to a violent battering with some kind of blunt object.

"Naturally the post-mortem examination revealed other things about the subject of a purely medical kind, and I have confined myself to those which seemed relevant to this hearing."

"Thank you, Dr. Bourget," McKiel said. "A few supplementary questions, if you would be so kind. Did you find any evidence that the victim had struggled against her suffocation? Or do you think that she was perhaps already unconscious?"

"There was no sign of a struggle—no broken fingernails, for example, no evidence of hair or skin under the fingernails, nothing of that kind at all. No evidence of blows other than those inflicted after death. However, it is possible that the victim had been struck a blow which had been sufficient to stun her before she was killed. In combination with the alcohol she had ingested, this might have left her incapable of defending herself before she lost consciousness completely."

"Did you see any evidence that the body had been moved from some other location?"

"There were no abrasions that would have been consistent with the body's having been dragged. Nor any tearing of her clothing. If she had been carried, of course, none of these signs would have been left."

"In other words, all of the evidence which you found was consistent with the victim's having been murdered where the body was found?"

"Yes, but it would not rule out the body's having been moved provided it hadn't been dragged. By car, for example."

"In your opinion," McKiel asked, "would the victim have bled much as a result of the injuries that were inflicted?"

"No," Bourget said. "I think that there would have been virtually no bleeding."

"In other words, the murderer would not likely have had bloodstains on his clothing as a result of his attack."

"Probably not."

"You testified that the victim was pregnant," McKiel said. "Was that far enough advanced that the victim would inevitably have been aware of it?"

"Nothing, I suppose, is inevitable," Bourget said. "But if she did not know it, she must have been singularly ill-informed on the subject."

There was a titter of laughter in the court, which was silenced by Thurcott, who so far had listened without comment to the testimony.

"The injuries to the ankle," he now asked. "What do you think caused them?"

"Some small animal, I should think, such as a dog or a fox," Bourget replied, and then allowed himself a small, macabre joke. "Not, I feel sure, by the murderer himself. And a bear would have done more damage and would probably have dragged the body, which there was no sign of, as I have said."

"I see," Thurcott said. "Horrible."

"Quite so," Bourget said. "The surprising thing is that not more damage was done given the time the body lay exposed."

"And that it was not found by some person in that time," Thurcott said.

"Perhaps," Bourget said. "I am not familiar with the locality."

"Members of your laboratory also conducted an examination of articles of clothing seized from Private Williams," McKiel said. "Could you give us the results of that examination?"

"On July 6, Staff Sergeant Grant turned over to the laboratory a Canadian Army battle dress uniform, three shirts, two neckties, two undershirts, three pairs of shorts, five pairs of socks, four handkerchiefs, and a pair of boots, which I was told were the property of Private Owen Williams. All of these articles were tested for blood stains, and none were found. We also examined the boots for blood stains or other human matter and found nothing. We also examined the traces of earth on the boots, but found nothing that could be of any use in determining whether the wearer had been in the gravel pit where the body was found."

"The boots, of course, could have been cleaned," McKiel said. "And even if these were the clothes worn by the murderer, the absence of bloodstains would not be surprising."

"That is so."

"The only material found on the clothing that might be of some relevance were faint traces of semen on the inner seam of the fly of the trousers," Bourget continued. "But how long exactly these had been there, there was no way of knowing since the trousers had been recently pressed."

"Nor," Bourget added, "could one know by what means the stains came to be there."

"They could be consistent," McKiel said, "with someone's engaging in an act of sexual intercourse without taking off his clothes, as might happen if the act were taking place in a semi-public place."

"Of course," Bourget said. "But there could be other explanations."

"I understand that," McKiel said. "I was merely suggesting this as a possible explanation. Not everyone goes around, after all, with dried semen on their trousers."

Bourget glanced at Williams with his sad, sardonic eyes and made no comment.

"Thank you, Dr. Bourget," McKiel said. "Your evidence has been most useful. And, as always, presented with exemplary brevity and lucidity."

Bourget inclined his head slightly in acknowledgement of the compliment.

"I have no further questions," McKiel said.

Thurcott turned to Dorkin.

"Lieutenant Dorkin, you are at liberty to ask any questions you may have."

"Thank you," Dorkin said. "I have no questions."

Thurcott studied his pocket watch and considered.

"It is nearly twelve o'clock," he said. "If it is agreeable to everyone, I think we should adjourn for lunch and recommence promptly at two o'clock."

Even as Thurcott was speaking, there was a clatter of chairs as the newspapermen began edging their way out to get copy filed. Thurcott glanced at them with distaste, rose and departed, and the courtroom became an uproar of voices.

At their table, Whidden's entourage were packing their briefcases, and as Dorkin rose to leave, he became aware that he had become the object of Whidden's attention. Ignoring Dorkin's awareness of him, he continued his study, then came across and held out his hand.

"Dorkin," he said, rolling the name around in his mouth. "Dorkin. We've met somewhere before."

"Yes, sir," Dorkin said. "You spoke at the law school three or four years ago. I was introduced to you afterwards."

"That's right," Whidden said. "Saint John boy, weren't you?"

"Yes, sir."

"Father was a butcher, was he not?"

The tone of voice was bland, innocent of malice, the put-down adroit. Dorkin was ashamed to feel the flush that overspread his face.

"No," he said. "He's a tailor."

"Yes, yes," Whidden said. "Had a little shop in one of those streets down near Market Square."

"Yes," Dorkin said. "He still does."

"Good," Whidden said. "Good. Ken Meade sent you up to keep an eye on things here, did he?"

"Yes," Dorkin said.

Whidden chuckled.

"Good old Ken," he said. "How is he?"

"Fine, I believe."

"Good," Whidden said. "That's good. Yes. Well, give him my regards when you next see him."

He chuckled again to himself and strolled back to join McKiel. He murmured something to McKiel, and McKiel paused in the packing of his briefcase and glanced up at Dorkin, who was still standing where Whidden had left him, feeling a fool and filled with an impotent and ancient rage.

CHAPTER FOUR

Back at the armoury, Dorkin went along the landing to the bathroom, stripped to the waist, and ran water, still cold, into the basin. Then, looking at his face in the mirror, he experienced an unsettling moment of dissociation. The face that looked back at him seemed suddenly unfamiliar—not the face that he had accustomed himself to see and that he assumed that others saw, but a different face, somehow lesser, somehow ridiculous, like the shameful faces foisted upon the ego by adolescence.

Although he did not look it, Bernard Dorkin was Jewish. He had dark-blond hair, blue eyes, broad features, so that if he looked anything definitive, he looked Slavic, as in part no doubt he was. Moreover, his father was a socialist and a militant atheist, and Dorkin had been in a synagogue only once in his life. Nevertheless, in the eyes of the world he remained intransmutably Jewish, and, if only because of that, he was Jewish in his own eyes as well. He would have preferred not to have been Jewish in anyone's eyes, not because of any sense of shame or inferiority, but simply because it involved him in difficulties (such as his brush with Whidden) that got in the way of what he wanted to do with himself.

His father had been born in the Ukraine, the son of a village tailor, and at the age of thirteen he had already been working with his father for three years and might well have lived out his life as a village tailor if it had not been for a bizarre accident. One morning, just before dawn, his father, Dorkin's grandfather, a pious man, had gone out alone to a remote millpond, perhaps for some private act of purification, and when he had not returned three hours later, a search was begun from the village. Somehow, in some way no one was ever to know, he had been caught in the millwheel. When they found him, his body had been beaten to a pulp, and Dorkin's father had decided that whoever it was who ruled the world, it was not the God of Israel, nor any other god an honest man would want anything to do with.

For another three years, Dorkin's father had tailored on in his village, and then in the chaos in Russia before the First World War, he had uprooted himself, and following in the wake of someone else from his village, had arrived one bitter winter morning in Saint John, speaking not a word of English. But he was a good tailor, and he did well and married and after a while set up his own shop and continued to do well.

He had two daughters, and one son, Bernard. He was still peasant enough to value sons above all else. He made Bernard a reader like himself and like himself a person who thought about things, and Bernard did him proud. He led classes. He won prizes. He got a scholarship to university and went on to law school. Unlike some of his contemporaries, he did not see the law as a stepping stone to grand political office. Nor did he see himself as a trial lawyer. His intention was to do the kind of office law that would offer him security and leisure for the things he enjoyed, such as books and music. After he graduated, he had practised with a Saint John firm for six months to establish his credentials, and then he had enlisted. He would soon have been conscripted anyway, but he knew more than most people what was going on in Nazi Europe, and he had enlisted out of conviction. But instead of finding himself in Europe as part of the crusade against fascism, he had found himself part of the legal apparatus in Camp Utopia, dealing not with the kinds of things for which he had primarily prepared himself but with the petty criminalities of the stupider levels of the Canadian Army.

And now, just when his prospects for escape had begun to look good, the business of Williams had come up, and it made him very nervous. But with luck, in a day or two at most, he would be out of it. And H. P. Whidden, K. C., could go fuck himself.

At five to two, Dorkin was back in his place in the courtroom. Whidden, McKiel, and company were already there when he arrived, Whidden and McKiel conferring in low voices while the underlings unpacked the briefcases. They did not look up when Dorkin arrived, nor even when Williams, abject and untidy, shuffled in with his escort.

As Williams was seated in his chair, Dorkin studied his face. But Williams's face told him nothing. The mere fact of his being accused was producing symptoms indistinguishable from those of guilt, as accusation always did, even in the pettiest of charges. Jaywalkers, shoplifters, murderers, the most purely innocent—hailed before the law, they all presented one face or another from the same limited repertoire: fear, shame, confusion, unconvincing indignation.

At two o'clock, punctual again almost to the second, Thurcott took his place, and McKiel rose and outlined his agenda for the afternoon. He intended to call witnesses to testify to the movements of Sarah Coile on the evening of July 1. He intended also to call witnesses to testify to the movements of Private Williams insofar as these could be known. The police had interviewed a very large number of people whose knowledge had some bearing on these questions, but since he was sensible of the painful nature of the case and also of the need not to waste the time of the court, he intended to call only those witnesses whose testimony he considered essential rather than merely supplementary. The prosecution, he said, was hoping to complete its case before the end of the afternoon.

Dorkin had expected the hearing to last at least two days. This unexpected brevity could only mean that the prosecution's case was so strong that it had far more evidence than it needed. No doubt, there would also be a concern on Whidden's part to orchestrate his presentation in such a way that his own appearance at the trial itself was not an anticlimax. Dramatic surprises of some kind would have to be held back. It would all be very skilfully structured.

McKiel's first witness was Lavinia Page. Appearing tiny even in her high-heeled shoes, she walked with small, mincing steps to the witness stand. She was wearing a long-sleeved navy blue dress and a little white and navy tam perched jauntily on one side of her head. She sat down and smoothed her dress over her knees.

McKiel suavely put her at her ease. Her name was Lavinia Page, but she was known to her friends as Vinny. She lived on the Bangor Road a quarter of a mile from the Hannigan Road. She had known Sarah Coile for many years, but they had just become close friends over the last three years. Sarah was a nice person. She laughed a lot, and she was liked by everyone who knew her.

McKiel then led her through the events of the evening. Vinny described how Sarah had dropped in on her in the afternoon on her way home from town, how they had arranged to go to the dance along with Vinny's boyfriend, Brick, how Sarah had danced with Owen Williams, how Sarah and Williams had gone out at intermission and not come back. This had happened at ten-thirty, the usual time for the intermission.

"Tell me," McKiel asked in a gentle, understanding tone of voice, "did you and your friend and Sarah have anything to drink?"

"Yes," she said after what struck Dorkin as a perhaps carefully calculated hesitation. "We all had a drink of rye."

"And did Williams have rye with him too?"

"I think so. The soldiers always did."

"So she may have drunk more while she was with him?"

"Yes."

"Would you say that Sarah was someone who was accustomed to handling a fairly large amount of alcohol in an evening? Did she generally drink very much?"

"No, she didn't usually. Just a drink or so at a dance. Nothing to get drunk on."

"But on this particular night, things may have turned out so that she had more than usual and might not have been able to defend herself if anything untoward happened?"

"Yes, I think that could be."

"Now," McKiel said, "I'm going to have to turn to a more delicate question. Did Sarah ever confide to you that she was going to have a child?"

"No, never."

"Were you surprised when you learned about her condition?"

"Yes, I was very surprised. I don't know how it could have happened. She was a good girl. She was a very religious girl."

"You have no idea who the father of her child might have been?"

"No."

"Someone she met at one of the dances perhaps."

"Perhaps."

"Thank you, Miss Page," McKiel said. "You have been very helpful."

Vinny Page was followed by a terrified little lance-corporal who was on the stand to testify to only one thing. He had been in charge of the orderly office when Private Williams returned on the Saturday night of July 1 at 12:33 AM.

"We turn now," McKiel said, glancing at his watch, "to witnesses who will testify to some of Private Williams's movements between the time he left the dance hall with Sarah Coile and his arrival back at the armoury."

Mrs. Linda Clark was a big-boned, ample woman of forty, with a bold, broad face and flaming red hair. She spoke in a deep voice roughened, Dorkin guessed, by a quarter of a century of Buckingham cigarettes with some help perhaps from Messrs.

Seagram & Co. She was the proprietress of The Maple Leaf canteen on the Bangor Road.

"Mrs. Clark," McKiel said, "we have heard that Private Williams came to your canteen the night of the dance. What time was that?"

"It was about ten to twelve. I remember because I close at midnight, and when he came in, it was getting late, and I looked at the clock."

"At the time I understand that there was only one other person in the canteen, a Mr. John Maclean. So please tell us what happened."

"The soldier bought a glass of ginger ale from the fountain and went into one of the booths at the back to drink it. I told him he couldn't stay long because I was going to close in a few minutes."

"Did he seem to be drinking?"

"I figured he probably was, but he wasn't staggering or nothing like that."

"How did he behave? Did he seem nervous or upset?"

"Not exactly nervous. But quiet. He seemed to be thinking pretty hard about something. But I didn't pay much attention to him. I was cleaning up so I could go home. Just about the time I was getting ready to tell him and John that I was closing, he left."

"You are certain that Private Williams arrived just before midnight?"

"He arrived at ten to twelve, just like I said. I looked."

"And how long do you think it would it take someone to walk from The Silver Dollar to your canteen?"

"Fifteen minutes, maybe twenty minutes."

"So that if someone set out at ten-thirty to walk from the dance hall to your canteen, you would expect him to arrive about ten to eleven rather than ten to twelve."

"Yes, unless they walked awful slow."

She was followed on the stand by John Maclean. He was wearing an old suit that looked like the kind of thing people picked up at the Salvation Army and that left half an inch of sock showing above his boots, making him look even more like a scarecrow than he might have looked anyway. Dorkin guessed that he was somewhere in his fifties, but his face looked as if it had been knocked around a good deal—by cheap booze or rough weather or whatever—so he wasn't easy to place. But when he began his evidence, Dorkin was surprised by how well he spoke, as if the scarecrow image were some kind of joke he had decided to play on the court.

"Mr. Maclean," McKiel said, taking it slowly as if he were talking to someone who wasn't quite all there, "we understand that just before midnight on Saturday, July 1, you were at The Maple Leaf canteen when a soldier whom we know to have been Private Owen Williams came in. I wonder if you could you tell us everything you can remember about what he looked like, how he acted, what he did while he was there? Can you do that?"

"I'll try to do my best," Maclean said, in a tone with just the faintest edge of sarcasm.

If there were witnesses who were intimidated by the setting, he didn't seem to be one of them.

"He came in," Maclean continued, "and I was sitting on one of the stools at the counter talking with Linda. He ordered some pop, and Linda gave it to him in a glass, and he went back into the corner to drink it."

"Excuse me," McKiel said. "But did you notice anything particular about his appearance?"

"When he went off to sit down, I turned around to have a look at him, and I noticed that he had dirt on his uniform. Not a lot, not mud or anything like that, but bits of leaf and grass."

"Did he seem to you to be drunk? Was he staggering?"

"No, he wasn't staggering that I could see, but I think he must have been drinking some because he had a bottle with him. There's a little mirror on the wall behind the counter, and I could see him back there. He drank a little out of the glass, then got a pony of rye out of his pocket and dropped some of it into the pop. Then he sat there and drank it. He wasn't there very long, just five or ten minutes. But all the time he was there, he never looked up at all. He just sat there scowling at the other side of the booth. Then he got up and left.

"After he'd gone, I went back to the booth to get the glass so Linda wouldn't have to do it, and I found that he'd left the empty rye bottle lying there in the corner of the seat. I took the glass and the bottle back to the counter for Linda and left. When I got out, I could see the soldier maybe a furlong down the road walking towards town. And that was the last time I saw him until I saw him here today."

He glanced at Williams, who looked back at him wide-eyed then turned away.

"The court will note," McKiel said as Maclean rose, "that Private Williams left The Silver Dollar at approximately ten-thirty. He arrived at The Maple Leaf canteen less than a mile away over an hour and a quarter later at ten to twelve. There is nearly an hour unaccounted for. I wish now to try to shed some light on that missing time."

The Reverend Zacharias Clemens of The Church of the Witnesses of the Lord Jesus Christ sat hunched forward a little in the witness box, heavy and shapeless, his large hands in his lap. His face might have been that of a farmer—plain, rather featureless, with a broad straight mouth and a nose that was a little too large. His hair, greying at the temples, was black and long. His eyes under heavy, black brows were pale blue, and as McKiel established for the court who he was they kept drifting vaguely away over the spectators to far corners of the room. He was dressed in a dreadful brown suit, white shirt, and a broad, funereally black tie.

"I appreciate how painful this must be for you," McKiel said, "and I shall try to be as expeditious as I can. In your deposition of July 7, two days after the body of Sarah Coile was found, you stated that you had occasion to pass the intersection of Broad Street and the Hannigan Road, sometime around eleven o'clock on the night of July 1, that is to say, not long after Sarah Coile and Private Williams left The Silver Dollar. First of all, I wonder if we could try to pin the time down a little more exactly if that is possible. I am sure you understand the importance of this."

Clemens considered, then began to speak in a rather nasal baritone with touches of what seemed to Dorkin a southern accent.

"I'm not sure how exact I can be," he said. "But I'll do my best. It was a Saturday, and on Saturday after supper, it is my practice to go to my church to think about my sermon for the next morning."

"Perhaps you could tell us where your church is, Reverend Clemens," McKiel interrupted.

"Yes, of course. I'm getting ahead of myself. My church is on the corner of Lloyd Street and Broad Street. You may know that Sarah Coile was a member of my church and that she was buried from there."

"And the gravel pit where Sarah Coile was found," McKiel said, "is between Lloyd Street where your church is and the Hannigan Road."

"That's right."

"So you went to your church that evening. What time was that?"

"I think around half-past seven. I had supper and did a few chores and then drove to the church. I remember that it was very hot. I worked in the church for a couple of hours. I don't pay much attention to the time when I'm there like that. Sometimes I stay for just an hour, sometimes much longer. That night it was dark when I left, but it hadn't been dark very long."

"Perhaps ten o'clock?" McKiel suggested.

"I would think so. Yes. Sometime about then."

"And then?"

"I got into my car and drove along Broad Street and up the Hannigan Road a little way to the home of Ada and Thomas Salcher. Some people here may know them. They are an elderly couple who paid me the honour of attending my church but who are now not very well, and so sometimes, every week or so, I visit them. We talk and pray together, and I try to make their lives a little brighter by reminding them they are not alone."

The pale eyes drifted away from McKiel to the mass of spectators, rested momentarily on Dorkin, then Williams, then drifted back.

"I stayed there about an hour and then drove back to the church. It must have been about eleven when I left. When I had been back at the church for a while doing a few final chores, I did look at my watch, and it was around eleven-thirty."

"So, allowing for your uncertainties, you would have left the Salcher house, let us say, somewhere between ten to eleven and ten after. Would that be fair to say?"

"Yes, I think that would probably be right."

"Now would you tell us what you saw on the way back to the church that has a bearing on this enquiry?"

"Yes. As I was turning off the Hannigan Road onto Broad Street, I saw a soldier and a woman in a light-coloured dress standing by the side of the road just on the corner by the old churchyard. They were under one of the trees, and I think that they must have been standing there talking."

"You are sure of the location?" McKiel asked. "This is a matter of great importance. Private Williams said that he left Sarah Coile at the point where Birch Road joins Hannigan Road fifty yards further down. You are sure that the couple you saw were not at that point on the road?"

"Yes, positive. I didn't drive that far. I turned left onto Broad Street, and they were there on the corner."

"As if they might have been going to walk along Broad Street?"

"Maybe. But I couldn't say that. They could have gone other ways too. They weren't walking. They were just standing there.

When I came along, they turned away, as if they didn't want anyone to see who they were."

"And did you recognize them?"

"I recognized Sarah Coile."

"And the man?"

"I didn't recognize him, but I could see that he was a soldier in uniform."

"Is he someone whom you see in this court?"

"I couldn't say that. I really didn't see his face at all. He turned away before I could get a look at him."

"Could you tell us what he looked like? Was he tall, short, medium?"

"Not tall. A little taller than Sarah. He wasn't very big. I mean he wasn't a heavy man, just average. And he had dark hair. I could see because he didn't have his cap on."

"Was his appearance consistent with that of Private Williams?" McKiel asked. "You understand that I am not asking whether or not you can say definitely that it was Private Williams, merely whether there was anything about his appearance that would make it evident to you that the person whom you saw could not possibly have been Private Williams."

"Perhaps Private Williams might stand up," Thurcott said.

Carvell got Williams awkwardly to his feet, and Clemens studied him.

"If he turned around," Clemens said.

Carvell put a hand on Williams's shoulder, and Williams turned.

"I do not want to be guilty of bearing false witness," Clemens said. "The man I saw could have been Private Williams, but he would no doubt resemble other people in this room too. I didn't notice anything special."

"But you can definitely state that somewhere near eleven o'clock on the night of July 1, you saw Sarah Coile standing on the corner of Broad Street and Hannigan Road by the old churchyard with a soldier in uniform."

"Yes, that is so."

"Thank you," McKiel said. "I must compliment you on the care which you have taken to be accurate in the evidence you have given."

Clemens descended, and Thurcott glanced at the pocket watch on the bench in front of him. It was now four o'clock, and the sitting had been going on for two hours without interruption.

"I have only one more witness," McKiel said. "With your permission I would like to recall Corporal Drost of the RCMP."

"I understand," McKiel said when Drost had taken his place, "that under your supervision an investigation was conducted of the people known to have been at the dance at The Silver Dollar on the night of July 1. I would be grateful if you would give us the results of that investigation."

With nothing substantial to base it on, Dorkin had conceived a dislike for Corporal Drost, though he could not help but admire the meticulousness of the investigation that his office had conducted into the movements of everyone who had been at the dance hall or had been seen around it. Of all the men known to be at the dance hall, Drost concluded, only Private Williams remained unaccounted for for any substantial period of time between 10:30 PM and 2 AM.

"But is it not possible," Thurcott asked, "that there could have been a man or men outside the dance hall whom you did not find out about?"

"Yes," Drost said. "That is possible, but in view of our detailed enquiries, it seems very unlikely."

"In the light of Reverend Clemens's testimony that he saw Sarah Coile on the Hannigan Road with someone whom he took to be a soldier about 11 PM," Thurcott asked, "did you check the movements of soldiers other than those at the dance? I am thinking of other soldiers in the garrison and soldiers who may have been home on leave."

"We questioned all the other soldiers at the armoury," Drost said, "and were satisfied that they were not at the dance hall that night. We have no way of knowing for sure how many other soldiers may have been in the area on leave, but we did make enquiries. We learned of five soldiers who were on leave, and we questioned all of them and found nothing to suggest that they had been anywhere near the dance hall on the night of July 1."

"I see," Thurcott said.

McKiel's summary of the evidence against Private Williams was a model of clarity and brevity. He began with what he took to be the indisputable facts. So far as Sarah Coile was concerned these were that at around 10:30 PM, she left The Silver Dollar in the company of Private Williams and was not seen again by anyone whom the police questioned other than Private Williams until her body was found four days later in the gravel pit off Broad Street, some half a mile or so from the dance hall. She had been dead since the night she disappeared or very shortly after.

So far as Private Williams was concerned the indisputable facts were that he left the dance hall with Sarah Coile at approximately 10:30 PM and was next seen at approximately 11:50 PM, an hour and twenty minutes later, at The Maple Leaf canteen, which is only some fifteen or twenty minutes' walk away. Evidence by one witness at the canteen suggested that Private Williams had been lying on the ground. When first questioned about his whereabouts that night, Private Williams said that he had left the dance hall with Sarah Coile and had walked her along the track behind the dance hall which became Birch Road until they came to Hannigan Road, where he left her to walk home by herself while he went down the Hannigan Road to the canteen and then back to the armoury. When subsequently confronted with the fact that his description of his movements left nearly an hour unaccounted for, he testified that he had been drinking and must have left the dance hall later than he had thought and that he and Sarah Coile had stopped for a while outside the dance hall to talk before walking out to the Hannigan Road. None of the witnesses who saw Private Williams that night considered him to have drunk excessively.

Reverend Clemens testified that at approximately 11:00 he had seen a girl whom he recognized as Sarah Coile with a soldier, not at the junction of Birch Road and Hannigan Road, where Private Williams asserted on two occasions that he had left Sarah Coile, but some fifty yards further up the Hannigan Road at the junction with Broad Street. Assuming that the girl was Sarah Coile, McKiel asked whether it were really plausible that she had left the dance hall with Private Williams at 10:30 and within half an hour appeared with a different soldier who nevertheless resembled Private Williams in general height and build, while Private Williams vanished into thin air for nearly an hour before re-materializing at The Maple Leaf canteen.

Surely, McKiel said, the truth was more simple, and the truth was that Private Williams left the dance hall with Sarah Coile at 10:30, was seen with her some half an hour later by Reverend Clemens on Broad Street, and then lured or chased her to the nearby gravel pit where he assaulted and brutally murdered her for reasons which he alone knows, perhaps because she had resisted his advances, perhaps because he was the father of her child.

McKiel remained standing briefly, then returned to his place and sat down beside Whidden, who rolled his leonine head to one side and said something into his ear. McKiel pursed his lips and nodded. As he spoke to McKiel, Whidden's eyes rested on Dorkin, unseeingly, as they might have rested on the tabletop or a section of the wall.

At six-thirty, Thurcott sat on the bench, unhappily, as he had seemed to do all day.

"I must ask you, Private Williams," he said, "if there is anything you wish to say about the evidence which has been given here today."

Williams stood up, and, his voice threatening to break, said, "I didn't do anything to Sarah Coile."

At the back of the courtroom, someone made a sound more like the growling of a dog than a form of articulate speech.

Thurcott cleared his throat.

"Nevertheless, Private Williams," he said, "in view of the evidence presented here today, it is my duty to commit you to stand trial in this court in the last week of September for the murder on or about July 1, 1944, of Sarah Coile. In the meantime, you will be confined in the county jail adjacent to this court. I declare this hearing concluded."

CHAPTER FIVE

In the uproar that followed, the pushing back of chairs, the scraping of feet, the sudden release of voices that all together sounded somehow inhuman and murderous like the sound of the sea among rocks, Thurcott rose and walked out of the courtroom, very straight and dignified with his papers under his arm. Williams, staring wildly around like someone who has just been violently awakened, was got to his feet by Carvell and guided out his different door.

Whidden placed his hand on McKiel's shoulder in a gesture of Olympian approval. Dorkin sat looking down at the random notes and doodles he had begun making during the afternoon. He was still contemplating them when Thurcott's clerk slipped up to his table, with his waiter's air of trying to seem invisible, and murmured in his ear, "Mr. Thurcott would like a word with you, sir, before you go, if that would be convenient."

Dorkin packed his papers into his briefcase and followed the clerk out of the courtroom. Thurcott was seated behind the desk in his office, looking very small and worried. He rose, directed Dorkin to an armchair, and sat down again.

"From now on, this case will be no affair of mine," he said, "but before you left I wanted to ask you to explain to Ken Meade how very unhappy I am about these proceedings. There should have been legal counsel, and if there were difficulties about getting one, the hearing should have been postponed until one was found. Given the evidence that was presented, I had no choice but to send the boy to trial, but there were a great many things that should have been questioned. Perhaps I should have intruded myself into things more than I did, but when you're on the bench, you really can't act as a defence counsel as well."

"Do you think Williams may be innocent?" Dorkin asked.

"I don't know," Thurcott said. "I don't know. The evidence presented today seemed to me far from conclusive. Whidden wouldn't have agreed to act as prosecutor if he hadn't felt pretty sure that he would win, but…"

He hesitated for several seconds before he went on.

"But—I probably shouldn't be saying this, and I would be grateful if you wouldn't repeat it to Ken—but with Whidden, feeling that he can win and feeling that the accused is guilty are not always the same thing…"

He hesitated again, as if there were more that he wanted to say, and Dorkin sensed the presence of an imperfectly suppressed anger. Then, with an almost imperceptible shake of his head, Thurcott changed the subject.

"Anyway," he said, "tell Ken about my unease with the hearing. Also, someone should see about getting Williams proper counsel. I understand that his uncle is here today. Perhaps you should talk to him now. Could you do that?"

"I could," Dorkin said, uneasily. "If I could find him."

"He's probably gone back to the jail. He was there earlier in the day. But Sheriff Carvell will know where he is, I expect. You could ask him."

Dorkin looked at his watch. It was already getting late for driving back to Fredericton. He could leave in the morning. And he would be able to tell Meade more clearly what the situation was.

"All right," he said. "I'll see what I can do."

Dorkin left the courthouse by a side door that led out onto a little walk that ran between the courthouse and the jail. The sidewalk, the far side of the street, the parking lot by the RCMP office, were still crowded with people, hanging around, gawking, drawn by the scent of death. As he walked the few yards to the jail and mounted the steps at the bottom of the squat tower, he was aware of their eyes upon him.

He found Carvell sitting behind his desk and explained his errand.

"Yes," Carvell said, "the uncle's here. Also his wife. They're in with Williams. You can wait and talk to them here if you like."

Dorkin sat down in one of the armchairs.

"What sort of shape is Williams in?" he asked.

"Not very good," Carvell said.

"What's the uncle like?"

Carvell shrugged.

"I don't think you're going to find he's much help. Nor the wife either. She's the blood relative. A sister of Williams's father. Their name is Whittaker. Hubert and Alice Whittaker."

Dorkin had only to look at them to recognize the accuracy of Carvell's assessment. Hubert was a heavy-set man of fifty or so, with a watch chain across his paunch, a bluff round face, and a walrus moustache. The wife was dark, small, thin-lipped. She seemed burning with rage, her black eyes under her straight, black brows, glittering like anthracite. They were both dressed in black, as if for a funeral.

Dorkin met with them in the room where he had talked to Williams. He sat on one side of the table, they on the other, stiff and hostile.

"Before I go back to Fredericton," Dorkin said, "I wanted to talk to you about arrangements for defense counsel for your nephew."

At the word *nephew*, Mrs. Whittaker glared fiercely at her husband.

"I understand," Mr. Whittaker said, "that I am not legally responsible to pay for lawyers in this business."

"No," Dorkin said. "You have no legal responsibility."

"I also understand that if I don't pay for a lawyer, the government will. Is that right?"

"Yes. He can't be tried without having legal counsel, and if no one else can provide it, the court will."

"Then why not let them?"

"You can let them. But your nephew would be better represented if he had his own lawyer rather than one appointed by the court."

"Suppose I did pay for a lawyer," Whittaker said, "and they decided that Owen didn't do it after all. Would I get my money back from the government?"

"No," Dorkin said, "I'm afraid not. That's between you and your lawyer."

"Do you call that justice?"

"No, probably it isn't, but it's the law. I didn't make it."

"The rich made it, Mr. Dorkin. The rich and the lawyers."

"That may be, Mr. Whittaker, but I can't help it. All I'm trying to do is find out what needs to be done in relation to your nephew."

"I already talked to a lawyer, Mr. Dorkin. I had a hard time finding one who would even talk to me. The one who did sent me a bill for twenty dollars for half an hour's talk. He told me that paying a lawyer for the trial could cost a thousand dollars or more."

"Possibly," Dorkin said.

"I don't have a thousand dollars, Mr. Dorkin, and I have two sons of my own that I have responsibilities to. I'm not going to mortgage my farm to defend a nephew."

Dorkin thought of observing that he had two farms if you counted the one he had possessed from Williams's mother for debts, but he let it pass. It wasn't his business.

"What was he doing at that dance hall anyway with that girl?" Mrs. Whittaker said.

"I don't know," Dorkin said. "It was a dance, that's all."

"Do you think he killed that girl?" Whittaker asked.

"I don't know," Dorkin said. "Possibly not."

"He says he didn't," Whittaker said.

"He never did a day's real work in his life," Mrs. Whittaker said. "Emma—his mother—spent every cent she had and a lot she didn't have putting him through high school so he could get a job in an office where he wouldn't have to get his hands dirty. And this is what it comes to."

"The army is a curse," Whittaker said. "His father was another fool. He couldn't wait to enlist, and in a year he was back with his lungs burned out so he couldn't ever really work again."

"Does Private Williams have any brothers or sisters?" Dorkin asked.

"No," Mrs. Whittaker said. "There were two boys before him, but they both died of the croup."

She made it sound as if this too were a well-deserved punishment for something or other. Dorkin looked at them exuding their air of greed and ignorance and decided that he had had enough.

"Thank you," he said, getting up. "I just wanted to be clear what the situation was."

The Whittakers looked at each other, too slow and gauche to disguise their relief at getting out of it so easily.

"It will all be looked after then," Whittaker said.

"Yes," Dorkin said. "Somehow it will be looked after. You needn't trouble yourselves." He saw them out the front door and watched them descend the steps. He felt sure that no one here would be seeing them again.

"A nice couple," he said to Carvell when he was back inside.

"Salt of the earth," Carvell said.

"I'd better see Williams for a few minutes," Dorkin said. "I can talk to him in his cell."

Carvell led him down the line of cells, and Cronk appeared from wherever he lurked and unlocked the door. Williams was lying on his bunk, curled up facing the wall. He turned over when they came in, and seeing Dorkin, started to stand, but Dorkin gestured him back, and he sat down on the edge of the bunk.

"Before I go back to Fredericton, I wanted to explain to you about what will happen now," Dorkin said. "I talked to your uncle, and it seems that he doesn't have the financial resources to pay for a lawyer for you."

"He always hated me," Williams said. "He didn't need our farm. He could have given it to me. I could have farmed. I probably wouldn't have been conscripted then."

"I'm sorry," Dorkin said. "I can't help that. He can't be made responsible if he doesn't want to be. He's not your guardian or anything like that, and you're not a minor. When I go back to Fredericton, I'll report the situation, and either the army or the court will pay for a lawyer for you."

"I didn't do anything to that girl," Williams said. "What's going to happen?"

He looked as if he were going to start to cry.

"Calm down," Dorkin said. "A preliminary hearing is not a trial. All it means is that there are enough grounds for suspicion to warrant a trial. In a trial, those grounds are going to be questioned by your lawyer, and you can't be convicted if there's any doubt whatever about your being guilty. They have to prove you guilty. You don't have to prove yourself innocent. The odds are all on your side."

Dorkin became conscious of his own voice, detached from himself, rushing along, filling the stale air with these pious half-truths—if they were even so much as half-truths. Williams was sitting looking down at the plank floor between his boots.

When Dorkin left the jail, the crowd was still there, though much thinned. The better dressed had gone home to their suppers, their newspapers, their respectable evening's rest, leaving behind the unashamedly, insatiably curious, those eternal, unoccupied watchers of life's calamities. Dorkin noticed that there was a surprisingly large number of women among them, mostly in their twenties, the age of women whose husbands would be in the army, fighting the war that Williams was refusing to fight. They all watched him in silence as he descended the steps, and he found himself hating them more than he could find reasons for, and also, to his surprise, fearing them a little.

Back at the armoury, he had hardly been in his room long enough to take off his tunic when there was a tap on the door, and he opened it to Sergeant MacCrae, who had waited for him on what Dorkin felt sure was merely the pretext of asking if he needed anything.

MacCrae was somewhere in his mid-twenties with one of those rectangular, plain, sun-roughened faces that Dorkin thought of as the regulation enlisted man's face of the Canadian Army. Unlike his flock of Zombies, he had a GS badge on his sleeve. He also had four ribbons on his tunic. Ribbons all looked the same to Dorkin, and as he wondered what they were, MacCrae worked his way towards what he had really come for, which was to get the inside story of what had happened at the hearing. Dorkin gave it to him, or all of it that mattered, because there were also things that he wanted to ask.

"Tell me about Williams," he said. "What was he like?"

"Well, he never caused no trouble, sir. He did what he was asked to do well enough, and he never drank or got into trouble in the town."

"Do you think he killed the girl?"

"No, I don't. There was something sneaky about him, but I don't think he was up to killing anybody. I never seen that girl in my life, but I heard she was a big, strapping girl, and one of the boys said that if her and Williams had got into a fight, she would have beat the shit out of him, if you'll excuse the expression, sir."

"But not if he hit her over the head with a rock first."

"No, I guess not. But he seemed pretty much the same as always before the Mounties picked him up, sir. And if he'd beat that girl to death, I don't think he could have come back here and acted as if nothing had happened."

"Did you ever hear who might have knocked her up?"

"No. The boys talked about that. Nobody had any idea."

"You don't think it could have been Williams?"

"I just know what I heard from the boys. They say all he ever did was dance with her a couple of times over the last two or three weeks."

"Did she run around a lot?" Dorkin asked.

"I guess so. She was supposed to be pretty well put together, and they say she liked to attract men. But she was supposed to be a cockteaser, sir, if you'll excuse the expression."

"Well, there's obviously someone around she didn't cocktease," Dorkin said.

"Yes, sir. Or someone who wouldn't take no for an answer."

"Could be. If you don't think Williams killed her, have you heard anyone make a guess about who might have?"

"No," MacCrae said. "I don't think it was any of the boys here. The Mounties spent two days questioning them. But that dance hall's a rough place. There are a lot of guys who don't go into the dance at all. They just hang around outside to drink and fight. Any one of those guys could have murdered the girl."

"But she was seen on the Hannigan Road with a soldier," Dorkin said.

"Yes, sir, but that could have been someone home on leave. Or someone in a tunic he'd picked up somewhere. It might not have been a soldier at all."

"Maybe. But there's more than an hour that Williams doesn't account for, and the Mounties say he lied to them."

"He was drinking, sir," MacCrae said. "So were all the other people out there. That guy Smith, the one they call Brick, ran his car off the road on the way home that night. I wouldn't put much stock in what any of them said about the time."

Dorkin thought about it and decided no. There were just too many people saying the same thing.

"So what do you think will happen, sir?" MacCrae asked.

"I don't know. It doesn't look very good."

"He didn't do it, sir. I just don't believe that he could have done that and come back here and for three or four days acted as if nothing had happened."

"You may be right, Sergeant, but that's not evidence that's going to cut much ice in court."

When he was gone, Dorkin opened the window and stood looking down at the parade square where a flock of ragged kids were chasing around kicking up the dust. MacCrae's protestations about Williams's innocence continued to roll around in his head. He also found himself remembering Thurcott's remark about Whidden, and he reflected that Thurcott's unease about making it imparted to it a strong ring of truth.

Shit, Dorkin thought.

A quarter of an hour later, driving the Jeep himself, he swung into the parking lot of The Silver Dollar and parked near the front door. There were no other cars in the lot, no signs of anyone around, but he felt as if he were being watched. He also had an odd sense of dislocation, as if somehow, notwithstanding the name proclaimed by the bullet-holed sign, he had stopped at the wrong place. The dance hall seemed smaller and meaner than the image he had formed of it from the testimony in court, and the parking lot with its dried-out potholes, its fringe of crushed weeds and grass, its litter of discarded papers and broken bottles, seemed smaller also and more squalid.

He walked along the side of the dance hall and then back towards the edge of the woods, trying to imagine what it would have been like that night. There were half a dozen paths leading into the woods, and he took one at random. Beside it there was the kind of litter one saw in alleys where rubby-dubs went to drink, and it was only the buzzing of flies that alerted him at the last moment and kept him from stepping into a pile of shit in the middle of the path.

After about twenty yards, the path swung off to the right and joined a wider track, which he realized must be the western remains of Birch Road. Gradually, this widened and became a sort of road, if two wheel tracks with grass and weeds down the middle could be called a road. In a place where there had been a puddle, he saw in the softened dirt the tread marks of a car or a small truck, and the testimony of summer nights began to reappear. The road was obviously a place to park and drink and, no doubt, make love. There were also several small clearings where a car could pull off the road, or where lovers could find privacy, and he passed three footpaths leading off to his left uphill into the woods, one of which looked well travelled.

When he got to the Hannigan Road, he looked at his watch, saw that it was ten past nine, and realized that he had forgotten his intention to time how long it took him to walk from the dance hall to the Hannigan Road. He guessed perhaps no more than ten minutes, even walking slowly and looking around, but in the dark with a girl in dance shoes it might have taken a little longer.

This was the corner where Williams claimed to have left Sarah Coile, and across the road and fifty yards further up was the corner of Hannigan Road and Broad Street, where the Reverend Clemens testified that he had seen someone whom he took to be Sarah Coile standing under a tree with someone whom he took to be a soldier and whom the Crown took to be Owen Williams.

Dorkin walked up the road until he was abreast of Broad Street and then crossed over. Near the corner, just outside the rail fence that ran along the churchyard, there was a large, ancient pine, presumably the tree under which Reverend Clemens had seen his couple. Beyond that there was a line of younger maples, then the scrub below which would be the gravel pit.

There were no streetlights out here, and there were no houses close enough to the corner to provide any real light. At eleven o'clock at night, even with a moon, it would have been very dark under those trees.

Dorkin looked at the weathered, boarded-up church, the weathered, toppling tombstones, then walked on along Broad Street. Like the dance hall, the road down to the gravel pit was a diminished version of his imaginings, neither so long nor so steep, scarcely forty feet. Even without the photographs he had seen in court, he could probably have identified the spot where Sarah Coile's body had lain. It was a little hollow among the mounds of earth that had slid down from the lip of the pit, and it seemed to Dorkin almost like a shallow grave. (Had her murderer thought that too?) What marked the place now was that all around it, the grass had been tramped away as on a footpath. Only in the middle where the body itself had lain was the ground still soft as it would have been then.

He stood above it, remembering the photographs he had seen that morning, filling the grave again in imagination with its terrible occupant. He wondered if McKiel had ever come out here, and he felt sure that he had not. And he was surer still that Whidden had not. They lived, both of them, in a world of words.

He crouched down and brushed his hand over the surface of the hollow and picked up a smooth pebble of sandstone a little bigger than the end of his thumb and put it in his pocket. Almost at once, in the real presence as it were, the questions began to swarm, and he again remembered Thurcott's fussy unease with McKiel's compelling logic.

If Sarah had been the cockteaser MacCrae had described and this was her night for cockteasing poor, dumb Williams, what possible reason could she have had for bringing him here? And even if she did intend to let him make love to her, why would she walk past a dozen more comfortable places in the woods and in the churchyard in order to come to a gravel pit? It made no sense.

The pathologist had been quite definite that she had not been dragged, but she could have been killed somewhere else, and then either carried here bodily or brought in a car. And Williams could have done neither. He was too small to have carried her even a short distance, and he had no car nor any likely access to one. What was more there was no real certainty that the body had been brought here the night of the dance. It could have been the next night or even the night after. He recalled Bourget's expressing surprise that the body had not been more badly mauled by wild animals than it had.

He found himself in a wilderness of speculation, and he was too tired to try to think it through now. The pit was already a deep pool of darkness, but the long summer evening was good for another hour of half-light, and Dorkin walked back the way he had come, timing it this time (it took fourteen minutes) and fixing the route between the dance hall and the pit more clearly in his mind.

At The Silver Dollar, he got into the Jeep, drove back down the Bangor Road, and turned off up the Hannigan Road. As he turned, he checked the odometer. As he recalled from this morning's evidence, Daniel Coile's place would be about a mile from the intersection.

Dorkin was almost past it when he noticed the homemade wooden mailbox with the single word *COILE* printed on it in green paint. He drove on, found a place to turn where a culvert led to an old woods road, and came back more slowly for a better look.

The house was a long way back from the road behind a snake rail fence. Dorkin recognized the early nineteenth-century colonial style, but whatever colonial elegance it may once have had was long gone. It hadn't been painted for decades, and there was a string of crude sheds, one of them half fallen down, that had been tacked untidily onto one side.

Lower down on the Hannigan Road, below the Coile place, there were a number of smaller houses that had never seen good times. In one of these, the Reverend Clemens had visited his sick parishioners on the night of July 1 before driving back down this road as Dorkin was now driving it, except that then it would have been after eleven o'clock and pitch dark.

When he reached Broad Street, Dorkin turned left onto it and realized for the first time that Broad Street did not meet Hannigan Road exactly at a right angle, so that the effect was that of a shallow hairpin turn. Gawking around as he approached, Dorkin was surprised by it. Even if he knew the road, someone making that turn in the dark would have to have his wits about him.

Yet in the second or two he would have had, the Reverend Clemens had recognized Sarah Coile and had seen that her companion was a soldier and had seen him turn his face away. He had known Sarah, so that was at least plausible. But the soldier in his dark clothing in the dark?

At nine o'clock the next morning, when he should have been well on his way to Fredericton, Dorkin was standing in the visitors' room at the George County jail looking out the window at the rain, a steady rain that was falling straight down as if through holes in the bottom of a bucket. When he was very young, it was in some such fashion that he had thought that rain must happen. It was to the sound of this rain that he had awakened a little before six after only three or four hours of sleep.

When he had arrived back from his excursion to the Hannigan Road, he had sat by the window of his room while the nighthawks and swallows and the last light disappeared from the sky. He went over again and again what he had heard during the day and what he had seen that evening, and he was drawn back inescapably to two conclusions. The first was that it was very doubtful if Williams had killed Sarah Coile. The second was that if he let matters take their course, Williams would almost certainly be hanged. It was the second of these conclusions that he fought to escape from. He was not God and neither was he a policeman, and he had done everything he had been asked to do and more. The rest should be left to the system. It was not his business.

Somewhere, from some corner in the depths of the mind, uninvited and unwelcome, there floated up Marley's dreadful cry in Dickens's *A Christmas Carol*: "Mankind was my business."

Shit, he thought again.

He could imagine even more clearly than he had before the kind of defence lawyer the system would be likely to provide Williams. He could, even when he thought about it, bring up particular names and faces—weakly ambitious, incompetent little men for whom the merest nod of approval from the great H. P. Whidden would matter more than their obligations to any client, let alone someone like Williams.

He went back and forth over it all night, sleeping, then waking up to it again, then going back to a sleep troubled by obsessive anxiety dreams from which he now retained only vague memories of flight and imprisonment and humiliation.

The upshot of the night's excursions into these labyrinths was that he was back again at this ugly little jail.

There were steps along the corridor, and then Williams was standing in the doorway with Carvell towering behind him. He hadn't shaved, nor even combed his hair. He saluted his perfunctory salute. He seemed sullen and suspicious.

"Sit down, Private Williams," Dorkin said when the door had closed. "I'd like to have a talk with you before I go back to Fredericton."

For a moment, Williams remained by the door, then he slouched over and sat down, and Dorkin sat down opposite him.

"When I go back to Fredericton," Dorkin said, "I'm going to try to get the army to provide a lawyer for you, and it will make it a lot easier if I can give them a clear idea of what actually happened the night of the dance."

Williams sat, looking down into his lap, and said nothing.

"Look," Dorkin said, "I can't make you talk to me if you don't want to, but I'm trying to help you."

"Begging your pardon, sir," Williams said, "but I don't know that. I don't know what side you're on. You told me to say nothing in court, and it didn't do me any good. How can I tell who you are?"

"I'm a lawyer. I spend my time trying to keep soldiers out of jail when they knock out store windows and get in fights with civilians. I was sent here by headquarters in Fredericton to give you what advice I could and to see what was happening and report back. When I told you to say nothing in court, I was telling you what any lawyer would have told you. If you had started talking, you would only have got yourself in more trouble. Without any defence lawyer to protect you, McKiel would have taken you to pieces. I'm on your side, or I'm trying to be."

Dorkin had begun to raise his voice angrily. Williams blinked.

"What is it you want to know about, sir?" he asked.

"I want to find out what actually happened the night of July 1," Dorkin said. "The Mounties think that you lied to them."

"No, sir, I didn't," Williams said. "I was mixed up about the time I left the dance hall. I wasn't paying any attention to the time."

"Okay," Dorkin said. "Tell me what happened. You went to the dance with some of the other soldiers from the armoury, and you met Sarah Coile there. How did that happen? Did you know her before?"

"I saw her around, and I'd danced with her once before, that's all."

"You weren't the one who knocked her up?"

"No, sir, I didn't."

"Okay, so what happened the night of the dance?"

"I danced with her a couple of times, and we went out and had a drink. Then we went back in for a while and danced some more. Then there was an intermission, and we went outside again. She smoked a cigarette, and we had another drink. I heard the music starting up again inside, but she said she didn't want to go back in because she wasn't feeling good. She said she must have drunk too much and that she wanted to go home and would I walk her partway. She said she knew a shortcut through the woods, so we walked along a sort of trail from back of the dance hall out to the Hannigan Road, and I left her there, and she walked up the Hannigan Road, and I walked the other way. That was the last time I saw her."

"Then on Tuesday, Corporal Drost came to question you?"

"Yes, sir."

"And you told him the story you just told me?"

"Yes, sir. But not exactly. There were a lot of little things I didn't tell him. I didn't think they made any difference."

"Did Corporal Drost caution you that what you were saying might be used as evidence against you?"

"No, sir."

There wouldn't be any reason to at that point, Dorkin reflected. Still, it might be something for a defence to keep in mind since they were using what Williams had said as evidence.

"Okay," Dorkin said. "What did you tell me just now that you didn't tell Drost the first time he questioned you?"

"I don't remember exactly. I didn't say anything about stopping outside for a drink."

"And what did you tell them the second time? The same story you told Drost before?"

"Yes, sir. Just about."

"And they got you to sign a paper with all that on it?"

"Yes, sir."

"Did you ever tell them the other things that you've just told me?"

"Not all of them, sir. I'm not sure. They confused me. They never gave me time to think."

"What did they say?"

"They said that I lied to them. They said if I left the dance the time I said, I would have been at the canteen a lot earlier and that I must have stopped somewhere along the way."

"When did they tell you that they had found Sarah Coile? Right at the start?"

"No, sir. Not until later. I didn't understand what it was all about at first."

"So what did you say when they accused you of lying?"

"I told them I hadn't paid much attention to when I left the dance. I knew it wasn't anywhere near the time I had to be back at the armoury, so I wasn't paying any attention. It must have been later than I thought. Maybe eleven-thirty. Or later."

"Did you tell them about going outside for a drink?"

"No, sir, I don't think so."

"Why not?"

"I didn't think. They never gave me time to think and get things straight before they asked me another question. If I didn't answer a question right off, they would ask a different question, and then come back to the first one later on."

"Okay. So you had your drink, and you heard the music start up after the intermission and you left to walk to the Hannigan Road. That would still only make it a quarter or twenty after eleven. It still took you a long time to get from the dance hall to the canteen."

"I wasn't walking very fast when I was with her. We just sort of strolled and talked."

"What did you talk about?"

"Nothing much."

"What?"

"Well, I guess I told her about the army, and she told me about where she worked. Just stuff like that."

Dorkin put his hands behind his head and leaned back and looked at Williams. The unshaven black beard made it look as if the lower half of his face had been dirtied with coal dust like the face of a miner, and it struck Dorkin that there was indeed something subterranean about Williams. He was in there somewhere, but a long way down, a long way behind the eyes he was looking out through.

He met Dorkin's eyes for only a second, a look furtive and questioning, and then he looked down at his hands with their bitten fingernails resting on the edge of the table. Dorkin let the silence spin itself out. Inside the jail it was stuffy in spite of the rain, but the windows were closed, no doubt nailed and unopenable.

"Private Williams," Dorkin said finally, "I don't believe that you murdered Sarah Coile, but I also don't believe the story you've just told me."

Williams blinked, looked past Dorkin at the window, then down again at his bitten fingernails.

"No one saw either you or Sarah Coile in the dance hall or outside after the intermission started," Dorkin said. "I think that you left the dance hall when you said you did the first time the Mounties questioned you, and that means that no matter how slowly you walked, there is at least half an hour that isn't accounted for."

Williams sat, and Dorkin waited.

"What do you want me to say?" Williams asked.

"I'm not here to teach you to say anything. I'm trying to find out what the hell happened that night, so that I can do something about finding someone to save your life."

There was another long silence. Williams squirmed in his chair like a delinquent schoolboy.

"Tell me," Dorkin asked, "did you stop somewhere in the woods with Sarah Coile?"

Williams glanced up at him, then down again.

"Did you?" Dorkin asked again. "I've got to know what happened."

"Yes," Williams said.

"All right. Now tell me what happened."

"Well, we went out. We were just going to have a drink from my bottle when some of the local guys who hang around out there started shouting stuff at us and making dirty talk, so we went around the corner as if we were going back inside. Then we went off along that trail back of the dance hall and found a place, a sort of little clearing."

"Did she seem to know where she was going?"

"Yes, sir. She said she knew the way because it was a shortcut back to her place."

"Okay. So then?"

"Well, we stood there and had a drink."

"Did she seem to be drunk?"

"I don't know, sir. A little maybe."

"So what did you do after you had your drink?"

Williams hesitated, at the edge evidently of some kind of brink. Through all this, he had never once looked at Dorkin directly.

"God damn it, Williams," Dorkin said. "It's important that I know. What did you do?"

"We kissed some."

"What else? Were you standing up or did you lie down?"

"After a while, we laid down."

"And? What did you do? How far did you go?"

Under the prison pallor, Williams was blushing now, and the hands moved nervously on the table, apart, then back together.

"Look, god damn it," Dorkin said, "you're not the first person in the world to pet with a girl in the bushes. What happened?"

"She let me touch her tits. Just through her dress. And her leg."

Dorkin waited out yet another silence.

"Then she wouldn't let me do it anymore. She said that we should get up. She said it was time for her to go home. She said that she must have drunk too much because she wasn't feeling very well."

"And then?"

"We walked out to the road, and she went off towards home."

"You didn't walk up the road with her to the corner by the churchyard?"

"No, sir."

"You didn't see her meet anyone up the road?"

"No, sir. But I didn't look. I just walked the other way down the road."

Dorkin studied him, wondering. There was an habitual unease, a kind of perpetual shiftiness about Williams that made it seem even when he was answering the simplest question as if he were hiding something. As if he were an actor performing a role that he was not yet entirely comfortable with.

"When you were with Sarah in the woods," Dorkin asked, "were you aware of anyone else around? Did you think you were being followed or watched?"

"Well, sir, there were a lot of people around out there, drinking and stuff."

"But did you think that anyone was actually following you? Did you have the sense that Sarah might be aware of someone around whom she knew?"

"I don't know. When we were lying down, she seemed to hear something that made her listen, but there were people all over out there."

"Did you ever get the feeling that she might actually be waiting for someone else?"

"No, sir. I never thought of that. But I suppose she might."

"Who do you think murdered her?"

"I don't know, sir. There were guys all over out there."

"But she didn't want you to walk her home?"

"No, sir."

"So you left her there, and you went off to the canteen. That all happened the way you've said it did?"

"Yes, sir."

"And you didn't hear anything about her until Corporal Drost came to talk to you on Tuesday about her being missing?"

"No, sir, I never heard anything."

Dorkin sat. He hadn't run out of questions, but he felt that he had run out of capacity to make sense of the answers.

"What's going to happen to me?" Williams said.

"I don't know. I'll see what I can do about arranging a defence when I get back to Fredericton."

"But I didn't do anything to that girl. All I did was leave the dance with her."

"Not quite," Dorkin said. "You also lied about it afterwards to the Mounties."

An hour later, Dorkin was sitting beside his driver, cramped into the passenger seat of the Jeep with the top up and the flimsy doors closed as best they could be and the rain drumming heavily on the canvas overhead. The road wound uphill and downhill, and they kept catching up with lumbering farm trucks, which they often had to follow for miles, and what with the road and the rain and the scuffed, inadequate windshield wipers on the Jeep, it took them nearly two hours to get back to Fredericton.

Throughout, Dorkin kept turning it all over in his mind, wondering, "Do I dare?" and "Do I dare?" And wondering also and more fundamentally, "Ought I to dare?" At officers' training, there had been much talk of initiative, but he had been in the army long enough now to know that in practice the exercise of initiative was a good way to get your ass burned and that the best way to have a quiet life was to do what you were told—certainly no less but certainly no more. When he got to Fredericton, he had still decided nothing.

If Meade had been impatient for his return, he was too polite to show it when Dorkin finally arrived in the early afternoon. He waved away Dorkin's salute at the door with a sweep of the arm as a thing unnecessary between them and motioned him to a chair. Then he summoned his CWAC corporal and had coffee brought, offered Dorkin a cigarette, which Dorkin declined, lit one for himself, sipped his coffee judiciously, approved, and settled back in his swivel chair to listen.

Dorkin did his best to keep to essentials, but even so, it took him almost an hour to summarize the evidence that had been presented at the hearing and to report on his meetings with Thurcott and Williams's uncle while Meade sipped and smoked and swivelled thoughtfully now and then in his chair.

"The evidence is entirely circumstantial," Dorkin said when he had finished, and only then recognized how much he had been colouring his account in Williams's favour.

"Most evidence is," Meade said. "It isn't very often people are brought red-handed into a courtroom. And even when there are witnesses, you can't always be sure they're telling the truth. Or know what the truth is."

Dorkin hesitated, drawing closer to the brink. He had said nothing yet of his conversation with MacCrae, of his own reconnoiterings of the site, of his second talk with Williams. He had the feeling that he was being carried forward against his better judgement, but he decided to go on. Sooner or later, Meade was going to hear about some of that from someone anyway. So in another half an hour, he gave Williams's later version of the events and what he had found out from his own investigations.

Meade stopped swivelling and sat with his chin in his hand watching him closely as he talked. When he had finished, there was a long silence that Dorkin broke himself.

"I don't think he did it," he said.

"Then who did?" Meade asked.

"I don't know. Probably someone who was hanging around outside the dance hall—someone the Mounties didn't check because they didn't even know he was there. There isn't even any real evidence that the body was left there that night. It could just as easily have been a night or two later. I suspect that she may have been dropped there out of a car."

"And Williams's lies to the Mounties?"

"I believe what he said. The first time, he didn't know that there was anything at stake, and he was too embarrassed to talk about necking with the girl. The second time, Grant put the heat on him. He was confused, and he was afraid to admit that he had lied the first time. Assuming that Grant ever gave him the chance."

"I suppose that's possible," Meade said. "But those lies are going to be awfully hard to undo in court."

"It's possible that they may not be admissible," Dorkin said. "I'm not sure the Mounties were all that careful about warnings."

Meade swivelled and thought.

"What do you think will happen about defence counsel?" Dorkin asked.

"Well, if the uncle or someone else in the family can't look after it," Meade said, "the court will have to appoint a defence counsel."

"Is there any possibility that the army could provide it?"

"It's never been considered so far as I know."

"Suppose a request were made? Would it be possible?"

"In theory. But there would be some very strong opposition to it."

Dorkin paused, gathered his courage, and not sure why he was doing what he was doing, and with a small voice deep inside telling him that he was a god-damned fool, he jumped.

"Assuming that Williams agrees, I would like to be allowed to act as his defence counsel," he said. "I would like to request that, with respect."

Meade considered.

"Well," he said at last. "That might take some doing."

"I understand that," Dorkin said.

"And Whidden is a pretty tough customer. Not to mention McKiel."

"I understand that too. But I don't think their case is that strong. What's more, I believe that Williams is innocent. I suspect that a counsel appointed by the court will not. I'm not sure he would even want to win given the fact that Williams is a Zombie."

"I'm not sure I'd go that far," Meade said, "but there may be something to what you say. But I thought you were anxious for an overseas posting."

"It can wait another three months."

"The war may be over by then."

"I don't think so," Dorkin said.

"No," Meade said. "In spite of all Montgomery's big talk, I don't think so either. But that's another matter. There's a meeting tomorrow about the Williams case. I'm scheduled to report on what's happened, and I can convey your request. But I think that any final approval is going to have to come from Ottawa."

He hesitated and then added, "You're a very capable young chap. That's why they've been hanging onto you at Utopia. I think I should warn you that taking this case may not do you any good no matter what the outcome is."

"It doesn't matter," Dorkin said. "I don't intend to pursue a military career."

"I wasn't just thinking of the military."

"I'll take my chances."

"Okay," Meade said. "If that's what you want, I'll put it to them tomorrow and see what I can do."

CHAPTER SIX

At the sound of the approaching engines, Dorkin turned and saw coming up over the tops of the trees at the edge of the camp a chunky little aircraft with a fuselage like a fat cigar and two fat, very noisy, radial engines—a Lockheed Hudson, one of the fleet that flew off the airbase at Pennfield Ridge two miles away to patrol the approaches to the Bay of Fundy for German submarines. Until a year before, the war zone had begun within sight of land here, and there had been one night in 1942 when people along the shore had spent hours watching a red glow like a stormy sunrise where a torpedoed ship was burning somewhere just over the horizon. The subs were operating further out now, but the Hudsons that had helped drive them there still flew off Pennfield in endless succession, varied now and then by training aircraft like Harvards and Ansons, more rarely by a wandering Lancaster or Mosquito, once by a Spitfire trailing its clouds of glory.

For two and a half weeks, Dorkin had gone about his usual duties, without hearing anything from Meade. As the days had gone by, he had become convinced that some other arrangement must have been made for Williams's defence, and he had begun to feel a sneaking sense of relief like that of a soldier who has volunteered for some more than ordinarily suicidal mission and has then been absolved from the consequences of his heroic folly by the mission's being scrubbed.

Then yesterday the signal from Meade had arrived. It read:

> *I have received permission from Ottawa to assign you the responsibility of defending Private Williams, and he has agreed to this. I have made all necessary arrangements for your temporary transfer to Fredericton HQ effective immediately, and for your accommodation, etc., in Wakefield. To preserve you from having your guts shaken out in a Jeep I am sending a staff car to pick you up at your quarters at 0900 hours tomorrow, Saturday, August 19. He will bring you here, and we can discuss further details then. Lt. Col. K. Meade.*

And so, at 0855 hours, Dorkin was standing in front of the officers' quarters, shoes polished to a metallic sheen, trousers pressed to a razor crease, face carefully shaved, hair flawlessly parted, nails clipped and filed. He watched the Hudson climb and bank away towards the coast, and then promptly at 0900 hours, as if it had been lying in wait just out of sight, there appeared, not a drab, khaki-coloured staff car, but a shiny black Packard 120 with military plates. It slid to the curb, a corporal got out, circled the back of the car, and standing by the right rear door, snapped Dorkin an excessively smart salute.

"Lieutenant Dorkin, sir?"

Dorkin returned the salute.

"Corporal Bennett, sir. Colonel Meade has sent me to pick you up, sir, as was arranged."

He opened the door, and Dorkin hesitated. He always rode in the front beside any driver of his own, but there was something emphatic in Corporal Bennett's manner that made it clear that in this car with this driver that kind of familiarity would have marked him as someone who was not quite all an officer should be. So Dorkin got into the back and the door was closed, with just the necessary firmness, behind him.

Three hours later, he was seated at Meade's special table in the officers' mess in Fredericton. They had finished lunch and were sipping coffee. Nothing had been said so far about the Williams case. It had all been very casual as if they were enjoying nothing more than a pleasant social occasion.

"So, tell me about yourself," Meade was saying. "You're not married?"

"No," Dorkin said.

"Anything on the horizon? Any flame burning?"

"Not now," Dorkin said. "There was, but it broke up in the spring. She didn't want to marry and then sit around for years if I went overseas. And she didn't want to be widowed at twenty-three."

"Too bad," Meade said. "But I can see her point, I suppose. It's hard for them. What about you? Much hurt?"

"I thought I was for a few weeks," Dorkin said. "But I'll live."

"A good time for romance, wars," Meade said, "but a bad time for marriages, I guess. Anyway, we should probably get down to business. Why don't we take a little walk down to the shore, and then I'll tell you what's been happening."

There was a path above the river, which on the other side of a light screen of trees was as smooth as a lake, and they strolled back and forth while Meade smoked a cigarette. Behind the officers' quarters, some benches had been set up facing the river, and when Meade had finished his cigarette, they settled there.

"Well," Meade said, "as you've probably guessed from the time all this has taken, there's been a good deal of debate here and in Ottawa about Williams and about your request. The movement to have Williams given an immediate dishonourable discharge hadn't given up by any means. It was obvious that this would represent a clear prejudgement of the case, but it still wasn't easy to get that into the heads of certain members of the officer class, and it all took time.

"Then there was the question of whether or not the army was responsible for providing Williams with a defence counsel. It seemed to me and others that so long as he was in the army, he was the army's responsibility, but in the end, it came down as much as anything to a matter of how things were going to look. It's a very political situation, and it's going to get more political every day this uproar about overseas conscription goes on. Anyway, the final consensus was that the best thing for the army to do in the circumstances was to present itself as putting the well-being of any soldier whatever, even a Zombie, above mere self-interest—unlike our esteemed Prime Minister. So it was finally arranged that you should be relieved of other duties and transferred directly to my command here. No one raised the question of assistant counsel, and I decided to take what I'd got and run. Needless to say, you can come to me for advice unofficially whenever you wish.

"I've also arranged a clerk for you from Fredericton. His name—believe it or not—is John Smith. I'm told he's a good typist and can run an office pretty well. He can also double as a driver. I've explained to him that this is a delicate case and that if he doesn't keep his mouth shut about it, he'll find himself shovelling snow on the Alaska Highway.

"I understand you weren't very well accommodated when you were up there for the preliminary. It probably wasn't anybody's fault, but there's an officer's room next door which is better than what you had. There isn't any officers' mess there, so you can eat in the town. I've also arranged with Fraser for an office for you and Smith and for any equipment you need. And you'll also need transport, so I've arranged for a car from the pool in Fredericton. It isn't very grand, but again it'll be better than having your guts shaken out in a Jeep. Does all this sound all right?"

"Yes, sir," Dorkin said. "It sounds fine. I couldn't ask for more."

"I've also been doing a little legal spade work for you," Meade said. "I've had a talk with the prosecutor's office, and I've had them pass over to me copies of the various depositions which the Mounties took in Wakefield. I'll give them to you before you leave. I've also got approval for you to examine the evidence that the Mounties collected on the site. I understand they brought in everything they found in the gravel pit but the birdshit."

"Thank you very much," Dorkin said. "I think I would have had trouble getting that material on my own."

"I wouldn't be surprised," Meade said. "Whidden isn't known for giving away his advantages if he can help it."

He gazed briefly at the river, then said, "You genuinely believe he didn't do it?"

"Yes," Dorkin said. "I do."

"You don't have to, you know. All you have to do to fulfil your duty as defence counsel is to say everything on behalf of your client that can be said. And, if necessary, do whatever you can to get the charge and the penalty reduced."

"He didn't do it. I'm certain of it. For one thing he just isn't the type."

"In the right circumstances," Meade said, "we're all the type."

The next morning Dorkin arrived in Wakefield equipped with everything that Meade had promised—Private John Smith, amanuensis and spear carrier, the Ford staff car, the files with the depositions from Whidden, McKiel, and Co., a large envelope containing copies of the orders that had been dispatched to Captain Fraser concerning his accommodation and working facilities, a copy of the letter arranging for his board at the Carleton Hotel compliments of His Majesty, copies of letters that had been dispatched to Sheriff Carvell and Corporal Drost informing them of his appointment as defense counsel and respectfully hoping for their co-operation.

On the parade ground at the back of the armoury, he found Sergeant MacCrae drilling the company of Zombies. They were in full battle dress, complete with steel helmets and Lee-Enfields. This, Dorkin learned from MacCrae, had become a regular morning routine as a cure for what Captain Fraser considered a general lack of discipline. When Dorkin presented himself to Fraser, he found that Fraser's manner towards him had become stiffly, grudgingly correct. Someone, Meade probably, had obviously roasted his ass for him, and the drilling outside was, no doubt, his way of kicking the cat.

Instead of the bare cell to which he had been consigned on his first stay, Dorkin found himself with a room completely furnished with bed, dresser, clothes press, desk, easy chair, floor lamp. Some tasteful predecessor, perhaps back in the heady days of 1940, had put his own imprint on it, repainting it a restful cream and filling it with this unmilitary furniture requisitioned from god knows where. Even nicer than the furniture was the luxurious sense of privacy. It was the first time in over two years that he had had a room that was not part of some barrack line of similar rooms into which someone might burst unannounced at any time of the day or night.

His office was also pleasant—a second-floor room at the front of the building with two windows that looked down on a quiet residential street. It all seemed so fine that it completely overwhelmed his soldierly persuasion that good fortune was merely fate's way of softening one up for the bad fortune to follow.

Even Private Smith had been accommodated with a room of his own—a tribute perhaps to the magical little GS badge on his sleeve. He would have volunteered for overseas, Dorkin reflected, secure in the knowledge that no one in his right mind would have turned him loose with a loaded gun. He was tall, gangling, awkward, with a perpetual air of vague abstraction as if struggling unsuccessfully to remember something. But Meade's CWAC secretary had repeated the assurance that he was a good clerk, and that was what mattered.

For starters, Dorkin put him to work getting their office set up, and after lunch he went to the jail for his first meeting with Williams.

The building was every bit as ugly as he remembered it, and as he mounted the front steps under the squat, crenellated tower, a quotation began floating around somewhere just out of reach of consciousness. It came to him as he was pushing open the door, a snippet from Browning that had struck him as fine stuff when he had come across it in a second-year English course:

In a sheet of flame,
I saw them and I knew them all. And yet
Dauntless the slug-horn to my lips I set.
And blew. "Childe Roland to the Dark Tower Came."

Inside, he became aware, as before, of the smell of dust, and behind that, not altogether masked, another smell, stale and pervasive, perhaps the smell, infused into the very woodwork, of years of unwashed, vomiting rubby-dubs.

He found Carvell in his office reading the newspaper. Here too Meade's letter had smoothed his way.

"So," Dorkin said when they had shaken hands, "how is he?"

"Not good," Carvell said. "I think he's getting a little stir-crazy. Sergeant MacCrae and some of the other soldiers from the armoury come to see him. Otherwise nobody. And the Mounties don't want him exercising with the other prisoners because they're afraid he may be attacked."

When they got to Williams's cell, Henry Cronk appeared with his ring of keys. He seemed even grosser than Dorkin remembered him. Perhaps all by himself he was what made the place smell so bad.

Dorkin was shocked by Williams's appearance. He hadn't shaved that day, nor maybe the day before either, and there was something sick about his eyes. He also seemed to have lost weight. The three weeks since the preliminary hearing seemed to have broken him. The sullen belligerence was gone and had been replaced by despair, terror, god knows what all.

"What's going to happen, sir?" he asked Dorkin when they were alone together in the visitors' room.

"I'm going to get you acquitted," Dorkin said. "But I can't do it unless I get some help from you. I know it's hard, but the first thing you should do is to try to pull yourself together. The more you let yourself go to pieces, the more people are going to think you're guilty. You could start shaving regularly for one thing."

"The water they bring me isn't hot enough," Williams said. "It hurts my face to shave in cold water."

"Perhaps you should change your razor blade more often."

"They don't let me have a razor, sir. They bring it with the water, and it's always dull."

"Okay. I'll see what I can do about it."

"That man Cronk hates me," Williams said.

"What does he do?"

"He treats me as if I were a dog. He won't come if I need him. He leaves my pail sometimes all morning before he empties it."

Whom the gods intend to destroy, they first make contemptible. But there was also something inherently craven about Williams, and Dorkin felt the sense of irritation with him that he had felt before and was to feel many times again.

"All right, I'll see about that too," Dorkin said. "You mustn't just sit here and brood. Do you read at all? Would you like me to bring you some books?"

"I used to read magazines some."

"Any particular kind?"

"I used to read cowboy magazines."

"I'll get you some. Is there anything else?"

"No, I can't think of anything else."

"All right," Dorkin said. "I'll be seeing you often. Maybe next week we can go over what happened again when I've had time to look through the testimony from the preliminary hearing. Think about that night and try to remember everything you can. Even little things may turn out to be important."

He had almost said, the difference between life and death.

"So how did you find him?" Carvell asked when Dorkin was seated back in the office.

"Not good," Dorkin said. "I don't want to seem to be asking for special treatment for him, but I'd like to ask a couple of favours."

He told him about the water and the razor blades.

"I'll buy some fresh blades myself," he said.

"No, that won't be necessary," Carvell said. "I'll see to it."

"I wondered about a radio. I haven't said anything to him, but it would help to pass the time."

"It's not usually allowed because of the noise. But if he keeps it down, I can make an exception."

"He seems to think that Cronk is being deliberately unpleasant to him," Dorkin said.

"Could be. Henry's a bit of an asshole. But being a jailer isn't a job many people want. And he had both his boys killed in the Great War, and he has to do something. The other guys back there treat him as a clown, so I suppose he welcomes the chance to bully somebody. I'll see what I can do."

He smoked his cigarette and studied Dorkin.

"So how did you come to be involved in this affair?" he asked. "Orders from on high?"

"No, nothing like that. I asked to do it."

"Why?" Carvell asked. "Or should I be minding my own business?"

"Not at all. I was very uneasy after that preliminary hearing. And I thought the chances of Williams getting a lawyer who was really interested in his case weren't very good. So I volunteered."

"Out of a sympathy for the underdog?"

Dorkin shrugged.

"I suppose. Something like that."

"And a dislike for H. P. Whidden?"

"Maybe that too," Dorkin said. "Although I never thought about it. Thurcott was also very unhappy about that hearing. And he didn't seem to have a very high opinion of Whidden's integrity."

"Neither do I. I wouldn't trust him around the corner. Well," he added after a thoughtful pause, "as sheriff I'm under certain constraints when it comes to an affair like this, but if there's anything I can do to help you that's within the constraints, I'd be happy to do it. You've taken on quite a load."

That night, Dorkin slept well in his new room, got up just after eight when the clatter on the drill floor below had moved outside, shaved, showered, and dressed, taking his time over everything. He had breakfast at the hotel, then set off to find the store that Carvell had recommended.

It turned out to be a plain wooden building, one of a line of similar buildings that ran unbroken for a whole block off Main Street. The sign across the front, rather grandly painted with little gold curlicues at the corners, proclaimed: *MELTZER'S FURNITURE. J. Meltzer, Prop.* (Jacob? Joseph? Jonathan?) Below in the window beside the door a smaller sign, hand-printed on cardboard and a little faded by the sun, more modestly read: *Furniture and Furnishings Bought and Sold.*

Dorkin opened the door and went in. He took in the store in a glance—the jumble of furniture in every stage of newness and decay, the stoves and heaters, the tables full of clocks and pots and dishes and god knows what, the ranks of old books, the piles of old magazines—and he knew it instantly for what it was, a place where a precarious living was made in a dozen small ways, buying, selling, trading up, trading down, repairing or having repaired, cleaning, scraping, upgrading, sometimes perhaps lending a little money.

From a glassed-in office at the back, a man emerged. He was in his fifties, small, grey-haired with a high, receding hairline, sad, lustrous eyes, a slight stoop, the sort of man his father might have become if he had let life break him. Dorkin caught the slight break in the man's step, the faint flicker of surprise, as he saw the officer's uniform. Then he came on, smiling, deferential.

Dorkin explained what he was looking for. A radio, not too expensive, something for temporary use. He said nothing about Williams and let Mr. J. Meltzer, who presumably this was, assume that the radio was for Dorkin himself. There were a number of radios, and for three dollars Dorkin chose a small one that picked up CFNB in Fredericton and WLBZ in Bangor. The CBC was so far away it would have needed an aerial, and Williams would never have listened to it anyway. Then Dorkin went quickly through a pile of magazines and picked up half a dozen cowboy pulps for a nickel each.

Somewhere midway through all this, Dorkin detected the shift in Meltzer's manner and realized that he had been recognized. How? he wondered. Meltzer himself was easy: the eyes, the colouring, the shape of the face, the nose, although these might also have been something other—Lebanese, for example, or Armenian. But he, Dorkin, who had none of these markers, was not easy at all, and yet somehow through some indefinable giveaway, they always came after a few minutes to know him as one of them.

Dorkin sensed Meltzer's urge that they acknowledge each other, but the uniform and the two pips still daunted him.

Dorkin hesitated, then held out his hand, and Mr. Meltzer brightened and took it.

"I'm from Saint John," Dorkin said. "And you? Have you always lived here?"

"Yes. My father came here just before the turn of the century. But he married a girl from Saint John, and I still have relatives there."

For a quarter of an hour, they compared notes on whom they knew and whom they didn't. Mostly they didn't, but Meltzer had heard of Dorkin's father, whose firm opinions on just about everything had made him well known. And it turned out that Dorkin's older sister had been a friend of a distant relative of Meltzer's.

"She inherited a bit of my father's character," Dorkin said. "She used to boss me around when I was younger. And still would if I let her."

Then Dorkin paid him, they shook hands again, and Meltzer walked with him to the door.

CHAPTER SEVEN

When he had delivered his purchases to the jail, Dorkin crossed the street to keep the appointment he had made with Corporal Drost. Before he tackled the pile of depositions, he wanted to see whatever remained of that night to be seen.

In the outer office, he found Constable Hooper two-fingering a report on an old Underwood typewriter. In spite of the height and the muscle, there was something of the puppy dog about Hooper. He was the kind of Mountie who spent spare evenings coaching kids' softball teams. He raised his wide blue eyes to Dorkin, and there followed a little dance that Dorkin had danced a dozen times with fresh Mounties. His uniform confused their reflexes. It did not have a spot in their particular hierarchy, but it was an officer's uniform all the same, and it triggered a saluting instinct that Dorkin let float around in its confusion for a second or two before he turned on the cordiality.

"I'm Bernard Dorkin," he said. "You may remember me from the preliminary hearing. I've been made responsible for Private Williams's defence, and I've arranged with Corporal Drost to have a look at the stuff you collected."

Hooper fetched Drost from an inner office. Dorkin shook hands with him, but his game didn't work so well with Drost. In the more ordinary matters of simple assault and low-level property damage, Dorkin would now have sat down with his Mountie, and they would soon have come to feel that they were after the same thing—which was to do whatever needed to be done in the interests of justice and the public peace in whatever way was the least trouble and expense to everybody. But in this more exalted matter, he and Drost were not after the same thing at all, and Drost was carefully keeping his distance, the more so because it was obvious that he had been chewed out by Grant for not securing the murder site more effectively and was not going to risk being chewed out again by being any more helpful to the defence than he had to be.

And yet, at the same time, Dorkin sensed in Drost's manner something more than caution—a kind of puzzlement, a kind of uncertainty of tone and gesture—and it came to him all of a sudden as they were still dancing their dance of introduction that Drost might be wondering if perhaps they were indeed on the same side, if perhaps Dorkin's role as defence was a put-up job by the army. Hence all these extraordinary privileges of access.

In this atmosphere of equivocality, Drost led Dorkin down a hall to a small, windowless room with shelves filled with boxes around three walls. The only furniture consisted of two straight-backed chairs and a large table.

"I'll start with the clothing," Drost said.

He took down a box from a group of four, set it on the table, and began emptying it, carefully taking out the items one by one rather like a travelling salesman displaying his wares. There was a trashy looking white dress made out of some kind of satiny material with a V-neck and a little red cloth flower crudely sewn into the angle of the V. There was a white slip, stained slightly yellow by the wearer's armpits, and a heavy white brassiere similarly stained, a white garter belt, a pair of rayon stockings, one with a long tear up the back, one ripped almost in two near the ankle. And there was a red belt and a small leather handbag and a pair of scuffed, black shoes. Very sad, Dorkin thought.

After a few seconds, he picked up one of the shoes. The heels were not as high as he had imagined from the photographs he had seen in court—not more than half an inch higher than the heels of ordinary walking shoes. They would not seriously have impeded her on the forest paths.

"And there weren't any pants?" he said.

"No," Drost said. "They weren't anywhere around the pit, and we looked along the route back to town, but we didn't find anything. But you can't look under every rock, and they could have been thrown into the creek."

"What about the purse?" Dorkin asked. "Were there any fingerprints?"

Drost hesitated, shifted uneasily.

"Yes," he said. "Some."

"But none of Williams's?"

"Not that they could tell."

"Some of hers?"

"Probably, but it was hard for them to be sure."

"Any others?"

"Yes, a couple. But we've no way to know whose. They could be anybody's. We can't fingerprint the whole town."

"No," Dorkin said, "I suppose not."

"This is what was in the purse," Drost said, taking a smaller box out of the bigger one and putting the stuff out on the table: a dollar bill, some change, a lipstick, her wartime identification card, two photographs, one of a girl, one of a soldier.

"That's her," Drost said. "The other one is of her brother."

Looking at the photograph of Sarah, Dorkin had the feeling he often had when looking at photographs of the dead: the sense of the instant fixed while the flow of time out of which it had been lifted drove inexorably on. She was standing in front of some chokecherry bushes, full-leaved, heavy with fruit, on what must have been, given that and the fall of the light, a late afternoon in mid-summer. She was standing with her feet apart, her hands crossed in front of her, wearing a snug, sleeveless summer dress. The bare arms were plump, the breasts pressed together between them heavy, the face round. She was laughing, looking straight into the camera, and the impression was of a big, strapping country girl, the sort of girl who from that kind of background was almost certain before very long to get herself knocked up by somebody.

The autopsy report had said that she was five-foot-six and weighed a hundred and fifty pounds, and she certainly looked as if she weighed all of that. Dorkin recalled MacCrae's remark that if Williams had tried to assault her, she would have beaten the shit out of him.

Dorkin looked at the other picture.

"What about the brother?" he asked.

"He's overseas," Drost said.

Not good for Williams, Dorkin thought. The sister of one of the boys who was risking his life for his country.

When Dorkin had looked his fill, Drost packed up the stuff and brought down two more boxes.

The first contained the squalid debris from the pit: cigarette packages and chocolate bar wrappers in varying states of decay; a squashed shoebox; a copy of *The Daily Gleaner* dated June 5, 1944, which had been soaked and dried; bottles broken and unbroken; a woman's stocking left behind from some earlier midnight amour; a man's cap left behind probably by some drunk; the rubber ring from a condom; two entire condoms, the contents dried, the sides stuck together.

The final box contained Williams's stuff: his battle dress uniform, his wedge cap with its Seaforth badge, three pairs of undershirts and shorts, three pairs of socks, two regulation dress shirts, a regulation necktie, a handkerchief, two regulation towels, and a regulation face cloth. And a tin of Sheiks.

"Could you open that?" Dorkin asked.

It contained two condoms in their little cardboard sleeves. One of the original three was missing. Williams had not had occasion to use a condom. And whoever had raped Sarah, if it was rape, had not used a condom. Dorkin wondered what had become of the third condom. He made a mental note to ask when the time was right.

"Okay," he said. "I guess I've seen it all."

He waited while Drost packed up the stuff and put it back on the shelf.

"You don't think he did it," Drost said, when they were back in the office.

His air of uncertainty persisted, and he was obviously fishing.

"A defence attorney always thinks his client didn't do it," Dorkin said.

They both made as if to laugh.

"But there's still the missing hour," Drost said.

Dorkin hesitated. He had no intention of giving anything away to Drost, but he wanted to pick his way. So long as Drost believed that he was on a fool's errand—or that he was being used by the army to make a pretence of caring for even the humblest Zombie that fell—he would be co-operative, perhaps more co-operative than he realized. But the minute he began to feel that Grant's case, and therefore his own ass, was being seriously threatened, he would shut up like a clam.

"There's not really that much time missing," Dorkin said. "They dawdled along talking. If you think about it, it's hard to see how he could have had time to do what was done."

Dorkin watched it work. Drost put him down as either a fool or a surreptitious accomplice. Either would do. Dorkin left feeling pleased with himself.

By the middle of the afternoon, the Zombies under the direction of Sergeant MacCrae and Private Smith had his office ready. The room was far larger than he needed, and he would much rather have had two smaller rooms—one for himself and one for Smith—but he had ordered them to use a couple of filing cabinets and a bookcase to make a divider that reached halfway across the room and gave at least an illusion of privacy.

He sat down at his desk to make a beginning. He circled in red on his calendar Tuesday, September 26, the day on which the trial was now scheduled to begin. He had exactly five weeks in which to prepare. The printed evidence that Meade had secured for him made a thick pile at one corner of his desk. He laid out a foolscap pad, took off at random the first deposition, and began to read:

"On Saturday, July 1, I, Lavinia Jean Page, of Wakefield in the County of George…"

The sun shone all that week, and most of the next, but August was waning, the overnight temperatures dropping towards frost, the first leaves turning. Every morning, Dorkin got up early, breakfasted at the hotel, then came back to his desk in the armoury to work on the case, reading, reflecting, making notes, getting up now and then to look down into the street in front of the armoury—a street of picturesque Victorian residences, tended lawns, beds of flowers.

Inside the armoury, the atmosphere was less poetic. Captain Fraser's campaign of persecution against the Zombies went on unabated, and twice a day, rain or shine, MacCrae marched them for half an hour in full kit up and down the parade square at the back. There was also a blizzard of petty orders and a daily trail of bedraggled miscreants to Fraser's office to be put on charge and confined to barracks. It was all vaguely insane, and every minute Fraser was in the armoury, his paranoia pervaded the atmosphere like the smell of something dead in the woodwork. Fortunately, at four o'clock every afternoon, he locked his desk and went off to the local golf club to work on his cirrhosis of the liver. Immediate command of the armoury then devolved on MacCrae, the air cleared, and a great calm would descend, which would last until nine o'clock the next morning.

Although they didn't see much of each other around the armoury, Dorkin had quickly come to like MacCrae. In spite of his bluff, lumberjack face, he came across to Dorkin in their occasional chats as an intelligent, capable man, who, although he would never say it out loud of a commanding officer, saw as clearly as Dorkin did what a worthless shit Captain Fraser was. And in conversation with Carvell one day, Dorkin learned that one of the little ribbons on MacCrae's tunic was the Military Medal, which he had got for hauling wounded men out of the water when their landing barge had been hit by a mortar bomb off Dieppe. He was so badly wounded himself that he was later invalided home. Poor old Fraser, Dorkin thought. In addition to having to put up with a snotty-nosed Jewish lieutenant, he was saddled with a non-com factotum who was a decorated war hero.

Fraser's attitude toward Dorkin remained one of imperfectly concealed resentment and rage, but Dorkin pretended blandly not to notice. He saluted Fraser whenever they met and made the kind of regulation small talk about the weather and the war that a subordinate makes to a superior officer. But mostly he did his best merely to stay out of his way, closeting himself in his office with his papers.

He began by going carefully through everything: the transcript of the preliminary hearing, the depositions from the people who had been at the dance and those who had seen Williams in the hours and days afterwards, Williams's own, partially perjured statement about that night, Clemens's statement about Sarah (if it was Sarah) and the soldier (if it was a soldier), the dreadful autopsy report with its still more dreadful photographs, the forensic reports on the examination of Sarah's clothes and those of Williams.

He took his time, letting things settle of their own accord, not pushing, trying not to impose theories too soon. When he had gone through everything, he shuffled the pile of depositions so that he could deal them to himself in a different order and went through them all again. What he was searching for was the raw material out of which he could construct an edifice of reasonable doubt, but his more extravagant hope was that hidden somewhere in the criss-cross of evidence there would turn out to be some corner undiscovered by the Mounties in which the real murderer lurked.

Sometimes after lunch he took a walk around the centre of the town, becoming something of a familiar figure, exchanging nods and comments about the weather with storekeepers who occasionally stood outside their doors, soaking up the sun. Sometimes in the afternoon or in the early evening, he took his staff car and drove out into the country. Late one afternoon, travelling further afield than usual, he drove across the bridge to the other side of the river and up over the side of the valley eastward along a gravel road.

He drove for almost ten miles, the road deteriorating with every mile but still drawing him on, until he came out at last at a small settlement—a miserable collection of a dozen unpainted houses with swayback rooftrees and collapsing porches strung out along the road.

In one of the yards, watched by an enormous boy as shapeless as a slug, he turned the car around and headed back.

The valley came upon him suddenly. The road mounted a long, shallow rise, and at the top of it the trees abruptly opened out on both sides into hayfields, and there below was the river with the big island that the Zombies guarded so faithfully, the open land of the valley, the town with its roofs and steeples. He stopped the car and got out to look.

As he stood there, a three-ton truck turned out onto the road from a side road further down and began slowly climbing the steep gradient towards him, its engine labouring heavily in bottom gear. As it passed, the face above the steering wheel looked out at him with brazen indifference, a round face with several days' growth of beard under a dirty cloth cap. The body of the truck had four-foot-high slats on the sides and a slatted gate at the back, and it smelled like the yard of a slaughterhouse.

A little way up the hill, the truck stopped, turned on a culvert, and came crawling back and parked behind Dorkin's car. The driver got out.

He wore a checked shirt and trousers made out of some woollen material so heavy that they looked as if they could have stood up by themselves. He was perhaps five foot six, bowlegged, pot-bellied but with powerful shoulders and arms like a wrestler.

"Ya got trouble? Ya got a flat?" the man asked.

"No," Dorkin said. "No trouble. I'm just admiring the view."

The man threw a glance down at the river and then looked at Dorkin as if he thought he was being made the butt of some joke. He let it pass.

"I'm Louie Rosen," he said. "You probably heard of me."

"No," Dorkin said. "Not yet."

"No?" the man said. "I thought everybody knew Louie Rosen."

"I'm not from here," Dorkin said.

"I know who you are. Everybody knows Louie Rosen. Everybody but you anyways. And Louie Rosen knows everybody. Around here, everybody and everything. You're a Saint John boy. I got a sister in Saint John. Married. Two nice daughters. Her name's Abrams now. Her husband works in his father's furniture store. You know him?"

"No," Dorkin said, "I don't. I know the store. And one of the girls went to school with me."

"So," Louie said, "what are ya doin' up here defendin' a sex murderer?"

"It's part of my job," Dorkin said.

"You're gettin' us a bad name."

"Oh? What 'us,' Louie?"

"You know what 'us,' for Christ sake. Us. God's chosen people who have to make a livin' around here."

"What have you got in the back of the truck, Louie?" Dorkin asked. "I could smell you coming half a mile away."

"Hides. Cow hides mostly. A couple of pigs. You know. You kill a cow. People eat some of it. Foxes eat some of it. Some of it gets ground up for fertilizer. The hides you make leather out of. I collect them and clean them and send them off to the guys who make leather."

"You mean if I defend this guy, no one is going to sell you their cow hides? Who are they going to sell them to?"

"It ain't that exactly. It just don't look good. People say you want some dirty work done, go find a Jew. You've heard it?"

"Sure. I've heard lots of things. We boil babies up and eat them at midnight. Only sometimes it's Catholics who do that. Unless you happen to be a Catholic and then it's the Orangemen."

"You bought him a radio," Louie said.

"So who knows besides you and Mr. Meltzer?"

"Everybody in town."

"Having heard it from you and Mr. Meltzer."

"Who knows? Everything gets around."

"Louie," Dorkin said, "you're talking a lot of shit. Anyway it isn't dirty work. The boy didn't do it."

"Are you gonna prove that?"

"Maybe," Dorkin said. "Anyway, if you know everything, tell me who knocked the girl up before she got killed."

"Now *that* I don't know," Louie said.

"Any ideas?"

"No. I thought it must have been the soldier. And he killed her because he didn't want to marry her. She put the heat on him."

"No," Dorkin said. "He didn't knock her up. Somebody else did, and I'm wondering who. Did you know her?"

"Sure. I mean I knew her, but I never talked to her. I knew her to see. I bought some hides from her old man a couple of times. But I don't know nothin' about the girl's boyfriends."

"Would you tell me if you did?"

"Maybe," Louie said. "If you didn't let on to nobody where you heard it. I gotta live here, remember."

He looked at his watch.

"I gotta go," he said. "A man's waitin' for me. Take it easy."

He climbed back into the truck, and Dorkin watched it labour up the hill and drop away over the crest.

By the middle of the second week, Dorkin had been back and forth over the written evidence half a dozen times. It told him nothing. He had found no nook where the real murderer might lurk. There was no neat, self-referencing little group whose members might have conspired to lie for each other. The only person unaccounted for during the hour between Williams's departure from the dance and his arrival at the canteen was Williams himself. Whoever had murdered Sarah (assuming that it wasn't Williams) had come from somewhere outside the magic circle that the Mounties and Whidden had drawn, perhaps from among the drinkers, the fighters, the loonies who had hung around outside in the woods or on the roads, someone perhaps whose act had been one of random violence to which no path of logic could lead.

There was one other angle that Dorkin had not yet explored, and that was the possibility of having Williams's statements to the Mounties thrown out of court on the grounds that Williams had not been properly cautioned. Dorkin had visited Williams every day since he had come back to Wakefield to see if he needed anything and to cheer him up as best he could, but he had avoided discussing the case until he had finished his search through the evidence. Now, he decided, it was time for another talk.

Williams still did not look good, but he was clean-shaven and as neat as it was probably in his nature to be.

"I want to talk to you about the second time the police questioned you," Dorkin said. "Did they warn you at the beginning that what you said might be used as evidence against you?"

"I don't remember," Williams said. "I don't think so."

"All right," Dorkin said. "Tell me what happened first. What did they say to you?"

"Corporal Drost asked me to tell him again about when I had last seen Sarah Coile the night of the dance. He told me what he remembered that I had said before and asked me if that was right and I said yes."

"You didn't know at that point that she had been murdered?"

"No, they only told me later."

"When?"

"I'm not sure now exactly."

"Did they warn you that what you were saying might be used as evidence against you?"

"I'm not sure."

"Who was there? Anyone besides Drost?"

"The other guy from town."

"Hooper?"

"Yes, I guess so. He was writing things down."

"What about Sergeant Grant? Was he there?"

"No, not then, I don't think. But the door was open, and I could hear people outside."

"How did Drost talk to you? Did he accuse you of anything? Did he say that he didn't believe you?"

"No, he just asked about what happened."

"So then?"

"I'm not sure. I guess after a while Hooper went out, and Drost just talked to me about that night. How many people were at the dance. If there was a lot of drinking. Stuff like that. He just seemed to be making conversation. Then Hooper came back with a paper. They'd typed up what I said, and they asked me to read it and see if it was right. So I read it and said yes."

"Even though it left out the fact that you'd stopped in the woods with Sarah?"

"Yes, I guess so. I didn't think it made any difference. And I was afraid to change what I said before."

"Did they warn you that the paper might be used as evidence against you? Did they say that specifically?"

"I'm not sure what you mean."

Shit, Dorkin thought.

"All right," he said, "never mind. So then what happened?"

"I signed the paper. Then Hooper took it out, and Sergeant Grant and another Mountie came in. Sergeant Grant had a copy of the paper, and he read it and asked me again if that was what happened. And I said yes. And I remember he asked me again if that was *exactly* what happened, and I thought of telling him about stopping, but I didn't. I was getting scared. Then, I guess he told me that people had said I had left the dance hall about ten-thirty and that the waitress at the canteen had said that I got there about midnight and where had I been for an hour and a half? He started shouting after a while, and he told me that Sarah Coile had been found murdered and that I was the last person to see her alive. And he asked me if I had gone to the gravel pit with her. And where had I been all that time."

"How long did they question you?"

"I don't know. Two hours. I don't know. Sometimes Grant and the other guy would go out and just leave Drost and sometimes Hooper, but Hooper didn't say anything, just sat there. Drost didn't shout or get mad. He said it would be better for me if I told the truth about things. He said things like what happened to Sarah happened sometimes, and people did things without really meaning to and the law understood that. Stuff like that. Then when I said that I had left Sarah on the road and I hadn't gone anywhere or done anything, Grant would come back. And he kept asking me about the time."

"And what did you say?

"I said that we hadn't walked very fast, and we stopped to talk for a while along the path in the woods. And he said that I hadn't put anything about that in my statement and I was making it up now."

"And?"

"Nothing. It just went on and on, the same things over and over. After a while I didn't really know what I was saying I was so tired. Then they stopped, and they told me that I was being arrested and charged with murdering Sarah Coile."

Dorkin looked at him. Shit, he thought again. It was hopeless.

"Okay," he said. "There are a couple of other things I want to ask you about. When they found Sarah, she wasn't wearing any pants, and they never found them. Do you know if she was wearing pants when you were with her?"

Under the dirty prison grey, the familiar blush of embarrassment spread over Williams's face.

"It may be important," Dorkin said.

"Yes, she was," Williams said.

"You're sure?"

"Yes."

"When you were petting with her, did you touch them?"

"Yes."
"Did you take them off?"
"No."
"Do you know what they were made of? Cotton? Rayon?"
"I don't know. Some slippery stuff."
"Okay," Dorkin said. "Something else. There were only two safes in the tin the police took from your kit. What happened to the other one?"

More blushing, even deeper, and a long look at the table.

"I took it out to see what it was like. I unrolled it and couldn't get it rolled up again, so I threw it away."

"When was that?"

"I don't know. Maybe a month before. When we started going to the dances."

"It had nothing to do with Sarah?"

"No."

Dorkin sensed something odd in Williams's manner, a kind of wobble. A lie finding its footing? Or merely Williams's habitual embarrassment?

"One thing you have to understand," he said, "is that the prosecution may know things they haven't told me. And if I go into court, and they spring things on me that you should have told me about and didn't, it's not going to do you any good at all."

"I'm telling you the truth," Williams said.

The next day Dorkin went to the library at the courthouse and spent all day reading whatever he could find about the admissibility of evidence. The day after that he drove to Fredericton and spent another day in the provincial law library doing the same.

It was evening when he got back to Wakefield. He parked the car behind the armoury and went up to his office and sat down at his desk. He had found nothing he didn't know already. The police had an obligation to warn suspects before taking evidence from them, that was all, and there were a thousand loopholes. Williams hadn't been a suspect the first time he was questioned, and he was so confused about the second time that it was hard to be sure what had happened. If Dorkin put him on the stand, in ten minutes Whidden would have him in such a state that he wouldn't know his own name. And the prospect of putting him on the stand to explain to a jury that he had spent the hour that was unaccounted for rummaging around in Sarah Coile's underwear didn't bear thinking about.

For the first time, Dorkin allowed himself to acknowledge the fears that had been gathering, quietly, surreptitiously, for over a week. He looked at the pile of paper, so neat, so ordered, so satisfying in its illusion of completeness, and he thought of the wilderness of possibility outside. In other circumstances, he might have been able to invoke those possibilities—to weave a plausible alternative explanation for Sarah's death at the hands of someone she had met on the road. But this was a case where everyone felt that someone deserved to be hanged, and a culprit once settled upon was not going to be ungrudgingly given up because of unsubstantiated possibilities.

Dorkin put his head down in his hands and sat. He saw that he had been deluding himself about the vulnerability of Whidden's case. Even if he could construct an edifice of reasonable doubt (and he was not sure now that he could even do that), he felt certain that it would not be enough—not in these circumstances and not against the likes of Whidden and McKiel. What he needed was a real, live, alternative culprit to serve up to the jury, not just some theoretical phantom. He thought about it, and he was drawn back to the idea that from the beginning had hovered around the edge of everything he had thought about the case. Somewhere out there, there was someone who had knocked Sarah up, and if reality were behaving itself, that someone ought also to be the murderer.

CHAPTER EIGHT

Dorkin began his quest the next morning with the United Farmer's Dairy. Its manager, a brisk bantam of a man, was wary at first, but he settled down and led him back through the dairy with its overwhelming noise of flapping drive belts and clattering milk cans and introduced him to the two girls Sarah had worked with.

Their names were Dora and Jackie. Dora was plain and shy and had a set of very false-looking false teeth. Jackie was homely but brazen. They were both awed at being talked to by an army officer about a murder.

But they knew of no particular boyfriends Sarah had had, and they had not been aware that she was in trouble. (At this question, much blushing by Dora, much sly sideways glancing by Jackie.)

"Did she seem any different in May or June?" Dorkin asked. "Did she seem upset or worried?"

"She was talking about going to Saint John or somewheres," Dora said.

"Did she say why?"

"She said she could make more money," Dora said.

"The other reason she wanted to go to Saint John," Jackie said, "was to get away from her father."

"Oh?" Dorkin said. "Why was that?"

"She said he never did any work, and he took most of her money," Jackie said.

"I think he hit her, too," Dora said. "She had a bruise on her cheek once that she said she got running into a cupboard door, but I think someone hit her, and I think it was her father."

"When was that?" Dorkin asked.

"In the spring sometime," Dora said. "Three or four months ago."

"You've no idea why he hit her?"

"No," Dora said. "Maybe she wouldn't give him her money."

"What else did she say about her father?" Dorkin asked.

"Nothing," Jackie said. "Nothing that I remember."

"Do you remember what you used to talk about with her?"

"Nothing special. Just movies and clothes and stuff like that," Jackie said.

Dorkin gave the girls a quarter each for a coke and a treat and, as if in afterthought, got the names of three girls who sometimes chummed with Sarah.

All that afternoon and most of the next day, Dorkin plied the town and the surrounding country, hunting out the girls whose names he had picked up and picking up more names from them. When he had finished, he had talked to another Jackie, two Bettys, a Mary, a Daisy, a Mildred, a Pearl, and a Ruby. He had found out that Sarah liked Gene Autry and Roy Rogers, but not Wild Bill Elliott. She also liked Wilf Carter and Hank Snow. She thought Frank Sinatra was a sissy. Her favourite colour was blue. She liked cats. And other than that nothing that he hadn't already heard. She didn't like her father or her job, and she was talking about moving away. But no one knew of any serious boyfriend. Sarah's lover remained as invisible as her murderer, his act perhaps as single.

The next morning, taking a different tack, he drove to the Hannigan Road and began calling systematically at every house there and along Broad Street, inquiring about anything anyone might have seen on the night of July 1 or the three nights following. His hope was that someone would remember seeing a vehicle driving down into the pit on any of those nights. Even if his witness couldn't identify it, the mere fact of such traffic could serve to sow doubts in a jury's mind about Williams's role as sole suspect. There was also the possibility that someone would remember even at this distance some unconsidered, crucial trifle that would put one end of the thread in his hands. And it seemed to him too that the mere fact of his enquiries, the mere idea that an investigation was still going on, might make his murderer nervous enough to do something that would give him away. So at every house he visited, he contrived to suggest that there were still unanswered questions about Sarah Coile's death and facts that the public in general did not know.

His uniform with its magical pips on the shoulders meant that no one slammed a door in his face, but most of the people he talked to were cautious, suspicious, wary of some trap. A few were garrulous, made to feel important by being involved however distantly in a murder investigation, but they told him nothing that was of any use. No one had seen vehicles driving down into the pit, or parked cars, or suspicious late-night walkers of the roads.

Near the end of the afternoon, he stopped at a house on Broad Street near the entrance to the gravel pit. It was small, merely a one-room cabin, to which had been added a screened-in verandah at the front and a couple of rooms at the back.

As Dorkin got out of his car, he saw a man sitting on the verandah watching him. He made no move to get up until Dorkin had climbed the steps, tapped on the screen door, and pushed it open. Then he heaved himself out of the chair, came to attention, and snapped Dorkin a mock-smart salute.

"Private Alden A. Bartlett, sir," he said, coming down hard on the *sir*. "Number two-two-six-four-nine, 10th Canadian Infantry."

He laughed, and Dorkin made a vague pass at returning his salute. Ex-private Bartlett was fifty, maybe older, shorter than Dorkin, lean, wiry, with dark hair thinning and going grey.

"Lieutenant Dorkin, I presume," he said. "Have a chair. I been wonderin' when you were gonna get to me. I been watchin' you all afternoon. And one of my neighbours hiked around this mornin' by the back way to warn me you were comin'."

"Oh?" Dorkin laughed. "What did he warn you of?"

"This smart young army lawyer goin' around askin' everybody questions."

"Do you mind?" Dorkin said.

"Not a bit. But you'll probably be wastin' your time. I told the Mounties everythin' I knew—which was nothin'. You could have saved yourself a lot of time by just talkin' to them."

Dorkin had already heard that he was treading a path that the Mounties had trod before him, as he should have known.

"I like to hear it for myself," he said.

"Don't trust them, eh?" Bartlett said. "Don't think I would neither. Anyway, why don't we sit? I don't stand too good."

They sat, and Bartlett pulled up his right pant leg. The leg had been amputated just below the knee, and an artificial lower leg and foot were attached by an ugly arrangement of straps.

"May 12, 1917," Bartlett said. "Just after Vimy. It wasn't no big battle or nothin'. We were just settin' behind an old blowed-up house, and the next thing we knowed there was a jeezless great bang, and we were all knocked ass over teakettle. Broke my ankle all to pieces. They took me back to England to a place called Bradford. A hospital full of cripples and lunatics, and they tried for a while to fix it. But it went bad, and so they took it off. I'd sooner of had two legs than one, but I was gonna be alive anyways. Not goin' back to get my head blowed off instead. And I didn't even need to be over there in the first place, but I was young and stupid. And it was all for nothin' that I could ever see. Does anybody know what it was all about? Do you know?"

"No," Dorkin said, "I don't. The vanity of a few hundred old men, I guess."

"Yes, that'd be it, all right," Bartlett said.

"What did the Mounties ask you about?" Dorkin said.

"Wanted to know if I'd seen your soldier on the road that night. Or him and a girl goin' down into the pit. But I hadn't. I couldn't have seen that far in the dark even if I'd been standin' up lookin'."

"Did they ask about anyone else?"

"No. Just him. But I hadn't seen nobody else neither."

"Did you see any cars on the road that night?" Dorkin asked.

"Some, but I don't know whose. On Saturday, some of the boys come around, and we sit out here when it's warm and play cards and have a beer or two. Nothin' too fierce at our age, you know. So I sort of notice cars going by without payin' much attention."

"You didn't happen to notice any cars late that night? After midnight?"

"You think somebody might have brought the girl there in a car?"

"Could be. It might even have been a night or two afterwards."

"I wondered about that too," Bartlett said. "But I never seen anythin' any of them nights. I sleep pretty sound, and it's a ways up the road. But, you know, I seen that girl out here that Saturday she was killed. I wouldn't have paid no attention to it, but I remembered it after they found her."

"What time was that?" Dorkin asked.

"Middle of the afternoon, maybe a little later. I expect she'd been to town to see the parade. She went along the road out here, and then she took the shortcut across to the Bangor Road. It goes off just beyond the end of my lot here. I expect she was goin' to see her friend, that Page girl."

Dorkin recalled Vinny Page's testimony at the preliminary that Sarah had come to her house and they had arranged to go to the dance together.

"Did you often see her on this road?" he asked.

"Every once in a while. It's a quarter mile longer if she goes and comes by the Bangor Road, but she'd be more likely to pick up a ride out there. And I used to see her sometimes on Sunday goin' to that church over there."

He motioned down the street to where the metal spire of Clemens's church rose up between the trees.

"Her family went there. At least her mother did and the other kids. I never seen Dan very often. But sometimes the mother and Sarah and the rest of them would walk there. Sometimes see the mother in the evening too. They have church at funny times, them people. And sometimes in the summer when they got the doors open, you can hear that fool Clemens halfway to the American border hollerin' about being saved. I don't care much for that kind of religion myself, do you?"

"No," Dorkin said. "Not much."

"Not a religious man?"

"No," Dorkin said.

Bartlett hesitated, uncertain.

"I understand you're of the Jewish faith."

"Not exactly," Dorkin said. "I'm Jewish, but I'm not of any faith."

"Me neither," Bartlett said. "Not since the war."

"Did you ever see Sarah Coile going by here in a car?" Dorkin asked.

"Sometimes with her father. He's got an old Ford truck. Sometimes with that Page girl."

"You've never heard anything about who may have knocked her up?" Dorkin asked.

"No. Just thought it must have been your soldier, and he killed her to get out of it."

"He didn't kill her. He didn't knock her up, either."

"Had to be someone with a car, you figure?"

"Probably."

"You think you can get your soldier off?" Bartlett asked.

"Yes," Dorkin said.

"A lot of people gonna be disappointed," Bartlett said.

"Yes," Dorkin said, "I expect there will be."

"Anyway. I ain't been much help to you."

"Worth a try. Thanks for your time."

"Time I got lots of."

He got up and saw Dorkin to the door with his cripple's gait, the lower right leg swinging forward dead from the knee.

"If I find out anythin' might be of any use, I'll let you know," Bartlett said. "But I wouldn't be too hopeful."

Dorkin walked to his car. He visited three more houses, ritualistically, hardly listening to the same useless answers he had already gleaned two dozen times, and all the while he was thinking about Vinny Page. One thing he had heard from almost all the girls he had talked to the day before was that if anyone knew something that others did not know about Sarah Coile it would be Vinny Page. She was the prosecution's witness, but it was not about the testimony she had given in court that he wanted to ask her. He debated it with himself the rest of the afternoon. After supper, he made up his mind. The days were trickling relentlessly away. He no longer had time for the higher refinements of legal ethics.

Half an hour later, he was sitting facing Vinny Page across the parlour of the Page house. Outside in the hall, just out of sight beyond the doorway, their presence betrayed by the faintest of sounds, her father and mother hovered, listening.

She had brought an ashtray with her, and she sat smoking and listening with an elaborate show of attention as Dorkin explained that he was not here to discuss the testimony she had given at the preliminary hearing but simply to find out more about the background of Sarah Coile. Everyone he had talked to, he said, had told him that she was Sarah's closest friend. Everyone had told him that if Sarah had confided in anyone it would be Vinny Page.

"Yes," she said. "Yes, I suppose that's true. For the last couple of years anyways."

"Some of the people I've talked to," Dorkin said, "have told me that over the last few weeks Sarah was talking about leaving Wakefield. Did she talk to you about that too?"

"Yes. Quite a lot."

"One of the girls she worked with at the dairy said that she wasn't getting along very well with her father. Do you think that was one of the reasons she wanted to leave?"

"Yes, I guess maybe."

"What was the problem between her and her father?"

"I don't know. A lot of things, I guess. He didn't work much, and he used to take a lot of her money."

"Did Sarah ever say anything to you about his beating her?"

Vinny puffed her cigarette.

"Yes."

"Do you remember when Sarah told you about his beating her?" Dorkin asked.

"Not too long ago. I think he did it more than once, but that time there was a mark on her face. Maybe that's why she told me."

"Do you think Sarah was talking more about leaving here in the month or two before she was killed than she had before?"

"Yes. I think she was gettin' serious about it. One day I said that she would need some money to get started somewhere else, and I asked her did she have any saved up. And she said she'd saved a little, but she knew where she could get some more."

"Did she say where?"

"No. She said it was a secret. She said she might tell me sometime but not now."

"You haven't any idea who she was going to get the money from?"

"No, I don't know. I thought maybe she was gonna steal it or somethin' like that. But she never did things like that before."

"You don't think it might have been from whoever got her in trouble?"

"I don't know. I didn't know anythin' about that then."

"Did she ever say she might be going away with someone? A man, I mean?"

"No, she never said nothin' about that."

"Did she have any steady boyfriend that you knew of?"

"No. She used to see people at the dance, but she never went there with anyone."

"And she'd never said anything to you about being in trouble?"

"No, never. I just heard about it afterwards."

"If she were going to confide in anyone, I guess it would have been you. I wonder why she didn't."

"I don't know. I've wondered too."

"You've no idea who it might have been who got her in trouble?"

"No."

"Not Williams, you think?"

"I don't know. It could have been, I suppose."

"She never talked about Williams?"

"No, nothin' that I remember."

"What did you think of Williams?"

"I didn't know him except just to see. Sort of shy, I guess."

"Why do you think Sarah was dancing with him that night?"

"I don't know. Maybe some of them other guys was pesterin' her, and he was a way of keepin' clear of them. He was someone she could manage maybe."

Dorkin sat and thought. He had come up with nothing that he hadn't heard from the others. He wondered if Vinny were hiding things from him, but he decided not. Nor the others either. The silence was too complete. No sense of a chink in it anywhere.

He rose and thanked her for her co-operation.

"I know it must be a painful thing to have to remember."

"Yes," Vinny said. "She was my best friend."

Dorkin had the sense that she would have liked to have managed a tear, but none came.

Three hours later, after his solitary dinner at the hotel, Dorkin sat at the desk in his office, meditating on the futility of the day's enquiries. The darkness was beginning to gather, but he didn't turn on the lamp. What was needful now, he decided, was a long systematic think.

Begin with the indisputable facts, he told himself. These were few and simple. First, Williams left the dance with Sarah around ten-thirty, they stopped to make unconsummated love for half an hour or so, then walked out to the Hannigan Road. Sarah walked up the road towards home, and Williams walked back to the canteen and then to the armoury. Second, Reverend Clemens testified that he saw someone whom he took to be Sarah with someone whom he took to be a soldier and whom everyone now took to be Williams. It was possible, of course, that Clemens was mistaken and that the girl whom he saw was not Sarah at all. Third, on Wednesday, Sarah was found in the gravel pit, raped, suffocated, and badly beaten, having been dead for about three days—meaning that she might have been killed within an hour of leaving the dance or as late as the next morning. And meaning also that the body might have been conveyed to the gravel pit any time during the next three days.

The puzzling thing about the first set of facts was what Sarah was doing walking away from the dance with Williams in the first place. Dorkin had found no evidence that Williams had ever had anything to do with Sarah before the dance the previous week and no evidence that he was the father of her child. It was also strange that she should choose him for a little lovemaking when she clearly had other, more attractive choices. He had wondered from time to time whether she had used Williams merely as a blind to cover her leaving the dance so that she could meet someone else, choosing Williams because he would be easy to get rid of, as Vinny Page had suggested. But if that were the case, she would not have stopped to make love with him as she had. Whatever her motives may have been for going off with Williams, it seemed obvious that she had no plans then for meeting someone else. To make way for her real interest, she might have paid Williams off with a kiss or two but not with the heavy petting he had described. Whoever Sarah had met after she had left Williams, it seemed clear that it was a meeting that she at least had not planned.

Assuming that Clemens had indeed seen what he said he had seen, almost immediately after leaving Williams on the Hannigan

Road, Sarah had met someone who seemed on the basis of a quick look in the dark much like Williams in general appearance. And then? And then things started once more not to make sense. If Sarah had gone voluntarily to make love with this new partner, why had they not simply gone into the churchyard where they would have had privacy enough? Why go on to the gravel pit, whether down through the bushes or around by the road? And if Sarah had been running from whoever it was, the last place she would run to would be down into the darkness and seclusion of the gravel pit instead of along Broad Street where there were houses and lights. On any assumption, it seemed inconceivable that Sarah had voluntarily gone down into the gravel pit. Either she had been murdered in the churchyard and her body carried down through the bushes into the gravel pit—something that would have required a man a good deal bigger and stronger than Williams—or she had been murdered somewhere else altogether and her body brought back, presumably by car.

There was something else that seemed likely too, and that was that whoever Sarah had met, it had been someone whom she knew. The rage of violence against her dead body that Bourget had described was not likely the rage of some stranger. It was the rage of someone in whom she had bred somehow—by infidelity, by demands for marriage or for money, by threats of exposure—an insane, ungovernable hatred. Someone had lurked somewhere outside the dance hall, awaiting his opportunity. Their meeting on his side would have been no accident, however unexpected it may have been on hers.

But suppose Clemens had been mistaken and the girl he had seen was not Sarah at all. That could have happened easily enough in the circumstances. Dorkin had had enough experience with eyewitnesses to know how fallible they were, how little they often really saw, how easy it was for them, while quite unconscious of any act of fabrication, to create in their own minds a coherent, meaningful picture that had only the most tenuous connection with the half-apprehended events that had actually taken place. Like nature, the mind abhors a vacuum, and what it does not see or does not remember, it invents. So Clemens sees a man and a woman and later decides that it was Sarah whom he saw. Sarah and a man who comes to look more and more like Williams. And at a time too that gets moved closer and closer to the time Sarah and Williams would have been there.

And if Clemens were mistaken in his identification of Sarah, a whole new range of possibilities opened up. She could have gone on her own to some house on Hannigan Road or Broad Street or somewhere even further away. She could have been picked up by someone in a car as she walked up Hannigan Road. She might have gone home and been murdered there by the irascible Daniel Coile in one of his fits of drink.

There was also the possibility, of course, that Clemens was lying. Having decided that Williams was guilty, he could be doing what police themselves sometimes did. He could be fabricating testimony to ensure that a murderer did not go free for lack of evidence. Dorkin looked at the date of Clemens's deposition. It was Friday, July 7, two days after Sarah had been found—more than enough time for him to have heard from the rumour mill everything he needed to know to fabricate the scrappy details he had provided. But whatever the truth might be about Clemens, several things now seemed clear. Like the facts he had started with, they were simple. Sarah had left Williams, and somewhere, probably by chance on her part, had met, not some random stranger, but someone whom she knew—presumably, if reality were indeed behaving itself, whoever it was who had fathered her child. She had had sexual relations with that person, whether willingly or under compulsion, and she had then been savagely murdered sometime between midnight on July 1 and the next morning, and sometime between then and Wednesday her body had been taken to the gravel pit.

There was still one thing that stubbornly baffled Dorkin. Why had Sarah gone off and engaged in the abortive lovemaking with Williams? When he was in high school, Dorkin had had a physics teacher who had been in love with science and who had said something that Dorkin had always remembered. In any search for the truth, it is the circumstance that does not seem to fit that points the way. Dorkin thought about that now, and he thought about Sarah's choice of Williams. And abruptly, out of the darkness and the silence, he had an inkling of what it might mean.

CHAPTER NINE

At nine o'clock the next morning, Dorkin was standing at the window of the visiting room at the jail. He listened to the jingling of Henry Cronk's ring of keys and the opening of Williams's cell door, and he turned as Cronk shuffled Williams in. They saluted perfunctorily, a ritual that Dorkin had decided was best kept up, and Williams sat down. He looked pale and tired, and he seemed still to be losing weight.

Dorkin tried to lay down some smoke by making small talk, but he could see that Williams wasn't fooled. He obviously sensed at once that something was up, and he was wary, watchful, withdrawn somewhere deep inside himself in that unsettling way he had, unsettling especially since every once in a while it made Dorkin wonder if perhaps, just perhaps after all, there really might be a murderer hiding away in there.

"I've been thinking again about what happened that night between you and Sarah," he said, "and I want to make sure I've got it straight so we don't find ourselves getting caught out in court."

"I told you," Williams said.

"I know," Dorkin said, manoeuvring behind the smoke, "but there are still things that puzzle me, especially about Sarah. You said that she might have been a little drunk but not very. She wasn't staggering or anything?"

"No."

"Did she seem nervous at all?"

"Nervous?"

"Yes. As if she might be afraid of someone. Or trying to get away from someone."

"No, I didn't notice."

"I'm puzzled," Dorkin said, "about why she would lead you on the way she did and then stop it. Do you think she might have heard something?"

"I don't know," Williams said. "Maybe. She might have."

"But you're not sure?"

"No."

"There's something about it," Dorkin said, "that just doesn't seem to hang together. I can't help feeling that there's something in the situation that we've missed—something that might make sense of it."

He paused. Williams met his eyes briefly then looked away, and Dorkin let the silence stretch out, letting him sweat. He shifted uneasily in his chair, still avoiding Dorkin's eyes. I'm going to get the truth out of you this morning, you shifty little bastard, if I have to break both your arms, Dorkin said to himself.

"Let's go through it again slowly," he said at last, "and see if we can turn up whatever it is we've missed. You left the dance hall at intermission. You had a drink outside and necked a little, and she suggested that you go somewhere more private. This was her idea, you said?"

"Yes."

"But you were willing, so you went along a track to the Birch Road, but there were people around, so you went along to another place that she seemed to know about. Okay?"

"Yes."

"Then you lay down?"

"Yes," Williams said.

His face was flushed now.

"So she let you touch her breasts and her leg, and then she wouldn't let you go any further. Why do you think that was? Did she hear somebody, do you think? Or did she suddenly change her mind? When she told you to stop, what exactly did she say? What were the words she used?"

"She said she didn't want to go all the way."

"Were those her exact words? 'I don't want to go all the way'?"

"Maybe not exactly. Something like that?"

"I see. So what did she do exactly?"

"She got up, and I walked with her to the road and left her there, the way I said."

"You told me before that she said that she wasn't feeling well," Dorkin said.

"Yes," Williams said.

"That was probably why she wanted to stop and go home?"

"Yes, I guess so."

"It just came over her all of a sudden?"

"Yes, I guess so."

Dorkin let another silence hang. He got up and looked out the window at the swatch of scarlet maple leaves on the tree outside and at the hollyhocks along the side of the house next door with their little drums of seed, their last brilliant trumpets of the season, their traffic of bees shopping for winter. Or was it spring? The war might be over by then. He came back and sat down across from Williams and looked at him.

"Private Williams," he said. "You're lying to me. You've been lying to me every time we've talked, and I'd like you to start telling me the truth."

Williams stared at him, and the blood that had flamed his face drained away.

"I'm trying to save your god-damned life," Dorkin said, his voice rising, "and you're playing some kind of stupid game with me. I've had enough of it. I'm not sure what the truth is, but I'll know it when I hear it because you're too god-damned stupid to make up a lie that will go on looking like the truth. And if you try, I'm getting out of this, and you can find yourself another lawyer."

Williams looked so frightened that Dorkin was stricken again by the thought that the truth might turn out to be that he was indeed the murderer.

"I've told you everything that matters," Williams said.

"What the hell do you know about what matters? You tell me the truth, and let me decide what matters. Let's take it again for one last time. You walked along the Birch Road and found somewhere more private. Is that true so far?"

"Yes."

"So then what happened? What did you do? What did she say? Don't fart around with me. There are things one doesn't forget, and this is one of them. Tell me what happened."

William hesitated, not looking at Dorkin. A minute passed, then another, as he evidently fought out some excruciating battle within himself. When he finally began, Dorkin was aware of his own heart drumming heavily.

"It was sort of a little clearing we went to," Williams said, "and there was a place in one corner where there was some tall grass. She got me to take my tunic off, and she sat on that so she wouldn't get stains on her dress, and I just sat on the grass. After a while we stretched out."

"Did you talk? What did she say?"

"She said she liked me, and she asked me if I liked her. I said that I did."

"And did you?"

"Yes, I guess so."

"Why? Why did you like her?"

"I don't know. She was sort of fun to be with."

"Okay," Dorkin said, "so what else did you talk about?"

"I remember she asked me what I was going to do after I got out of the army, and I said that I would probably go back to Fredericton and get another job like the one I had. And she said she'd never been as far as Fredericton. And she said she'd like to go away and live somewhere bigger. She said she didn't like Wakefield."

"Anything else?"
"Not that I remember."
"So then?"
"She kissed me."
"And?"
"She let me touch her, like I told you before. Then she asked me if I wanted her to take her pants off, and I said yes."
"And she did?'
"Yes."

Williams shifted in his chair and looked out the window.

"Tell me the rest," Dorkin said. "I'm sorry, but I've got to know everything that happened."

"Well, you know…"

"You touched her."

"Yes. After a few minutes, she asked me if I wanted to go all the way. And I said yes. I'd bought that tin of Sheiks from one of the other guys. We'd got a lot of lectures about VD and about getting girls pregnant, and I wanted to be careful. But when she saw what I was doing, she said she didn't like those things. And I said I didn't want to get her into any trouble. And she said that couldn't happen because it was the wrong time of the month. She said girls can only get pregnant at certain times in the month between their periods and that this was a safe time. I was scared of VD as well, but I didn't want to say that, so I just said I still wanted to be sure nothing happened. We argued for a little while, and then she said all right, I could go ahead and use it. But I think she was sort of mad at me. I had one of the Sheiks in my billfold, and I got it out, but it was dark, and I couldn't see very well, and I had trouble getting it on."

He stopped, blushing furiously, still not looking at Dorkin.

"So?" Dorkin said.

There was a long pause.

"Tell me," Dorkin said. "I've got to know."

"Well, before I could get it on, it happened. You know?"

"Yes," Dorkin said. "Don't worry about it. You're not the first."

Jesus Christ! he thought, relaxing for the first time since Williams began. All of this had come about because of nothing more than that.

"So then?" he asked.

"She didn't realize what had happened at first, and I had to tell her. Then she did get mad. She got up and put her pants on and left."

"She put her pants back on?" Dorkin said. "You're sure?"

"Yes."

"You didn't walk her out to the road?"

"No."

"Did you see which way she went?"

"Yes, she went out towards the Hannigan Road. When I got my tunic back on, I went the same way."

"How long did that take?"

"I don't know. A minute or two. I didn't realize she was leaving. I thought she might just have gone a little ways."

"So when you got out to the Hannigan Road, did you see her again?"

"No."

"Have you any idea where she went?"

"I don't know. She could have been walking up the Hannigan Road. It was dark, and I couldn't see very far."

"Did you look?"

"Yes, but not very hard because I knew by then that she didn't want me to walk her home. I thought of going back to the dance, but I didn't feel like it, so I went down the Bangor Road and stopped at the canteen."

"You never stood with her anywhere on the Hannigan Road?"

"No, I never saw her again after she left."

It sounded like the truth.

"Did you see anyone else on the Hannigan Road?" Dorkin asked.

"No. But it was pretty dark."

"Why do you think she didn't want you to use the safe?"

"She said she didn't like them," Williams said.

"Maybe," Dorkin said. "But she was also in need of a husband."

Williams had to think before taking it in.

"Why didn't she get whoever got her pregnant to marry her?" he said.

"That's the interesting question," Dorkin said. "That's what I'd like to find out."

Dorkin parked on Broad Street near the pine tree under which Clemens had testified that he had seen Sarah and the soldier. He got out of his car, crossed the Hannigan Road, and walked down to the entrance to Birch Road. What he wanted first was to find the clearing on the upper side of the road where Williams had said that he and Sarah had made abortive love. A hundred yards in, he came to a track running off up into the woods to his right that looked as if it might once have been a woods road but was now partly overgrown. A hundred yards beyond that, just where Birch Road was itself beginning to deteriorate into a mere track, he came to a clearing that fitted Williams's description—a ragged semicircle of tall grass and devil's paint brushes, sundrenched now but at night no doubt private enough for quickies for dancers with nowhere more comfortable to go. Dorkin wondered if Sarah had used it with others before Williams.

At the back of the clearing, not visible from the road, he found a path, hardly more than an accidental pattern in the trees. Curious, he followed it in, and when he came to a fork, he bore right in the general direction of the Hannigan Road and at a second fork bore right again, realizing that what seemed from the road a uniform and impenetrable mass of trees had in fact a network of tracks and paths as intricate as the network of streets and alleys in some old, unplanned city. After a few minutes, he came to a wider track that he realized must be the overgrown woods road he had noticed earlier.

He deliberated and then decided to follow it to see where it came out. As the track meandered among the trees, he began to lose his sense of direction and was thinking of retracing his steps when he heard quite close off to his right the sound of a car on what he realized must be the Hannigan Road.

He emerged onto it a quarter of a mile above the entrance to Birch Road and well beyond Broad Street and the churchyard. Just at the end, the track widened out, and there was an old cedar culvert over the ditch where a car might easily pull off and park. It struck Dorkin that after leaving Williams, Sarah, knowing the woods as she evidently did, might well have taken this shortcut along the hypotenuse of the triangle rather than walk all the way out to the Hannigan Road and then up. If that were the case, she would never have passed the corner of Broad Street where Clemens had testified that he had seen her. It struck Dorkin also that it may have been along this track that her murderer, knowing these woods also and having waited his chance, intercepted her.

To be sure that he had not confused one track with another, Dorkin followed the track back and came out where he expected to on Birch Road. He walked back out onto the Hannigan Road and up to the churchyard. He circled the desolate, boarded-up church, threading his way among the tombstones that stood up to their waist in the long grass, reading here and there an inscription, the testimonials of long-dead love: beloved wife, beloved husband, our dearest daughter, our precious flower, whom God gave us for 2 years, 10 months, and 3 days.

At the back of the churchyard, Dorkin cruised the decaying cedar-rail fence, looking for any kind of path on the other side that might lead down through the bushes into the gravel pit. He had not been mistaken. There were no paths, only a few places where it would be possible to push down through the bushes. There was no doubt in his mind now that Sarah, alive or already dead, had been taken down into the pit that night or a night or two later by the road in a car or truck.

He climbed over the fence at the side of the churchyard and walked along Broad Street and down the road into the gravel pit. For a few minutes, he stood looking at the grassy depression in which she had been found. Then he went back to his car.

Just south of where the Bangor Road entered town, there was one of those areas to which, as a town grows, there drift all those things that nobody wants around, together with some of the people whom nobody wants around either. As he bounced along the potholed gravel road, Dorkin noticed an asphalt plant belching smoke and hot dust, a small iron works with a lot of rusting machinery standing around in the yard, a field of cars in various states of demolition, a pen full of cattle. Among these and off on little mud sideroads, there were clutches of jerry-built shanties with weedy dooryards full of woodpiles and flapping laundry and dirty-faced kids.

At the edge of the flat ground at the foot of a steep, wooded hill, the road made a loop back on itself, and just off the loop down a mud road flanked by ditches full of burdocks and chokecherries, Dorkin found what he was looking for. The crude, hand-painted sign on the board fence said L.R. ROSEN. *Hides Bought and Sold. Bottles. Scrap Metal. Fox Feed. General Trucking.*

He drove through the open gate and parked in the big yard inside. In the middle stood a great, weathered, two-storey frame shed that had started to lean to one side and was held from flattening itself out across the yard by three triangles of eight-inch timber like flying buttresses. Behind it was a scattering of smaller sheds, and just inside the gate a little shack with a tin smokestack that looked like an office. Louie's truck was backed up to the door of the big shed in the centre of the yard.

Inside, Dorkin found Louie, squat, bow-legged, black-armed, as solid as a bear, standing on one side of a pile of hides. A tall, young Indian was standing on the other, and they were turning the hides over onto a second pile. The Indian fixed Dorkin with his unflickering black eyes, and Louie turned.

"Well, well," he said. "To what do I owe such an honour as this?"

"No honour, Louie," Dorkin said. "I wonder if I could talk with you for a few minutes."

Louie considered, while the Indian continued to watch, immobile.

"This here's Cat Polchis," Louie said. "He works for me."

"How do you do," Dorkin said.

The Indian nodded. He seemed so much the inscrutable Indian that Dorkin wondered if he were playing at it.

"Okay," Louie said. "Let's go over to the office. But I ain't got much time."

"Toady!" he shouted, and a fat teenage boy emerged from somewhere out of the shadows at the back of the building. "Help Cat go through that stuff."

"I'm gonna fire that useless son of a bitch the end of the week," Louie said when they were out in the yard. "Cat don't like him, and he ain't worth a shit. But it's hard to get anybody these days. Fuckin' war's fucked up everything."

"Where did you get the Indian?" Dorkin asked. "Out of a movie?"

"Cat? No. He's from down the river. His father and mother got killed in a car just before the war, and he went to live with an uncle. But the uncle drank and treated him bad, so Cat left. He was kickin' around, and I hired him. He lives out back and looks after the place when I'm not around. He pitches for the local baseball team, what's left of it."

The office shack was a single room with an old oak desk, three armchairs, all different, and a pot-bellied stove with a teakettle on top. The walls were decorated with an assortment of calendars, some with woods scenes, some with coy pin-up girls in shorts. The desk was scattered with old magazines and newspapers. There was no sign of bookkeeping.

Louie sat down behind the desk and lit a cigarette.

"So?" he said.

"You told me the other day that you know everybody around here," Dorkin said. "Tell me what you know about Dan Coile."

Louie raised his eyebrows and studied him through the cigarette smoke.

"Why should I want to do that?" he asked. "I mean is it the law that I have to?"

"No," Dorkin said. "I'm not a cop. There isn't any law."

"Then why should I stick my neck out?"

"As a favour, Louie."

"I don't owe you any favours. And I can't see that I'm ever likely to."

"Look, Louie, I'm only after what's public knowledge, the kind of things everyone in a place like this is going to know. I can probably get it from other people, but it will take a lot more time, and I haven't got a lot of time."

Louie sighed and coughed and looked out the window.

"Okay," he said finally. "What do you want to know?"

"Well, for a start, tell me about Dan Coile. Where does he come from?"

"He don't come from nowhere. That farm belonged to his father, and he got it when the old man died. Long time ago. Twenty years ago or more. He had some brothers, but they went away and never come back. But there's still lots of other Coiles around here. Cousins and stuff."

"It doesn't look like much of a farm."

"It ain't. They grow their own vegetables and sell a few. And he raises a few beef cows and some pigs to get cash. He don't work no more than he has to."

"And the wife?"

"She's a Fowler from out at Sherburn. About five miles further out near the border. I heard he knocked her up, and that's why they got married. They were both pretty wild when they were younger. But she got religion, and now she don't drink or smoke—nor nothin' else neither maybe."

"Does Coile drink?"

"Off and on. He's supposed to have got religion too, but I don't think it means much. He may be just goin' along with his wife to keep the peace."

"What's he like when he's drunk?"

"Mean. I hear he used to knock the wife around, but I don't know whether he still does now that she's become a saint."

"What was he like with the kids? Did he knock them around too?"

"I wouldn't be surprised. But I never heard nothin' particular."

"How many kids are there?"

"There's a brother in the army. And there's a girl a bit older than Sarah was. Named Sheila. And a younger one. And another boy."

"Are the other two girls still home?"

"The young one is. The other one's livin' with an aunt out at Sherburn."

"Do you know why she moved out?" Dorkin asked.

"No, I don't think I ever heard," Louie said.

"Did you ever hear anything about Dan Coile messing around with her—or with Sarah?"

"I'm not sure I'm understandin' what you're askin'."

"It's called incest. Getting into bed—or the hay or whatever—with your own daughter."

Louie raised his eyebrows.

"It goes on, Louie," Dorkin said.

"I know. I know," Louie said. "Some people even do it with cows. 'Once I was happy but look at me now, in the Dorchester pen for fuckin' a cow.'"

"I don't care about the cows," Dorkin said. "I'm wondering if you've heard anything about Coile and his daughters."

"No, I haven't. But that's not the kind of stuff that gets talked around too much, is it?"

"Probably not. You can end up in jail for it if anybody wants to take the trouble. But sometimes it gets around all the same. You've never heard anything like that?"

"No," Louie said. "Nothin' like that."

"Have you ever been around their place?"

"Some. I bought some hides from him a few times. You think he's the one who knocked the girl up?"

"It's possible. It helps to explain a lot of strange things."

"And you think maybe Coile killed her to keep her quiet?"

"It's crossed my mind. But don't talk that around."

"Don't worry," Louie said. "I don't intend to."

"I'd be interested in talking to the older girl and the aunt," Dorkin said. "Do you know where they are exactly?"

"Sure. They're out in Sherburn, where the Fowlers come from. The aunt's married name is MacMillan. Fern MacMillan. But I think you better be careful. This is rough stuff you're talkin', kid. You better understand that there are people that fancy uniform ain't going to protect you against even in broad daylight, let alone after dark."

"Like Dan Coile?"

"Maybe. Or maybe just somebody who wants your boy hanged and don't like you messin' around with stuff they think ain't your business. Maybe just somebody who don't like Yids."

"Are there lots of those around here?"

"Enough," Louie said. "There's always a few of them around everywhere. Especially if you stir them up by actin' as if you were a real, honest-to-god, Anglo-Saxon human being."

"These ones are mostly Irish and Scottish."

"Whatever."

"So tell me about Aunt Fern," Dorkin said. "Has she got religion too?"

"Not that I know of, not that kind anyways," Louie said. "A spitfire. Them Fowler girls out there are hot stuff, if you know what I mean."

"And Mr. MacMillan?"

"He farms. And works in the woods. And traps a little too."

"Kids?"

"No, no kids."

"You don't think it would be smart for me to go out there?"

"I don't think it's smart for you to even be here," Louie said. "I don't think any of it's smart."

"Okay," Dorkin said. "I'll think about it. But draw me a little map anyway in case I decide not to take your advice."

CHAPTER TEN

"Turn right," Dorkin said, and Smith stopped, looked both ways along the deserted road, cornered carefully, and started slowly down a long slope.

Bringing Smith along as driver on this expedition was being done merely to give him something to do. Once they had got their shop set up in the armoury, it had taken Dorkin only three or four days to realize that he didn't particularly need Smith, apart from the fact that having a subordinate around enhanced his image a little in the eyes of the awful Captain Fraser. So Smith did some typing, filed some papers, ran an errand now and then, but mostly sat unobtrusively in his little nook reading the books (surprisingly sophisticated) that he had had the foresight to bring along.

At the bottom of the slope, the road curved away and emerged abruptly from the forest into open country at the bottom of a shallow little valley with a creek and a covered bridge, and a couple of dozen houses scattered among fields along half a mile of road.

This was Sherburn Falls, and the creek that ran through it was the same that flowed past the back door of Dan Coile's place except that here it was smaller, cleaner, more a brook than a creek, and the falls just below the covered bridge was not so much a falls as a rapids—a long slope of smooth rock down which the river flowed in sheets.

From Louie's description, Dorkin had imagined somewhere primitive and barbarous, as befitted a place on the far side of so much forest, and it was to give himself the protection of a witness as well as to shore up his crumbling prestige that for the first time he pressed Smith into service as a driver. But what he saw seemed unthreatening. These were not the big, affluent farms of the river valley, but the houses were solid, the fields and fences well tended.

"The other side of the bridge," Dorkin said. "Take it slow."

He saw no one, but by the time they had crossed the bridge, he felt sure they were being watched. With Louie's crude map to guide him, he counted off the houses left and right until he found a homemade wooden mailbox with the name *JOHN MACMILLAN* hand-painted in block capitals.

The house stood almost up to the road in one corner of a three-acre field, its borders marked by low walls of stone. The main house, cedar-shingled, was square, plain, two-storeyed. Attached to it in a long line were a summer kitchen, a woodshed, and a grey barn. From a small paddock beside the barn two immense workhorses stood with their heads hanging over the fence watching Dorkin's car as it came into the yard, driving before it a flock of chickens and rousing from its sleep by the back door the farm dog, mongrel and large, who barked dutifully but didn't look likely to attack.

At the far end of the garden that ran beside the dooryard, a man who had been digging potatoes stood watching the car also, a big man dressed in work pants and a plaid shirt. He stuck the fork in the ground and made his way unhurriedly towards Dorkin.

Close up, John MacMillan turned out to be even bigger than he looked at a distance, towering half a head above Dorkin. Dorkin guessed that he would be about forty, with jet-black hair, a jet-black moustache, and soft, remote brown eyes. If he was surprised at Dorkin's appearance in his dooryard, he didn't show it.

Dorkin had come with a carefully prepared plan of inquiry beginning with a variation of the familiar evasions. He had been assigned the duty of representing Private Williams. Part of that duty naturally entailed examining the evidence against Williams, and in doing this he had come to the conclusion that there was a possibility that Private Williams was innocent. He was particularly interested in identifying anyone whom Sarah might have been seeing regularly. Naturally, it was awkward for him to talk to her parents, and he was hoping that he might be able to talk with him and his wife and perhaps Sarah's sister, who he understood was living with them.

Watching the strange, soft eyes, Dorkin couldn't tell whether any of this oily froth was being believed or not. When he had finished, the eyes drifted away, then back.

"My wife's inside," MacMillan said. "She knows more about all this than I do. I think it might be better if you talk with her."

"It won't upset her?"

"No, I don't think so. We've sort of got used to it."

The wife was in the back kitchen. Against one wall there was a black woodstove on which two great pots were steaming. There were preserve bottles everywhere and an overwhelming smell of vinegar.

Fern MacMillan was standing in the middle of the room awaiting them. She was short and compact with the sharp, clean features of a much younger woman and dark blonde hair tied back in a bun. She gave the impression of being a woman who took a good hard look at the world before she dealt with it, and she gave Dorkin a good hard look now, her head cocked to one side, her lips pursed. MacMillan explained who Dorkin was, and Dorkin went through his act once more.

"I understand," Dorkin said, "that all this is very painful to talk about, and you aren't under any obligation to do it if you'd rather not. But I would be grateful if you would. Nothing you say will be repeated, and there isn't any question of your having to appear in court or anything like that. I'm merely hoping for information that might give me some guidance."

He trailed off, aware that he was beginning to flounder.

Fern MacMillan glanced at her husband and considered.

"All right," she said. "Let's go inside where we can all sit down."

In the main kitchen there was a long pine table down the middle, and they all sat.

"So," she said, "what are you tryin' to find out exactly?"

"Well," Dorkin said, "I'd be interested in anything you might know about any boyfriends Sarah might have had in the last year. Anyone she might have been serious about. Perhaps she might have said something to you."

"No," she said. "We never saw her much in the last couple of years."

"She never talked to you about her trouble?"

"No, she never said nothin' about that. I only heard about it after the court hearin'. After that it was all over the country. That and a lot of other stuff. Crazy stuff."

"What kind of crazy stuff?" Dorkin asked.

"They were sayin' that they said in court that that soldier ate off part of her leg."

Dorkin recalled Bourget's macabre joke, but decided to let it pass since the truth was almost as bad.

"Do you think Sarah might have talked to her mother about her trouble?" he asked.

"I don't know. I wouldn't think it," she said. "You don't think that soldier was the one who got her in trouble?"

"No," Dorkin said. "It's not possible. He'd never had anything to do with her until a couple of weeks before that night."

"You don't think he murdered her?"

"No," Dorkin said. "I don't."

"You think she may have been murdered because she was in trouble?"

"It's possible."

"I suppose. It wouldn't be the first time. More than are known about, I wouldn't be surprised."

All this was just a diversion. Cautiously, Dorkin began to move towards his real objective.

"I heard a rumour," Dorkin said, "nothing very specific, that Sarah might have had some plans for leaving Wakefield. I've been wondering if there was someone she might have been planning to go away with—or someone who might have persuaded her that he was going to take her away somewhere."

"I don't know. I never heard nothin' about that."

"I also heard that she wasn't getting along very well with her father."

"Oh? Where did you hear that from?"

"A couple of the girls who knew her," Dorkin said. "It was just gossip. The trouble is that I have no way to tell what's just gossip from what may be the truth."

Fern glanced at her husband. He shrugged, and she sat for a moment looking down at the table, her mouth tight.

"Nobody gets along with Dan Coile," she said. "Not for very long anyways. Sarah was no exception."

"Did she ever say anything to you about it?" Dorkin asked.

"Sometimes."

"Recently?"

"Once last winter. I just happened to meet her in town on Saturday. I told her she could come out here if she wanted. But she had her job at the dairy, and she didn't want to give it up because then she wouldn't have no money at all. And there's not much to do out here. And it's hard to get to town, especially in the winter."

"She did stay out here once a couple of years ago for a few weeks one summer," MacMillan said. "And once when she was real little, just five years old maybe before she went to school, she lived out here for six months. We never had no children, and Matilda had more than she could really handle. There's a picture of her here."

He took a framed photograph from a collection on a cupboard and handed it to Dorkin. It showed a round-faced child in a neat white dress standing by the porch with a dog whose shoulder was almost level with her own.

"We would sort of liked to adopt Sarah," MacMillan said, "since we didn't have no children, but Dan wouldn't hear of it."

"That bastard!" Fern exploded. "He came out here and got Sarah two years ago before any of this happened—before she started runnin' round, I mean. I should have had John run him off the place, but he was the father, John said, and he could have set the law on us, so we let her go. She didn't want to then. If she'd stayed, none of this would have happened. She'd still be alive."

"Her sister Sheila," Dorkin said. "Is she living out here because of trouble at home?"

Fern pursed her lips and stared furiously at the black cookstove and then out the window. Dorkin looked at MacMillan.

"Dan wouldn't leave her alone," MacMillan said.

"That bastard!" Fern said again. "I told Matilda not to marry him. He was never any good—prancin' around and bootleggin' and thinkin' that every woman who saw him go by in a car was crazy after him. The only woman fool enough even to look at him, let alone marry him, was Matilda."

"She would have been a good girl, Sarah," MacMillan said, "if she'd had half of a chance. A real happy little girl, she was. Just full of fun. Good looking, too, right from the start."

"Who do they think she might have been going to run off with?" Fern said.

"That's what I never found out," Dorkin said. "Maybe no one."

"Someone useless the way her mother did," Fern said. "It's funny how the same things go on happenin' in families."

"Would her sister Sheila possibly know something about what was happening?" Dorkin asked.

"No, I don't think so," Fern said. "She's been out here for over a year now, and she ain't seen Sarah for a long time."

"Once when we'd gone into town one time back in the spring," MacMillan said, "Dan came out here and tried to get her to go back home with him, but she's of age, and he ain't got no say over her now, so she told him to get off the place and threatened to shoot him. She ain't been home since."

"She's workin' days for a woman over in Leach Settlement who just had a baby," Fern said. "She don't like to talk about any of this.

She's got a boyfriend now who's serious, and she don't want ever to see Dan or any of them again or have no part of anythin' to do with them."

Dorkin considered and decided not to push it now. Later, he thought, if he really needed to, he could try to talk to the sister.

"Well," he said, getting up, "I won't bother her. I'm sorry about Sarah and about all the trouble you've had. And I'm grateful for your help."

MacMillan got up too and followed Dorkin out into the yard.

"You don't think it was the soldier got Sarah in trouble?" he asked when they were out of earshot of his wife.

"No," Dorkin said.

MacMillan considered.

"You're thinking it may have been Dan," MacMillan said.

"I've been wondering."

"Do you think Dan murdered her?"

"I don't know," Dorkin said, cautious.

"That would be awful hard on everybody," MacMillan said.

"Yes," Dorkin said.

He hesitated, afraid of pushing too hard.

"Have you any idea how far things went with Sheila?" he asked.

"She never talked to me about it, just Fern, and Fern didn't say too much. I think he just kept hanging around her and trying to peek at her when she was getting dressed. Or outside. Things like that. And trying to get alone with her when Matilda wasn't around."

"Nothing more?"

"I don't know. You may have heard already. He got into trouble once years ago because of a girl twelve or thirteen years old. She lived down the road from his place, and her father beat Dan up."

"Was it taken to court?"

"No, they just let it go at that. I guess they figured it would be too hard on the kid to have it spread around any more than it was already."

"Was she pregnant?"

"No," MacMillan said. "I don't think it ever got that far."

"I see," Dorkin said. "Well, that's interesting to know."

"If Dan did do it," MacMillan said, "how would you ever prove it?"

"I don't know," Dorkin said.

"I wouldn't want Fern to have to go into court," MacMillan said. "Nor Sheila."

"I can promise you that that won't happen," Dorkin said. "I just wanted some information for guidance."

"You'd guessed some of it anyways."

"Yes," Dorkin said. "Some of it."

It was dusk by seven-thirty now, and as Dorkin rounded the corner onto Broad Street, he saw that the lights were on in Bartlett's little bungalow, brighter light at the back where the kitchen was, dimmer, more orange light on the porch where Dorkin guessed that a kerosene lamp must be burning. It was Saturday night, and Bartlett and his old comrades would be starting their weekly get-together. From the tin pipe that served as a chimney, a wisp of smoke ascended to become part of the faint smokiness that tinged the air from the autumn's first bonfires.

He parked in Bartlett's drive and lifted out the case of twelve pints of beer, which he had chilled in the big icebox in the armoury kitchen. Bartlett opened the door and was waiting for him as he mounted the steps with the case under his arm. Behind him, in the warm lamplight, two other men watched.

"Well, now," Bartlett said, "what have we got here?"

"A few bottles of beer," Dorkin said. "I thought we might have a sip and another talk about some of the things we were talking about earlier. If you wouldn't mind?"

"No, I don't mind. I got a couple of the boys in here, but there ain't nothin' I know that they don't know. Or that anybody else don't know for that matter. You may be wastin' your beer."

"It won't matter. You're welcome all the same. Somewhere or other the world must owe you at least one free case of beer."

"Well, as long as you feel that way about it, there ain't no harm done."

"This here's Lieutenant Dorkin," he announced when they were inside. "Who you've all heard about by now. And this here's two old pals of mine from a long ways back. This here's Earl Scourie. And this here's Herb MacClewan. They're old soldiers too. And ain't none of us died yet anyways."

They got up from their chairs, awkward in the presence of the officer's uniform, unsure whether to shake hands or not. Earl was a little man, completely bald, with a wide mouth, so that he looked like the man in the moon in a cartoon. Herb was bigger, tougher, with fading red hair, a red face, and big red hands.

"Earl," Bartlett said. "You got two good legs under you. Why don't you take this beer out to the kitchen and pour us out a little and put the rest to keep cool."

Earl went off, and Dorkin sat down on one end of the old couch that Bartlett used as a sofa. They cut some of the edges off the awkwardness with talk of the coming of fall until Earl came back with the beer.

"Down with the Kaiser," Herb said, and they all drank.

"Were you together in the war?" Dorkin asked.

"No," Bartlett said. "Earl here was at Vimy, but we was in different outfits. Herb didn't come over until after I was on my way home. He got wounded in the leg at Cambrai. Didn't break nothin'. Earl here never got a scratch."

"Got gassed a little once," Earl said. "That's all."

"So," Bartlett said, "what's the news?"

"No real news," Dorkin said. "But I'd like to ask you some more about Dan Coile."

"Sure," Bartlett said. "Don't know whether we'll be able to answer."

"I hear that he had a hankering after little girls," Dorkin said.

Bartlett and the others exchanged glances.

"Yes," Bartlett said. "Ain't no secret about that. There was some trouble a few years ago nearly landed him in jail. You heard about that?"

"Yes," Dorkin said. "I hear he's also had trouble with his own girls."

More glances.

"What kind of trouble?" Bartlett asked.

"I'm not sure. But some of the things I've heard make me wonder if things might not have gone on there as well that could have landed him in jail if it got around."

Bartlett whistled.

"Boys," he said, "you been gettin' an earful."

"He's a dirty old son of a bitch," Earl said. "No doubt about that."

"One thing I did hear out at the garage one day," Herb said, "is that the older girl's got a boyfriend, and he's supposed to have told Dan that if he ever comes near that girl again, he's gonna shoot him."

"Any idea why?" Dorkin asked.

"Well," Herb said, "I heard that Dan figures she should be home helpin' her mother. But I wonder if there ain't more to it than that. But I ain't never heard nothin'."

"You're thinkin' that Dan maybe knocked that girl up who got murdered," Bartlett said.

"I'm wondering if it might not be possible," Dorkin said.

"And if he was the one who murdered her?"

"I don't know."

"Boys, oh boys!" Bartlett said.

"It's only speculation," Dorkin said. "I'd rather you didn't talk it around."

He knew even as he was saying it that they would. But he didn't have time to be cautious. And it crossed his mind again that it might not be a bad thing to throw a scare into Dan Coile—if it was Dan Coile.

"You didn't see his truck around that night?" he asked.

"No," Bartlett said, "I don't think so. We was all here, and I don't remember noticin' it. Either of you boys?"

They both shook their heads.

"Lots of stuff goes by here on a Saturday night," Herb said, "but we'd probably have noticed Dan if he went by. Everybody in the country knows that old truck, and nobody ever drives it but Dan."

"If he'd gone by, we'd have remembered it, sure," Earl said.

"You didn't see him any of the next three nights?" Dorkin asked.

"No," Bartlett said. "I'm sure I'd have remembered it if I had."

"And you never saw anybody else driving down into the pit?"

"No. I'd have remembered that too. But half the town could have gone down there, and I wouldn't see after dark."

"What about Clemens?" Dorkin asked. "You didn't see him driving around that Saturday night?"

"Not as I noticed," Bartlett said.

"But that's different," Herb said. "His car's just an ordinary Ford. We probably wouldn't pay much attention to it."

"Tell me about Clemens," Dorkin said. "Who is he? Where does he come from? How long has he been here?"

"I heard he come from down in the States to begin with," Bartlett said. "I don't recall where. May never have heard. And he was somewheres up the Miramichi before he came here. He's been here four, maybe five years."

"Did he start that church?" Dorkin asked.

"No," Bartlett said. "That church has been there twenty years or more. A man named Sidlaw built it first, but there's been half a dozen since him. They don't seem to stay very long. It didn't amount to much for the last ten years before Clemens came, but he's built it up. He's got quite a congregation there now."

"Some of them women think he's God," Herb said. "He's supposed to have cured one woman that the doctors had given up on just by prayin' over her. Maybe so. But I don't believe it."

"He makes a good livin' out of it anyways," Earl said. "Lots more than any of us will ever see."

"They say he gouges them ladies pretty good," Bartlett said. "But I don't suppose they have to give him money if they don't want to."

"Go straight to hell if they don't," Herb said.

"The Coiles go to that church," Dorkin said.

"That's right," Bartlett said. "If he never did nothin' else, he got Matilda off the booze. They say she hasn't touched a drop in three years."

"And Dan?"

"Well, he don't drink as much as he used to," Bartlett said. "But every once in a while, he goes on a tear. I saw him in town one day last winter so drunk he couldn't hardly stand up."

"Does Clemens have a family?" Dorkin asked.

"Yes," Bartlett said. "He's married. His wife's a skinny little woman never leaves the house hardly except to go to church. And he's got a daughter twenty or so, maybe more. She wouldn't be a bad-lookin' girl if she was dressed up in some decent clothes and prettied up a little. But I guess that would be a sin. You don't see her around much either except in town sometimes when he takes her in to buy groceries and stuff. I think they get a lot of stuff—eggs and the like—from the congregation."

"Do you think Clemens would lie to protect Dan Coile?" Dorkin asked.

"You're thinkin' about what he said about seein' the girl that night with a soldier," Bartlett said.

"Yes."

"Maybe. I don't know."

"They're a pretty tight crew, that congregation," Herb said. "I think that Clemens has got them all believin' that they're right and everybody else is goin' straight to hell. I doubt if he'd put himself out much just for Dan himself, but he might do it for Matilda's sake."

"But if Clemens didn't see them," Bartlett said, "how would he know that Sarah had ever been with a soldier at all that night anywhere?"

"Clemens didn't describe anything that he couldn't have picked up from hearsay," Dorkin said. "He didn't go to the Mounties until two days after Williams was arrested. By that time, it was all over town."

"Maybe Dan told him everythin' he needed to know," Earl said.

"Maybe," Dorkin said. But he doubted if it would have been that crude. And for Clemens, it would have been catastrophic if Dan were arrested and it all came out. If he were lying to protect Dan—and not just to hang Williams—he would probably be doing it on his own because he had guessed what had happened. More likely, Dorkin thought, he had deceived himself before he had deceived anyone else, and the easiest way to get at his testimony might be to call into question his estimate, vague at best, about what time he had left the Salcher place.

"Clemens was supposed to have been on his way from visiting a couple named Salcher when he saw Sarah and the soldier," Dorkin said. "Have you ever seen him driving by here at night?"

"I see him now and then." Bartlett said. "He does a lot of chasin' around visitin' people. I never paid much attention."

"Tell me about Salcher."

"Nothin' much to tell. They live up near Dan. He'd be seventy nearly. She's about the same, and she's a little simple. Has been for a long time, and now she's got somethin' wrong with her so she can't walk except maybe across the room."

"Clemens testified that he visited them fairly regularly."

"Could be. I never heard."

"Seems an odd time to be visiting."

"I guess so. But they're an odd outfit. Maybe you should go talk to Salcher and see what he says. Maybe Clemens was never there at all. Anyone ever check?"

"No," Dorkin said. "Not that I know of."

"Well, well," Bartlett said. "Now ain't this all somethin'."

On Monday morning, Dorkin drove back to the Hannigan Road. He had marked the house a long time before—an ugly storey-and-a-half affair with metal roofing and grey asphalt siding faked up with lines to make it look like shingling.

He parked just beyond the mailbox and walked down the dirt driveway into the dirt yard. At the back, there was a big vegetable garden, a decaying shed, a two-door privy, a chicken coop whose chickens were foraging over the yard, and a pigpen. Dorkin picked his way among the chickens and climbed the back steps onto a rickety porch full of pots and gardening tools.

He knocked on the screen door and heard a mumble of voices from inside, then the scrape of a chair on the floor and a shuffle of booted footsteps. The man who peered at him through the screen was small with a straggly, grizzled beard, receding hair, and black eyes that had something strangely dead about them. He made no move to open the door.

"Mr. Salcher?" Dorkin said. "My name is Dorkin. I'm representing the army in the Sarah Coile case. I wonder if I could talk to you for a few minutes. There are some things you may be able to help me with."

The dead eyes continued to peer, then cautiously the door was opened.

The smell hit Dorkin as soon as he stepped inside, a smell concocted out of god knows what—unwashed clothes, unwashed bodies, stale cooking, sour scrubwater, mould, dank rot, dead rats in the walls. He was led into the kitchen where a grotesquely fat woman was sitting at an old drop-leaf table drinking a cup of tea. Her hair, mouse-coloured, was so thin that Dorkin could see the shape of her skull through it. Her face was an unsunned pinkish white.

"He wants to talk about the Coile girl," Salcher shouted at her. And then to Dorkin, "This here is my wife, Ada."

"You're a soldier," she said smiling, childishly delighted, with what remained of her teeth. "We don't see no soldiers here much no more. Not since the war stopped. You been in the trenches?"

"No," Dorkin said. "Not yet."

"She forgets things," Salcher said.

"So do we all."

He had a sense already of the futility of asking what he had come here to ask.

"Mr. Salcher," Dorkin said, "on the night that Sarah Coile was murdered the Reverend Clemens said that he saw her standing on the corner of Broad Street with a soldier. He'd been visiting you, and he was on his way home. He was a little unclear about the time, and that's what I thought you might be able to help me with. Do you happen to remember what time he left here that night? It was Saturday night, July 1. Dominion Day."

"That's a long time ago," Salcher said. "He do come here sometimes."

"I know," Dorkin said. "But I thought you might remember that night in particular because of the murder."

"No," Salcher said, drawing out the vowel. "No, I can't say I do remember that night in particular."

Mrs. Salcher looked at them back and forth as they talked, uncomprehendingly, like a deaf woman.

"He's askin' about Reverend Clemens," Salcher said.

"In overalls," Mrs. Salcher said.

"No, Ada," Salcher said. "He don't wear no overalls. He's our minister. He wears a suit."

"Does Reverend Clemens visit you often?" Dorkin asked.

"Now and then. Ada can't get to church no more because of her legs, so he comes here to see her and talk to her. It does her good. Gets her mind off things."

"When does he usually come?" Dorkin asked.

"Evenins mostly," Salcher said. "No particular time. He could have been here that night."

"Would it have been as late as eleven or eleven-thirty?"

"Could be. Our clock don't work good, so we don't pay much attention. We ain't usually goin' nowhere. Especially Ada."

He gestured at an old pendulum clock on the cupboard. The pendulum was swinging away, and the clock said a quarter to four. It was, in fact, just after ten.

Shit, Dorkin thought.

"You must have known Sarah Coile," he said.

"Sure," Salcher said. "We knew all them Coile kids."

"Did you know Sarah after she grew up?" Dorkin asked.

"Well, not knowed exactly," Salcher said. "I seen her goin' back and forth on the road sometimes. And sometimes I seen her over to their place. I've knowed her father from a long time ago, and we sometimes do each other little favours."

"I hear Sarah grew up to be a good-looking girl," Dorkin said.

"Yes, sirree," Salcher said. "The last three or four years. She filled out into a woman pretty early. I tell you the young fellers sure watched her pretty close when she went by, swingin' that ass of hers."

He dropped his voice.

"Old fellers too, come to that," he said, glancing sideways at Mrs. Salcher, who seemed now to have drifted off into some world of her own and forgotten all about them.

"Any old fellers in particular?"

"Well, now, it wouldn't do for me to say that," Salcher said, winking, "but if I was a few years younger, I'd have some thoughts about it. She'd give a man a ride he wouldn't match again in a hurry, I'll bet."

Dorkin studied him, trying hard to keep up an expression that suggested a man in good, manly talk with one of his fellows.

"Well, she'd evidently given somebody a ride," he said.

It took Salcher a second to pick it up.

"Yes," he said, "I guess so."

"You've never heard any talk about who it might have been?" Dorkin asked.

"Well, everybody says it was that soldier, the one who killed her."

"I don't think so. I think it must have been someone else."

"Well," Salcher said, "if it wasn't that soldier, I don't know who. But there's lots of boys around here would be up to that all right. Them ones who go to the dances. She'd have had lots of chances, all right, a good-lookin' girl like her."

"Do you think her father knew anything about her being knocked up before she was killed?" Dorkin asked.

"No. I wouldn't know. I wouldn't know nothin' about that."

"Mr. Coile never said anything to you?"

"No, no. We never talked about nothin' like that. Never talked about his kids at all. Except for the one in the army. We talked about him a little. He's over in France now."

"In the trenches," Ada said.

"You didn't happen to see Dan Coile around in his truck that night?" Dorkin asked.

"No, I wouldn't think so," Salcher said. "But that was a long time ago. And I don't pay much attention to what goes by. We mostly set back here in the kitchen."

"I thought perhaps if he'd been out that night, he might have seen something that would be helpful to me. He didn't happen to drop in on you that night?"

"Not as I remember. He do drop in now and then, and we sometimes have a little snort if he's got somethin' with him. But I don't remember that night. Long time ago."

Dorkin looked at the dead eyes and at Ada, wallowing in her chair, communing with her fantasies of the past.

Shit, he thought again. Shit. Shit. Shit. Two months ago, these leads would all have been fresh. Now it was a cold trail. God damn the god-damned Mounties. This was what they should have been doing.

He was wasting his time. He thanked Salcher and got up from the table, and Salcher walked with him to the door. Outside on the porch, out of earshot of Ada, he sidled up to Dorkin and put his hand on his arm.

"We got plenty to eat here," he said. "Ain't no trouble about that. But I don't come in the way of much cash. You don't suppose you could let me have fifty cents, so that if I get into town, I might have the price of a little somethin' to drink? I'd take that as real kind."

Dorkin took out his billfold and found a fifty-cent piece.

"Thank you, sir," Salcher said. "That's real kind. If I hear anythin' I figure you might want to know, I'll get it to you sure."

Dorkin strode down the driveway, scattering chickens in front of him, resisting an urge to kick them, furiously angry and aware behind the anger of the gathering panic. In one week from tomorrow the trial of Owen Williams was scheduled to begin.

On the flat floodland along the river on the south side of town, Dorkin drove along a dirt road between houses that descended from respectability through humble to a final cluster that was something like a slum. Among these was the house where he had learned from Bartlett that he might find John Maclean. It was a two-storey tenement building with a long verandah that was starting to fall away from the rest of the house. A couple of fat teenage girls were sitting on the verandah on an old hammock. Chewing away methodically at their gum, they stared at Dorkin as he mounted the steps.

He had scarcely reached the top before a woman of forty or so appeared at the door.

"I'm looking for Mr. John Maclean," Dorkin said. "Is this where he lives?"

"Yes," the woman said, "this is where he lives, but I ain't sure he's in his room right now. What did you want to see him about?"

"I just wanted to have a talk with him," Dorkin said. "If he can help me out, there'd be some money in it for him."

The woman eyed him and considered.

"All right, I'll see if he's in," she said finally and disappeared into the house, leaving Dorkin to wait outside while the two fat girls on the hammock chewed and watched.

After nearly five minutes, the door opened again, and Maclean came out. He was dressed in an old blue mackinaw, heavy work pants, and ankle-length work boots. For a moment, he studied Dorkin warily.

"You wanted to see me about something?" he said.

"I'm Lieutenant Dorkin," Dorkin said. "You may remember me from Private Williams's preliminary hearing."

"No," Maclean said, "but I've seen you around up town."

"I'd like to talk to you for a few minutes," Dorkin said. "Nothing to be alarmed about. Nothing to do with you. Just some information. Why don't we go sit in the car?"

Dorkin opened the door for him, then went around and got in behind the wheel.

"You wouldn't have a cigarette?" Maclean asked.

"No," Dorkin said, "I don't smoke. But I can get you some. Is there anywhere close by?"

"Down the road here," Maclean said. "There's a little store."

Dorkin drove back down the street. At the store it turned out that for some reason, perhaps a scribbler full of bad debts, Maclean didn't want to go in, so Dorkin went in and bought a twenty-pack of Turrets. When he drove back, he went past the boarding house and on a further couple of hundred yards to where the road petered out in a stand of alders by the riverbank. Maclean lit a cigarette and took a deep drag.

"That's good," he said. "Doctor tells me I shouldn't smoke, but I don't pay much attention. Got gassed in the war. At Wypers. Ever hear of Wypers?"

"Yes," Dorkin said.

"First spring of the war. Hardly got there. The Germans sent that gas over, and nobody knew what it was then. We had English on one side of us, and some kind of French black troops on the other, and them fuckers all just ran off and left us there."

"So I heard," Dorkin said.

"Anyways, I got a little pension out of it," Maclean said. "They probably didn't know I was going to live so long when they gave it to me, or they wouldn't have done it. You ain't over there killing Germans."

"No, not yet."

"Be smart and stay home. Let them fuckers fight their own wars."

Dorkin took out a two-dollar bill, the price of a couple of bottles of cheap port, and passed it to him.

"I want to ask you about the night Sarah Coile was murdered," Dorkin said. "You were out on the Bangor Road that night, and I'm wondering if you might have noticed Dan Coile's truck anywhere out there. Do you know it?"

"Oh yeah, I know it. But I don't remember that I saw it that night. And if I'd seen it, I think I'd have remembered it because I'd have looked back when I heard about the girl."

"You didn't see him anywhere else?"

"No, not that night."

"What about the next two or three nights? Did you see him anywhere then?"

"I don't think so. I think I'd have remembered."

"You know him well enough to recognize him?"

"Oh, sure. I've seen him a thousand times. I even used to know him a little. You think he may know something about what happened to the girl?"

"I don't know," Dorkin said. "I just thought that if he were around out there, he might have seen something that he hadn't said anything about to the police for some reason."

Maclean meditated for a minute on these manifest lies and let them pass. Dorkin didn't need for him to believe them. They were merely a way for them both to avoid implicating themselves in specifics, as Maclean no doubt understood.

"I hear Dan Coile used to bootleg a little," Dorkin said, fishing.

"Yes. I guess."

"What do you think of him?"

"Just between us?"

"Just between us."

"A mean son of a bitch. Used to sell watered stuff. May still do if anyone's fool enough to buy it. Once sold a pal of mine a bottle that didn't have hardly anything in it at all. Just water with some flavour of some kind. Figured he was too drunk to know the difference."

"Do you think he would be up to killing someone?" Dorkin asked.

"Maybe. If he was drunk enough or mad enough."

"I don't think the soldier killed Sarah Coile. You've never heard anything about anyone else?"

"No. Nothing like that."

"Do you know Reverend Clemens?"

"Oh, yeah. But just to see."

"He testified that he saw Sarah Coile and a soldier out near the dance hall that night. You didn't happen to see him anywhere out there?"

"No. I heard what he said in court. But I wasn't anywhere near where he said he saw the girl and the soldier."

"You don't know of anyone else who might have seen Dan Coile or Clemens that night?"

"Not right now. But there could have been, I suppose."

"Do you think you could find out?" Dorkin asked. "It would be worth ten dollars to me to know if anyone saw either of them driving around out there that night. Or any of the next three nights. I'd particularly like to know what time it was when anyone saw Clemens the night of the dance. Do you think you could ask around?"

"I might. But it'd be tricky. I wouldn't want to ask right out. But I suppose I could make up some story and see if anybody gainsaid it. I could say I'd heard talk that Dan was hanging around out there and see if anybody would say yes or no. Same with Clemens. But I wouldn't be too hopeful if I was you."

"It's worth a try."

"There's only one thing," Maclean said. "I don't want to have to end up talking to the police. Or getting anybody else in a spot where they have to talk to the police."

"That won't happen. Once I find out what happened, I can get it proved some other way."

"Well, I'll see what I can do. But I don't expect to see any ten dollars."

"I'll give you five just for trying," Dorkin said and dug out a bill.

Back at the boarding house, he let Maclean out and watched him as he mounted the rickety steps, slowly, with the drunkard's habitual exaggeration of care. He knew that nothing was likely to come of this, but it was important, he reflected, if only for his own subsequent peace of mind, that all the stones be turned.

CHAPTER ELEVEN

The next morning, Dorkin sat in his office, looking out the window at a dark, unwelcoming day, autumnal raw, with a low cover of dirty grey cloud. He had gone late to breakfast at the hotel, ate slowly, killing time, and now sat, killing more time, afflicted by a gathering sense of depression.

He was still sitting, as if waiting, it seemed to him afterwards, when the phone rang.

It was Carvell, and Dorkin sensed at once from the calculated care in his voice that something bad had happened. His immediate thought was that it was Williams. He had killed himself, or tried. But it wasn't Williams.

"Louie Rosen's been killed," Carvell said. "His truck went off the road. I thought you'd probably want to know."

It was too abrupt for Dorkin to take it in all at once. It also seemed somehow too improbable. Louie didn't seem the sort of person to die of anything but extreme old age.

"When did it happen?" Dorkin asked.

"A couple of hours ago," Carvell said. "I've been out of town, and I just heard about it now. He went down into a gulley. The cab of the truck was smashed in, and they only got him out a few minutes ago. I heard about it from Drost. The truck's still there, and they're trying to haul it out. I thought I'd better go out and have a look in case there's an inquest."

"Where did it happen?" Dorkin asked.

"The Berkeley Road. It's about four miles out the Bangor Road on the right. You know it?"

"Yes," Dorkin said. "I'm going to go out too."

There was nothing much on the three-quarters of a mile of the Berkeley Road—no farms, no cleared land, just a couple of small hunting cabins and one ramshackle tarpapered house. It was probably a logging road that had later been fixed up a little to make a shortcut between the Bangor and Hannigan roads. In its better stretches, it was gravelled. In its worse ones, it was just dirt. It started flat from the Bangor Road and then climbed steeply through the woods for half a mile. It was near the bottom of that hill that Louie had gone off the road.

Dorkin saw the wrecker and the collection of cars and trucks that marked the spot as soon as he turned off the Bangor Road. Carvell was already there, and Constable Hooper, and a couple of dozen other men, garagemen and onlookers in mackinaws and slickers. The drizzle had now turned into a light, steady rain, and the road, which was dirt here, shone dully.

Louie's truck was at the bottom of a little gulley maybe twenty feet deep that angled down across the face of the hill. The side and bottom of the gulley were scattered with granite and sandstone boulders dropped by the glaciers, some of them the size of basketballs, some of them bigger than the cab of Louie's truck. The truck was lying on its side between two of the larger boulders, the top crushed, the engine driven partway back into the cab. The door on the driver's side, which was the one that was turned up, was twisted and crumpled, hanging on one hinge. The windshield was completely broken out except for a fringe of pointed shards. The wooden body was smashed to pieces.

For a quarter of a mile on either side of the gulley, there weren't even ditches, and the road was bordered closely on both sides with evergreens, slender-trunked, soft-branched, into which Louie could have driven and hardly scratched a fender.

"He sure picked his spot," Carvell said.

There were lines from the wrecker hooked onto the back of the truck, and as Carvell and Dorkin watched, the wrecker started up. The lines pulled taut, the wheels of the wrecker spun on the wet road, spitting mud and small stones. Louie's truck did not budge. The wrecker stopped, and the driver got out.

"I'm gonna take the clutch out of her," he said.

Down in the bottom of the gulley, two other garagemen stared at Louie's truck, meditating their next move, while Constable Hooper looked on.

Carvell began to descend the steep bank, cautiously over the wet grass and weeds, and Dorkin followed him. There was a trail of devastation where the truck had gone down—vegetation gouged and sheared off leaving raw clay, small rocks dislodged, pieces of broken slats from the back of the truck, shards of glass, unidentifiable bits of metal, cow hides, pig hides, a shovel, a peavey.

"Not much left of her," Carvell said to Hooper.

"No," Hooper said.

"What happened?" Carvell asked.

"I don't know."

"He lost control on the hill maybe."

"Maybe," Hooper said.

Dorkin leaned over the corner of the truck and looked down into the cab. There was blood everywhere, the seat and the floor soaked, the twisted steering wheel and the dash smeared.

"He was broke up pretty bad," one of the garagemen said.

"I can imagine," Carvell said.

"He wouldn't have suffered none anyways," the garageman said. "He wouldn't have known what hit him when he got to the bottom here."

Hooper, after another turn around the truck, was looking at the left front tire.

"That could have been what put him off the road," Carvell said.

"Maybe," Hooper said.

The tire was partway off the rim, the red inner tube protruding. The tire and the tube had both been given a thorough mauling as they had been rolled around under the rim, but there was no obvious reason for the tire to have gone flat.

Hooper went over it inch by inch. When he had finished, he sent one of the garagemen back up to the wrecker for a tire iron, and he carefully got the tire and tube off the wheel himself. He put them on the ground and took out the tube. As Carvell, Dorkin, and the garagemen watched, he extracted a small blob of metal. Dorkin did not at once recognize what it was.

"A .303?" Carvell said.

"Yes," Hooper said. "Or a 30/30. Something like that."

It was a small, unpretentious frame house among other unpretentious houses on the lower side of a little street without paving or sidewalks that ran for a quarter of a mile along the side of the valley just downhill from Main Street and just uphill from the CPR tracks. All the curtains were drawn.

Dorkin tapped discreetly, and the door was opened almost at once by a man whom Dorkin recognized as the owner of a clothing store on Main Street, a small, brisk, balding man, a sidewalk talker and joker, now solemn and officious. Dorkin introduced himself.

"I know, I know," the man said. "I'm Milton Geltman. It's an honour to have you come. A terrible thing."

"Yes," Dorkin said.

He was led into the living room, where a dozen people were crowded together.

"Ruby," Geltman said, "this is Lieutenant Dorkin. Mrs. Rosen."

She had a long face, a long nose, a small mouth, full-lipped but narrow, one of those homely faces that looks as if it were being seen in a distorting mirror. She lifted her heavy eyes and a long hand.

"I'm sorry," Dorkin said.

"You knew him?" she said.

"A little," Dorkin said. "We met a couple of times."

Geltman took him around the room, and names flew by in lowered tones. Among the mourners, Dorkin recognized J. Meltzer, from whom he had bought the stuff for Williams. Apart from Meltzer, they all seemed a little intimidated by him, and he had the feeling that his arrival had broken an atmosphere of intimate grief that would only be restored by his departure. He stood awkwardly in the silence.

"What will I do?" Mrs. Rosen suddenly burst out, sweeping the room with her eyes. "I have nothing. Nothing. We only had what he made. He never even bought the house."

"Everything will be all right," Geltman said. "You have your friends. You will have your house. We will see to it. You should lie down for a while."

He gestured behind him, and two of the women helped Mrs. Rosen to her feet and walked with her out of the room to the stairs.

"Do they have any children?" Dorkin asked Meltzer.

"One boy," Meltzer said. "He was no good. He and Louie didn't get on. He went away five or six years ago. Nobody knows where he is. In the States somewhere. I suppose we'll have to try to find him, but I don't know how. What a terrible thing."

"Yes," Dorkin said again.

He stayed on for another half an hour and drank coffee, unable to effect an exit that would not seem rude, regretting that he had come, filled with guilt and rage. He felt sure that if he had not talked with Louie, Louie would not now be dead.

It was early afternoon when Dorkin arrived at Louie's yard. The big double doors in the fence were closed, but to one side there was a smaller door, like a house door, and Dorkin let himself in. The doors to the big warehouse were also closed, and there was a general air of desertedness. Dorkin picked his way among the rain-filled potholes in the yard, tried the door of the office and, finding it locked, went across the yard and around to the back of the warehouse. In the far corner of the yard, almost up against the fence, there was a small shack.

When he was still a dozen paces from the shack, the door opened, and Cat Polchis stood watching him.

"I'd like to talk to you about Louie," Dorkin said.

Cat continued to stand, as if he hadn't heard him. His eyes were so black that there was no sense of there being an iris and a pupil, only blackness, uniform, opaque, impenetrable. After an uncomfortably long pause, he stepped back, holding open the door.

"Okay," he said.

Except for a cubicle in one corner, presumably the bathroom, the shack was one big room. There was a black cookstove for heat as well as cooking, a pine table, some pine chairs, a big pine cupboard with pans and dishes, a single bed, and an old Morris chair, the kind of thing that Louie might have picked up somewhere. On the wall above the table, there were two pictures of baseball teams and one of Cat by himself in a baseball uniform. Everything was very neat, very clean, with an almost military orderliness.

Dorkin sat down at the table.

"You want to be more comfortable?" Cat asked, motioning towards the Morris chair.

"This is fine," Dorkin said.

Cat sat down opposite him.

"You heard that somebody shot out Louie's tire?" Dorkin said.

"Yes," Cat said. "I heard. It's all over town."

"You didn't hear anything about who might have done it?"

"No."

"Any idea?"

"No," Cat said. "Not yet."

"Do you think somebody might have been waiting for him?"

"Could be. I don't know."

"Do you know if anybody phoned him this morning?" Dorkin asked. "Do you know if somebody might have set it up?"

"No," Cat said. "I was over in the warehouse. I don't know who he talked to."

"Did he say where he was going when he left?"

"Across the river to a couple of places. After that, I don't know. Might not have been set up anyway. Somebody might just have been out with a gun and seen him comin' and took a shot."

"Just for the hell of it?"

"Maybe. Maybe for some reason."

"Such as?"

Cat shrugged.

"The talk around town is that you think it may have been Dan Coile himself who killed his daughter and that you were out here questionin' Louie. Louie fired Toady a couple of days after you were here. He probably spread it around."

"I talked to a lot of people," Dorkin said, suddenly turning defence lawyer on his own behalf, trying to deflect the accusation against himself that he himself had already made. "Why should someone pick on Louie?"

"Because he knew stuff," Cat said.

"He didn't tell me anything that I couldn't have found out from almost anyone," Dorkin said.

"I know that," Cat said. "But Dan Coile and his pals didn't know that."

"I don't understand," Dorkin said.

"Louie knew that Coile was messing around with his daughters," Cat said. "A couple of years ago, he was driving into the Coile place, and he saw Dan and the sister of the one who got killed coming out of the barn. Louie could tell that something funny was going on, so he pretended he hadn't seen them and kept on going and parked up by the house, but he could tell from the way Coile acted afterwards that he knew Louie had seen him and the girl."

In the doorway, as Dorkin was leaving, Cat said, "You should have left Louie out of it. It didn't have nothin' to do with him."

Outside the window, the rain poured down, sweeping along the street in gusts, bringing down with it cascades of sodden leaves. In spite of the rain, Dorkin had walked from the armoury to the RCMP office, and his raincoat now hung on the rack by the door, dripping water onto the floor.

Carvell was sitting in his chair against the wall. Hooper was manning the desk with the phone and the typewriter. Drost was seated behind the desk where they did business with their assorted visitors, willing and otherwise. Dorkin stood in the middle of the room. Except at a distance, he had not seen Drost since the day he had gone through the boxes of evidence. He had not liked Drost from the day he had first seen him in court, and he sensed clearly enough that Drost did not like him.

"Whoever did it," Hooper said, "was ahead of him up the road on the left-hand side. The bullet went in just by the corner of the tread and then hit the back of the wheel. If he'd waited until the truck was a little closer, it would have gone out the other side, and we'd probably never have known it wasn't just a flat tire."

"You've no idea who it was?" Dorkin asked.

"No," Drost said.

"I doubt if whoever it was intended to kill him," Carvell said. "It was just Louie's bad luck that it happened on a wet day and he went off the road where he did. Someone could have been out with a gun and just decided to play games."

"A dangerous game," Dorkin said.

"Yes," Carvell said. "But it isn't the first time somebody's shot a tire out just for the hell of it."

"You don't think that it might have been someone who had something against Louie?" Dorkin asked.

"Could be," Carvell said. "Louie could be pretty sharp when it came to dealing with people. I imagine he'd made his share of enemies. But I still doubt if anyone intended to kill him."

"You said that you had some information that you wanted to give us," Drost said.

"Yes," Dorkin said. "I don't think it was just a prank. I've found out that Dan Coile was molesting his daughters, and Louie knew it. He caught Coile and the older daughter coming out of the barn a couple of years ago."

"So Coile shot his tire out?" Drost asked.

"I think it's worth looking into," Dorkin said. "I think it's worth finding out where Coile was this morning."

"Have you ever heard anything like that about Coile?" Drost asked Carvell.

"Not about the daughters," Carvell said. "But he was in trouble over a young girl out there a few years ago. A neighbour's kid. But it blew over, and he was never brought to court or anything like that."

"Who told you about the daughters?" Drost asked. "That's a pretty serious accusation."

"I'd rather not say," Dorkin said, "but it was from someone reliable."

"Louie?" Drost asked.

"No," Dorkin said, "not Louie."

"But it was Louie who told you about him seeing them coming out of the barn."

"No," Dorkin said. "That wasn't Louie either. In fact, he deliberately didn't tell me about it when I was talking to him about Coile. It was Cat Polchis who told me about it this afternoon after Louie was killed."

"Bernie," Carvell said, "let me tell you something."

It was the first time Carvell had ever called him by his first name, let alone this nickname, which he had always hated, and the effect was paternal, at once affectionate and superior.

"I know that Louie was a likeable guy," Carvell said, "but he was a storyteller. He was full of them. Some of them were true, but a lot of them weren't. He liked to talk. He liked to weave tales. And most of the time he never expected people to believe half of what he was saying."

"But he didn't talk this one around," Dorkin said, irritated by Carvell's manner. "The only person he told was Cat, and so far as I know the only person Cat has told is me. Louie may have told tales around town for the fun of it, but this wasn't one of them. He didn't spread it around because he was afraid of Coile."

"But even if it's true," Drost said, "why should Coile all of a sudden two or three years afterwards decide that he's going to shoot up Louie's truck? And how would he even know that Louie was going to be there?"

"He could have phoned and set it up," Dorkin said.

"I'm sorry," Drost said, "but I can't see it. He was going away from the Coile place, not towards it. Do you think that Coile got him to come out to his place and then when he'd left got a gun and ran through the woods faster than Louie could drive in his truck and waited for him?"

"Coile has relatives by the dozens," Dorkin said. "He could have worked it out with one of them. Or more than one. They could have staked out the road and waited. When they shot his tire out, they may not have intended to kill him, but I think they certainly intended it as a warning."

"But why all of a sudden now?" Drost asked. "Even if what Louie said is true, why all of a sudden after two or three years?"

"Because," Dorkin said, "whatever reason he may have given to anyone he had help him, he had another reason of his own."

"Oh?" Drost said. "What was that?"

"I think that he was the one who killed Sarah, not Williams," Dorkin said. "I think that he was the father of the child that she was carrying, and I think that he waylaid her that night and killed her and left her body in the gravel pit."

Carvell whistled softly.

"Do you have any evidence to support this?" Drost asked.

"Not court evidence," Dorkin said. "Not yet anyway. But I know that Williams could not possibly have got Sarah pregnant, and I know that he didn't kill her. I know that whoever got Sarah pregnant was someone she couldn't marry. I know that Coile had been messing around with her and that he had also been messing around with the older sister before that. I know that Coile knew that Louie had seen him in compromising circumstances with the older girl. I know that Coile knew that I had been talking to Louie. And this was now dangerous stuff for him if he had killed Sarah."

There was a long silence. Drost looked down at his desk. Carvell looked thoughtfully at Dorkin.

"Did you ever check on what Daniel Coile was doing the night of the murder?" Dorkin asked Drost.

"No," Drost said. "I had no reason to. But we checked everyone who was in or around the dance hall. Hooper spent almost a week doing nothing else."

"But you didn't check Daniel Coile."

"The town is full of people we didn't check," Drost said. "We checked everyone who was on the road that night."

"But Daniel Coile isn't just anyone in town," Dorkin said. "Most people who are murdered are murdered by their own relatives, as you well know."

"Or by their boyfriends," Drost said.

"Do you think that Williams was the father of Sarah's child?" Dorkin asked.

"I don't know," Drost said.

"Did you ever find any evidence that Williams had ever had anything to do with Sarah Coile before that night?" Dorkin asked.

"I don't see that we needed to," Drost said. "We weren't trying to find out who knocked her up, we were trying to find out who killed her. I don't think there has to be any connection. She could have been screwing everyone in town. She probably was."

"You have no evidence for that," Dorkin said. "The truth is that once you decided that Williams was guilty, you ignored everything else and simply concentrated on assembling a case against him."

Drost flushed.

"Why are you telling me all this?" he said. "Tell it in court."

"I intend to," Dorkin said. "But I'm telling you now because I want you to do two things. I want you to find out where Daniel Coile was the night of the murder. And I want you to find out where he was when Louie's tire was shot out."

"I can't just haul people in off the street for questioning," Drost said.

"There are ways if you want to use them," Dorkin said. "What you're worried about is that you may get heat from Grant if you start interfering with his case against Williams and perhaps spoil his record for having solved a murder in six hours."

"I don't have to listen to this," Drost said. "You have no authority to order me around. You have no right even to be in this office. If you have a case, go make it in court."

"I've got a case," Dorkin said. "Unlike the prosecution, what I don't have is a police force at my disposal to collect the evidence. I can understand the pressures you may be under, but I think you should also consider what will happen if it turns out that you've been a party to hanging the wrong guy in spite of everything I've told you."

"I don't hang anyone," Drost said. "The judge and the jury do."

"That's bullshit," Dorkin said.

Drost pushed his chair back angrily and stalked across the room. He stood looking out the window at the rain. There was a long silence.

"Do you intend to reopen the investigation of the murder or not?" Dorkin said.

"On the basis of what?" Drost asked without turning around.

"On the basis of what I've just told you," Dorkin said.

"I have to have some evidence."

"I've given you evidence." Drost looked at him.

"You've picked up some rumours about Dan Coile messing around with his daughters, so you've decided that he was the one who knocked Sarah up and then murdered her to keep her quiet. That's evidence?"

"Tell me," Dorkin said, "did you ever make any serious attempt to find out who got Sarah Coile pregnant?"

"We were investigating a murder, not a paternity suit. Anyway, how do you know it wasn't Williams? Because he said it wasn't?"

"Not one person ever saw Williams with Sarah Coile outside the dance hall except that night," Dorkin said.

"Maybe not, but there are plenty of other people who could have knocked her up. It doesn't have to be Dan Coile."

"You're not going to check on any of this?"

"No," Drost said. "Not unless I hear something more convincing than anything I've heard here. I wouldn't be given the authority from Fredericton anyway."

"You're not going to ask?"

"No, I'm not going to ask."

"And what about Louie? Do you intend to talk to Dan Coile about that?"

"I don't know," Drost said. "I don't know who we're going to talk to. I'll take account of what you've told me. What we do with it and how we handle that investigation is none of your business, so far as I can see."

"In other words, you're going to do nothing," Dorkin said.

"God damn it!" Drost said. "I've had enough of this. You've told me what you've come to tell me. I'll make a report of it. Now I've got other things to do."

Without looking at Dorkin, he went back to his desk and sat down. Dorkin hesitated, then angrily picked his coat off the rack and put it on. Carvell rose and followed him out.

On the porch, before they went their different ways into the rain, Carvell put his hand on Dorkin's shoulder.

"I'm sorry about Louie," he said. "I don't think you should conclude that it was necessarily your fault. He was a sharpie, and there were all sorts of people who had grudges against him of one kind or another."

"And he was a Jew," Dorkin said.

"Yes," Carvell said. "I suppose there's that too."

"You don't think that quite apart from anything he may have known about Dan Coile," Dorkin said, "someone may just have taken a random shot at him because they wanted to take a shot at me and didn't quite dare?"

"I don't know, Bernard," Carvell said. "It's possible. Just about anything is. The world's an evil place."

"I don't want to see whoever it was get away with it," Dorkin said.

"I don't either particularly," Carvell said, "but he probably will unless he's foolish enough to brag about it."

He hesitated.

"You may be right about Coile and the girl," he said. "I just don't know. I probably shouldn't be saying this, but I think maybe that under the stress of all this you're losing control of yourself a little. I'm saying this by way of being a friend. I wouldn't want you to take it any other way."

The next day Dorkin found that there was a further blow in store. A message had come through that he was to phone Meade's office on a matter of urgency.

He got the CWAC clerk.

"Colonel Meade would like you to meet him for lunch at the officers' mess here at 1200 hours tomorrow," she said.

Meade himself would certainly have phrased it so that it did not sound so peremptory, but peremptory it certainly was. Something was in the wind, and Dorkin felt certain that it would not be good.

Dorkin dined with Meade by a window in the mess. Outside there was a stretch of immaculately tended lawn ending in a thin screen of twelve-foot Lombardy poplars. Beyond them, the river flowed by, unruffled today under a cloudless sky.

Dorkin could remember this site as it was in the spring of 1940 when it was under construction and he was still at university: banks of raw earth, excavations, mud, water, piles of lumber, mess. Now, over four years later, it had an air of permanency that made it seem as if there had never been a time when there had not been the war.

They dined on salmon steaks, big and fresh, and Meade was moved to ask Dorkin if he fished (which he did not) and then went on to tell him about the fishing trip that he had made every June for the past twenty-five years, war or no war, to the wilderness of the Big Sevogle River. From there, the talk drifted inevitably to the war. On Sunday, the British had dropped a parachute division on Arnhem, and it was beginning to be obvious that something was going badly wrong. Whenever the press releases started describing Allied troops as "valiant," one knew that they were being beaten. And the Canadians, grinding and sloshing up the coast, were not doing all that well either. The casualties, Meade said, leaning forward across the table and dropping his voice, were much heavier than was being let on. Any day now the conscription issue was going to blow up again. Did Dorkin know that MacKenzie King had been booed by Canadian troops when he had inspected them overseas?

When they had finished dessert and coffee, they walked for a quarter of an hour back and forth along the line of poplars by the river, and Meade smoked a cigar. Then, casually, he brought them at last around to his office. He settled himself behind his oak desk, and Dorkin took the chair that he had sat in when Meade had ordered him to attend Williams's preliminary hearing. Through dinner and their post-prandial perambulations, not a word had been said about Williams.

"Well," Meade said, "I hear that you've been brewing up quite a storm up there."

The tone was affable, indulgent. Caught off guard, Dorkin fished for some appropriate reply, and he was still fishing and beginning to realize that there was no appropriate reply when Meade continued.

"I'm afraid that I've had to call you down," he said, "because I've had complaints from Whidden and the Crown prosecutor's office. I've wanted to leave the case entirely up to you since this was what seemed to me proper, but I've come under considerable pressure to speak to you about your handling of some matters."

He paused. Dorkin said nothing, and he went on.

"Whidden is very upset that you've been talking to Crown witnesses."

He consulted a pad on his desk.

"To Miss Vinny Page, who I understand was a friend of Sarah Coile. And to a Mr. John Maclean, who testified about seeing Williams the night of the murder. I don't suppose there's any law against this so long as you weren't putting any kind of pressure on them, but it's generally regarded as unethical. Whidden is making noises about your tampering with witnesses."

"I'm sorry," Dorkin said. "I did talk to them because it seemed to me important. But I wasn't tampering with the evidence they gave at the preliminary. I never discussed that with them at all. I was talking to them about matters which were different altogether."

"Well," Meade said. "Whidden could not have known that. Could I ask what you did talk about?"

"I was talking to Miss Page because I thought that she might be able to help me find out who was the father of the child that Sarah Coile was carrying. I talked to Maclean about whether he had seen a truck that I was interested in tracking down on the night of the murder."

"Are these not things that you could have asked in cross examination at the trial?"

"I felt that by then it would be too late for the information to be useful to me."

"And did you get any information from them?"

"Some. What they said helped me to clarify my ideas about what might have happened that night."

"I understand," Meade said, "that there are rumours about that you think that it was the girl's father who murdered her. Do you really think that?"

"Yes," Dorkin said. "I'm sorry that it's got around. I didn't intend it to, but I think that people began to realize what the point of my inquiries was."

"Do you have any real evidence of this?" Meade said.

"That's what I've been trying to find over the last couple of weeks."

"What you have then is a suspicion?"

"Yes," Dorkin said. "A very strong suspicion."

"I think you had better tell me about it," Meade said.

Dorkin hesitated. He didn't like this at all, but he decided that he had no choice.

He talked without interruption for almost three-quarters of an hour, laying out as persuasively as he could what he had found out, what he suspected. When he had finished, Meade sat back.

"As I understand it then," he said, "your case against Coile is that he is believed to have molested his daughters and that therefore he might have been the father of Sarah's child and might have murdered her to keep this quiet."

He studied Dorkin from across the desk.

"That's very thin stuff," he said. "You have no actual evidence of his having seen her that night after she left to go to the dance?"

"No. That's what I've been trying to collect."

"I understand that you went to see the Mounties about it."

"Yes."

"I've had a complaint from them too," Meade said. "Inspector Gregory phoned me yesterday. He was very angry. He felt that you were using your rank in the army to bully his officers into conducting investigations for you that they did not feel were justified."

"I hadn't intended to bully. But I'm very unhappy about the initial investigation that Grant conducted into the murder. Within an hour or two, he decided that Williams was guilty, and they never pursued any other line of investigation."

"But they have been co-operative," Meade said. "They have made available to you all the evidence they have collected. You don't feel that they've withheld anything?"

"No. But it's the evidence they haven't collected that concerns me."

"Bernard, I appreciate your concern for Williams. A lawyer should fight for his client. But you are not a policeman. It's not your job to chase around the country trying to catch murderers. Your job is to go into court and attempt to convince a jury that the evidence which the prosecution is presenting is not enough to prove beyond any reasonable doubt that your client is guilty. If he is found not guilty, then it is up to the police to chase around the country and try to find out who *is* guilty. I gather from what you say that you feel that the case which the police have built is a weak one founded on very questionable circumstantial evidence. If that is so, then that is what you tell your judge and jury. You tell them that on the basis of the evidence that has been presented it is easy to construct an explanation of the girl's death other than the one the prosecution is presenting."

"I don't think it will be enough," Dorkin said. "There's too much prejudice against Williams because of his being a Zombie. I think that it's going to be very difficult for him to get an impartial hearing from any jury up there, or anywhere else for that matter."

"I take it that you are convinced that Williams is telling the truth," Meade said. "Have you ever really seriously considered the possibility that he may not be?"

"Whenever I've talked to him it always comes out the same. I don't think he's capable of being that good a liar."

Meade considered, shifted a pencil around on the desk. For the first time, Dorkin caught a flicker of irritation in his manner, but when he spoke, his voice was still level and reasonable.

"Bernard," he said, "I have great admiration for you, and I respect your concern for Williams and your energy in doing what you believe is right. But in the time that remains, I want you to confine yourself to your proper duties as a defence counsel and to stop acting as if you were a private investigator. I don't like doing it this way, but in view of the representations that have been made to me from higher up, I'm afraid that I'm going to have to put that in the form of an order. Even if you were a civilian defence counsel, some of your approaches would have been a little improper. But you are an army officer, and in addition to the normal considerations, you also have to take into account the obligations you have not to do anything to bring your uniform into disrespect. You should not be roaming the countryside in a staff car knocking on doors and fishing around for the local gossip about Daniel Coile and his family."

He stood up and held out his hand.

"I'm sorry," he said, "but these things had to be said. I would have had to say them even if I didn't want to because of the directive I've been given. I hope that it will not cloud our good will towards each other."

"No," Dorkin said. "Of course not. I understand your position."

"Do your best," Meade said, "as I'm sure you will. And remember that a lawyer is a little like a doctor. He can't save everybody, not even everybody who is saveable, and if he can't accept that, he'd better get out of the profession or he'll go crazy."

He came around from behind the desk and put his hand on Dorkin's shoulder and walked with him to the door. As Dorkin emerged into the outer office, the CWAC corporal studied him from over her typewriter, briefly, but in a way that made him feel that she was looking for bruises. Or burns. In a phrase that had made its way from the RAF through every branch of the forces, he had just, however politely, been shot down in flames.

After leaving Meade's office, Dorkin had driven downtown, parked his car, and walked the city for almost two hours—one hour while Meade's dressing-down in all its implications sank in and another hour while he came to terms with it as best he could.

Now it was ten o'clock and dark, and he sat in his office with only the old army-issue gooseneck lamp on his desk turned on. The papers he had been through so many times were neatly piled in their place in front of him. Beside them lay the stone he had picked up from Sarah's shallow grave at the gravel pit.

It was a flat oblong of grey and white sandstone, half an inch thick, an inch and a half long, almost perfectly symmetrical, rounded at the edges and polished as smooth as any craftsman could have done. He picked it up and held it in the palm of his hand.

Somewhere, perhaps a hundred million years ago, the sand it had been made of had been laid down at the edge of some shallow sea, then buried, compressed, hardened, pushed up, twisted, broken, shattered into innumerable pieces of which this was the remains of one. Then sometime, perhaps about the time of the first *Homo sapiens*, it had been picked up by a glacier, ground along, dropped as the glacier retreated and for thousands of years rolled back and forth in a stream or on some shore. Finally it had been buried in the deposit of gravel that had been dug into twenty or thirty years ago to make the pit where Sarah was to be found.

Turning it over in his palm, closing his fist on it, he had an abrupt, vivid sense of the immensity of time and of the brevity of the tiny spark of the individual human life and of its piteousness and sanctity. He found himself remembering the photograph that MacMillan had shown him of Sarah as a child standing beside an enormous dog in the sunlight of that one unique day. Her face floated before him, alive and dead, followed by other faces. Louie. Daniel Coile. Whidden and McKiel, Grant and Drost, for whom it was all a game, a competition to be won for the gratification of their egos. Meade was probably right in suggesting that perhaps he wasn't cut out for this.

Meanwhile, there was this. There was Sarah and Louie and Daniel Coile. And poor, dumb Williams. He would have to fight it out in court, but one way or another he was going to win. He was going to put Daniel Coile behind bars.

CHAPTER TWELVE

At two o'clock on the first day of the case of the King v. Owen Thomas Williams, Dorkin sat at his long oak table in the Central Court Room of George County. Beside him sat Private Smith, the keeper of his papers. To his right at the other long oak table sat H. P. Whidden and Donald McKiel. And beside them sat their much grander establishment of junior counsels, secretaries, factotums, dogsbodies—a force that seemed to Dorkin grotesquely excessive in terms of the objective it had been assembled to crush.

Dorkin had not succeeded in getting Williams a new battle dress uniform. The best he had managed was to get him a new shirt and tie and to have his work uniform cleaned and pressed. This was what he now wore as he sat, well-groomed, clean-shaven, but cowed and bewildered, like a delinquent schoolboy, between Carvell and a strange Mountie in dress scarlet who had been brought from Fredericton to be his keeper during the trial.

Facing Williams across the courtroom, in two rows of seats banked one above the other, sat the twelve men who were to pass judgement on him. As Dorkin had noted them down that morning during the selection process, they consisted of three farmers, two store clerks, the owner of a furniture store, a carpenter, a bookkeeper, a truck driver, a sawmill hand, a stable keeper, and a man of general business. They were all dressed in dark suits, their expressions solemn, as if in church. The two businessmen, the clerks, and the bookkeeper looked at ease in such clothes. The rest looked awkward and nervous, their voices hardly audible when they were polled.

Behind Whidden's entourage sat two rows of newsmen, more even than Dorkin had feared, for in the minds of many it was not just Williams who was on trial but Zombies in general—the cowards, the slackers, whom the public was paying to hang around and screw the girls whom the real men had left behind. And, for Williams, the news from overseas was not being very helpful. By now it was obvious that the Allied attack on Arnhem had been a catastrophe and that there was going to be no quick and elegant end to the Germans in the west. The Canadians were going to continue dying in the canals and ditches of the Lowlands, and as the lists of casualties continued to roll in, the conscription crisis was once more making its way to the front pages of the newspapers, as Meade had forecast.

It was this patriotic consideration, and not just the fascination of a sex-murder, that had brought out such crowds of people. They filled every seat on the floor and in the gallery above, those in front leaning forward with chin in hand, looking down over the balustrade at the arena. Even without turning around, Dorkin had a vivid sense of them, pressing down on him, heavy and malevolent. He had a vivid sense also of a little block of half a dozen men in a back corner of the room in rough, plaid mackinaws and cowhide jackets. One of them was Daniel Coile. He was there today by choice, but in two or three days he would be there because Dorkin had secured a subpoena requiring him to appear as a defence witness.

Before all these at his raised bench, in front of a portrait of the King in naval uniform, sat Judge Percy Dunsdale, who for some reason unfathomable to Dorkin had been chosen to try this case. Once a hack lawyer with a dismal trade in mortgages, foreclosures, and torts, a bagman and general errand-boy for the Conservative Party, he had been paid off by being appointed to the bench when the last Conservative government was in its feeble death throes.

Now in his sixties, he had had a decade of presiding over inconsequential trials for assault, break and entry, car theft, horse theft, boat theft, deer jacking, salmon poaching. He had never in his life presided over a murder trial.

The mills of the law grind always exceeding slow, and with Dunsdale in charge they ground more slowly still. Deeply impressed with the solemnity of what was taking place, he had that morning examined every scrap of paper that had come before him with a furious intensity of concentration like that of a drunk man trying to eat peas.

When the preliminaries finally were over, Whidden rose, bowed ceremoniously to Dunsdale, made his way with a measured pace to the middle of the court, paused, and then began.

"Your Honour, gentlemen of the jury, I will be brief. It is the intention of the Crown to prove that the accused, Owen Thomas Williams, did on the night of July 1, 1944, accompany Sarah Elizabeth Coile from a dance at The Silver Dollar and did brutally murder her and leave her body in the gravel pit where it was found some four days later. The evidence which we will bring to substantiate this charge is largely circumstantial, but we believe that it will establish the guilt of the accused beyond any reasonable doubt."

Whidden sat down, and it was McKiel, tall, suave, and clinical, who was given the task of handling the early witnesses. He began with Corporal Drost and Staff Sergeant Grant, both resplendent in dress scarlet. With the help of a large map, they told of the discovery of the body of Sarah Coile and the questioning and arrest of Private Williams. Following the transcript of the preliminary hearing, Dorkin saw that they were repeating almost verbatim their earlier evidence. Not for them the fatal shift of a detail.

Halfway through Drost's testimony, the brown envelopes with the terrible photographs of Sarah Coile's body were put into evidence. Watching closely, Dorkin saw that as the photographs passed from hand to hand through the jury, each juryman in turn looked up at Williams.

Dorkin had also virtually memorized the transcript of the preliminary hearing, and he had come with his own careful agenda. His first objective was to hammer away as best he could at the weaknesses of the prosecution's case. He still did not believe that he could win by fighting on that ground alone, but he could sow the beginning of doubt at least in the minds of the jurors, softening them up in preparation for the real attack in two or three days' time.

When McKiel had finished leading Drost through his testimony, Dorkin rose and moved out to the centre of the court, disguising as best he could the sudden nervousness that he felt as a lone figure under the scrutiny of so many eyes.

"Corporal Drost," Dorkin said, "when you first questioned Private Williams, did you caution him that what he said might be used as evidence against him in a criminal trial?"

He watched Drost's eyes flicker past him to the prosecutors, then back.

"No," Drost said curtly. "There was no reason to. At that time, I thought we were dealing with a simple case of a missing person."

"Nevertheless, no caution was given?"

"No."

"Let us suppose," Dorkin said, "that Private Williams is innocent of Sarah Coile's death but that after leaving the dance hall, they stopped somewhere in the woods together, if you understand what I mean. Now, since you had given him no reason to believe that anything serious was at issue, do you not think it possible that Private Williams didn't tell you about stopping with Sarah Coile simply because he was embarassed and told you only what he thought was relevant to your inquiry—which was that he had left Sarah Coile that night, alive and well, and had not seen her since?"

"I don't know," Drost said. "I would prefer not to speculate."

"Tell me, Corporal Drost, when you questioned Private Williams did he seem panic-stricken?"

"He seemed nervous."

"I feel sure he did, but you know, and I'm sure the members of the jury know, that whenever anyone, however innocent, is questioned by the police, they tend to be a little nervous. But Private Williams wasn't so nervous that you felt any suspicions about him at the time?"

"No," Drost said, after a moment's hesitation.

"Here is a person," Dorkin said, "whom you believe has brutally murdered a girl just four days before. Yet when you arrive without warning to ask him about that girl, he behaves exactly the way you would expect any innocent person to behave in the circumstances. Don't you think that remarkable?"

"Guilty people behave in different ways."

"Do you really think that if he had murdered that girl, he could have behaved as calmly as you describe?"

"I have no way to judge that."

"If you had sensed that Private Williams had been guilty of some criminal act in relation to Sarah Coile, you would have immediately instituted a more energetic search for her and investigated Private Williams's story more closely. But you did neither of these things because, as an experienced police officer, you sensed nothing suspicious in Private Williams's manner. Is that not so?"

"I suppose," Drost admitted grudgingly.

With Grant, Dorkin tackled the question of the propriety of Williams's interrogation.

"Tell me, Sergeant Grant," he said, "how many were present at the questioning of Private Williams?"

"There were five: myself, Corporal Drost, and Constables Hooper, Reynolds, and Kroll."

"And Private Williams was accompanied by whom?"

"By no one."

"He had no legal counsel, no source of advice?"

"No."

"Did you ask him if he wanted legal counsel?"

"I believe I did."

"Private Williams does not seem to remember being asked this," Dorkin said.

"Perhaps he did not understand."

"Perhaps he was not meant to understand."

"I resent that imputation."

"No doubt," Dorkin said. "Nevertheless, however it came about, Private Williams was subjected to a long interrogation late at night by five officers without benefit of any legal advice."

"He was warned that anything that he said might be used as evidence against him and that he had the right to remain silent."

"Do you recall at what point that warning was given?"

"Not exactly. It was quite a long interrogation."

"You make it clear in your testimony that Private Williams was confronted with his earlier statement to Corporal Drost."

"Yes."

"Even though that statement had been made without any warning that it might be used against him."

"At the time, there was no reason for a warning."

"But you were nevertheless now using it against him," Dorkin said.

"It was the investigation of a very serious criminal offence. If we took some liberties in order to get at the truth, we considered them justified."

"Did you suggest to Private Williams that if he now altered his original informal statement, he would be guilty of perjury?"

"I don't recall anyone saying that."

"I suggest to you that Private Williams was subjected to an extended grilling until late at night by a team of five RCMP officers without the benefit of any legal advice, that he was confused and unnerved, and that he was bullied into repeating a statement which he had made earlier when he had not been given any legal warnings and when he did not understand that anything criminal was at issue."

"That is a distortion of what took place," Grant said.

"As I understand it, you are suggesting that Private Williams deliberately lied in his initial statement in order to cover a criminal act?"

"Yes."

"But, Sergeant Grant," Dorkin said, "it wasn't a very clever lie since it could so easily be checked and disproven, as indeed it was. On the other hand, if Private Williams had told you that he and Sarah Coile had stopped somewhere along the way to the Hannigan Road, as we shall see that they did, the time which you so alertly discovered had not been accounted for would have been taken care of. If he had really murdered Sarah Coile, do you not think that is what he, or anyone with a grain of sense, would have done?"

"Not necessarily," Grant said. "Criminals often panic and say things to incriminate themselves."

"But we have just heard Corporal Drost testify quite emphatically that Private Williams was not panic-stricken when he made that statement and that there was nothing in his behaviour to suggest that he had done anything wrong. I suggest to you, Sergeant Grant, that the only reason Private Williams is in this courtroom now is that when first asked about Sarah Coile he was too embarrassed to admit that he had stopped in the woods with her after they left the dance."

Grant was followed by the manager of The Silver Dollar, who testified that the time of the intermission at the dance was approximately ten-thirty, by Mrs. Clark of The Maple Leaf canteen who testified that Williams arrived at the canteen at ten to twelve, and by Maclean, who told about the grass and dirt on Williams's uniform.

Maclean had never got in touch with Dorkin, and after his interview with Meade, Dorkin had made no attempt to get in touch with him. When he was seated, he glanced at Dorkin and almost imperceptibly shrugged his shoulders, as if to say, what can a man do? Dorkin felt sure that after their talk someone had given him a hard time.

The final witness of the afternoon was the pathologist, Dr. Pierre Bourget, impeccably dressed now that it was autumn in a darker suit than he had worn in July. Like Drost and Grant, he repeated his earlier testimony virtually without alteration.

"I would like the jury to be absolutely clear about one point," McKiel said. "It is your testimony that Sarah Coile had lost virtually no blood, that there were no signs that she had struggled, and that her assailant could therefore have emerged from the encounter without any incriminating signs either on his person or on his clothes. In other words, the fact that your laboratory found no incriminating evidence on Private Williams's clothing does not preclude the possibility of his having murdered Sarah Coile."

"That is correct," Bourget said.

"And the traces of semen on Private Williams's trousers. Would these not be consistent with an act of intercourse that took place while Private Williams was still clothed—as would almost certainly be the case if he had assaulted Sarah Coile?"

"That is also correct," Bourget said.

"Thank you," McKiel said.

"Do you think," Dorkin asked when Bourget had been turned over to him, "that the absence of incriminating evidence on Private Williams's clothing would be consistent with his having assaulted Sarah Coile in almost total darkness in the bottom of a gravel pit?"

"If he had knocked her unconscious at the very beginning, yes," Bourget said.

"You have given evidence that the body of Sarah Coile showed no signs of having been dragged," Dorkin said. "I wonder if you have any reflections on why Private Williams and Sarah Coile should have walked past numerous places where they could have had privacy and some degree of comfort in order to go to a gravel pit?"

"People sometimes have extraordinary tastes," Bourget said and drew a ripple of laughter.

"Would you consider it possible that the body of Sarah Coile might have been brought to the gravel pit by car, perhaps sometime that night, perhaps as much as two nights later?"

"That is certainly possible. Many things are possible. It might, for example, have been thrown over the back of a horse or lowered gently from a balloon."

This time the laughter was louder, more general. Dorkin waited it out.

"Quite so," he said. "But Private Williams doesn't own a horse or a balloon any more than he owns a motor car, and since Sarah Coile by your evidence weighed one hundred and fifty pounds to Private Williams's one hundred and forty, it seems unlikely that he carried her there bodily."

Behind him, Dorkin heard the scrape of a chair.

"Your Honour," McKiel said, "my learned friend is conducting a line of questioning with this witness which is quite out of order. Dr. Bourget is a pathologist, not a policeman."

"Quite right, Mr. McKiel," Dunsdale said.

"I apologize," Dorkin said. "But I am trying to make it clear that it is a great deal more likely that Sarah Coile, alive or dead, was driven to the gravel pit in a car rather than chased or even walked there. One final point. The traces of semen on Private Williams's trousers. In the preliminary hearing, I believe you made it clear that it was impossible to know how long they had been there. I believe you also suggested that there were ways they could have come there other than by an assault on Sarah Coile?"

"I don't recall."

"What you suggested, Dr. Bourget," Dorkin said, "is that young men without access to female companionship sometimes make their own satisfactions and that such furtive activities could easily account for the traces of semen on Private Williams's trousers. Would you not still agree that that could be so?"

"Yes. I suppose so."

"Thank you. In other words, there was absolutely nothing in your examination of Private Williams's clothes to connect him definitively to the murder of Sarah Coile?"

"I suppose not, but nothing in the world is definitive, Lieutenant Dorkin."

"No doubt," Dorkin said. "But if we are going to convict someone of murder, we would like to have something a little more definitive than anything arising from your testimony."

The afternoon was fading, the sun now shining almost level through the tall windows into the faces of the public in the gallery. Dunsdale consulted his watch, consulted Whidden, then declared the court adjourned until nine o'clock the following morning.

Except for the judge's chambers and the jury room, all the other rooms in the courthouse, including the small, bare office that Dorkin had been assigned, were at the front of the building and could only be reached by leaving through the same door as the public. Dorkin collected his papers slowly to give the crowd outside time to disperse before he and Smith made their way out, but the crowd was not in a dispersing mood, and he found the lobby and the corridors still filled with people.

As he made his way through them, Dorkin became aware of Daniel Coile and his cronies standing together by the front door, watching him silently. He met one pair of eyes, not those of Coile but of a younger man, hulking, stooped, wearing a coarse mackinaw jacket, fixing him with a look of cringing hatred, a look which if it were to seek its fulfilment would seek it silently, anonymously, from ambush, as he or someone like him had done with Louie Rosen.

Dorkin ate his supper alone in the mess at the armoury after the others had finished, picking without much appetite at some kind of fish covered with some kind of white sauce accompanied by the usual overcooked vegetables.

There was a strange quiet in the armoury. Captain Fraser had decreed that for the duration of the trial everyone except Sergeant MacCrae should be confined to barracks when they were not out on essential duties. The effect was to make the armoury seem a little like a prison.

As he ate, Dorkin read the newspaper. The front page was full of news of Arnhem. The British were reporting that General Horrocks's Second Army had reached the Meuse and was proceeding against Arnhem. The Germans were announcing that they were mopping up the remnants of the British paratroopers. Dorkin was inclined to believe the Germans, and it seemed obvious that, as with Dieppe, the British were preparing to present a calamity as a victory in disguise.

CHAPTER THIRTEEN

Next morning, the stage having been prepared for him, Whidden took over, rising and advancing grandly to the centre of the courtroom like a great actor. One might almost, Dorkin thought, have expected a round of applause.

His first move was to recall Corporal Drost. Unlike the other witnesses, the Mounties sat near the front of the court, and this afternoon, not only Drost but Hooper was there. While Drost was being sworn in, Hooper took the map of the Hannigan Road area from the stand where it was displayed and replaced it with a sheet of bristol board covered with rows of numbers.

Once again, as at the preliminary hearing, Drost described the meticulous interviews to establish the whereabouts of everyone who had been at or near the dance hall the night of the murder, but this time there was an additional twist. When all of this testimony had been collected, it was transferred to the chart that was now before the court. In this chart, everyone who was at the dance was identified by a number. After each number, there followed the identification numbers of the people who had accounted for that person's movements in the period after the intermission when Sarah Coile had left the dance hall.

Standing in front of the chart, with a pointer like a school teacher, Drost showed that if the list were examined it was clear that there was no small group of people accounting for each other. Dorkin saw that the Mounties had examined the depositions exactly as he had done, and like him they had found no other potential murderer lurking among those whom they knew to be at the dance hall that night. But unlike him, they were not disposed to move outside that circle of suspects, and Dorkin saw that what they and Whidden were engaged in was the fabrication of an artificial world, like that of an Agatha Christie novel, with a carefully circumscribed locale and a carefully defined roster of suspects, so that conclusions could be removed from the untidy realm of the merely possible and rendered undeniable.

"Of all the people known to be at the dance that night," Whidden said, "I take it that there was only one whose movements were not accounted for by anyone during the critical period, and that person was Private Williams, who was seen to have left the dance hall with Sarah Coile?"

"Yes, sir."

"I should explain also," Drost added, "that we asked everyone at the dance if they had seen anyone who was totally strange to them in the area and in particular if they had seen any such person with Sarah Coile. In all cases, the answer was that they had not."

"In summary," Whidden said, "this exhaustive investigation produced only one possible suspect, and that was Private Williams."

"That is correct."

"Corporal Drost," Dorkin said, "I'm sure that everyone joins the Crown in its admiration for the thoroughness with which you and your constables conducted this part of the investigation. However, there are a number of questions which trouble me. As you yourself have made clear, there were people outside the dance hall that night who never went in. You have identified some of these, but would you not agree that there could have been others out there in the darkness who remained unidentified?"

"Yes," Drost said, "in theory, I suppose, that is possible."

"Is it not also possible that some such person could have waylaid and murdered Sarah Coile after she and Private Williams separated?"

"In theory, perhaps."

"Is it not also possible that Sarah Coile met someone on her way home, someone perhaps with a car or a truck, that she was murdered wherever that person took her, and that her body was taken to the gravel pit, perhaps that night, perhaps even a night or two later?"

"In theory."

"Corporal Drost, the case you have created against Private Williams is also only theory. You don't have one scrap of concrete evidence connecting Private Williams with Sarah Coile's death."

Drost hesitated, considered, then let the comment pass.

"Corporal Drost," Dorkin went on, "an article of Sarah Coile's underclothing was not with the body and was never found in spite of a thorough search of the entire area. Nor was it found among Private Williams's possessions at the armoury. How do you explain that?"

"Private Williams could have disposed of it on his way home. It could have been thrown into the creek, for example, as he crossed the bridge."

"But why should Private Williams carry off this item of underclothing and then simply throw it away somewhere?"

"It's possible that he was not in a rational state of mind."

"Is it not more possible that it was taken off somewhere other than in the gravel pit in the company of someone other than Private Williams and that it was used to suffocate her and then disposed of?"

"Many things are possible."

"Corporal Drost, there is someone who had a very good reason for killing Sarah Coile. Could I ask you if you ever made any attempt to find the person responsible for getting Sarah Coile pregnant?"

"We questioned all of her close friends," Drost said. "None of them were aware of her condition. And none of them knew anything which would be of help in identifying the person in question."

"Does it not strike you as odd that this person has never come forward?"

"There could be many reasons for that."

"So your conclusion is that it was mere coincidence that Sarah Coile should be pregnant and that she should be viciously assaulted and murdered?"

"We felt that her pregnancy had nothing to do with her death," Drost said.

"The jury might be interested to know," Dorkin said, "that at the preliminary hearing the Crown floated the suggestion that the reason Private Williams murdered Sarah Coile was that she was pregnant by him. It was only when they came to find out that Private Williams could not possibly have been the father of Sarah's child that they decided that Sarah's death and her pregnancy were unrelated. I suggest that the Crown was right the first time. Sarah Coile's pregnancy and her death were related, and the author of both is still at large somewhere. For all we know, perhaps among the public in this very courtroom."

This produced a stir and a tap of Dunsdale's gavel, and Dorkin went back to his place well pleased with himself.

Whidden's next witness was the Reverend Zacharias Clemens. While Drost removed his chart of names, Clemens extricated himself from the middle of a row of seats at the back and plodded heavily to the witness stand. Dorkin saw that he had undergone something of a transfiguration since the preliminary hearing. He had a new, dark-grey suit and a dark-green tie. He had even had a haircut. The overall effect was to make him look more like a benign United Church minister than a shaggy evangelist prophet.

"Now, Reverend Clemens," Whidden said, "perhaps we can turn to the night of July 1, and you can tell the court in your own words what you saw that is of relevance to these proceedings. I have had the map of the area placed before the court again, and you can perhaps refer to that to make your account clearer."

The Reverend Clemens cleared his throat and turned slightly in his chair so that he was addressing the jury. Once again he went painstakingly through his account of working at his church, of visiting the Salchers, of departing to return to his church somewhere around eleven o'clock, and of seeing at the corner of the Hannigan Road and Broad Street the couple whom he identified as Sarah Coile and a soldier whose appearance was consistent with that of Private Williams.

All through this, Dorkin watched Clemens closely—watched the eyebrows, the muscles at the side of the face, the hands resting on his knees—looking for telltale signs of a lie that he had still not become entirely comfortable with. But there was nothing. The impression created was that of an honest citizen who had become a part of these painful proceedings out of a sense of duty. Dorkin could see that the jury found him totally convincing.

Dorkin looked at Williams. He was staring at Clemens in a sightless sort of way, his face a blank, and Dorkin wondered how much of all this he was really taking in.

In the middle of the courtroom, his arms negligently sweeping the air, Whidden was engaged in a peroration on Clemens's conscientious accuracy as a witness. When he had finished, Dorkin rose. If Clemens was apprehensive about being cross-examined, he didn't show it, and Dorkin knew that he was going to have to deal with him very cautiously if he was not going to antagonize the jury.

"Reverend Clemens," he said, "I too must compliment you on the scrupulous care you have taken in giving your testimony, and I am not for a moment questioning your conscientiousness in describing what you believe you saw that night, but I am wondering if perhaps you may have been mistaken about what you saw. You said that when you came around the corner, the couple you saw were talking to each other, and when they saw you, they turned their faces away towards the graveyard."

"Yes, that is so."

"So you had only a brief glance at their faces. Are you sure that that glance was enough to allow you to be sure that the girl was Sarah Coile?"

"It wasn't just that. She was someone whom I had seen many times."

"You're absolutely certain that the girl whom you saw was Sarah Coile? Are you sure you didn't leap to the conclusion that it was Sarah Coile on the basis of a few superficial similarities and then later fill in the rest of the detail from your own imagination? That happens, you know, and there are numerous cases where witnesses have done that in court. These were not people who were attempting to deceive. They genuinely believed what they said, but other evidence proved incontrovertibly that they could not possibly have seen what they testified to. Are you sure that you have not deceived yourself in this way about Sarah Coile?"

"I believe that the girl whom I saw that night was Sarah Coile. I wish that it had not been."

"Beyond doubt?"

"Yes. Beyond doubt."

"Reverend Clemens," Dorkin said, "if you look at the map which has been prepared of the area, you will notice that the way the intersection of Broad Street and Hannigan Road has been drawn is not quite accurate."

Clemens looked at the map.

"I don't understand," he said.

"The map shows the intersection as a right-angled turn, but in fact that is not a right-angled turn. Broad Street joins Hannigan Road at a slight angle, so that if you are coming down the Hannigan Road and making a left turn onto Broad Street, you are making a slight hairpin turn. Is that not correct?"

"I believe it is," Clemens said. "I hadn't thought about it before."

"This means," Dorkin said, "that since you are coming down a hill, that is a slightly difficult turn which does not leave you a lot of time to look around, especially in the dark. It also means that when you are around the turn, anyone standing on the corner will already be slightly behind you, over your left shoulder. I know because I went out there and drove that corner several times in the dark, and I could not see very much of the tree under which the two people you saw were standing."

"The girl was wearing a white dress, which stood out," Clemens said. "I suppose that was what caught my eye. I am also a very slow, cautious driver. I expect I don't take corners as quickly as you might do."

"Please understand," Dorkin said, "that I am not for a moment questioning your attempt to describe accurately what you believe you saw, but I must point out that even allowing for your driving slowly, in that very brief period of time, only two or three seconds, the two people had time to see you and turn their faces away, and you had time not only to recognize Sarah Coile but to note the details of what she was wearing and to see the height and build of the man, the fact that he had dark hair and was not wearing a cap, and the fact that he was dressed in army uniform even though that also would be dark."

"I can't say how long it took," Clemens said. "It may have been longer than you say, but anyway that was what I saw."

"I believe it was on the Friday, two days after the body was found, that you went to the police," Dorkin said.

"That is so."

"By that time, there had been a good deal of talk about what had happened. You would have heard this too."

"Yes, that is why I recognized that it was my duty to tell the police what I had seen."

"I take it that by then you would have heard all about the body and how it was clothed. And you would have heard all about Private Williams."

"I'm not sure now of everything I heard."

"Did you hear descriptions of Private Williams?"

"I don't recall."

"If you did, you might later have projected those characteristics back onto the man whom you saw at the corner."

"I have described the man as I saw him," Clemens said, for the first time with a trace of annoyance.

"Was there anything about the appearance of Sarah Coile that night as you described her to the police that you could not have heard from common gossip?" Dorkin asked.

Clemens coloured faintly.

"I don't know," he said. "I described what I saw."

"You haven't said anything about the possible age of the man whom you saw. Did you form any impression about that?"

"I don't know. As I said, I never really got a look at his face."

"So he might, for all you know, be a man in his forties or fifties?"

"Except for the uniform."

"Except," Dorkin said, "that you thought he was in uniform. I must say that I'm very uneasy about that. What was it made you think it was a uniform? What sort of jacket was he wearing? One like the one Private Williams has on now?"

"No. Like the kind you see on the street. One that fastens at the waist."

"But could that not simply have been an ordinary waist-length jacket such as anyone might wear?"

"Well, I don't know. Perhaps."

"Are you sure that after learning that Private Williams had been arrested, you did not fill in in your own mind what you felt you ought to have seen—but which, in fact, you did not really see at all?"

"My impression was that it was a uniform."

"But you might have been mistaken?"

"I suppose."

"To come back to the question of the age of the man. Apart from the question of the uniform, you saw nothing that would be inconsistent with its being a much older man than Private Williams?"

"No, I suppose he might have been older."

"Older and not in uniform. In fact, quite possibly not a soldier at all."

Clemens lifted his shoulders slightly in a gesture of impatience and looked down at his hands.

"I should make it clear to the jury," Dorkin said, "that I am not suggesting that Reverend Clemens has engaged in any deliberate untruth. But I think that the members of the jury should ask themselves whether he has imagined that he saw a good deal more than he possibly could have seen in the brief time he had while turning the corner onto Broad Street. One final question. In your testimony, Reverend Clemens, you estimated that you could have gone past the intersection as early as ten to eleven."

"I think it would have been closer to eleven."

"Nevertheless you did accept that estimate on the part of the prosecutor. You didn't happen to check a clock at the Salchers' house as you left?"

"They do have a clock, but it doesn't keep time."

If he recognized the question for the trap it was, he gave no sign of it.

"I see. So you are only guessing at the time you left their house and went past the intersection a few minutes later. It is very easy to misjudge time, as everyone knows, and is it not possible that you could have gone past the intersection where you saw the couple as early as twenty to eleven—by which time, even in terms of the evidence given so far, Private Williams and Sarah Coile could not possibly have arrived there yet? Could that not be so?"

"I don't think it was that early. I think it was closer to eleven o'clock."

"But you are only guessing."

"Yes, I suppose."

"Thank you," Dorkin said. "I have no further questions."

As Dorkin was going back to his place, Whidden rose.

"A supplementary question," he said. "I take it, Reverend Clemens, that in spite of what has just been said, you still have no doubt that the girl you saw was Sarah Coile and that the man was at least not inconsistent in appearance with Private Williams?"

"Yes," Clemens said. "That is what I was trying to make clear."

"And you have no doubt that you went past the intersection at around eleven o'clock."

"I'm sure it was about that time."

"So am I," Whidden said, then turned to the jury, leaning forward, his hands clasped behind him beneath his gown.

"I should make clear, however," he went on, "that I am not for a moment disputing the possibility so ingeniously raised by my learned colleague, that within half an hour of leaving the dance hall Sarah Coile got rid of Private Williams (who then disappeared into thin air for nearly an hour) and found herself in the company of a different man altogether who just happened to be of exactly the same build as Private Williams and to be dressed in something that at least looked like an army uniform. We are certainly not disputing that such wild improbabilities as these do from time to time occur in the course of a century."

It took a second or two for it to sink in, then the smiles spread through the jury, and there was a scattering of laughter among the public.

Clemens was the last witness of the morning. Dorkin collected his papers and with Smith ploughing a path for him made his way through the crowd.

The afternoon session began with Vinny Page. Like Clemens, she had also been repackaged for the trial. At the preliminary hearing, she had come across as a vivacious flirt. Now, the sexy little flick of the ass that she had shown when she had walked to her place on the stand two months before had been suppressed, and she was costumed in a discreet two-piece suit and a modest little hat. The note struck was that of a demure maiden who might have dropped in on her way to church.

Whidden, as elaborately gallant as a stage-colonel out of a Hollywood movie about the Old South, treated her as someone who even after three months was still in deep mourning for the loss of her childhood friend. Gently, he guided her through the events of the fatal night. Once again, she described her arrival with Sarah and Brick at the dance, discussed Sarah's drinking habits, which had become even more moderate since the preliminary hearing, went through the events at the dance leading up to the departure of Sarah and Williams at intermission. Once again, she testified that Sarah had not known Williams well.

"Would you say," Whidden asked, "that while she might agree to go outside with Private Williams for a breath of air, she would not likely consent to anything more than that and might even resist if Private Williams were to make advances?"

"Yes," Vinny said.

"You said that Private Williams had danced with Miss Coile once or twice. Do you think he may have conceived an attraction for her?"

"Yes, I think that he might have. He seemed very keen to dance with her that night."

"Tell me. What did girls like you and Miss Coile think of Private Williams?"

"We thought he was very shy. And sort of funny. Sort of strange."

"Someone who was probably not very attractive to girls?"

"Yes."

"Someone who might easily misunderstand and think a girl was more inclined to be friendly with him than she really was?"

"Yes."

"And who might be inclined to be angry—perhaps even violent—when he discovered his mistake?"

"Yes."

Enough was enough. Dorkin rose.

"I must object to this. The prosecution is putting words into the mouth of the witness and leading her into areas of speculation about which she can have no possible knowledge."

"Objection sustained," Dunsdale said. "Mr. Whidden, you must stick to the facts."

Whidden shot a look at the jury, slyly and endearingly suggesting a mischievous boy caught with his hand in the cookie jar. Dorkin saw two of the jurors smile.

"Tell me, Miss Page," Whidden said. "Was Private Williams someone whom you would have been uneasy to be alone with?"

"Yes," she said.

"Would you say that you would be wary about being alone with Private Williams?"

"Yes."

"You might even be afraid of him?"

"Yes."

"Miss Page," Dorkin said, when Whidden had resumed his seat, "you testified at the preliminary hearing that Sarah Coile never told you that she was going to have a child. Am I correct?"

"Yes," she said, hesitantly.

She had obviously been thoroughly coached but not evidently for this line of questioning.

"I understand that you were her closest friend," Dorkin said. "Do you have any idea why she did not confide in you about this?"

"No, I don't."

"And you have no idea who the father of her child might have been?"

"No."

"You know of no one whom she was going steady with?"

"No."

"It seems very strange to me," Dorkin said, "that she should not have said anything to you about being in trouble. Do you imagine that this was perhaps because the father was someone whom she was too afraid—or too ashamed—to acknowledge?"

"Your Honour," Whidden said. "I cannot understand the purpose of these questions. Private Williams is not being tried for being the father of Sarah Coile's child, but for murdering her."

"I hope that the purpose of these questions will appear in due course," Dorkin said. "I am trying to make it clear to the jurors that while Private Williams had no obvious motive for murdering Sarah Coile, there is someone who did have a very strong motive for doing so."

"Very well," Dunsdale said. "You have made your point. Have you further questions?"

"Just one, your Honour. I have heard, Miss Page, that Sarah Coile was talking about leaving Wakefield."

"Yes."

"I understand that she also talked about getting money from someone to help her get settled somewhere else. Is that correct?"

"Yes, I believe so."

"She never told you who she was going to get the money from?"

"No."

"Why do you think she was so secretive with you?"

"I don't know."

"She never suggested that she was going to get money from Private Williams?"

"No."

"Given the unknown father of her child and this talk of getting money and going away, it would seem that there were some very mysterious things going on in the life of Sarah Coile in the couple of months before she was murdered," Dorkin said.

"Yes," Vinny said, "I guess so."

"My next witness, your Honour," Whidden said, when Vinny Page had stepped down, "is Mr. Hubert Whittaker."

This took Dorkin completely by surprise. What followed Vinny Page's name on the list of witnesses was not that of Hubert Whittaker, but half a dozen names that Dorkin recognized as those of residents of the Broad Street and Hannigan Road area.

He rose.

"Excuse me, your Honour," he interrupted, "but my list of witnesses does not include Mr. Whittaker."

"Your Honour," Whidden said, "we changed our plans somewhat. I believe my learned colleague was given a list of the changes this morning."

"I was given a list," Dorkin said, "but it is the same list that I was given yesterday."

"Ah," Whidden extravagantly apologized, "a thousand pardons. There has been some mistake. Mr. Cosgrove, will you give my colleague the new list?"

He motioned and one of his minions rose and brought Dorkin a sheet of paper, on which the names of Mr. Hubert Whittaker and a Dr. Martin Sachs followed that of Vinny Page.

"These little slip-ups are bound to happen now and then," Whidden said, smiling his wicked-schoolboy smile at the jury, and Dorkin recognized that all of this had been carefully choreographed beforehand.

"We may proceed then, Lieutenant Dorkin?" Dunsdale asked.

"Yes," Dorkin said. "I trust I may have a list of tomorrow's witnesses."

"I'm sure you will," Whidden assured him.

While all this was going on, Hubert Whittaker was edging his way uncertainly down the aisle. Dorkin had not seen him since the day of the preliminary hearing when he had absolved himself from any responsibility for the plight of his nephew.

Whidden waved him on, and he took his place on the stand, carefully not looking at Williams or Dorkin.

"Mr. Whittaker," Whidden said, "would you be so good as to explain your relationship to the accused?"

"I am his uncle by marriage. His father was my wife's brother."

"Thank you," Whidden said. "Before we proceed, I think that I should explain to the court that it was only with the greatest reluctance that I summoned Mr. Whittaker as a witness in these proceedings, and only with the greatest reluctance that he agreed to appear. But he has information which I hope to show is relevant and which no one else could easily provide.

"Now, Mr. Whittaker, I would like you to help me develop for the court an outline of Private Williams's background. Tell me first of all about Private Williams's relationship with his mother."

"Well," Whittaker said, "his father died when he was quite young, and he was brought up by his mother. He had two brothers, but they died when they were only two or three years old, so he and his mother were the only ones."

"Would you say that his mother had a strong influence on young Williams?" Whidden asked.

"Yes. He pretty much did what she said."

"A mummy's boy, as people sometimes say?"

"Yes, you could say that."

"And Mrs. Williams? What sort of woman was she?"

"Very religious. Very strict. Like many people from the old country. From Wales, I mean."

"And she communicated these feelings to her son?"

"Well, she made him abide by them anyways. I couldn't say what he thought of them."

Through all this, Dorkin watched Whittaker, who never once so much as glanced at Williams. Once his eyes met Dorkin's, and he looked quickly away. As for Williams, the anger he had expressed about Whittaker a few weeks before seemed to have been crowded out, and he stared at him now with something between stupefaction and bewilderment.

"Tell me," Whidden was saying, "did young Williams have many friends among the other boys?"

"No, not as I ever saw. He didn't play games or fish or hunt or anything like that. Kept home to himself a lot."

"I see. And girls? Was he popular with girls? Did he have girl-friends when he got to be high-school age?"

"I don't believe so. I think his mother disapproved."

"And after high school?"

"No, not then either, so far as I ever heard. But I couldn't be sure of that because he was away working in Fredericton then."

"Was Williams much affected by the death of his mother?"

"Yes, I would say so."

"So much that her views about life—about girls and that—could continue to affect him even after she had died?"

"Yes, I wouldn't be surprised."

Dorkin was on his feet.

"I must object to this. How can this man pronounce on such a question? Once again you are inviting this witness to speculate about matters which are beyond his—or anyone else's—capacity to know."

"Objection sustained," Dunsdale repeated. "You must stick to the facts, you know, Mr. Whidden."

"Did you notice any change in Williams's manner or mode of life after his mother died?" Whidden asked.

"No," Whittaker said.

"Thank you. You have been most helpful."

"I have not had the advantage of having coached this witness like my learned friend," Dorkin said, borrowing Whidden's term a little sarcastically, "but perhaps I might use him to fill in some other aspects of Private Williams's background. You mentioned that Private Williams's father died when Williams was very young. Perhaps you might tell us what he died of."

"He died from lung trouble."

"As a result of being gassed in the Great War?"

"So they said."

"I believe that two of the senior Williams brothers were also killed in the war, were they not? And a brother of Mrs. Williams also?"

"Yes."

"All, I believe within a few months of each other, so that it is not perhaps surprising that Mrs. Williams may have discouraged her only remaining child from volunteering for another war."

"Maybe not."

"Tell me, Mr. Whittaker, what happened to Mrs. Williams's farm when she died?"

"It came to me."

"What do you mean, it came to you?"

"I helped her out, and when she died the farm came to me to pay off the debt."

"How much was that debt?"

"I don't remember."

"You are under oath."

"Three hundred dollars."

"You already had a large farm of your own?"

"Yes."

"It didn't occur to you that since this woman was your sister-in-law you might have let her son have the farm rather than seize it for debts which were a fraction of its worth?"

"I object," Whidden said. "These are matters which have nothing to do with this trial."

"I must agree," Dunsdale said.

"I am establishing," Dorkin said, "that this witness is hostile to my client as people often are towards those whom they have wronged and that his testimony, which has obviously been orchestrated by the prosecution, is not to be trusted. Reluctance or no reluctance, I ask the jury to reflect on the character of a man who would agree to come into a court of law in order to slander a nephew who is on trial for his life in the way that Mr. Whittaker has done here today."

"You are out of order, Lieutenant Dorkin," Dunsdale said. "Do you have any further questions for this witness that are of relevance to these proceedings?"

"No," Dorkin said, turning away with contempt. "No, your Honour, I do not."

"Very well," Dunsdale said. "You may step down, Mr. Whittaker, and we will have your next witness, Mr. Whidden."

Like the Mounties, Dr. Martin Sachs had not been sitting at the back with the commoner class of witness but had a place just behind Whidden. He was a small, middle-aged man in a dark pinstripe suit. His head was bald almost to the crown and the few strands of black hair that were left were combed straight across the top. He had a small moustache and wore round, steel-rimmed glasses, a combination that gave him a superficial resemblance to Heinrich Himmler.

As he took his place in the witness box, he studied Dorkin briefly, then looked calmly away, as if to say that none of this was about any of that. Whidden led him through the credentials that established his status as an expert witness: degree in Psychiatry from the University of London, two years of study in Vienna, several years work as a consultant in London, now for some twelve years a psychiatrist in practice in Montreal and a consultant with a special interest in criminal psychiatry, in which capacity he had appeared as an expert witness in trials in various parts of eastern Canada.

He answered Whidden's questions in a precise, measured voice with a trace of a British accent but also with something slightly guttural as if his native language had been something other than English—German perhaps. Or Austrian? As he spoke, his eyes moved about the courtroom, fixing one point after another, then, as if having categorized them to his satisfaction, moving on: Williams, Dorkin again, the crowds behind and above Dorkin, the jury, Whidden's entourage, and back to Whidden himself.

"Now, Dr. Sachs," Whidden said, "I would like to pose a number of purely theoretical questions before we turn to pertinent areas of the present case. First of all, I would like to ask you if it is possible for someone to commit a murder—even a very violent murder—and then to all appearances behave normally."

"Yes, that is certainly possible. Not common, but possible. There are numerous authenticated cases of this phenomenon."

"Perhaps you could explain what sort of person would be capable of this."

"Certainly," Sachs said, settling himself in. "It requires a personality which is capable of profound acts of repression. He divides his mind into two compartments, and he relegates to one part anything which is inconsistent with the image he has of himself in the other part. It will be easier to understand this if I point out that we all do this in some measure. We all create a certain image of ourselves and try to realize that image in our lives, or at least in our fantasies, but we all do things which are inconsistent with that image and which therefore we do not approve of. We then employ various mechanisms to reconcile ourselves to these actions. The simplest mechanism is just to forget what we have done. Another mechanism is to dissociate ourselves from the action. One often hears people say, 'I don't know what made me do that.' Or more significantly, 'I was not myself when I did that.' In the case of someone continuing to behave normally after committing a murder, you have an extreme case of that. The murderer has convinced himself that it was not really he who committed the murder, and so afterwards he behaves as if indeed he had not. Needless to say, such a person is extremely dangerous since he has no moral controls placed upon his actions."

Sachs delivered all this in a formal, academic tone, looking slowly back and forth over the crowd as if giving a lecture to a class of low-level undergraduates. Dorkin wondered if he were, in fact, repeating one of his own lectures.

"Would such a person remember what he had done?" Whidden asked.

"Generally, yes. But he has dissociated himself from it. He knows that it happened, but does not regard himself as having done it."

"And at the time of the murder, would such a person be aware of the criminal nature of what he was doing?"

"Again, I would say generally, yes. In some cases, it would be precisely because he regarded the act as criminal that he was doing it. It would represent an escape from the restrictions which he normally places upon himself. I should perhaps have explained that one of the mechanisms behind such a person's ability to dissociate himself from actions he disapproves of is that he has been brought up in an intensely repressive environment. He will have been brought up to believe that so many things are wrong that the only way he can live with himself and his own frailties is to develop an extreme capacity for dissociating himself from his own actions."

"A number of witnesses in the present case," Whidden said, "have commented on the fact that in the days immediately after the dance, Private Williams behaved perfectly normally. I take it that this does not preclude the possibility of his being the murderer."

"No, it does not. But I could not say with any definiteness whether Private Williams would have been capable of behaving in such a way without conducting a detailed examination."

"I understand. Now another question. You have familiarized yourself with the facts of this case. On the basis of these facts, what would you conclude about the personality of the murderer?"

"Most obviously, the degree of violence done to the body was far in excess of what was needed merely to kill the victim. It seems evident that the murderer was not merely concerned with preventing her from identifying him as having raped her. He was clearly activated also by a violent, irrational hatred. Such violence is not uncommon in cases of rape."

"Could you explain the reasons for this?"

"There can be many. But the most common is that the rapist has a fundamental hatred of women. After the sexual act is completed, he experiences a violent sense of revulsion, but instead of directing this against himself, he displaces it and directs it against his victim."

"Perhaps you could explain the kind of background that is likely to produce such attitudes."

As Dorkin studied him, Sachs sat up a little straighter in his chair and launched into another lecture.

"It arises most commonly from a situation in which the individual has a strong attachment to the mother. This precludes his having normal relationships with girls his own age, but the sexual drive is often still there and may be all the stronger for being repressed. In the event that he does have sexual relations, whatever the circumstances, he feels that he has been unfaithful to the mother and experiences a consequent sense of guilt. This he displaces by regarding the girl as dirty and as having led him into an act he is now repelled by. In the extreme case of the rapist, this often leads to murder, as I have already explained. I should say also, perhaps, that the individual who has this kind of strong attachment to the mother also in the unconscious part of his mind hates his mother because of her emotional domination of him, and the hatred and violence he may direct against other women is fuelled in part by this subconscious hatred of his mother."

"You have heard," Whidden said, "that Private Williams was in effect an only child with a strong attachment to a possessive mother, who was also very strict about moral matters. Would you say that this is the kind of background which might produce the kind of psychological abnormalities which you have been describing?"

"Yes, such a background does often result in this kind of psychological maladjustment, but it does not, of course, necessarily lead to the commission of violent criminal acts."

"I understand," Whidden said. "I am merely trying to establish that the apparent normality of Private Williams's behaviour after the dance is not necessarily inconsistent with his being the murderer and that his background is not inconsistent with his being the kind of person who might commit such a murder. Are those fair statements?"

"Yes."

"Thank you," Whidden said. "You have been most informative."

Dorkin had listened to all this with gathering anger. Just as Whidden had waved his magic wand and replaced the untidy chaos of the night of Sarah's murder with the neatly defined world of Drost's charts, so now he was replacing the actual Williams with this fictional monster dredged up from Sachs's psychoanalytic ideologies. Dorkin could not imagine that Whidden himself believed this windy bullshit. As for the jury, he could not be sure. In other circumstances, with their ploddingly literal view of the world, they almost certainly would not, but in these circumstances most of them would be prepared to believe almost anything that would help justify retroactively the condemnation of Williams that Dorkin felt sure they had decided on before they had ever entered the courtroom. All of this, Dorkin felt sure, Whidden would understand only too well.

"Dr. Sachs," Dorkin said, keeping his voice as level as he could, "this is a trial in which a human life is at stake, and you have consented to come here and with no examination whatever of the accused—without ever having so much as laid eyes on him until you saw him here this afternoon—you have used your professional stature to conduct a campaign of vicious innuendo designed to establish in the minds of the jury an image of him as a pathological monster."

"I have done no such thing," Sachs said, his voice quite unruffled as that of someone long accustomed to attacks by the ignorant. "I have merely given answers to a series of hypothetical questions about the minds of certain kinds of murderer. I have said nothing whatever about Private Williams himself, as I was careful to point out."

"If you are giving testimony that is not supposed to relate to Private Williams," Dorkin asked, "might I ask you what it is you think you are doing in this courtroom?"

"I have already explained," Sachs said, unperturbed.

"Your Honour," Dorkin said to Dunsdale, "I am astonished at the dishonesty of what is taking place here. I ask you to instruct the jury to disregard all of this testimony as having no basis whatever in fact."

"Well now, Lieutenant Dorkin," Dunsdale said, "I do think that Dr. Sachs has made clear that what he has said doesn't necessarily relate to Private Williams, and I am sure the jury will keep that in mind. Do you have any further questions, Lieutenant Dorkin?"

"I have not," Dorkin said.

As he sat down, he saw that Whidden had leaned over to talk to McKiel. Watching them, Dorkin sensed the falsity in their manner, as if in a badly rehearsed play, and realized that something more was up.

"Your Honour," Whidden said, turning back to the bench, "we have decided not to wear out the patience of the court and of our good jurors with a parade of supplementary witnesses. This therefore concludes the case for the prosecution. Tomorrow, we will turn matters over to the learned counsel for the defence."

It was obvious to Dorkin that, like the calling of Whittaker and Sachs, this had been the strategy all along and that the names that had followed theirs on the list of witnesses had been merely a blind. It was the latest move in a campaign in which he had been outmanoeuvred at almost every turn. And so, abruptly, a day or more before he had expected it to happen, he was going to have to fight his fight. Always, always, one of his instructors at officers' training had said, keep your enemy off balance. Surprise. Surprise. That, gentlemen, is the secret of victory.

CHAPTER FOURTEEN

Following his meeting with Meade the week before, Dorkin had done what he knew he should have done a long time before. Affirming the certainty of Williams's innocence, cajoling, beseeching, sometimes bullying, he had combed Carnarvon and Fredericton and had managed to assemble a little contingent of witnesses willing to testify on Williams's behalf.

Carnarvon had been settled by Welsh fleeing the depression that had overwhelmed their valleys at the end of the Napoleonic Wars. Dorkin had imagined it as a neat little village, rather like the ones on the lids of cookie tins, but there was no village, only a ruined schoolhouse, a decaying chapel, and a succession of farmhouses strung out along two miles of road, most of them set among fields whose edges were being eaten away by the forest. Though he did not know then that Uncle Hubert had yielded up his services to the prosecution, Dorkin had avoided him and found instead a cousin of Williams's mother. A pig-farmer, sixty years old, balding, greying, half-toothless, guileless, awkward, he was to tell again the story of the massacre of Williams's family in the Great War, and Dorkin hoped that his rustic simplicity would strike some responsive chord in a rustic jury.

From Carnarvon Dorkin had also managed to pluck forth a Presbyterian minister, a short, black-haired, round-faced man, who in the twenties had fled another depression in the Welsh valleys and fired by some youthful Celtic idealism answered the call of

Carnarvon's little flock. He knew Owen for a good boy always, not drinking or fighting, a model son to his mother.

In Fredericton, Dorkin had found a history teacher with socialist leanings (which Dorkin had prevailed upon him to disguise) who had taught Williams and was willing to attest to his character and conscientiousness, if not his intellect. He had also found a fellow worker from the lumber company where Williams had worked who was willing to testify that Williams had never exhibited any evidence of murderous intentions towards anyone. ("Williams wouldn't have lasted two minutes with my grandmother, or anybody else's grandmother.") But Williams's boss had refused to testify, and when Dorkin had tried to pressure him had turned patriotic and ugly.

When Dorkin had set about arranging for testimony from some of the soldiers in Wakefield, Captain Fraser had also turned patriotic and ugly, and it was only through veiled threats of court orders that Dorkin had persuaded him to grant the necessary leave from duties. Later, Dorkin knew, Fraser would make them pay, but there was nothing he could do about that. Only Sergeant MacCrae, the untouchable hero of Dieppe, would perhaps escape, and perhaps once again get a few others out with him.

Now all of them, civilians and soldiers, sat in a row at the back of the court waiting their turn, a motley crew, badly coached, insecure in their honesty.

The preliminaries over, Dorkin rose and began working his way through his roster, beginning with the witnesses from Carnarvon and Fredericton. His purpose was to dislodge the image Whidden and Sachs had created of Williams as a subhuman monster and to replace it with the image of an ordinary human being, shy and awkward, but fundamentally normal.

On his side, Whidden picked away, dressing up the image of Williams as the maladjusted outsider waiting only for the circumstances that would transform him into a homicidal maniac. But with the exception of the history teacher, whose social persuasions Whidden shrewdly intuited, these were witnesses with whom he had to go easy if he were not to alienate the worshipful members of his jury, and some of his darker hints about Williams's suppressed perversions went over the heads of both the witnesses and the jury.

With the outcast Zombies from the armoury he was on happier ground, and he once again played to a fully appreciative house as he swept back and forth across the front of the court, by turns whimsical, sarcastic, scornful, never for a moment letting his audience forget that these were the cowards who lounged in Wakefield while their sons and brothers were fighting and dying in Europe. What he sought to elicit from them without bewildering subtleties was evidence to establish Williams as a sullen and dangerous misfit.

Dorkin's concern was to emphasize once again that following his return from the dance Williams behaved normally and that no one saw any physical evidence of any kind that he had murdered Sarah Coile. He wound up the morning with Sergeant MacCrae. In his battledress uniform complete with his campaign ribbons and the ribbon of his Military Medal, he was a formidable presence—someone not even Whidden could cross with impunity. He had no evidence to add to what the other soldiers had said, but his saying it removed the taint that their being Zombies had given it.

"So," Dorkin said in conclusion, "as sergeant in charge of that platoon, you would be familiar with the behaviour of Private Williams, and you saw no change whatever in this in the days following the dance?"

"No, sir," MacCrae said. "None."

"Do you believe that Private Williams murdered Sarah Coile?"

"No, I do not."

"Thank you," Dorkin said.

"Sergeant MacCrae," Whidden said, "as part of your training, did you have any training in psychology?"

"No, sir," MacCrae said.

"So your assessment of Private Williams's behaviour is not rooted in any kind of professional training?"

"No, sir."

"Yesterday, Dr. Sachs, a professional psychiatrist, testified here that there was not necessarily anything inconsistent in Private

Williams behaving normally and his having murdered Sarah Coile. I take it that you would agree that Dr. Sachs would be more knowledgeable about such matters than you would be?"

"I suppose he would be."

"Thank you," Whidden said.

And then Dorkin had a stroke of luck. Not content to take what he had and run, Whidden pushed for more and made one of his rare false moves.

"Sergeant MacCrae," he said, "I think that almost everyone here must be aware of your heroic military record. I am wondering what you think of men who refuse to fight and leave men like yourself to bleed and die in defence of our country while they loaf and go to dances?"

Before answering, MacCrae looked down at Whidden with a dislike that he was at no pains to diguise.

"I don't think that anyone should be forced to go overseas who does not want to, sir," he replied. "And I don't think that people who are not going themselves have the right to make judgements. Some of the men who do not go have very good reasons for what they are doing."

"Such as Private Williams?"

"Private Williams's father died because of the Great War, sir, and three of his uncles were killed. That seems to me enough for one family."

Somewhere at the back of the gallery someone—an old veteran perhaps of the Somme or Passchendaele—applauded briefly.

"You are a very tolerant man, Sergeant MacCrae," Whidden said, recovering what he could. "More tolerant, I dare say, than I would be in your place."

"Before I leave, sir," MacCrae said, "I'd like to point out that Dr. Sachs did not know Private Williams and I did, and I still do not believe that he murdered Sarah Coile."

"Thank you," Whidden said. "I have no more questions. I am sure that the jury, like myself, cannot help but admire your loyalty to your men."

MacCrae was Dorkin's last witness of the morning. He felt that he had not done badly. But it was the afternoon that would tell. First there would be Coile. And then if he could not break Coile, enough at least to lodge an irremovable doubt in the minds of his jurors, there would have to be Williams. The day before the trial began he had spent the whole day with him, going over everything that had happened, fishing, probing, trying to find out anything that still remained to be found, trying to be sure that in court there would be no unpleasant surprises.

When he was away from Williams, Dorkin's feelings towards him were ones of compassion, but when he was with him, what he often felt was irritation, and he sometimes experienced a curious shock of displacement, as if the person he had committed himself to defend had been supplanted by some shabby imposter. And he would ask himself whether, if he could go back to July, he would do this again. He wasn't sure. And sometimes he found himself asking what difference Williams made anyway. In a world where millions were being shot, blown up, drowned, tortured, frozen to death, hanged, gutted, what difference would one more make?

Dorkin walked for a quarter of an hour before going back to the armoury, where he ate a sandwich and washed and changed his shirt and then set off for the jail for a final talk with Williams.

Everything was more formal now. Dorkin was met by a Mountie and ushered to Williams's cell. He found him sitting on his bunk, looking very small and frightened. He looked up suddenly at Dorkin as if he were the hangman come to lead him the few steps to the gallows.

"Dear God," Dorkin thought, "if there is a God, don't let him go to pieces yet. Keep him together for another three or four hours."

Dorkin stood in the centre of the court, as in an arena, conscious as always of the weight of people above and behind him, and watched Daniel Coile make his way down the aisle. The companions who had been with him every day at the back of the courtroom were still there in their rough mackinaws, but Coile was dressed up in a grey tweed suit that fitted him well enough but still didn't look as if it belonged on him. He walked with a belligerent, I-don't-give-a-shit-for-anybody slouch.

As he sat down in the witness box, he turned on Dorkin a look of sullen hatred. Dorkin noticed that his eyes were small and set too close together, and everything about him suggested something petty and mean, a scavenger rather than a predator.

"Mr. Coile," Dorkin said, "I wonder if perhaps we might begin with what you can tell us about Sarah's movements during the day of July 1. This was a holiday, so I presume she did not go into town to her job at the dairy."

"That's right," Coile said after a moment's hesitation, as if searching Dorkin's question for some clever trap.

"She was home all day?"

"No, she wasn't home all day. She went into town sometime before noon."

"To see the parade?"

"I don't know what she went in for. I didn't ask. I didn't know she was gone until after."

"I see. And what time did she come back from town?"

"End of the afternoon sometime. Four o'clock maybe."

Coile slouched in a corner of the witness box partially turned away from Dorkin, answering him across his right shoulder as a man might who had been accosted in the street by someone he didn't like.

"And after she came home," Dorkin said, "what happened then?"

"We had supper, and I went out to do my chores. Then I come back in."

"And did you see Sarah again?"

"Yes."

"And?"

"She was all dressed up to go out."

"To the dance?"

"Yes. But she didn't say nothin' about no dance. She said she was goin' to the movies with Vinny Page."

"Why would she do that, do you think?"

"Because I didn't want her goin' to that dance hall."

"But her friends all went there. Like Vinny Page. It seems a normal activity for a girl her age."

"I didn't want her goin' there because I thought she was gonna get herself in trouble," Coile said. "And she did."

"Perhaps," Dorkin said. "But we don't know that. Tell me, Mr. Coile, did Sarah have any steady boyfriends that you know of? Anyone she went out with regularly? Anyone who came to the house to pick her up, for example, to take her to a movie or a dance? Anyone like that?"

"No, not that I know of."

"That seems a little strange. From all accounts, she was an attractive girl. It seems odd that she shouldn't have had someone. Have you any idea why?"

"No. I wouldn't know."

"You have no idea who it was who got her in trouble?"

"Sure," Coile said. "It was him."

He pointed at Williams.

"Why do you say that, Mr. Coile?"

"It stands to reason."

"No, Mr. Coile," Dorkin said. "I'm afraid it doesn't stand to reason at all. Whoever was the father of Sarah's child, it was certainly not Private Williams. You say that you know of no regular boyfriend. I enquired extensively, and I could find nothing about a regular boyfriend. With the exemplary thoroughness which we all saw put in evidence here yesterday, I presume that the RCMP conducted an even more extensive enquiry about this than I did, and they obviously did not come up with the culprit either. It's all very odd. Somewhere there is a wonderful, invisible man whom it would be very interesting to talk to. You have no idea who it might be?"

"No," Coile said. "I still think it was him."

"Well, let's leave that, since you aren't able to help us, and turn to a different question."

Dorkin hesitated. This was the thin ice, and he wasn't sure how far he would be able to skate out onto it. But he was banking partly on the fact that in so small a place most of the jury would already have heard about Coile and his earlier troubles with little girls and would need nothing more than a reminder to set their minds in motion along lines that might produce the reasonable doubt that in theory at least was all that was needed. He was also hoping that Coile was unsavoury enough that the jury might find him an acceptable alternative to Williams as a sacrificial victim on the altar of their righteous indignation.

"I would like," Dorkin said, "to try to get some sense of Sarah's habit of mind in the weeks or months before her death."

In the witness box, Coile twisted, shifting his weight from one buttock to the other. Dorkin saw his eyes flicker toward the back of the court where his friends were sitting.

"Mr. Coile," Dorkin said, "I am interested in the way Sarah behaved at home. Did she get on well with you?"

"Sure. Why not?"

"You never had fights?"

"Nothin' to speak of."

"Mr. Coile, let me remind you that you are under oath and that there are severe penalties for perjury. Did you and Sarah frequently have fights?"

"Yes."

"Almost daily?"

"I suppose."

"What were they about?"

"Things."

"What things, for example?"

"About her hangin' around dance halls. Carryin' on."
"Did you ever actually strike your daughter?"
"Not as I remember."
"Mr. Coile, you are under oath."
"Maybe once or twice."
"I understand that it was a good deal more often than that. Is that not so?"
"It could be."
"I understand that sometime not long before she was murdered, you hit her so hard that you bruised her cheek. Is that not so?"
"I guess so."
"Did you have a fight with Sarah that night before she went to the dance?"
"Yes. I told her not to go."
"Did you fight about anything else that night? Or earlier that day?"
"Not that I remember."
"Did you ever fight over the fact that she was pregnant?"

Coile hesitated. His eyes flicked again to the back of the court, then to the jury, then back to Dorkin.

"I didn't know she was pregnant," Coile said. "She never told me nothin' about it."

"You are under oath."

Another hesitation.

"She never told me nothin'."

"You didn't know any of the circumstances that resulted in her being pregnant?"

"I don't know what you mean."

"Mr. Coile," Dorkin said, "you have a second daughter, Sheila, who is not living with you now but at your sister-in-law's. Did she leave because of disagreements with you? Let me remind you again that you are under oath."

"Yes," Coile said.

"Did you attempt to bring her back and did she refuse to come?"

"Yes."

"I understand, Mr. Coile, that some years ago you were the victim of a serious assault. Is that correct?"

"I don't know what you mean."

"I mean that you were beaten up by one of your neighbours."

"Yes."

"I understand that the reason for this was that the neighbour felt that you had behaved improperly towards his thirteen-year-old daughter. Is that correct?"

There was the scrape of a chair as Whidden rose, but before he could speak, Dunsdale had spoken for him

"Lieutenant Dorkin, I cannot allow such a question. You are dealing in mere hearsay apart from anything else. The jury must ignore all of this."

"I apologize again," Dorkin said. "I would like, if I may, to turn back to the night of the murder."

"Very well," Dunsdale said.

"Mr. Coile," Dorkin said, "you live only a short distance from where the body of your daughter was found. I am wondering if perhaps you happened to drive down the Hannigan Road that night and saw anything suspicious. Anything that might have a bearing on the murder. Were you out that night?"

"Yes," Coile said. "I was out."

"Could I ask you what time?"

"I didn't write it down."

"Make a guess."

"Eight o'clock. Maybe half past eight."

"I see. And where did you go?"

"I went out to a friend's place to see about some things."

"And where did your friend live?"

"Across the river on the Gulch Road."

"You drove past the corner of Broad Street and Hannigan Road to go there?"

"There ain't no other way unless you drive all over the county."

"Quite so. And when did you come back?"

"Twelve o'clock or so."

"Did you see anything on the way back that might have a bearing on the murder of your daughter?"

"Not that I know of."

"Did you see your daughter when you came back?"

"No, I never seen her again after she left for the dance until I seen her at the hospital when I went to identify her."

"You didn't happen to pick her up in your truck?"

"No, I didn't because I didn't have no truck. The clutch went bad the middle of that week, and it was settin' in the yard. I went out there in my friend's car, and that's what I come home in, me and him and two other boys."

For the first time, Coile looked straight back at Dorkin without looking away. A smirk of triumph. Dorkin had the sense that he had been waiting for these questions.

"And when did you get your truck fixed, Mr. Coile?" he asked as coolly as he could.

"The next Wednesday. I couldn't get no one to do it in town because I owed money. I ordered a clutch and me and two of the boys put it in ourselves."

"When you came home with your friends," Dorkin asked, fighting for some time to think, "did they come into the house with you or did they go straight back across the river?"

"No, they come in."

"And how long did they stay?"

"A couple of hours. It was Saturday night. There weren't no hurry."

"Your friends, of course, can confirm all this," Dorkin said.

"They already have," Coile said. "The Mounties spent two days questioning everybody but the dogs. Why don't you ask them?"

"Could I ask you, Mr. Coile," Dorkin said, "when these questionings took place?"

"Last week," Coile said.

Dorkin stood. He deliberately kept himself from looking at the jury. And he especially kept himself from looking at Whidden or the Mounties sitting behind him.

"Thank you, Mr. Coile," he said.

"Your witness, Mr. Whidden," Dunsdale said.

Whidden rose grandly.

"I think, your Honour, that this witness has been harassed enough in this courtroom. I have no questions."

"Your Honour," Dorkin heard himself saying, "I would like a recess of perhaps fifteen minutes before calling my next witness."

Dunsdale looked down at him, shuffled his papers, looked at his watch, then at Whidden.

"Mr. Whidden," he said, "do you have any objection to a brief recess?"

"No, your Honour," Whidden said, half rising. "No objection whatever. If Lieutenant Dorkin feels that he needs a recess, then a recess we shall have. With your permission, of course."

He had the air, unmistakably, of having won.

Dunsdale banged his gavel.

"We will have a recess of a quarter of an hour."

There was an explosion of chatter. One way or another, it had been a sensational half-hour. Not looking at anyone, Dorkin walked down the aisle towards the main door. Halfway there, he heard—was probably meant to hear—someone behind him say, "If I was him, I wouldn't go drivin' no back roads at night. Nor daytime neither."

Dorkin closed the door to his little room and sat down. It was a room for temporary use: a table, three chairs, a coat rack. From one wall, the yellowing photograph of some long-dead judge looked down on him.

Dorkin had no doubt whatever that Daniel Coile had been molesting his daughters, or trying to, but was it still possible that he had murdered Sarah? He tried to collect his thoughts.

In the end, what he had said to the Mounties had alarmed them enough that they had conducted the investigation of Daniel Coile that Drost had said they had no right to conduct. In spite of the breakdown of his truck, in spite of the testimony of his cronies, there were no doubt still a dozen complicated ways in which Daniel Coile, alone or in company, could have murdered Sarah. The whole drunken crew of them could have picked her up and gang-raped her, dropped her in the pit, and then gone on to Coile's place to wind up their evening.

But could they have conspired to tell a story that would stand up to the sudden descent of the Mounties almost three months later? Probably not. Almost certainly not. And the Mounties were obviously very sure of their ground. However much they may have hung back earlier from turning up evidence inconvenient to their conclusion that Williams was the murderer, once the alarm had been sounded about Coile, Dorkin knew them well enough to know that they would not have buried evidence against him no matter how much they would have liked to.

Daniel Coile may have screwed Sarah, he may have knocked her up, but it was very unlikely that he had killed her. In the end, this worst thing of all seemed to have happened—that it had no logic, that it made no sense, that her murder had been as random an act of violence as being trampled by a runaway horse on the street.

Now there was no alternative. He would have to do what he had dreaded all through the last six weeks. It would have to be Williams. There were things that only he could tell and that Dorkin could not now risk leaving untold, if only for his own peace of mind. But the thought of what some of Williams's evidence entailed appalled him. Even in murders such as this people sometimes found a certain villainous grandeur (witness Jack the Ripper), but the truths that Williams was going to be made to tell were neither villainous nor grand, merely squalid and ignominious. Perhaps, Dorkin thought, their very squalor might serve to convince, since the jury might feel that someone who was going to lie would choose lies that were less humiliating. Or would they think that this was just what was so clever about the lies?

There was a tap on the door, and before Dorkin could move to open it, Carvell stepped in.

"I came to tell you that they're just about ready to reconvene," he said.

Dorkin looked at him with surprise. It was not Carvell's job to run such errands.

"I'm sorry about the Coile thing," he said. "I didn't know. They didn't let me in on it either."

"Thanks," Dorkin said. "I set myself up for it. I shouldn't have lost my temper with Drost."

"Still," Carvell said. "They were doing what you had asked them to do. They should have told you the result."

"I guess so," Dorkin said, "but the damage is done now."

"I'm sorry," Carvell repeated. "What are you going to do now?"

"I'm going to have to put Williams on the stand," Dorkin said. "I haven't any choice."

"No," Carvell said, "I suppose not."

With the courtroom as quiet as any room with three hundred people in it could be, Dorkin walked Williams to the witness box. His voice as he was sworn in was barely audible. He looked at the clerk of the court. He looked at Dorkin. Otherwise he sat slumped in his chair looking down at his hands. There is something in almost everyone, thanks to the power of fairy tales, childish and adult, that says that innocence does not look like this, but is clear-eyed, upright, God's truth shining from the face for all but the wilfully blind to see.

Dorkin took it slowly, carefully, little by little, the easy things first, the date and place of his birth, the names of his mother and father, the fact of his growing up an only child, the death of his father of lung disease as result of gas, the prior deaths of the uncles, his schooling, his job in the lumber yard, his conscription.

"And why did you not volunteer for overseas service?"

"I was helping to support my mother. She didn't want me to. And she remembered what happened to the others."

"And after your mother died?"

"I felt that if they wanted me to go overseas, they should have conscripted me."

"If the government ordered you to go, you would go?"

"Yes."

Then on to the night of July 1, following the group of them going to the dance, recounting the dances with Sarah, following them on their walk along the path behind the dance hall and along Birch Road, coaxing him gently through the humiliations of their three-quarters of an hour of abortive lovemaking and of her leaving him angrily to walk away by herself towards the Hannigan Road. Finally, he took him through his interviews with the Mounties.

As the questioning went on, Dorkin glanced now and then at the jury. They were listening intently. He couldn't tell whether they were believing what they heard or not, but it seemed to him to be unfolding with the ring of truth. He began to hope.

It was not Whidden, but McKiel, who rose to cross-examine. He walked slowly around the table and stood in front of it with a pad of long, legal-size paper. He scanned the top page once, then a second time, before turning to a second and then a third page. Finally, after a minute of silence, he turned to Williams.

"Well, Private Williams," he said in his toneless, clinical voice, "we have seen a very polished performance here in the last hour or so. I must congratulate Lieutenant Dorkin. I don't think that the most experienced criminal lawyer in Montreal could have done it better. But I do have a few trifling reservations about what we have heard you say under the expert guidance of your learned counsel. A few trifling reservations and a few trifling questions."

He studied the notepad again, more briefly, then put it down on the table behind him.

Then for a quarter of an hour, he made Williams repeat his account of his abortive lovemaking with Sarah, spinning out the episode of the condom, peppering him with questions about every detail, pretending not to understand answers, forcing him to repeat them, reducing him to a state of incoherence.

"Well," McKiel said, "perhaps we'd better go on. Now let me see if I've got this straight. Miss Coile left you for whatever reason and walked away, and you never saw her again. But when the RCMP first questioned you, that is not what you told them. You told them that you left the dance hall and walked Miss Coile straight out to the Hannigan Road and left her there. Why did you tell them that?"

"I didn't think it made any difference. I didn't know anything had happened to her."

"But why not tell them the simple truth—if it was the truth—even if you didn't think it made any difference? What would have been wrong with that?"

"I didn't like to."

"But tell me, Private Williams. Why the additional lie of saying you walked with her as far as the Hannigan Road? Why not say that you walked her partway there and that you left her to walk the rest of the way by herself? Why the extra lie?"

"I don't know."

"Or perhaps you really did go to the Hannigan Road with Miss Coile, where you were seen by the Reverend Clemens, and that little bit of the real truth remained embedded in your lie. So anyway your story is that when you first talked to Corporal Drost you lied because you were too embarrassed to tell the truth."

"Yes."

"But you lied again when you were interviewed by Sergeant Grant. Why was that?"

"I didn't know there was anything wrong."

"You also signed a statement attesting to all these lies and saying that you left Miss Coile on the Hannigan Road. By that time, surely, you had been told what had happened and warned that what you said might be used in a criminal prosecution against you."

"No, I still didn't know anything."

"You're telling me that you signed the paper without being warned that it might be used in a criminal proceeding. But the clear evidence of the RCMP officers is that you were warned. They have no particular reason to lie. Are you sure you have not forgotten the sequence in which things occurred?"

"I don't know. There were a lot of policemen. They confused me. They told me if I changed my story I would be in trouble."

"When did they tell you that?"

"I don't know. After a while. It was a long time before they told me about Sarah Coile. I didn't understand what it was all about."

"And you are telling the court that when you signed that statement, you had not been warned? You yourself have just said that you were very confused. Are you sure of that?"

"I don't know. Maybe I didn't hear it. Maybe I didn't understand."

"I see. I suspect you understood perfectly well. But however that may be, you did sign a false statement?"

"Yes, but…"

"Never mind the 'buts.' We have heard them already. You knowingly signed a false statement?"

"Yes."

"But the statements you have made here today are true?"

"Yes."

"Good. I just wanted to be sure. When I talk to you I sometimes find it difficult to keep track of what is supposed to be true at any given moment and what isn't. The statement that you walked with Miss Coile out to the Hannigan Road is false, but the statement that she left you and walked out there by herself is true? Have I got it right?"

"Yes."

"I see. So the true statement is the one you made after you learned at the preliminary hearing that the Reverend Clemens had seen you at the corner of Broad Street, fifty yards further up the Hannigan Road than you would have been if you had left Sarah

Coile where you said you had. I presume this statement was made first to Lieutenant Dorkin?"

"Yes."

"After you had come to realize that your first statement could not be made to seem true? Is that correct?"

"Your Honour," Dorkin interrupted, "I must object. Prosecuting attorney is bullying the witness. Under the kind of questioning he is conducting, almost anyone could be made to seem confused. Private Williams is saying that at a time when he did not know it made any difference, he was embarrassed by the circumstances of his experience with Miss Coile and disguised some of the facts about it. When he came fully to understand what had happened and when he was not being bullied by the police who had not troubled to tell him what the inquiry was about, he told me what had actually happened, and that is the evidence which he is giving in this court. There is nothing very mysterious about that."

"Perhaps," McKiel said. "But I would like to hear these things from the witness, not from his counsel, whose voice, it seems to me, I have heard speaking through the witness a good deal this afternoon already. Private Williams seems quite the ventriloquist's dummy."

"The jury should note Lieutenant Dorkin's objections," Dunsdale said.

"I am curious, Private Williams," McKiel said, "about when exactly you did tell what you say is your true story to Lieutenant Dorkin. Was it two weeks after the preliminary hearing? Three weeks? Whenever, you would have had plenty of time to construct and ornament a more plausible story than the one you told to the RCMP. Tell me, Private Williams, did Lieutenant Dorkin rehearse you in the story you were to tell here today?"

"He made me go over it."

"I object to this," Dorkin said. "The prosecuting attorney knows perfectly well that every counsel has a witness go over his evidence in order to get it clear in his mind so that he will not be nervous in court. If I had asked the Reverend Clemens, for example, if he had gone over his evidence with the prosecutors, I think you would find that he had."

"That is speculation, Lieutenant Dorkin," McKiel said.

"Would you like me to recall Reverend Clemens and ask?" Dorkin replied.

"That won't be necessary," Dunsdale said. "The jury will note Lieutenant Dorkin's objection."

"I don't wish to prolong this unnecessarily," McKiel said. "I am sure that by now the members of the jury understand clearly enough what has happened here, which is that Private Williams, however he managed it, lured Sarah Coile away from the dance hall and brutally murdered her in the gravel pit off the Hannigan Road. Is this not what happened, Private Williams?"

Williams stared at him, but as Dorkin started to rise, he said, "No," in a voice that was scarcely audible.

"I have no further questions," McKiel said.

"Have you any other questions you wish to ask of this witness, Lieutenant Dorkin?" Dunsdale asked.

"Yes," Dorkin said. "I think that the jurors may not clearly have heard Private Williams's reply to Mr. McKiel. Private Williams, did you murder Sarah Coile?"

"No," Williams said, once again almost inaudibly.

CHAPTER FIFTEEN

It was the worst by far of the bad nights that Dorkin had spent in Wakefield. For four hours, he worked in his office on the speech that he would make to the jury the next day, carefully getting it all in order: heading, subheading, sub-subheading. He felt exhausted and oppressed, and the words as he looked at them on the paper seemed to have an existence only in a world of words, without any relationship to any reality, to any truth. But it wasn't about truth anymore anyway, if it ever had been. It was a contest between himself and Whidden, in which what was involved for Whidden was not the guilt or innocence of Williams but his own ego and reputation, as Magistrate Thurcott had suggested after the preliminary hearing.

When he looked out the window, he saw that a rain that had been threatening all day had begun, very light, as yet hardly more than a mist.

Near midnight, he went to bed and turned on his radio and waited through some cowboy music for the news. You are my sunshine. The last paratroopers had been withdrawn from Arnhem, and someone British had issued a communiqué saying that the setback had been a gallant success. In four weeks, a new victory loan campaign would begin. The Tigers had taken a one-game lead over the Browns. A barn and all its contents had burned in the village of Stanley. Private Owen Williams, testifying in his own defence, had proclaimed his innocence in the death of Sarah Coile. The case would go to the jury tomorrow.

Dorkin turned off the radio and the light and let the demons of the darkness have their way. All the things that he ought to have done, all the things that he ought to have said, or ought not to have said, came swarming down on him. He woke and slept and woke and was not sure whether he had slept or not. The oppression that he had felt all evening was shot through now with vast, terrifying, insubstantial anxieties, and he thought that madness would be something like that. He remembered a house that he used to pass on his way to school where in warm weather they used to put out on the verandah a crazy old woman, who would sit all day rolling her head from side to side, in hell for the crime of having been born.

After one final half-sleep, longer than most, he was awakened by the familiar clatter of metal-shod boots and the familiar mutter of voices. In intervals of quiet, he could hear the whisper of the rain. He tried to go back to sleep again but couldn't and was at the same time exhausted and preternaturally awake when Smith knocked on his door an hour later to rouse him for the last day. One thing only gave his heart a faint lift, and that was the reflection that, however it turned out, in twelve hours or so, there would be an end.

When he descended for breakfast in the mess, he found the armoury strangely deserted.

"Where is everybody?" he asked the cook who made his breakfast.

"They've gone on a route march, sir, around the island."

"In the rain?"

"Yes, sir. Captain Fraser's orders, sir. Wars don't wait for the weather to be good, do they, sir?"

"I suppose not," Dorkin said. "Sergeant MacCrae too?"

"Yes, sir. Everybody but me, sir. I've got a bad knee. That's why I'm a cook."

When Dorkin entered the courtroom with Private Smith following dutifully a pace behind, he noticed that for the first time they had allowed spectators to stand, two deep, along the back of the court. The second thing he noticed as he walked down the centre aisle was the row of brass in the seats behind Whidden's entourage. Colonel Meade. Another, heavy-set lieutenant-colonel whom he had never seen before. A moustached lieutenant who had the air of an aide-de-camp. Captain Fraser, in the presence of all this authority, sitting hunched and obsequious. Behind them was a second row of VIPs, this one made up mostly of what were evidently men of the law who had come for the show.

Meade and his party were standing, and Meade was talking to Whidden across the little oak fence that separated the public from the official area of the court, introducing the others, chatting. Feeling that it would seem impolite not to acknowledge Meade's presence, Dorkin hovered, awkward and uncertain, waiting his opportunity. Finally, Whidden turned back to his place, and Dorkin came forward. He saluted the four officers, and Meade made introductions.

"Lieutenant-Colonel Hepworth. Lieutenant Keys. Captain Fraser, of course, you know."

Hepworth's manner was distant, and Dorkin guessed that he had been one of the officers who had not wanted the army involved in Williams's defence.

"So," Meade said. "Good luck. I'm sure you will acquit yourself well."

Hepworth stared straight ahead.

Sometimes over the previous two weeks, in the watches of the night, or in the interval between the dawn uproar of the soldiery and Smith's discreet tap on his door, Dorkin had fantasized eloquent speeches about such things as the presumption of innocence, and reasonable doubt, and the high principles of the British system of justice above all mere prejudice and personal inclination. But in the cold light of morning in front of his shaving mirror with his real self staring back at him, he knew that he was not an orator. For one thing, he was too young to mouth such high sentiments and make them credible. For another, he had come no longer to believe them.

And this morning, beneath the surface nervousness, he felt flat, uninterested, dead. Partly it was the lack of real sleep over the last couple of weeks, and especially over the last four days. Partly it was that he had been over it all too many times. If he was not an orator, he was evidently not an actor either with the talent to speak the same lines a hundred times as if the words had just that moment flooded into his mind.

Williams arrived, looking small and frightened, as usual, between Carvell and the Mountie. The jury filed in and were polled, the murmur of conversation faded, died, and Dunsdale entered through his little door behind the bench. All rose, all sat.

Dorkin had never addressed a jury before. The simple crimes of his innocents at Utopia did not warrant such an outlay of public money and were dealt with by a magistrate.

He went through it all again, slowly, reasonably, logically, point by point. It was the only choice he had anyway since the weight of feeling was going to be all on the other side. That morning on the front page of the local weekly paper there had been the faces of two more dead soldiers, and inside a last letter to his mother from a soldier now dead these two months outside Caen.

He talked of the unethicality of the RCMP interrogation of Williams, of the absence of any physical evidence connecting Williams to the murder, of the normality of his behaviour in the days following the murder, of the improbabilities inherent in the prosecution's contention that it was Williams who brought Sarah Coile to the gravel pit, of the grave potential for error in the evidence of Reverend Clemens, of the absence of any evidence whatever other than that of Clemens which was inconsistent with Williams's later account of his activities that evening, of the failure of the RCMP to locate as a potential murderer the father of Sarah Coile's child, of the numerous possible explanations of the indisputable facts other than that offered by the prosecution, of the airy insubstantiality of Dr. Sach's testimony and of the prosecution's attempt to create a profile of Williams as a psychopath.

It took him over two hours to cover the ground, and he knew that he was not doing it well. Now and then, he had the sense of listening to his own voice as if he were detached from it, and he was struck by how curiously flat it sounded. Looking at the members of the jury, he found it difficult to read their reactions, but the signs did not seem propitious. Most of them looked away after a moment whenever he met their eyes, and the three businessmen whom he had judged to be the hard cases made it clear from small signs—a pursing of the lips, a slight, abrupt tilt of the chin—that they did not care much for what he was saying.

Out of the corner of his eye, he was conscious of Whidden, his bulk sprawled casually in his chair, sometimes looking down at the table, sometimes upward at the high ornamental ceiling, with an air of indulgent amusement.

Twice he was aware of jurors watching Whidden rather than himself and realized that he was being upstaged. Now and then, he allowed himself a glance at the row of VIPs. Meade looked attentive and thoughtful, the other colonel impassive and stern. Fraser watched him with a kind of skulking hostility.

Towards the end of his speech, some of the spectators, even some of the newsmen, began slipping out. He finished and stood in a cavern of silence, the jurors in front of him looking down at their hands or their feet or the floor or at Dunsdale or Williams, anywhere but at him.

Dundsale tapped his gavel and adjourned the trial until two o'clock that afternoon.

At ten minutes past two, Whidden rose to a packed house. He waited for the stir he had created to wash back and forth across the courtroom, and then in an expectant silence moved out from behind his table like a great actor coming onto the stage.

Overweight, slightly awkward, shuffling, untidy in his baggy trousers and crumpled gown, he had the true popular touch. He was not just someone whom the jurors could admire but someone whom they could fantasize themselves as having become had a few of the cookies crumbled another way. And he himself, Lieutenant Bernard Dorkin, trim in his officer's uniform, precise in thought and speech, with the aura of the university still about him, was not someone whom they could imagine themselves being, even if he had not been defending the Zombie Owen Williams. Even if he had not been a Jew.

Whidden took them through the evidence again, but as he moved around, now staring down at the floor, now up at the ceiling, now at some space above and behind the banked spectators in the gallery, he seemed to be addressing, not just the jurors, but spectators, newsmen, the greater public outside, even history. What Dorkin had struggled to get through to the imagination of the jurors was that the evidence that had been presented to them was a chaos—a tangle of uncertainties on the basis of which no reasonable judgement was possible. What Whidden presented them with was an illusion of order. Weaving an alternate cosmos in which it was difficult not to believe once lured inside, he made vanish with his magic wand all the stubborn, squalid untidinesses that make life unsimple and ungreat and replaced them with something to free the imagination—the mythlike spectacle of a simple girl destroyed by an ogre. It was a myth, Dorkin felt sure, that almost everyone there already wished in some confused way to believe in—a myth that was all the more compelling in that it left open, for anyone who wished to imagine himself stepping into it, the role of winged avenger.

Dorkin listened with impotent rage at the unscrupulousness of what was happening. The context of Williams's untruths to the Mounties was ignored so that only the untruths remained, Clemens's evidence was treated as indisputable fact, the absence of any hard evidence against Williams was adroitly kept out of sight or transformed into further proof of guilt, all the shoddy insinuations based on Sachs's testimony were resurrected.

"We have been told," Whidden said, launching into his final peroration, prowling slowly back and forth across the front of the court as if struggling to contain his indignation. "We have been told by the defence, as if it were almost in itself conclusive proof of innocence, that Private Williams showed no evidence of guilt or remorse in the days after the murder as you or I would have done. But you must keep in mind that we are not talking about someone like you or I. We are not talking about an ordinary human being with ordinary reactions. We are talking about someone who could rape, suffocate, and beat to death an innocent girl with a savagery which went far beyond any mere need to kill her. When you are talking about a monster in human shape, is it reasonable to expect him to exhibit ordinary human signs of remorse? The mere fact that he was capable of such a murder means that an appearance of innocence no longer means anything.

"What happened on that fateful night was really very simple in spite of Lieutenant Dorkin's valiant attempt to make it appear complicated. Private Williams lured Sarah Coile away from the dance hall. What exactly happened then, how they came to go to the gravel pit, only Private Williams now knows, and as we have seen, he has not been very forthcoming on the subject. The learned defence counsel has tried to present this as a great mystery, but it is not difficult to construct plausible ways in which this could have happened. They could have gone into the churchyard, and Sarah Coile could have attempted to escape from Williams down through the bushes into the darkness. It was a warm summer night, and after they had been seen by Reverend Clemens, they could have continued to stroll along Broad Street and gone down into the pit by the road. Once there, Private Williams raped Sarah Coile. And when he had raped her, he murdered her, not just to keep her from exposing him but out of an insane rage against her because his peculiar background had bred in him a deep hatred of women.

"When this was done, he walked calmly back to the armoury where he behaved as if nothing had happened. When questioned by the RCMP, he lied. It has been suggested that if Private Williams had been guilty, he would have concocted lies that were more credible and less easily disproven. But it is important to recognize that at the time he told them they did seem credible in terms of what he knew. But he had not calculated on the fact that Sarah had gone to the dance with a friend who had noticed at exactly what time she had left, so that his account of his activities could be shown without question to be false. Nor had he calculated on being seen with Sarah Coile at the corner of Broad Street and the Hannigan Road. It was only after the preliminary hearing, when he knew the full extent of the evidence against him, that Private Williams in meetings with his defence counsel concocted a second story to take account of the evidence which his first story could not account for.

"Although the defence has sought to cast doubt on that evidence, who cannot believe that it was indeed Private Williams and Sarah Coile whom the Reverend Clemens saw that night? I ask you to think about it. Are we to imagine that in the very short space of time that is supposed to be involved, Sarah Coile parted from Private Williams and was then almost immediately joined by someone else who nevertheless exactly resembled Private Williams in height and build? Or, even more extravagantly improbable, are we to imagine that by some even more miraculous process some totally different couple consisting of a girl who exactly resembled Sarah Coile and a man who exactly resembled Private Williams took their places? I think not, and I am sure you think not.

"What Reverend Clemens saw that night was Owen Williams and Sarah Coile in the minutes just before Williams led or chased her down into the gravel pit where he murdered her. That, gentlemen, is the very simple set of facts that you have before you and on which you have what I suggest is now the not very difficult task of passing judgement."

He delivered the last of this standing directly in front of the jury, looking them straight in the eye. There wasn't a sound in the courtroom. He continued to stand for a moment longer, looking down at the floor now as if meditating, then turned and went back to his place. As he sat down, there was a little explosion of congratulation along the table. McKiel quietly shook his hand. From behind, Dorkin heard someone saying in a stage whisper, "Wonderful. Wonderful."

Dunsdale tapped his gavel. There remained now only his charge to the jury. After a ten-minute recess, he began, and for nearly two hours, in a subdued hubbub of people coming and going, he floundered aimlessly through the evidence and such legal matters as reasonable doubt and the propriety of the original police questionings of Williams, all of this well peppered with "you should perhaps consider," "you should perhaps ignore," "on the one hand," "on the other hand."

When he had finished and the jury had departed, Dorkin took advantage of the first hour, when nothing was likely to happen, to get away, leaving Smith to keep watch and summon him if need be. It was raining more steadily now, and he walked through it to the armoury for some early supper. He found Sergeant MacCrae in the mess drinking coffee—or what passed for coffee in the army.

"I hear you've been out for a walk," Dorkin said.

"Yes, sir."

"Your punishment for testifying yesterday?"

"I expect so, sir."

"I'm sorry. I had to do it."

"I understand that, sir. No harm done. I expected something of the sort."

"It doesn't do to say bad things about the war. It spreads alarm and despondency among the masses."

"I suppose so, sir," MacCrae said. "What do you think is going to happen to Williams, sir?"

"I don't know," Dorkin said.

"Not hopeful, sir?"

"No," Dorkin said, "not hopeful."

He took the staff car back to the courthouse. Smith was still there unfed, and he sent him back to the armoury for good and sat down at the table. Whidden and McKiel had both gone, leaving a skeleton crew of a couple of clerks. The VIP rows were empty. Like Whidden and McKiel—or perhaps with Whidden and McKiel—they would be off having drinks and dinner somewhere. In the seats further back and in the gallery, people came and went, leaving others to hold their seats. It was important to be there for the kill.

Dorkin turned over the papers on the table—notes, depositions, transcripts. He wanted never to have to look at them again. Now and then, he left the courtroom and went and sat alone in his little room. The corridors were full of people, including newsmen who asked him questions whenever he passed them. ("Do you have any forecast about the verdict?" "Will you appeal if there is a conviction?" "Do you think that there will be a recommendation for mercy?" "Do you believe in capital punishment?" "In view of Dr. Sachs's testimony, do you think you should have defended Williams on grounds of insanity?") He brushed them off. It was senseless. Even if he answered their questions, his replies would be crowded out by the real news. But if they weren't filling the air with words, they would be left alone with their own stupidity.

Once, Dorkin went outside by the back door and stood in the shelter of a little overhang. It was dark by then, and the street was almost deserted because of the rain. As he stood, he saw Constable Hooper come out of the RCMP office across the street and without noticing him lounging there, get into his car and drive off. Somewhere some husband had beaten up his wife, or some son had beaten up his father, or a couple of drunks were beating up each other, or someone had driven a car into the ditch. Life going on.

Twice while Dorkin was in the courtroom, the clerk who was waiting on the jury passed through and created a little flurry of excitement among the spectators and newsmen, but they were false alarms. It was nearly eleven o'clock when he came in and went first to Whidden's table and then to Dorkin's with the message that a verdict had been reached.

The news had obviously travelled elsewhere by other messengers. Almost at once Whidden and McKiel reappeared, and there was a rush of people into the courtroom—spectators, newsmen, lawyers, but of Meade's VIPs only Meade himself and Captain Fraser returned. Colonel Hepworth had evidently seen all he wished of the performance and did not want to break up his evening.

As the uproar began to subside, Williams was led back to his place, and the jury filed in. Dorkin had heard that if a jury had found an accused innocent, they looked at him as they came in, but if they had found him guilty, they did not. Except for a glance or two, quickly averted, they did not. They settled into their places, awkward and self-conscious. Everyone waited. Then the little door opened, and Dunsdale returned. He too sat without looking at Williams while the jury was polled. When it was done, he turned to them.

"Gentlemen of the jury," he said, "have you reached a verdict?"

The foreman rose. As Dorkin had expected, one of the businessmen had been chosen, the furniture-store owner, grey-haired, grey-faced, grey-souled, self-important, dressed as usual as if for church in a dark suit.

"We have," he said.

"And what is your verdict?"

"We find the accused guilty as charged."

"And is that the verdict of you all?"

"It is. But I have been asked also to inform you that three members of the jury felt that a recommendation for mercy should be made."

"I see," Dunsdale said. "And the rest of you not?"

"No, your Honour."

"Thank you," Dunsdale said.

He turned for the first time to Williams.

"Will the prisoner rise and stand before the bar," he said.

Carvell and the Mountie helped Williams to his feet, and Carvell walked with him to the centre of the court. He seemed stunned, hardly knowing where he was.

"Owen Williams," Dunsdale said, "you have been found guilty as charged of the willful and brutal murder of Sarah Coile on or about the first day of July, 1944. Do you have anything to say before I pass sentence?"

"I didn't kill Sarah Coile," Williams said, his voice trembling. "I told the truth. I never saw her after she left me."

He looked at the jury, who sat looking down at the floor, avoiding his eyes. It was not, they seemed to be thinking, supposed to happen like this. The prisoner was supposed to receive his sentence, as the newspapers always reported, without emotion.

Dunsdale shuffled the papers in front of him, embarrassed and irritated.

"Well," he said, as if afraid that Williams would go on. "Yes, well. However. Owen Williams, you have been found guilty as charged, and it is therefore my duty to order that you be taken from this court to the George County Jail, where you will be confined. From there on Monday, December 18, 1944, you will be taken to a place of execution and hanged by the neck until you are dead."

Williams swayed and almost fell, and Carvell steadied him.

The jury stared at him openly now, as if he had been in that moment transported across some gulf, to some remoteness, from which his eyes could no longer reach back to them. Without looking up again from the papers in front of him, Dunsdale made a vague, dismissive gesture with one hand at Carvell. He turned Williams around, and the Mountie joined him and between them, they half-walked, half-carried him across the court and out the door that led towards the jail.

Dunsdale discharged the jury, and they filed down out of their box, very subdued, not speaking, not looking at each other, as if suddenly, belatedly, ashamed.

CHAPTER SIXTEEN

Dorkin was aware of Dunsdale speaking, distantly, from the bench, then rising, departing back through his little door, unleashing an uproar of chairs, feet, voices, a terrific, unintelligible hubbub, which as the courtroom emptied began to fade so that there floated up out of it from somewhere just behind Dorkin the sound of a professional conversation. He heard the voice he had heard before repeating idiotically, "wonderful, wonderful, wonderful," then a deep, after-dinner-speech sort of voice mouthing very slowly, "That, gentlemen, was the most brilliantly conducted prosecution that I have ever seen."

Across the aisle, Whidden and McKiel were talking while the dogsbodies gathered up their papers and packed the briefcases. Whidden looked at Dorkin, then excused himself to McKiel and came across and held out his hand.

"A good battle, well-fought, young man," he said. "You handled yourself very well. Let me be the first to congratulate you."

Dorkin looked at him with amazement. Too surprised, too stunned, to have the resources to lose his temper, he rose and shook the proffered hand and sat down again.

When the courtroom was empty of everyone except a janitor come to clean up, Dorkin gathered up his own papers and went back to his little room to get his coat. He would have to go to the jail to see Williams before he went back to the armoury, but for the moment he couldn't face that, and he had composed nothing to say to him. He sat down.

There were two ashtrays on the table in front of him, one with a small chip out of one corner, and he stared at them, half seeing them, half not, realizing that in spite of all the warning signs, there had been a part of him that had continued right to the end not to believe that this could happen. Around the periphery of consciousness there hovered an inchoate rabble of reflections on his failure. But at the centre, infinitely more than the cumulative effect of these, there had gathered a sense of undefined, unbounded terror, as if he were lying beyond rescue at the bottom of a deep pit.

After a few minutes, there was a knock on the door, and before he could get up, it was opened, and Meade looked in. He was carrying his raincoat over his arm, and he had the air of a man who was still turning over in his mind some pleasantry he had just heard. When he saw Dorkin's face, his expression grew serious.

"You look, my son," he said, "as if you were dismayed."

"Yes," Dorkin said. "I guess so."

Meade hesitated. He had stood just inside the door in a way that made it apparent that he was expected somewhere. Now he came all the way into the room and sat down across the table from Dorkin. There was something over-deliberate in his movements, and Dorkin realized that he was a little drunk.

"I can understand your being upset," he said. "But you have nothing to reproach yourself with. You did very well. Everyone has remarked upon it."

"Williams is innocent," Dorkin said. "I have no doubt about it."

"Look," Meade said. "I know you're very upset, but in court you said everything on your side of the case that could be said. Whidden did the same, and on the basis of that, the jury made a decision. What else can be done? I know it's not a perfect system, and I know that sometimes it can fail, but it's the best there is in an imperfect world. And in a way, you know, the important question is not so much whether someone is justly convicted or not as whether or not he had a fair trial. That's all the system can hope to guarantee. Nobody is God. And if the system does fail sometimes, that's the price of being human. It's something one just has to accept."

He stopped, as if aware that he was beginning to ramble.

"I must say, however," he went on, "that in this case, I don't believe the system has failed."

"You think that Williams is guilty?"

"Yes," Meade said, "I do. I always have. Ever since I saw the evidence from the preliminary hearing. And everything I've heard since has only served to confirm it. I never expected you to win. No one did. You've let yourself get too close to Williams. When it comes right down to it, you know, all you had to defend him with was his word on everything that mattered."

"I don't think he's that good a liar," Dorkin said.

"You'd be surprised how good a liar someone can be when his life depends on it and he has nothing to do all day but sit and think about it."

"With respect," Dorkin said, "I would like to request the additional time to prepare an appeal on Williams's behalf."

"I'm sorry," Meade said, "but I can't do that. On Monday Williams is to be given a dishonourable discharge. After that, he's no longer any business of the army's, and your connection with the case comes to an end. As I explained in the summer, there were people who wanted Williams discharged after the preliminary hearing, and I had to explain to them that that would imply that he was guilty before he was tried. Now that he has been found guilty, the discharge will go through. The papers are all prepared."

"In anticipation," Dorkin said.

Meade shrugged.

"You don't think that his sentence might be commuted?" Dorkin said.

"I think it's very unlikely," Meade said.

"So do I."

Meade glanced at his watch.

"Look," he said. "Don't take it too hard. You did everything you could have been expected to do. And a good deal more. Now it's over. It isn't your affair any more. I suggested to you once before that a lawyer is like a doctor. Some of his patients are going to die, and as a professional that is something he just has to learn to accept. You can't take things too much to heart."

"No," Dorkin said, "I suppose not."

"Terrible things are going on in Europe, you know. The Germans apparently have murdered millions of people, more than anyone ever imagined. This is small stuff by comparison. Anyway, I'm afraid I have to go. Before you go back to Utopia, I think you should take a week's leave. I'll get onto Utopia and fix it up. Go to Montreal. Get right out of it. Or somewhere along the shore. It's still nice this time of year."

"Thank you," Dorkin said. "I may do that."

"Consider it an order," Meade said. "As well as a reward. I'll fix it up, and you can pick up the papers at the office in Fredericton on Monday morning."

He went out, leaving the door open behind him, and Dorkin continued to sit. He wondered if the powers that be in the army had agreed to his request to defend Williams because they felt certain he would lose. And he reflected that what determined whether or not someone was going to hang didn't really depend on whether or not he was guilty. It depended on what kind of prosecutor he faced and what kind of defence he had managed to obtain. Even without someone as charismatic and unscrupulous as Whidden, it seemed to him that the odds were all on the side of the prosecution. And thinking of Whidden, he found himself remembering Swift's definition of lawyers. "A race of men bred up from their youth in the art of proving by words multiplied for the purpose that black is white and white is black, according as they are paid."

Anyway, he told himself, he now didn't need to give a shit, and he was aware of a gathering, guilty sense of relief. It was out of his hands. He couldn't be responsible any longer even if he wanted to.

After a while, the janitor came to the door.

"Are you planning to be much longer, sir?" he asked. "I'm wondering what I should be doing about locking up."

"It's all right," Dorkin said. "I'm going now. Sorry if I held you up."

He put on his raincoat, picked up his case, and went down the hall to the back door. It was still raining, and the path out to the sidewalk was covered with sodden leaves. Everyone had gone home except for one little cluster of four men. There was an old church across the street from the jail. Its front door was seven or eight feet above the ground with a little porch and two flights of steps set against the wall, and the men were sheltering under them in the shadows, drinking probably, and having one last look.

Dorkin had decided that for tonight anyway he would say nothing to Williams about his impending discharge from the army, nor about his own removal from the case. Tomorrow would be time enough. Meanwhile, he could soothe him with talk of an appeal—which there still could be even if he were not in charge of it.

He had to ring at the door of the jail and was let in by Cronk, who made him wait while he went for Carvell. Dorkin sensed at once that something was wrong.

"He's had some kind of breakdown," Carvell said when he arrived from the cells. "He walked back here all right, but when he got to his cell he collapsed."

The guardian Mountie in his red coat was standing by the open door of the cell. Inside, Williams was lying curled up on his bunk, his knees against his chin, facing the wall. They had covered him with a heavy blanket, but he was shivering and making small whimpering noises like an animal.

"I've sent for the doctor," Carvell said. "Maybe he can give him something that will make him sleep. That minister he's been seeing—Reverend Limus or whatever his name is—has been here, but I didn't see that he was likely to do any good, so I told him to come back tomorrow. He might help then."

"There's nothing I can do?" Dorkin asked.

"No," Carvell said. "I don't think so."

On the bed, the whimpering gave way to a strange low hooting sound, and the shivering became more violent. Dorkin turned away and walked back down the line of cells to Carvell's office and sat down. He felt the terrifying depression that had assailed him earlier beginning again to gather, and he set himself to keep it at bay. He had never been someone who went to pieces. It was the first time that he had ever even thought of such a possibility.

Half an hour later, when the doctor had come and gone, having given Williams a small advance on oblivion, Dorkin was let out the front door into the rain by Henry Cronk. It was now well after midnight. The Mounties' car was back in their yard, and there was only one small light burning in the office. Except for those in the jail, it was the only light visible anywhere, and there was no sound except the rain, nothing but a dank silence that made the town seem less something that humans had made than an extension of some primal forest. The little cluster of men who had been loitering under the steps of the church were gone, but as Dorkin descended to the sidewalk what he had taken to be merely a darker corner of the darkness there moved, and the figure of a man emerged and came towards him, his shoes squelching through the wet leaves on the street. He was wearing an old black raincoat and a cloth cap. A moment before his face came into the lights from the jail, Dorkin recognized the high-footing drunkard's walk as that of John Maclean.

"Wet night," Maclean said.
"Hello, John," Dorkin said. "Yes, it is."
"Sorry I never got hold of you again," Maclean said.
"It doesn't matter."
"I didn't want you to think I just ran off with your money."
"It's all right. I understand."
"Look," Maclean said, "is there somewhere dry we can get to? I'd like to talk to you for a minute."
Dorkin hesitated. He didn't want to talk to anyone.
"Okay," he said. "That's my car. We can talk there."
"You look down," Maclean said.
"I am."
"Little snort would do you good."

"Maybe."

He unlocked the car, and they got in. Maclean had a dank smell like that of a wet dog. He fished out of an inside pocket a packet of Turret cigarette tobacco and set about carefully rolling himself a smoke.

"You don't happen to be carrying any tailor-mades?" he asked.

"No," Dorkin said. "I don't smoke."

"I remember. I just thought maybe. Anyhow, I wanted to tell you what happened. This guy came to see me a few days after we talked."

"Oh? What guy?"

"I don't know. He gave me a name, but I didn't catch it. I saw him in court. Behind Whidden and those other guys. Anyhow, he said he worked for the attorney-general or somebody like that, and he told me that I was a witness for the prosecution and that you had no right to be talking to me. He said I could find myself in serious trouble if I let you interfere with what I was going to say in court. I didn't like the sound of that much. I didn't want to let you down, but guys like me, you know, they can do anything they want to with. I can't afford any lawyers."

"It's okay," Dorkin said.

"I found out what you wanted to know about Coile. Later on, when I heard the Mounties had been asking about it too, I figured them or Carvell would have told you, but I guess they didn't."

"No. They didn't tell Carvell either."

"Well," Maclean said. "That's too bad."

"Yes. But it probably wouldn't have made any difference. Do you think one of Coile's pals could have done it for him?"

"Killed the girl? Don't think so. Doesn't seem to me to make sense."

"You didn't hear anything about Coile messing around with her?"

"A lot of talk. Especially about the older sister. Just talk, but I wouldn't be surprised."

"You didn't hear anything about who may have shot at Louie Rosen?"

"No. Not a word. I'd tell you if I had. Nobody seems to know anything. Lots of rumours though."

"Such as?"

"Louie knew too much about somebody and was telling you what he knew. But also that he'd been sharp with too many people too often, and that day he just happened to drive by one of them when he had a gun with him."

"Could be," Dorkin said.

He looked at his watch.

"While I was asking around about things," Maclean said, "I found out something else. Something sort of funny, made me wonder."

"Oh?" Dorkin said.

"It was back in the spring. Late May, maybe June, this guy I was talking to didn't remember exactly. In the woods back of The Silver Dollar. Nights they have dances, there's a lot of drinking goes on there. People from the dance. And guys who are just around out there to drink and fight, you know. And sometimes some of the boys go out on the chance of picking up a drink. Or maybe just sit around and listen to the music."

"Or roll somebody who's had too much?" Dorkin said.

"Well, maybe. I don't know. I don't go in for that stuff. But I've been rolled once or twice myself. Anyhow. This guy I was talking to went back into the woods a ways to take a leak, and he was standing there when this guy came sneaking along a path and was right on top of him before either of them saw the other. Then this guy looked as if he'd been caught with his hand in a store till and went back off the way he came. He was all dressed up in bib overalls and an old jacket and a railroad cap pulled right down to his eyes. You'll never guess who it was."

"Daniel Coile?"

"No, that minister Clemens. Very peculiar."

Dorkin's heart flipped over.

"Yes," he said. "Very peculiar. Was your friend sure?"

"Positive. He knew Clemens to see all right, and Clemens was right on top of him before he realized he was there."

"What did your friend think Clemens was doing out there?"

"No way to know for sure. But we think he was out there looking at the girls. There's a lot of screwing goes on out there. I've heard a couple of the girls who are regulars at the dances don't do it just for the fun of it, if you know what I mean."

"Sarah Coile?"

"No, I never heard anything about her. I don't want to go into names. It doesn't make any difference who. But anyway that night Clemens said he saw your soldier, he may have been out in the woods looking life over instead of talking about God to old Salcher and his crazy wife. Might even have been doing more than just look at the merchandise."

"Did your friend ever see him out there again?"

"No. Just that one time. And no one else saw him that I know of. But it stands to reason that if he was out there once all dressed up like that, he'd be out there again, doesn't it?"

"Yes, it does. Your friend didn't follow him?"

"No. No reason to. Didn't matter to him what Clemens was doing. Or where he went. But I thought about that, and I'll bet you that what he was doing was driving up to the Salcher place and leaving his car there and sneaking down through the woods."

"What else have you heard about Clemens?"

"Nothing. I never even heard this until I started asking around about the other stuff. Some of the boys joked for a couple of weeks about Clemens out there all dressed up looking at what he couldn't get at home, then they all forgot about it."

Dorkin sat listening to the rain on the roof of the car, trying to think it out. Maclean opened the window a crack and threw his cigarette butt out and immediately started rolling another.

"Anyhow," he said, "that's the news. I thought you might be interested. But it may be too late to do much good now."

"Yes," Dorkin said. "Maybe. But I'm glad you told me about it."

"Makes you wonder a little about that evidence Clemens gave in court. About the time he said he saw your soldier and all that."

"Yes," Dorkin said, "it does."

Maclean finished rolling his cigarette and lit it.

"It wouldn't be worth the price of a little pony of rum, would it?" he asked.

"Yes," Dorkin said. "Sure."

He fished out his billfold and took out a five, then thought, and added another.

"Well, now," Maclean said. "You don't need to do that. You paid me once before and never got anything for it."

"It's okay," Dorkin said.

"Well, I ain't going to argue. If you're going down back of the armoury, maybe you wouldn't mind just letting me off there. There's a place there where I think I may be able to get fixed up before morning."

In the parade square, as he was getting out, Maclean said, "Just one thing. I didn't mention any names, and I don't think this guy I talked to about Clemens would want to be talking to Mounties or anything like that."

"He won't," Dorkin said. "I don't know his name, and I'm not going to ask."

"I don't want to have to talk to any Mounties either."

"It's okay. There won't be any Mounties."

"Good," Maclean said.

He winked and closed the door, and Dorkin watched him walking down the alley in the rain, close into the shadows under the walls of the houses like a stray cat.

"It certainly does make you wonder," Carvell said. "But it's not very much to go on."

He sat with his elbows on the desk, smoking a cigarette.

It was nine o'clock the morning after the trial. Dorkin had been awake most of the night. Now he was sitting across from Carvell in the wooden armchair that he had come by habit to sit in over the weeks.

"We don't even know if he was in the woods that night," Carvell said.

"I think he was," Dorkin said. "Alden Bartlett told me that he saw Sarah Coile going along Broad Street in the middle of the afternoon on July 1 on her way to Vinny Page's. The parade had been over for two hours or more by then, and none of her friends that I talked to had any idea where she was in the early part of that afternoon. I suspect she had been to see Clemens. I suspect that he was the father of her child, and I suspect that she made him feel threatened enough that he decided to get rid of her."

"It's a house of cards," Carvell said.

"I don't think so. Not this time. And whatever she and Clemens said, it also made her uneasy enough that she went about setting Williams up to think that he was the father of her child."

"You were wrong about Coile."

"Half wrong. I talked to his sister-in-law, Fern MacMillan, and her husband, and they told me that Coile was messing around with the girls. That's why the older sister left."

"Could be," Carvell said. "But suppose Clemens did knock her up and then murder her, why on earth would he attract attention to himself by coming forward as a witness?"

"He may have felt that he was in more danger than we know. If Williams were convicted, that would be an end to it. And I don't think that Williams would have been convicted if it hadn't been for his testimony. Do you?"

Carvell considered.

"Possibly not. But he wouldn't know that."

"But he would. If he were the murderer, he would know better than anyone else how thin the case against Williams was."

"It would still be risky stuff," Carvell said. "He had no way of being sure of what the police knew and whether what he was telling them was going to fit."

"But he covered himself. He never said it was Williams. If something happened to prove that it couldn't have been Williams, or Sarah either, he couldn't have been accused of anything more than having made an honest mistake. It wasn't as if he'd said that he'd talked to them or met them face to face. It was a very adroit lie, and all the vaguenesses he built into it only made it that much more convincing to the jury."

Carvell smoked and studied the day beyond the barred windows. The rain had ended overnight, and it was a bright, limpid morning, full of the sounds of Saturday turmoil in a country town—of the normal world flooding back.

"I'll tell you a tale out of school," Carvell said. "Hooper has always been sceptical of Clemens's evidence, but he wasn't going to break ranks. You know what the Mounties are like."

"Would he talk to me?" Dorkin asked.

"He might."

"What about Drost?"

"Drost isn't here. He left for Fredericton this morning. He's being transferred to Ottawa. He only stayed on because of the trial. For the time being, Hooper's in charge. I don't think he'd go very far in bucking the brass, but at least there's no one on the spot to tell him what to do."

"Their car's in the yard," he said. "I'll get him to come over here, so he won't have to worry about MacDougal."

Dorkin let Carvell do the talking, and Hooper sat, his legs crossed, his cap with its yellow band and its buffalo badge perched on his knee. He listened without comment or question, every now and then eyeing Dorkin warily with his guileless blue eyes. When Carvell had finished, he studied the polished toes of his boots.

"We're not trying to get you in hot water," Carvell said. "But there are some real questions about all this. You've had some doubts yourself."

"Yes," Hooper said. "But nothing solid."

Carvell and Dorkin waited and watched as the two sides of his Mountie soul fought it out.

"Well," he said finally. "I've always wondered how much Clemens could really have seen that night coming around the corner. I thought we might have some trouble in court about it, so one night about eleven o'clock me and MacDougal went out there. It was a clear night the way it was the night of the dance, but there was probably more moon. We took a white towel along to act like Sarah Coile's dress. MacDougal stood where she and the soldier were supposed to have been standing, and I came down the road and made the turn. I could see the towel but not much detail. Then MacDougal stood there without the towel the way the soldier would have been, and I couldn't see much of anything. Just the shape of someone there. It's hard to see how Clemens could have seen as much as he said he did in that light. The only thing is that if there'd been another car coming up the road or even one behind him, there probably would have been enough light—more than enough."

"He didn't say anything about another car?" Carvell asked.

"No," Hooper said.

"And nobody asked?" Dorkin said.

"No," Hooper said uneasily. "Not that I know of."

Dorkin bit his tongue. It was no time to moralize.

"There isn't much I can do," Hooper said. "I can't haul him in just on this kind of stuff."

"Well," Carvell said, "I could poke around and see what I can turn up. Maclean and his pals may know more than they told."

"I haven't got a lot of time," Dorkin said. "On Monday I'm supposed to be out of here."

"We can still work on it," Carvell said.

"I know that," Dorkin said. "But I want to be here."

The phone on Carvell's desk rang. He picked it up, took the receiver off the hook, listened briefly, then pushed the whole apparatus across the desk to Hooper.

"It's MacDougal," Hooper said when he'd finished. "There's been a call. He has to go out, and I'll have to take over the office."

He stood in the middle of the room, vacillating, his cap in his hand.

"I'll do what I can," he said finally.

"He's in a tough spot," Carvell said when he was gone. "If he sets about to undermine their case and they find out about it, he's going to be in the shit with Grant. And if he really does help to prove that Williams didn't do it, everyone will run around saying nice things about him, but they'll never forgive him. The army and the lords of the law may not be all that pleased with you either."

"Probably not," Dorkin said.

"Well," Carvell said, "if Clemens did do it or was an accessory to it somehow, he's going to be thinking he's home dry, and it may rattle him into doing something foolish if he finds out that he isn't. Why don't we go shake the bushes a little and see what flies out?"

CHAPTER SEVENTEEN

They found Thomas Salcher out back of his house by the pigpen. Over the fence in front of him, two enormous pigs were standing with their snouts lifted in expectation of food.

"That's a couple of good-looking hogs," Carvell said.

"Yes," Salcher said. "Pretty good. Just about good enough to have their throats cut."

He giggled. But behind the chat he was studying them warily.

"We're thinking," Carvell said, "that you may be able to help us with a little problem we have. Why don't we go inside out of the wind?"

They sat around one end of the kitchen table. Ada Salcher sat in a rocking chair, her dropsied legs above her sneakers like a pair of corpse-white balloons filled with water, the rest of her a shapeless pile of breasts and belly. She eyed them as she might have eyed someone passing on the road. In spite of the cooler weather, the stink in the house seemed to Dorkin even worse than when he had been there before.

"The problem," Carvell said, "has to do with Reverend Clemens."

"Oh?" Salcher said. "What kind of a problem would that be now?"

"We've heard some strange things," Carvell said.

"Oh?"

"We've heard that sometimes on Saturday nights, he dresses up in a pair of old overalls and goes roaming around in the woods behind the dance hall. Have you ever heard anything about that?"

"Well, now," Salcher said, glancing back and forth between Carvell and Dorkin, "I don't know."

"You either know or you don't know," Carvell said. "Have you?"

"Well," Salcher said, "I guess I have. Yes."

"Seen it even, perhaps?"

"Well, yes. It's just that he told me I wasn't supposed to tell nobody about it. He said it wouldn't do to have it git around."

"What exactly was it that you weren't supposed to tell? What was he doing out there?"

"He didn't like that dance hall. He said it was a palace of sin. He was gonna git it shut down, and he wanted to be able to say what was goin' on there. So sometimes he went to spy on it."

"In an old pair of overalls and a railroad cap."

"Well, yes. That's right," Salcher said. "He said if he got recognized, and they knew what he was doin', he might git beaten up. Even killed. He said people were threatenin' him because he preached against the dance hall."

"I see," Carvell said. "He drove here to your place and parked his car, did he?"

"Yes. Out back there."

"What about the overalls?"

"Well, now, he used to leave them here. Outside the back door there with my coats and jackets and stuff. They just looked as if they was mine. He'd put them on and then go off down the path back there into the woods."

"How long was he gone?"

"I don't know. Maybe an hour. Maybe longer."

"You never thought that maybe the reason he was going down there was to have a peep at the boys and girls in the woods?"

"Well, I did once or twice," Salcher said. "But that ain't no crime."

He giggled.

"I guess not," Carvell said, "if that's all he did. Did he come here on the night of July 1?"

"Oh, I wouldn't know about that," Salcher said. "That was a long time ago."

"In court, he said he was here that night. He said he had a religious visit with you and Ada. That's how he happened to be driving the Hannigan Road."

"Yes, that's right. I just didn't remember the date."

"It was the night Sarah Coile was murdered. Did he go out spying in the woods that night?"

"Now, I don't remember that," Salcher said. "I didn't think nothin' about all them things at the time."

Before Salcher had even finished, Carvell's fist came down on the table so hard that everything on it jumped. Salcher jumped too.

"Stop horsing around," Carvell said. "I think you know goddamned well what all this is about. You tell me lies, and you're going to find yourself in more trouble than you've ever seen in your life before."

Salcher couldn't have looked more cowed if Carvell had picked him up and slammed him against the wall.

"Yes," he said. "Yes, he was here that night."

"So what happened?"

"Just like usual. He parked out back and came in and talked for a while and said a prayer for Ada and then put on the overalls and cap and went out. Off down the path behind the house."

"When did he come back?"

"I don't know. I didn't watch the time. An hour maybe. Maybe more. I don't know."

"But he did come back?"

"Yes. But he didn't come in. He didn't bring the overalls back neither. I just heard the car start up and drive off."

"Did you look out?"

"No. I just saw it go by under the windows."

"You didn't see if there was anyone in it besides Clemens?"

"No. I didn't look."

"And you don't know what time it was?"

"No. I never paid no heed."

"Did he bring the overalls back here later?"

"No. I never seen them again. And I don't know as he ever went into the woods again neither. Leastways, he never came here before he did. But he came a couple of times just to visit."

"Did you ever think there might be a connection between Sarah Coile being murdered that night and Clemens never going out spying again?"

Salcher hesitated. He was thoroughly scared now, sitting with his hands clasped tight in his lap.

"I wondered," he said finally. "But I thought maybe he was afraid to go there anymore with all the police around that might see him."

"Did he ever talk about Sarah Coile being murdered?"

"Once. I remember once he said it was a judgement."

"Oh? A judgement for what?"

"I don't know," Salcher said. "For goin' to the dance hall maybe. Or goin' out back with boys."

"Did he say anything else?"

"I remember he said somethin' about how now all her sins would be forgiven."

"Sort of a tough way to get into heaven," Carvell said.

Dorkin and Carvell mounted the steps of the small front porch of the Reverend Clemens's house on Broad Street, and Carvell turned the key of the doorbell in the centre of the door.

There was a long wait, and then the door was opened by a tall young woman dressed in a loose blouse, buttoned up to the neck, and an unpatriotically long skirt that reached almost to her ankles. She had a delicately boned, oval face completely without makeup, dark brown hair pulled back in a severe bun, very large, dark eyes, a long neck. This, Dorkin assumed, was the daughter whom Alden Bartlett had told him about, but Bartlett had not led him to envision such a strikingly good-looking woman. However, she was not working at impressing them with her looks. Her eyes were hard as she looked first at Carvell, then at Dorkin, studying his uniform with systematic disdain.

When she showed no sign of speaking, Carvell introduced himself and Dorkin.

"We would like to have a few words with your father," he said.

"Could I tell him," she asked, "what it is you want to have a few words with him about?"

The accent was unmistakably southern.

"I'm afraid that it's confidential," Carvell said. "I'm sure he'll understand."

She hesitated, glancing beyond them at Carvell's car parked in the yard behind her father's, then stepped back.

"Come in, then," she said, "and I'll see."

They stepped into a narrow hall fronting a flight of stairs and were ushered into a small parlour furnished with a horsehair sofa, several tightly packed, uncomfortable-looking chairs, and a lectern. There was a faint smell of damp as in a house where windows are seldom opened, and Dorkin had an unsettling sense of having passed into an alien world.

The girl vanished into the back of the house, closing a door behind her, and Dorkin and Carvell stood in the middle of the room, unspeaking and uncomfortable, studying the prints on the wall. There was one of Jesus with children, one of Jesus with the disciples, all of them suitably Aryanized, one of a sun-drenched landscape with a distant rainbow towards which some common folk in work clothes were making their way with rapturous, upturned faces.

From somewhere at the back of the house, Dorkin could just hear a murmur of voices. There was an interval of silence, then a man's heavy tread. Reverend Clemens was in shirt sleeves and braces, massive and softly shapeless, though not so massive as he had appeared from the eminence of the witness stand, nor, no doubt, from his pulpit.

He looked at Carvell, then more closely at Dorkin. If he had cause for alarm, he didn't show it.

"Sheriff Carvell," he said. "Lieutenant."

He made no move to shake hands.

"We'd like to talk to you for a few minutes about Sarah Coile," Carvell said. "We understand that you were her minister."

"I was," Clemens said, emphasizing the pastness of it in an odd way. "I'm sorry that I could not have swayed her more than I did. Then all of this might not have happened."

The tone of voice was distant, as if suggesting that he regarded Carvell and Dorkin as themselves part of the great worldly conspiracy against holiness that had destroyed Sarah. As in court, Dorkin caught the whiff of a southern accent, not as strong as the daughter's, but unmistakable all the same.

"Yes," Carvell said. "I'm sorry too. Everyone is."

"That dance hall is a curse," Clemens said. "I'm sure it has ruined more lives than hers."

"Probably it has," Carvell said.

"I'm not sure what it is you wanted to talk to me about," Clemens said.

"Perhaps we could sit down," Carvell said.

"Certainly."

Clemens carefully closed the door, crossed the room with his slow, heavy stride, and sat down in the middle of the horsehair sofa, leaning back, his hands on his thighs, elbows out, his chin lifted. Dorkin and Carvell took chairs across from him.

"We have come into possession of some information," Carvell said, "which tends to cast some doubt on the guilt of Private Williams."

Watching closely, Dorkin saw, or thought he saw, a shadow as brief as that of a passing bird cross Clemens's face.

"We thought you might be of some help to us," Carvell said.

"If I can," Clemens said.

His manner seemed guarded, perhaps wary, perhaps merely puzzled.

"I didn't like to question you in court about Sarah Coile," Dorkin took it up, "but we were hoping that just between ourselves here, you might feel free to tell us something about her."

"Perhaps. What was it you wanted to know?"

"We were wondering if perhaps you might have some idea who the father of her child might have been."

"I had assumed that it was Private Williams. But I gather from the trial that this seems doubtful."

"You didn't know that she was pregnant before you heard about it at the hearing?"

"No, I did not."

"You've no idea of any special boyfriends?"

"No."

"Was she someone whom you knew well? Someone you saw often?"

"Ours is a small church. Everybody knows everybody else."

"She still came to church?"

"Yes. Not as often as she used to."

"When was the last time you saw Sarah?" Dorkin asked.

He tried to pose his question in a way that suggested without making it too obvious that he might already know the answer. Clemens hesitated briefly—for a heartbeat or two, no more—and the look that he gave Dorkin was ambiguous. Was it wariness as he saw what he took to be a trap and realized that he dare not lie? Or was it merely an annoyed awareness that Dorkin regarded the question as a trap and was expecting him to lie?

"I saw her on the afternoon of July 1," he said.

Dorkin carefully restrained himself from looking at Carvell. Then as they both waited, Clemens went on.

"She came to the church. My wife and daughter were both there helping me prepare things for Sunday. I talked with Sarah in my office at the back."

"Would it be possible for you to tell us what she came to see you about?" Dorkin asked.

"No," Clemens said. "I'm sorry, but I can't do that. People come to me in trust for my advice. I am not going to betray that trust."

"Not even when they're dead?"

"No. I'm sorry. It would still be a betrayal, and it would destroy the faith that others have in me if it were known that I had broken a confidence. You are a lawyer, Lieutenant Dorkin. I believe you are under an obligation not to divulge what your clients tell you. Why should you think that my obligation as a man of God should be less?"

"I'm sorry," Dorkin said. "Of course, we respect your principles. It just seemed to us that there might be some special significance in her coming to you for advice on that particular day."

"Is it possible for you to tell us if what she came about could be connected in any way to her death that night?" Carvell asked.

"No," Clemens said, "it was not. Not in any way."

"I see," Carvell said. "Well, we don't want to press you about it. We were also wondering if you saw anyone suspicious in the general vicinity of the dance hall that night?"

"No," Clemens said. "I don't recall seeing anyone at all."

"There's been some talk," Carvell said, "about a strange man who was in the area that night and has never been identified. He was said to have been dressed in overalls and some kind of cap."

This time the shadow that crossed Clemens's face was not swift but slow spreading.

"No," he said. "I didn't see anyone."

"That's too bad," Carvell said, drifting blandly on as if he had seen nothing unusual in Clemens's reaction. "What time did you go to the Salcher place?"

"I'm not sure," Clemens said. "As I said in court. I wasn't watching the time. Sometime around ten o'clock."

"You weren't outside at the Salchers'?" Carvell asked. "Out back or anything like that? Nowhere you might have been able to see into the woods?"

"No," Clemens said. "I just parked and went into the house. It was dark. And when I was leaving, I came out and got into the car."

This time Dorkin did glance, as if casually, at Carvell. Carvell's face retained its look of deferential inquiry.

"That's too bad," he said. "Maybe there wasn't any man. When things like this happen, people sometimes let their imaginations run away with them."

"Yes," Clemens said. "That's true."

"When you were driving back," Carvell said, "you didn't happen to see any other cars on the road?"

"No," Clemens said.

"When you were going around the corner where you saw Sarah and the man, there weren't any other cars going up or down the road? No one else who might have seen something in their headlights?"

"No," Clemens said. "I didn't see anybody."

"All dark?"

"Yes," Clemens said.

When they were back in Carvell's office, Carvell had phoned Constable Hooper, and the three of them were now sitting around Carvell's desk.

"But the fact is that he lied," Dorkin said.

"Yes, he lied," Carvell said. "But it may not mean what you're trying to make it mean. Even if he were just roaming around in the woods looking at the girls, he wouldn't want to admit it. And for all we know, he may have been screwing one of those girls who pick up their pin money out there—in which case he certainly wouldn't be disposed to admit it."

"And he may only have been out there spying on the dance hall the way he told Salcher," Hooper said, "and didn't want to admit to that either."

"I don't think so," Dorkin said. "Something happened that night that scared him enough that he took away his outfit and never used it again."

"But even if he didn't commit the murder," Carvell said, "all the activity out there afterwards would have been enough to scare him off."

It was now nearly three o'clock in the afternoon, and for over two hours they had been hammering it back and forth.

"He could have been lying about the cars, too," Carvell said. "He had the wind up by that time. He didn't know what we were getting at, and he may have decided to say that there weren't any cars. Then if he had to, he could always pretend to remember later that there was a car. So there could have been a car, and he could have had light enough to see what he said he saw."

"It is just possible that he could have seen her without the lights from another car," Hooper said. "He knew her well enough that he wouldn't have had to see much."

Dorkin walked across the office and looked out the window at the church across the street and the little nook where Maclean had waited for him.

Shit, he thought. It went round and round.

"Look," he said, turning back to them, "he was out there that night, and the account he gave in court of what he did there was a lie. If he spent time roaming around in the woods, all that talk of what time it must have been when he left Salcher's place was just bullshit. He perjured himself. He had also been talking to Sarah that afternoon, and he never said anything about that until we bluffed it out of him."

"Could you bring him in," Carvell asked Hooper, "and tell him what we know from Salcher about his movements and ask him to make a new statement about what he did that night? If he is the one who murdered Sarah Coile, he's going to be pretty rattled after this afternoon, and it's possible he may go to pieces. And even if he didn't do it, the fact that his testimony in court was perjured would certainly ensure that Williams got a new trial. It can't just be let go now."

Hooper looked at him unhappily.

"I shouldn't do anything without getting permission from Fredericton," he said. "It isn't my investigation."

"But it isn't anyone's investigation now," Dorkin said. "Williams is in the jug. That investigation's over."

"I don't know," Hooper said.

"There's something else," Dorkin said. "If Clemens did kill Sarah Coile, we've put Salcher in danger by what we told Clemens this afternoon. If he's a killer, he may also kill Salcher."

"That would be pretty risky in the circumstances," Hooper said.

"It would," Dorkin said. "But Clemens doesn't know we talked to Salcher. We just said we'd heard a rumour about a man in the woods. He may think he's covering his tracks by getting rid of Salcher before we get to him. If he *is* the murderer, he's going to be desperate."

"I tell you what," Carvell said to Hooper. "If you get in hot water with Fredericton, tell them what Bernie and I did by going to Salcher and Clemens. Tell them that we're a couple of irresponsible assholes. It won't bother me if it doesn't bother Bernie. You were forced to act quickly because you were afraid for Salcher's safety. So you decided to talk to Clemens to get to the bottom of what really happened that night."

"I shouldn't be doing it," Hooper said. "Not without some authority."

"But if Salcher is killed after what we've told you," Dorkin said, "you'll be in even deeper shit."

"Not if I check with Fredericton first," Hooper said.

"Do you think you can explain all this stuff to them so they'll make a quick decision?" Dorkin asked. "They'll have to get hold of Grant and god only knows who else. It could take all night."

"Probably," Hooper said.

"And the truth is," Carvell added, "that when you look at what we've got, it doesn't necessarily add up to all that much. Particularly to someone like Grant who doesn't want to believe it in the first place."

"You're afraid that if I talk to Fredericton first," Hooper said to Dorkin, "they're going to tell me to leave it alone."

"Yes," Dorkin said, "I am."

"Okay," Hooper said. "But I don't want to make it look like an official interrogation by bringing him in here. If it blows up on me, I'll be in less trouble if I talk to him out there without any formalities."

"But I'd better have some kind of witness to what goes on," he said to Carvell, "so I'd like you to come along. It'll also make it more difficult for him to shift his story around from what he told you."

"I'm coming too," Dorkin said.

Hooper hesitated, gathering himself to say no.

"I was the one who started all this," Dorkin said. "I was the one who tracked all this down. I want to be there. I'll go in my own car."

"Okay," Hooper said. "But I'll ask the questions. I want you to stay out of it. I have the feeling that when this is over, I'm going to end up serving the rest of my career in the Northwest Territories."

Clemens's Ford was still parked in the yard where it had been earlier in the day, and they drove in and parked side by side behind it, first Hooper and Carvell in the RCMP patrol car, then Dorkin in his staff car. It looked a little like a raid.

Once again, they rang the bell, once again waited, so long this time that they began to wonder if it was going to be answered at all. When eventually the door was opened, it was again by the daughter. She looked one after another at their three faces.

"There were just one or two more questions which we thought your father might be able to help us with," Carvell said.

She stood with her hand on the door, looking past them at the cars in the drive, then above them, beyond the cars, at something higher—the tops of the autumn trees, a passing bird, perhaps merely the sky—a trifling act of seeming inattention whose import Dorkin only came to understand when he remembered it later.

"My father has been having a nap," she informed them. "If you want to come in, I'll tell him you're here."

She stood aside by the open door, and they filed in. She ushered them once more into the parlour and with a small nod slipped away, closing the door quietly behind her.

They stood together awkwardly in the middle of the room. They looked at their shoes, at the furniture, at the pictures on the wall. Dorkin found himself studying the awful milksop Jesus. Except for their own breathing, and the shuffle of their feet, there wasn't a sound in the room, nor from beyond the closed door, seemingly anywhere in the house. Their wait stretched to five minutes, then ten, and still there was no sound of Clemens's oxlike tread in the hall.

The realization of what this silence might mean came abruptly to all of them at once, but it was Carvell who moved first. He flung the door open and strode down the hall to the kitchen at the back. It was empty.

A flight of very narrow stairs, as steep almost as a ladder, led up from beside the back door.

"Take the front ones," Carvell said to Hooper.

He hurled himself up the stairs on all fours like an ungainly dog, and Dorkin followed. They met Hooper in the upstairs hall. There was a bathroom, a back bedroom, a storeroom, all empty. In the front bedroom behind drawn blinds, a small, grey-haired woman in a long-sleeved print dress was sitting on the edge of the bed with her hands folded in her lap. She looked up at them without surprise, as she might have looked at someone from the household who had happened to glance in at her while passing. Then she looked down again at her hands. She seemed so much older than Clemens that Dorkin thought for a moment that she must be his mother or some aging parishioner he had taken in.

"Mrs. Clemens," Carvell said, "we wanted to have a word with your husband. Do you know where he's gone?"

"I was afraid," she said without looking up.

"Your daughter," Carvell said. "Do you know where your daughter and your husband have gone?"

"I have no daughter," she said, almost as if she were talking to herself. "I had two sons."

"Is she always like this?" Hooper whispered to Carvell.

"I don't think so," Carvell said. "I've never heard anything about it."

"Your daughter Elizabeth," he said to her again. "She let us in. Do you know where she and your husband have gone? Have they gone to the church?"

"Yes," she continued in the same abstracted tone of voice. "To the church. I was afraid, and they couldn't wait. We were going home. At last, we were going home."

"There must be a path at the back," Carvell said to Hooper. And then to Dorkin, "You'd better stay here with her. We'll see if they're at the church."

At the door, he turned back to Mrs. Clemens.

"Mrs. Clemens," he asked, "does your husband have a gun?"

"Yes," she said without looking up. "Yes, we have a gun. There's always danger for us. Evil men."

"Shit," Carvell whispered to Hooper. "We should have got him to come back with us when we were here the first time. Come on."

They pounded down the front stairs and out of the house. Mrs. Clemens continued to sit, oblivious to the noise of their departure, oblivious to the presence of Dorkin. He did not want to be there, dropped out of what was really his show. He looked at Mrs. Clemens. She wouldn't know whether he were there or not, and there must be neighbours who could be sent in.

He descended the stairs quietly so as not to arouse her from her reverie and went out the front door. Across the street, a white-haired man was raking leaves, or pretending to, while he watched the goings-on at Clemens's house. Dorkin sprinted across to him.

"There's an emergency," he said. "Do you know the Clemenses?"

"Yes," the man said. "Sort of. They're neighbours."

"Mrs. Clemens is upstairs. Is there anyone—your wife or someone—you could send in to stay with her for a few minutes?"

"Well, yes," the man said. "My wife..."

He looked over Dorkin's shoulder.

"Jesus," he said. "Look at that."

Dorkin turned. A cloud of dirty grey smoke was boiling up above the trees and drifting off towards the creek.

"Send your wife in to stay with Mrs. Clemens," Dorkin said. "And phone the fire department. I think it's the church."

Dorkin set off down the street at a run. There were already other people running—children, men, a few women. From far away beyond the creek, Dorkin heard the faint sound of the bell in the tower of the fire station. His man would not have had time. Someone else had phoned already.

Clemens's Church of the Witnesses of the Lord Jesus Christ was on a little street only a block long, which ended in a thick wall of trees and bushes, beyond which would be the steep slope that ran down to the creek. Somewhere in there presumably was the path that Clemens and his daughter had taken from the back of the house.

The church stood in a little field, all mud and weeds and oddly reminiscent of the parking lot around The Silver Dollar. Like Clemens's house, the building had the appearance of having been cobbled together by some ragtag group of parishioners. It was a kind of rectangular shed perfectly plain except for the little tin-sheathed steeple, not more than eight feet high, that perched near the front of the shallow-pitched roof. The roof was also sheathed in tin, a fireman's nightmare. Once upon a time, the church had been painted white, but the paint was turning grey, flaking and peeling, leaving patches of bare wood. The fire was raging at the back of the building. There were half a dozen windows along the side wall. The last two had been broken by the heat, and dense smoke was rolling out. As it rose, it became grey, then white, but inside at its source it was black, as if choking for air, and inside the black there was an unholy, dark turbulence of fire. The smoke had also begun to seep out along the top of the wall under the eaves and around the base of the steeple, as the fire smouldered its way along the rafters.

Four steps led up to the front door of the church, but there was no porch, and Hooper was balanced on the top step, holding onto the little two-by-four railing and trying ineffectually to kick in the door. Carvell stood at the bottom watching. There were already dozens of people around the church and along the street, all talking and chasing around. More were arriving every second. In the distance, Dorkin heard the siren of the approaching fire engine.

"What's happening?" Dorkin asked Carvell. "Where's Clemens?"

"I think he's inside," Carvell said. "The girl too, probably."

"Are you sure?" Dorkin asked. "This could be a diversion."

"No," Carvell said, "I don't think so. One of the people next door said he thought he heard shots."

"They must have bolted it top and bottom," Hooper shouted.

He gave the door one final kick and retreated back down the steps, just as the fire engine rounded the corner of the street, sending the crowd scrambling for the ditches.

"You couldn't have done anything anyway," Carvell said to Hooper.

The fire engine turned into the yard and swung around. Half a dozen men in ordinary work clothes were hanging onto the back and sides. Two of them threw off a pile of black firemen's coats, hats, boots. The other four freed the ends of hoses from the back of the truck, and the truck drove off again down the street towards a hydrant, flip-flopping the two hose lines behind it, as the rest of the volunteer firemen began arriving in cars. They outfitted themselves from the pile of gear on the ground, and while they waited for water, a giant of a man mounted the front step with an axe, smashed the lock side of the door, kicked it in, and was promptly driven back by a rush of smoke.

"Do you think there's anyone in there?" he asked Carvell.

"Yes," Carvell said. "But I don't think there's anything you can do about them now."

"What the hell's going on?" the fireman asked.

"I'll tell you later," Carvell said.

"It sure got a start," the fireman said.

"I think it had some help."

Along the street, the hose lines snapped full and became fiercely alive, fighting the men who held the nozzles. They directed one of them through the windows at the back into the inferno inside, the other through the front door down the length of the church, sending rows of chairs tumbling end over end towards the pulpit.

Within a quarter of an hour, the main fire at the back was out, but it had already burned its way up into the low attic under the tin roof and was smouldering forward along the rafters. It took over an hour to get it out. The firemen cut a hole through the gable at the front of the church, ripped off sheets of tin roofing, and cut more holes and poured water inside. Gradually, the smoke ceased. Then, when it seemed almost out, the little steeple gave an oddly human groan and settled backward into the roof. The firemen scrambled off their ladders, but for a minute nothing more happened. The steeple stayed where it was, half sunk at a forty-five degree angle into the roof. Then with a final groan and a rending of timbers, the whole thing came down bringing part of the roof with it into the front of the church.

Through all this, Dorkin, Carvell, and Hooper stood beside the fire truck, waiting their time, now and then getting notices from the fire chief, a fat, garrulous man, who addressed Carvell casually as George. Finally, the firemen came down off their ladders, and the hoses were turned off.

"I'm going to put more water on it later," the fire chief said, "but if we're careful, we can go in and see what's there. You better put these on. It's going to be dirty and wet."

He got three sets of boots, coats, and hats off the truck, and Dorkin, Carvell, and Hooper got into them and followed him to the back of the church.

The back door had been smashed with an axe. All that remained was a single upright board, blackened by fire, still attached to its hinges. On the other side, a heavy bolt holding some blackened splinters of wood was still shot into its housing. The floorboards inside were unsafe, and the firemen had laid planks across the joists. The three of them followed the fire chief inside. The stink of wet, burned wood was overwhelming.

Inside the door, there was an entrance hall, and to the right of that a small room. The fire chief stood to one side of the doorway, and one by one first Hooper, then Carvell, then Dorkin looked in.

The fire had burned up through the ceiling, and shafts of sunlight fell down into the room from cracks and holes in the roof above. The room held a desk, sodden and half burned, covered with debris from the ceiling, two chairs both overturned, and a couch. It was here that the fire must have been at its most intense—intense enough to burn through the floorboards so that the legs of the couch had punched through and the frame was now resting on the floor joists. The figure on the bed had been covered with a blanket that had been drawn up under the chin as it might have been in sleep, but the blanket, the clothing, skin, and flesh were charred and soaked into a single mass without distinguishable borders. The face on the pillow was like that of an Egyptian mummy, black, shrunk by the heat, the lips drawn back over the clenched teeth. It was evident that the figure was that of a woman, and there was in the face and the general proportions of the figure nothing that was inconsistent with its being the woman whom presumably it had to be.

Dorkin had never before seen so swift a transition from life to death. He was badly shaken, and as he stepped back from the door, he reflected that it was probably in that room and on that bed that Sarah Coile had also died before being taken to the gravel pit to be stoned and left for the dogs.

At the back of the entrance hall, a second door, charred to a cardboard thinness but still in one piece, led onto the platform in the main hall of the church. The ruins of the steeple filled the area by the main door, and in front of the platform there was the pile of chairs tumbled forward by the force of the fire hoses. A steady rain of black water was falling through the ceiling from the charred timbers under the roof.

On the platform there was a pulpit, blackened but upright, and just beyond it, lying curled up on its side as if it had been kneeling and fallen over, much less burned, much more recognizable than the other, lay the body of the Reverend Zacharias Clemens. Just beyond it lay a small .32 revolver.

When Dorkin and Carvell arrived back at the Clemens house, there were cars parked along the street and a small crowd of people on the lawn in front of the house.

"The Reverend's flock, I expect," Carvell said.

Dorkin looked at them with a mixture of pity and distaste: men whose trousers stopped six inches above their boots, slatternly women in ill-fitting print dresses, people grotesquely fat or grotesquely thin, or cross-eyed, or wall-eyed, people whose limbs seemed somehow to have got hung on wrong. The misfits of the countryside whom Clemens had taught to see themselves as the chosen of God.

Inside, there were more of them. Elders, perhaps, or whatever the especially chosen were called.

"Hello, Ezra," Carvell said to one of them. "Is Mrs. Clemens still here?"

"Upstairs," the man said. "Upstairs with some of the women."

"Does she know what's happened?" Carvell asked.

"I don't know," the man said. "I don't know. I ain't been up."

He looked fearfully at Carvell, then at Dorkin.

"But *you* know?" Carvell asked.

"Yes," the man said. "I guess so."

Mrs. Clemens was still sitting on the edge of the bed where Dorkin had left her. There were three other women in the room, sitting on straight-backed chairs facing her. They stared at Dorkin and Carvell without getting up or speaking. Mrs. Clemens seemed hardly aware of them.

"I'm afraid we have some bad news," Carvell said to her.

She looked at him for a moment, then her eyes drifted away and fixed themselves on something only she could see. Then they became hard. She looked back at Carvell.

"That girl," she said fiercely. "That whore. She was even leading her own father into sin. Everyone knew it."

Carvell turned to the women.

"I'd like to talk to her alone for a minute," he said. "Could you wait outside?"

They glanced at each other and, still without speaking, rose and went out into the hall. Carvell moved as if to close the door, then changed his mind and left it open.

"Your daughter," Carvell began.

"I have no daughter," she said, repeating what she had said before. "I had two sons."

"Your husband's daughter, then," Carvell said. "Elizabeth."

"Nor his daughter either. She was his Bride in God. As I was. I first, then Elizabeth."

She looked at Carvell impatiently as at someone who lived in ignorance in some outer darkness, hardly worth her attention.

"He was a prophet," she said. "Like Abraham. He had the right to more wives than one. They freed him so that he could bear witness to God."

"And Sarah Coile?" Dorkin asked. "Was she also a bride in God?"

"That one! She took possession of his soul and left him no peace. She was destroying him. She clothed him in a coat of fire. She was a witch. An agent of Satan. She would have brought destruction down on our house. She would have scattered our flock and left them to the mercy of the storm. It was the devil in her that was destroyed so that her soul could be saved."

She stopped.

"I was afraid," she went on. "When the time came, I was afraid. The time came, as he always said it would. But I was afraid."

"I don't want to distress you," Carvell said. "But is there anyone we can get in touch with? Do you have relatives? I heard you were from the States."

"I have no relatives," she said. "I had a mother and a father and a husband and two sons, but I went out of their house because I had been shown the way."

"Can we get in touch with them?" Carvell asked.

"No. It was long ago. Long ago."

Downstairs, the people started to sing, raggedly, some hymn, and after a few bars, it was taken up by some of the people outside on the lawn.

"You should have heard him," she said. "You should have seen him. The light of the Lord was upon him. I was afraid. But I was honoured still more that he should come to me. In the night. In a cloud of fire."

Just before seven o'clock, Grant and his team arrived, three carloads of them. Dorkin stood at the corner on Broad Street and watched them drive up to the church and disembark. They had brought the tracking dog with them. They had also brought Corporal Drost. As he emerged from the back of one of the cars, he looked down the little street, and his eyes and Dorkin's met. Surprised, he stared briefly, but he made no sign of recognition, nor did Dorkin. Dorkin watched the first of them enter the ruined church, then turned away, back to his own car, and left.

Now he sat in his office, waiting for the call that Carvell had promised him. It was almost midnight when it finally came.

"So?" Dorkin said.

"So," Carvell said, "they spent over an hour talking to Mrs. Clemens. You were right. It was Clemens. You were probably also right about Coile. He was apparently messing around with Sarah, though it's hard to say exactly how far it went."

"Was it Coile or Clemens who got her pregnant?" Dorkin asked.

"It's hard to say, but I suspect it was Clemens. It's also hard to say exactly what happened. Mrs. Clemens wasn't very coherent, and there were probably things she just didn't know. It looks as if Sarah may have gone to Clemens about her father, and Clemens took advantage of her. Although I suppose it's possible that she took advantage of him. That's the way Mrs. Clemens sees it anyway, but I'm not sure I'd put much stock in that. Whichever way, he became involved with her, and it obviously got out of control.

Out of his control, I mean. It sounds as if he was out of his mind over her."

"What about the murder?" Dorkin asked.

"It's hard to know exactly what happened there either. Apparently, Mrs. Clemens and Elizabeth weren't at the church on the Saturday afternoon when Sarah went there to see Clemens as he said they were. It may be that she threatened him. She may have wanted money to get away with and maybe get rid of the baby. Maybe he didn't have it. Maybe he thought that if he started giving her money, there'd be no end to it. If Sarah was trying to set Williams up, she must have had doubts about Clemens looking after her, and she was looking for another way out. It's also possible that she told Clemens she was going to find someone else, and he was crazy with jealousy. But we're never going to know.

"I don't think we're ever going to know exactly what happened that night either. After she left Williams, Clemens obviously intercepted her somewhere, probably on one of the paths up through the woods. It's difficult to know how planned it may have been. Or where it happened. I suspect he may have lured her back to the church on some pretext or other. It's pretty doubtful that he killed her there in the woods. There were too many people around, and he couldn't have carried her very far given her weight. And it's hard to know when she was taken to the gravel pit."

"But there's no doubt that it was Clemens?" Dorkin asked.

"No. No doubt at all. Apparently the three of them talked about it. It's all crazy as hell."

"Have you told Williams about it?"

"No. I thought you might want to."

Dorkin hesitated.

"No," he said. "You tell him. I'll talk to him tomorrow before I leave. He's not my problem anymore."

CHAPTER EIGHTEEN

Dorkin sat at the front of the restaurant by the window, looking out at the square with its neat, geometric criss-cross of walks, its ornate, Victorian bandstand, its old-fashioned iron benches that had survived five years of patriotic scrap drives. These things were to him as old as his memory of himself, the setting of summer walks with his mother, of summer concerts and summer games. The bandstand was boarded up now for the winter, and the triangles of grass between the walks were covered with a thin pack of dirty snow. In spite of the raw cold there were, as always, a few men on the benches—bums and merchant seamen pausing to reflect on their further peregrinations through the city in search of warmth or liquor or love. And on the walks they sat beside, there was a continuous traffic of shoppers. It was Friday, December 22, and Monday would be Christmas Day, the sixth Christmas of the war. And perhaps not the last after all.

On the table beside Dorkin's coffee cup lay the morning newspaper, its front page full of calamity. Once more, as in the spring of 1940, the panzers had struck through the Ardennes. This time it was the Americans who had been smashed, and the headlines were ominous. NO HINT THAT GERMAN OFFENSIVE SPENT. GERMANS USING MORE TROOPS THAN WON BATTLE OF FRANCE. In the middle of the page, there was a photograph of long lines of American vehicles bumper to bumper pulling back. It was obviously a rout.

Whether as reward or punishment, Dorkin's request for a transfer to regular army duties in Europe had at last been granted, and he was home in Saint John on embarkation leave. It was strange as always to be back among these familiar surroundings, strangest of all to be back in his own room with its relics of childhood and the haunting background murmur of the city outside the window, pervasive and elusive, like some quality of the air itself. Inside, pervasive and elusive also, there was the sad Jewish atmosphere with its sense of distances of space and time, those distances whose memory his father fought so furiously to deny and bury. But for weeks now rumours of unimaginable massacres had been filtering into the news reports, and Dorkin was aware that his father was more talkative even than usual, about nothing, about trivialities, filling the air with words. Behind this also, Dorkin knew, there was his departure, hardly ever mentioned. Dorkin did not believe for a minute that he would not be back. Soldiers never did. Parents nourished no such illusions, finding themselves almost daily on the edge of an abysm of grief, every arriving mail a heart-stopping moment of fear, every telegraph boy on the street an agent of terror.

The inquest for Zacharias and Elizabeth Clemens had been held two weeks after their deaths. Since there was nothing that Dorkin could add to the more official evidence that Carvell and Hooper would give and since it was not directly an army matter, it was not thought necessary by the army that he be there. The inquest was also in effect a trial, and when it was over, the Reverend Clemens stood condemned and Private Williams exonerated. But the law does not so willingly let go those whom it has decided to remove, temporarily or permanently, from the world, and it was another two weeks before Williams was released and returned to the army, his crimes expunged from his record, the papers ordering his dishonourable discharge made quietly to vanish.

One evening in mid-November when Dorkin was in the officers' mess back at Utopia, a fellow lieutenant brought him a newspaper folded over to an inside page. The item was a single sentence, reporting that a body recovered from the St. John River below Wakefield had been positively identified as that of Mrs. Roseann Clemens. A week after that, a letter arrived from George Carvell, a long letter in a surprisingly elegant hand—by way, it said, of an epilogue to these late, strange events.

The day after Dorkin's departure, Mrs. Clemens had been taken to the hospital. She was given a room by herself, and she spent most of her time just sitting. Sometimes when the nurses spoke to her, she acted as if she hadn't heard. Sometimes she talked to herself, and sometimes the nurses had the impression that she was imagining that there were people in the room whom she was talking to.

Since there seemed to be nothing that could be done for her in the hospital, she was released and went to live with one of the families from the church. She stayed with them for a couple of weeks and seemed to be getting better. She helped with housework, and she started going out to do shopping. Then one day a man walking across the St. John River bridge from the far side saw a woman standing looking over the rail. She looked up at him, and when he was a dozen yards away, she climbed up onto the rail, let herself slide off feet first, and dropped the thirty feet into the river. About a week afterwards, some boys in a boat found her four miles downstream, wedged up against some bushes and frozen into the first skim of winter ice.

Constable Hooper had continued his search into her background. He knew that the Clemenses had come to Wakefield from a church on the Miramichi, and the people there said that they had come from Ontario, but no one knew where. The Mounties checked in Ontario and found nothing. They sent descriptions of Clemens and the two women to the FBI and found nothing. The FBI checked with state police in the south and found nothing.

Hooper thought that they had probably changed their names, perhaps more than once. Both the women had apparently been married before they went with Clemens and perhaps were being pursued by husbands and relatives. Somewhere in the States, there were obviously people through whom the story could be pieced together, but it seemed unlikely that they would ever be found and that anything would ever be known beyond what was known now.

"If you believed in spirits," Carvell wrote, "you might think they were a visitation from another world. As for Clemens, I suspect that his little room at the church was host to more female companionship than just Sarah Coile, and I wonder if there may have been other victims elsewhere."

On the Sunday morning after the fire, when he had gone to the jail, Dorkin found Williams sitting by the table in his cell reading a book printed on cheap, wartime, pulp paper. *The Seventh Angel*. A trashy religious tract, from his spiritual mentor no doubt, with a cover lurid with the lightning of the final judgement.

"Sheriff Carvell has told you what happened?" Dorkin said.

"Yes," Williams said. "When are they going to let me out of here?"

"I don't know," Dorkin said. "It'll be a few days, I expect. There will have to be some ruling made in Fredericton."

"Will I get compensated?" Williams asked.

"I don't know," Dorkin said.

"I should be. I shouldn't have been arrested at all. It wasn't fair."

"No, it wasn't fair. It wasn't fair at all. But life isn't fair. It wasn't fair to Sarah Coile either."

"She was a whore," Williams said belligerently. "All she wanted was to trap me into marrying her."

"No," Dorkin said. "She wasn't a whore. Just a poor, lonely girl life never gave a chance to. Now that you've been given a chance, you should start by showing some compassion."

Williams ignored him.

"Reverend Limus always said that God would save me," he said.

"It wasn't God," Dorkin said. "Don't flatter yourself. God had nothing to do with it. It was blind luck and one of the local drunks."

Back at the armoury, Dorkin had packed up his papers and his kit in preparation for his immediate and final departure from Wakefield. He had not been thanked, nor had he expected or wanted to be, and when he looked back on all that had happened, he felt more depressed than elated. He had, by mere luck, rescued an innocent boy, who was also a mean-minded, self-righteous little shit. Not that these were capital offences. But still. He had avenged Sarah Coile, but vengeance does not raise the dead. Louie Rosen, unavenged, was also dead. An end had been put to the Reverend Clemens, but his two wives in God had been taken down with him. Daniel Coile and his cronies were all alive and well. The irrepressible H. P. Whidden would no doubt go on to compensatory triumphs, the cool-blooded McKiel to still more.

The dark tower forever awaits, the knight errant forever rides out, and in the end the only thing he ever really changes is himself.

He finished his coffee, put on his great coat, and walked out into the cold. On the other side of the square, the movie theatres were advertising *Going My Way* with Bing Crosby and *Hollywood Canteen* with Barbara Stanwyck. He had no interest in either, but he noted the titles in case he might want to affect an interest in order to escape from the house for a couple of hours some evening.

He turned down King Street into the raw cold rising up from the harbour. At the corner of Dock Street, two merchant seamen, one very drunk, were arguing in a Germanic-sounding language, perhaps Swedish. A Canadian sailor and his girlfriend gave them a wide berth, and a policeman on the other side of the street had stopped to keep an eye on them.

Dorkin made his way past and walked out to the end of the slip and leaned on the rail to look across the harbour. The commercial docks on the other side were lined solid with merchant ships, squat, ugly, their paint peeling, leaving patches of rusted metal.

Down the harbour beyond the commercial docks, small clouds of mist shifted, dissipating, reforming above the ice-cold water. Once long ago, when he was in grade three or four, his class had been brought down here as part of an outing, and the teacher had pointed down the harbour to the place where nearly three and a half centuries before, Champlain's little ship had anchored. Now in the place, or near it, Dorkin could make out through the mist the shape of a destroyer, grey, low, clean-lined, and deadly, riding at anchor, awaiting its charges.

ACKNOWLEDGEMENTS

I wish to thank Patrick Murphy for his support and to acknowledge the meticulous and perceptive editing of the text by Kate Kennedy.

ABOUT THE AUTHOR

Allan Donaldson was born in Taber, Alberta, and grew up in Woodstock, New Brunswick. He is the author of the short-story collection *Paradise Sliding* and the novel *Maclean*, which was shortlisted for the 2005 Rogers Writers' Trust Fiction Award. He lives in Fredericton.